FRAGILE FACADE

NORDIKA NIGHT

FRAGILE FACADE [VILE HOUSE BOOK 2]

ISBN: 978-1-0691308-1-5

Cover Artist: Quirky Circe

Editor: Jenn Heathers

Editor: Sarah H

Interior Formatting: Nordika Night

Contact: nordika@nordikanight.com

FRAGILE FACADE

VILE HOUSE

BOOK 2

NORDIKA NIGHT

Cheers, Death.
Try Me.

MIND YOUR MENTALS

SEIRES MUST BE READ IN ORDER FOR BEST UNDERSTANDING

• Book 2 starts off very volatile. While still dark, the relationship aspect is not as harsh as Krypt and Remiel. Think: when volatile meets vulnerable.

• Riot and Ghost have more of a soft side. But it takes the harsh start to get them there.

• ASPD (Antisocial Personality Disorder // Sociopath) is a spectrum, and in this book, Riot sits on that spectrum. Please remember that not everyone with this diagnosis reveals the same traits, and not everyone with this disorder is a cruel person.

• Narcissism. Ghost has narcissistic tendencies, but again, not everything he does is narcissistic in nature.

• Their growth is selfish. Their personality traits make them both selfish people with similar ideals. This means they ARE similar characters, both with tendencies to put themselves first. They learn selflessness as they go, whether they mimic it or mean it.

• The Reaper Corp theme is continuous throughout the series

• Death, murder, violence

• Manipulation & selfish mindsets, big egos, god-complexes, actions serve their own purpose

• Dub/con, non consensual sexual act (non-penetrative) involving a paralytic

• Rough sex including blood during sex

• Torture scene, captive situation, slight description of torture

• Poison ingestion

• Forced drug use (not between main characters) which causes a hallucination

• Hanging/noose as a part of a harsh game

• Forced medical scans

• Explosive device, bomb

• Emotional turmoil/upset

• Obsessive, possessive MCs

• A sexual tension scene that involves a third person as a catalyst (game of chicken, essentially)

• Manhunt through town

• Insecurities, mental confusion

• Cutting - upper arms (not often mentioned)

• Continued mention of the suicide curse (no more after this book)

• Physical harm to non main characters

STARTING RANK

Book 2 picks up right after Riot drugged Ghost and took him from the Ambient Raven music shop in book 1

1. Seven
2. Ghost
3. Menace
4. Riot
5. Facts
6. Glitch
7. Monster
8. Krypt
9. Ransom
10. Kyd

Who will end up below Kyd's rank by the end of the book?! ;)

GHOST

1
BLINK

HE RIPS my hair when he pulls it, yanking my face from the tepid pond water. My eyes have been open the whole time, but I keep my lungs closed, refusing to suck in a breath until I absolutely can't help it. Until my body does it without my permission. Until death is so close that it's almost desirable.

"Breathe."

I don't.

"Breathe!"

Fuck death. Fuck it for trying. Fuck it for wanting me. Fuck it for failing.

I grin into the dark woods through the murky water, refusing to breathe, watching the shadows, hellions, and demons shroud the area around me. Creeping in from all directions to take me to the underworld and hold me captive for eternity, they'll laugh in my face if I fail. If I'm cursed and death is knocking, it can knock fucking harder. Try harder! Cut deeper! Fucking come for me, Death! Fucking try it!

"Breathe, Ghost!"

Despair is so cynical. Almost hypocritical. It's hopelessness mixed with misery, and pathetic because of its power. I feel it just to fight it. I experience it just to believe it. Because it's real, but I'm not its fucking prey.

Death is a promise, but life isn't a guarantee. I'll die, but life won't make me. Living won't force me into a grave before I'm goddamn good and ready to fall into one, kicking and screaming—laughing harshly.

Desire is taboo. Almost forbidden. To want and to take is the goal, but to yearn and be denied is the reality. I chase it to taunt it, but it chases me back to goad me into the grave I refuse to settle in.

Desire. Death. Despair. Round and round we go.

It's here. It's gone. It comes. It goes. I desire the chase to death and despair as the end result. Masking and hunting and thrill-seeking and sobering. It's all an unharmonious circle. An addictive chase that leads me nowhere and a pause in time that creates confusion.

Who am I and where am I going? What am I and what is the point of anything?

Where does it start and how does it end? If I die here, right now, what would have been the point of existing? If I live through this and delay death, what is the purpose of surviving?

Murder. Suicide. Here. Gone.

"Breathe!" His mouth lands on mine and his fingers pinch my nose. He exhales his air into my closed lungs, forcing them open until I accept his breath, choking on it because I don't goddamn want it! I wasn't close enough. Death was there, but she wasn't touching me.

The shadows all dissipate, and he's ruined it. He's ruined my dance with impermanence. He's fucked up my desirable hunt for death and filled me with despair because I was *almost* there. Almost looking into her eyes and telling her to fuck right off and try harder next time.

Desire. Death. Despair. Oh, this tango we do...

"You fucking prick." He breathes into my mouth again, and this time, I cough it back out. I expel his breath and the water in my lungs, the pond in my stomach. I hack it all up and turn onto my hands and knees in the shallow pond while he whacks my back and hates me.

I love the way he hates me. Desire and despair, mingled into something that thrives in a chase to death.

My face reflects at me, the rippling water morphing me into the version of myself I see inside my head. Warped and twisted, broken but glued together to near perfection. No one sees my cracks but me. My jagged parts are so artistically put back together that I've made myself a masterpiece. I'm tainted perfection and insane power, and nothing, not even the desire of death, has been strong enough to crack me into the undone puzzle I truly am. It's a grand illusion, and I am the magician who showcases the mirage of *me*.

Riot yanks on the back of my shirt, flipping me until my back slams onto the weedy shore of the small pond, his dark waves falling over his forehead. My lungs wheeze and gurgle, but my vision is just fine. His tumultuous grey eyes glare down at me with such a heady mix of emotions that all I can do is laugh. At him. At the sky. At the pond. At death. Because fuck him! He drugged me and took me from The Ambient Raven just to prove a point. That he's stronger than me. That he can push me to Death's doorstep and pull me right back.

But it's not him who pulled me back. It's *me.* Because I'm a Sauder man, blessed with a beautiful suicide curse, and I've been chasing it all my life. I'm not like my brothers. I'm not scared. I'm not afraid of dying and tempting fate. I'm eager for it! Come at me! Try and fucking take me!

Because I'm stronger than it—more powerful than a curse. I'm the illusion, right? So when I'm there, right on the precipice of desire and despair, a wish and a whisper away from the curse that's taken my father and my brothers, I'll laugh in its fucking face and trick it. *Haha! Joke's on you, Death! I'm already dead inside, broken and glued together with something so much worse than the finite end you promise.* And when she's confused by me, wondering why I won't cross over and join her in the afterlife, I will turn my back on her and make her chase me again. Harder.

Because I'm Soren Sauder, and nothing or no one will kill me until I've finally tempted the wrong devil.

I laugh even harder, my stomach cramping with the force of it. The stars all watch, and the moon spotlights my insanity. Riot sees it all, and instead of worrying about me, he laughs right back.

Because I'm chasing death.

But he's the hellhound nipping at my heels to herd me there faster.

He's fucking relentless.

He kicks my side so hard I buckle and sink into the sludgy mud. I hold my breath, my lungs already screaming, letting myself sink even more, the pond hugging me into its silky embrace.

The hug ends too soon when he straddles my legs, pinning me down with his strong body. He's not stronger than me, but I like wicked games, and they're even more fun when he thinks he's winning.

Grabbing the front of my shirt, he pulls me up until my face is out of the shallow water. "You think this is funny?" he asks, grey eyes stormy and amused. "How close were you?"

I cough up sooty muck and water. "Not close enough."

"One foot in the grave?"

"One foot in Hell, the other lifted to take the last step." I cough harder. "Wanna walk there with me?"

His grin is disgusting because it's full of all that death, desire, and despair I war with daily. It's a cumulation of everything I feel, displayed so perfectly in a smirk, made better when his tattooed arm comes up to push back his dark hair, amplifying the image of him. "Oh, we aren't walking there. We're running. You think you can outsmart death?"

I laugh because it feels good. The warm water laps against my skin and regulates my body temperature. I love attention, and I have all of his, so I keep laughing. "So far."

"Alright, Ghost. Fuck the bargain with our brothers. Here's the new deal."

"I don't make deals."

"Here's the deal," he repeats. "Whenever you tempt Death, I'll tempt her harder by pushing you straight to her. If you want to defy this curse, I'm going to defy *you*. Wanna see how hard you can push back without dying? Fine. Do it. But I'm going to press you until you finally learn that you aren't as powerful as you think you are. However close to Death you get, I'll take you one step closer. By the time I'm done with you, you'll have both feet in the grave, half your soul in Hell, and you'll be so beaten down that you won't be strong enough to resist it anymore. You won't be able to laugh in her face."

I suck in a breath before he pushes me underwater, holding me down until I'm half dead. My eyes bulge and my hearing muffles. When my lips pop open to tell him *no deal* and that he's delusional if he thinks he's stronger than I am, nothing comes out. No air. No words. Nothing. Water fills me. Riot tilts my head until one ear comes out of the water, but not my mouth to breathe.

"And when you're right there, finally ready to die for real, you'll submit to me and admit that I'm stronger than you are. That I win."

Fuck that. I want to laugh again, but I'm too dead to try.

Riot smiles down at me, one of those cocky, sure-of-himself grins that means he'll let me die right now if I don't accept this deal. I'm not ready to fully die. I haven't proven myself enough yet. I'm half there, losing air and unable to think clearly through the fog taking over my mind. It's not a *true death* I'm after yet—it's that one or two second precipice between.

"You tempt death. I tempt you. When I win, you admit I win. Agree. Blink."

I'm so close now. The shrouding shadows and all the hellions are coming back. The water is comfortable and the muck is hugging me tenderly, drowning me in warmth. Death is a she, I just know it, and when I meet her and she brings me a true death, I want to leave this fucked up world even more fucked up than it was when I arrived in it.

"Agree. Blink." He pushes down on my already still chest.

A flash of Remi flits through my mind and I try to shake it free. He's got Krypt. He's fine. This is the closest I've ever been to the afterlife, and I'm not pulling back now. I'm ready to laugh in the face of Death.

"Blink!"

But I can't laugh because there's no more energy to laugh.

"Blink!"

Blackness takes over and all I see are the shrinking grey spots of his intense eyes and the look in them that proves he hates me so beautifully.

Don't blink. Don't blink. We're so close, don't blink.

Remi. Selena. Remi. Selena.

Riot. Riot. Riot.

I suffocate on memories instead of water, trying to block them out so I can step on the doorstep of Death's lair and slam the door back in her face. I'm knocking, but she's not answering. She's laughing at me. Mocking me for trying to defy her.

I'll be back, you crafty bitch.

Then I blink. Not because of Remi and Selena. Because I'm selfish enough to live longer to prove I can outsmart Death—outsmart Riot. That's *my* new deal.

I fade out when he doesn't pull me up right away. He grins at me again, my vision disappearing until my eyes stop seeing but stay open, and I drown in the pond out on Carnival Hill. A fitting place to die. Probably more bodies in here than water.

It's not as peaceful as I thought it'd be. I can't feel the one or two second precipice.

But here I am. Dead. Smiling. Trying to laugh.

"Not today, sweetheart."

I gasp and throw up, looking into the eyes of the hound I've goaded into joining me on this trip to defy my finality. I have no control of my body, but he does. Riot holds me up, sitting in the pond, smiling at me like I didn't just die for a few seconds. "Call me that again..." It's hard to snarl while half alive, but I manage.

"Guess what this makes me?" he asks while I cough. Grabbing my throat and tilting my useless head up to look me in the eye, he says, "Your God." He squeezes so hard I feel my windpipe bend.

When he lets go, pushing me back down, he makes sure my upper body is on the shore. Then he leaves me out here in the middle of the woods on Devil's Night to think about my new reality.

I blinked. I made the deal.

Finally, my laugh comes back. Because it's going to be so fucking fun dragging him to Hell with me.

GHOST

2

REST IN PARALYSIS

HALLOWEEN IN MOROS isn't something to be taken lightly. A holiday that signifies the end of life in the form of summer and the start of death in the form of winter, bringing Pagan, Gaelic, and Celtic believers to our small town. Dressed in traditional costumes from the roots of Samhain, crowns made of sticks and branches, wispy robes and long willowy dresses fill the streets, heading to the cemetery for the celebrations.

Samhain. The signifying switch in seasons that leads us into the 'dark half' of the year. I'm a believer. I feel the darkness creeping in, but I'm not resisting its pull. I'm embracing it, letting it consume me, inviting it to fill me even more. Because I'm someone who is affected by the seasons, the weather, and old beliefs.

"What's wrong with you?" Krypt asks, handing me his joint. "The weather?"

I'm fucking humming on the inside. Agitated and alive, but unsure how the combination is going to snap. The rain breathes something into my bones, making me cold and dangerous, but the thunder and lightning amplify the feeling, creating an electric buzz in every cell of my body. I feel the switch in the season, the life of summer fading after harvest, ready to welcome the death of winter and the darkness of the days. The combination of Samhain, as well as the busy streets of Moros, brimming with costumes ranging from slutty get-ups to traditional Pagan, has me on edge. In a good way. Alive and dark about it. Sinister blended with gleeful.

I take the joint and inhale the taste of weed, letting it out through shaky lips. I ignore his question because there's nothing wrong with me and fuck him for asking. "Where's Remi?"

Krypt looks across the street. We're sitting on the roof of The Midnight Diner with an unobstructed view through the windows of The Ambient Raven, but I don't see my brother through the glass. Dusk makes the interior lights of all the shops turn on, aiding the streetlights and decorations in turning our main street, Death Row, as ominous as the night will be.

Then I see Remi coming from the back of the shop to the front counter. He hesitates by his cello, touching it fondly but refusing to take it off the stand. My heart recognizes his pain, but I don't hurt for him. I recognize his turmoil, knowing he wants to play, but also knowing it hurts him to play alone. I haven't played music with my brother since before I left The Ambient Raven to initiate for The Misfits. I long for it, but I fear it, too. Afraid that the combination of our sorrow, blending through notes and stringed instruments, will be too much for me to bear. I'm already jigsawed and shattered, barely glued together, and if we play together, I'll turn to dust and finally meet the death I've been toying with for years.

Because music is a way to speak without having to confess aloud.

"You miss it?" Krypt asks, nodding at the shop.

Yeah, I miss it, but he doesn't deserve to know that. I miss the energy of the family business and spending time with my brother. But I'm not built for all that. I'm made to create music, not talk about it with the public. Remi is more suited to the business, and Cain is the piece that brings the place to completion. Not me. As much as that irks me to admit. So, I don't admit it. I ignore Krypt's second question and move on.

I take another hit, handing it back to Krypt while we both spy on my brother. I hate that they're together, but I don't hate all of it. Krypt is a terrible person with no sense of boundaries, but who am I to judge? He's good for Remi because he refuses to let him die, and that's about all I could ever ask from someone. I don't want the responsibility of my brother's life on my hands, so having Krypt take the burden does me a favour anyway. I'm selfish, but Krypt is possessive, so he works better. Balance, I guess.

"You feel guilty for raping him yet?" I ask, side-eying him as lightning webs across the sky, charging me from the inside out.

Krypt simply glares at me with annoyance, barely a glance, before his eyes snap back to The Ambient Raven. Cain says something to Remi before leaving the shop to head home, where I know someone in a blue mask will be stalking him.

"Don't let him out of your sight tonight," I tell Krypt, standing.

"Don't tell me how to own him."

"You don't fucking own him."

Another glare, all his inner beasts coming to life. I grin at that and leave him on the roof, climbing down the back emergency ladder of The Midnight Diner. The Neon Demon Nightclub isn't open yet, but later tonight, it'll be as busy as the cemetery, where the harvest festivals take place. Moros is split on Halloween—half of us ritualistic and the other half all about the party. Some of us are even all about the fun for the kids. But pretty much all of us believe in the horror of it, the spooks and the scares, and the thinned veil between our world and the one we're heading to after.

Which is another reason I'm amplified tonight. A peek into the afterlife I've been taunting? Yeah, that intrigues me, and I know just the place to experience it.

"HELLO, DAD." I smile at his grave, nestled between my brothers, uncles, and cousins.

It's quiet here, with the rituals taking place on the opposite side of the cemetery. But I have no interest in them tonight.

Stepping over my dad and brother, I look at the plot reserved for me and Remi. A headstone already sits in place, blank except for the Sauder last name. I smile at it, feeling at home here in my eventual eternal resting place. There's a certain comfort in knowing where my body will end up, but the uncertainty of not knowing the state of my dead body is what titillates me.

How will I die? Will I be mutilated and unrecognizable, or will I be whole and at peace? I'm already a ghost in my living life, and a part of me knows I won't go to the grave silently. I'll fight my way there, holding onto the allure of death until the very last second when I'm finally forced to give in and accept that Death is a more victorious opponent than me. Until then, our game will continue to be a race—her trying to lure me there and me luring her to try harder. A worthy set of opponents.

Squatting at the end of my burial site, I lightly brush my hand over the dewy grass, wondering when it'll be disrupted by digging a six-foot hole. It's a nice plot near the edge of the forest, close to where Krypt assaulted Remi's throat over a dead girl's body, the treeline encroaching on the place reserved for me. I don't mind. I live and breathe for Moros, so if its tree roots want to keep me company in my coffin, I'll allow it.

I wonder what the sky will look like from my supine position. Might as well look. Standing, I turn my back to it, spreading my arms wide. With calmness in my mind and the lightning all around me, I fall backwards with my eyes closed just to be dramatic.

But the grass and dirt don't meet me with a hard impact. I fall through them, my heart jumping into my throat, and my morbid mind suspended in contrast, unsure if I'm happy to fall into my grave or pissed at it for tricking me.

The sod fooled me, the grass so alive I didn't realize it'd

already been disturbed. When I sink through it, letting it blanket my back, I panic internally but do nothing externally to prevent myself from falling into the hole already dug. I don't grasp at the roots protruding from the sides, and I don't turn my body to catch my fall. With a thump, I land on the grass I dragged in here, my ears ringing and my body jolted. Six feet of dirt surrounds me on all sides, the roots sneaking in to tickle me in a few places, caressing me and welcoming me home.

I don't move. I don't breathe. I'm in here, underground, so I might as well get a real feel for what it'll be like. My heartbeat disrupts my attempt at deadness, thudding in my chest hard enough to prove I'm still alive.

Why do I feel so dead inside?

"Knew you'd look good down there. Comfy, sweetheart?"

I sigh and close my eyes. I do feel comfortable, actually. I'm not sure if it's because death appears comforting or because my life is already so brutal and melancholy that any distortion in the monotony of my thoughts puts me at ease. I'm complicated that way. I love myself—I hate my mind. It's an internal war I've been waging for years, doing everything possible to mask my puzzle pieces in confidence and only show the outside world my prideful ego. Moros needs a ghost, and I *am* that ghost, but I need somewhere else to run, a different escape, because my mind is no longer a safe place.

"Can you see them?" Riot asks from above. "It *is* Samhain."

I open my eyes and look left, wondering how many

inches of soil block me from my brothers' dead bodies. I look right, wondering the same about my dad's casket of bones. Their souls aren't here, and to be honest, I wouldn't want to talk to them if I could. What would I say?

Sorry I fucked up and failed to notice your impending suicide because I was too selfish to think about anyone but myself?

No. I'm Soren Sauder, I don't apologize, and I don't fuck up and fail. Not outwardly. I bury my insecurities as deep as my family's bodies are buried, hidden from the intrusion of prying eyes, but never deep enough to hide from myself. And then I gaslight someone else into taking the blame and believing it.

"We both know you have no interest in talking to the dead," Riot says, making me turn my head straight, looking up at him peering down at me. Lightning flashes beyond him, and like he's God himself, he blocks the rain from hitting my cold but not yet dead body. His black clothing and dark, wavy hair drip rainwater down on me like he's the only thing powerful enough to affect me in my gravesite. "You want to flirt."

"Flirt with who?"

"Death."

My flirting with death isn't subtle or gentle. There are no coy looks or bashful blinking, no suggestive hints or licked lips. No, when I flirt with Death, I fucking scream at her. I throw dares at her, goading and riling her to step up her game. I want her flirting back just as brutally, making the trip to Hell seem so fascinating that there isn't a chance I'll be able to resist it. Honestly, she does a good job. Because it's not death I crave. It's the precipice, that ledge, the tipping point of *this* life and *no* life. It's the mingling of a beating heart and a body that functions to the realization that it's faltering, failing, shutting down. And when I get to that point, where all will be lost within a second or two, I want to take that second or two to actually experience it. I want to live in that second or two. Not alive. Not dead. Somewhere in the middle. I almost got it when Riot drowned me in the pond. *Almost.*

"Thought you were chasing me straight to her?" I ask him, goosebumps lining my skin when the thunder booms. "Seems to me like you're just following along. I got here all on my own."

His feet thud on either side of my body, jolting me, but he pins me down with a hand to my chest, straddling my hips. I don't fight him. Because the look he currently has in his eyes is exactly what I need from him. He's not like Director who wants to rationalize with me. He's not like Remi who worries for me. He's not like Krypt, who protects me subtly. He's Riot, ready and willing to indulge in my game and laugh with me when I make it to that one-or-two-second precipice. He's here, in my grave, ready to push me even deeper. For how dark and twisted the Vile Boys are, Riot is the only one who has ever found my morbid game tantalizing.

When he presses on my chest, settling his weight on my hips, I sink into my grave. His eyes are bright grey, so much brighter than the night, flashing silver at me every time the lightning strikes. But his smile? Fuck, it's one of his sickly charming ones. Not the same as the charm he throws at strangers to establish a bond of fake trust, but one that's so pleasant it can only hint at something sinister. It's so beautiful it's deceiving.

"You sure you wanna be down here when I die, Riot?" I shift my hips, making him settle his weight right on my cock. "Trust me not to drag you under?"

His smile deepens. "Don't trust you worth a shit," he says. His hands slide up my chest and over my shoulders, caressing. "You're making a mistake right now, Ghost."

I don't make mistakes. "Am I?"

Pulling something from above my head, he laughs at my nonchalance. When long roots of a distant tree wrap around my neck like a noose, I latch onto his wrists, pretending to stop him. Oh, I'm not making a mistake. He is.

"Think a little choking is a mistake? Asphyxiation is my kink, man."

Riot keeps smiling, tying the vine root off to something. When he snugs it up against my throat, tight enough to hurt but not tight enough to cut off all my oxygen, he looks at me. "Oh, this is just a restraint, but we can get kinky if you want." His ass wiggles on my lap, and my hips buck in an attempt to fight back. "Ever fucked in your grave before?"

"What would my father think?" I gasp. Literally, because his elbow pounds on my solar plexus, knocking the wind out of me while a tree strangles me. I cough, my eyes watering, my hands grasping at my throat.

That's when I realize my mistake. Both hands at my throat, wrists close together. Close enough for him to slap on a pair of cuffs and tighten them so much tighter than the noose.

"I don't think he'd be too surprised," Riot says as I struggle. "He knows his oldest remaining son is an attention whore who will fuck anything darker than he is."

Still gasping, I spit at him. "You think you're darker than me?"

"It says something that your mind went to me first." He pushes my bound wrists above my head, hooking the cuffs to the root sticking out of the soil. Leaning over me, his eyes narrow, his hair falls forward to drip more rain, and his smile stops being charming. "Oh, sweetheart, you have no fucking idea how dark I can be." He holds up a syringe, and *fuck*, I start to panic. "Wanna know what it really feels like to be dead down here?"

"Fuck you, Riot! What is that?" I kick my legs and buck my hips, but Riot is strong and muscled, entirely in control of his body *and* mine. He jabs the needle into my hip with a jolting sting and tosses the empty syringe down where my feet are. "You fucking prick."

"Just a paralytic."

No. No. No. *No!*

"Knock me out." Panic fills me this time because nothing scares me more than being entirely present while unable to do anything about it. Don't take my body away and leave my brain! Fuck! My mind isn't a safe space, remember? My body is my only weapon, and he's taking it from me, leaving me with my weakest part. "Knock me out!"

"Not a chance," Riot says while my legs go tingly. "Because you need to learn to think without having any of your other vices. I'll wait."

He leans against the soil wall, waiting for my body to numb. I feel my heartbeat slow, but I don't lose all feeling in my upper half. *Yet.* I don't like it. I don't like the feeling of being disconnected from my body, the one and only thing that actually keeps me alive. Because if my mind was in control, I'd have died years ago. The suicide curse lives in my brain, infecting it with its whispers of total oblivion. My body is the part that fights back. It's my skill as a ghost and my confidence in my strength that's keeping me alive long enough to tempt death but never actually achieve it.

I don't want to play the game without my body!

I can hear myself hyperventilating, but I can't feel it. Titling my head down, the root digs under my chin, and I witness my chest heaving. I tell my legs to kick, to knock Riot out, to stand up and climb out of here, but they don't do anything. Not even a twitch.

"You know what my favourite part about you is?" Riot asks, making my eyes shift to him. I hate him. I've hated him for a long time because his ego challenges mine, and I'm a sore loser. Not that I've ever lost to him, but if I ever do, I won't be able to handle it. "How pathetic you really are. You think no one notices?" He laughs, cruel and powerful. "Oh, I notice. It's all I notice about you. Poor Soren Sauder, a ghost who gets no recognition."

I might not be able to feel my body, but I feel the burn inside it. How fucking dare he. He plucked my biggest insecurity straight from my soul, and now he's wielding it like a weapon in my own grave.

"The narcissist who craves recognition but is forced to thrive in silence. Your talents go unseen, ironically, because you excel at them. The Ghost of Moros. The man who wants to live in the spotlight but thrives in the dark. You're a mindfuck, yeah?" He smacks my legs, but other than sensing my body jolt, I don't feel it. "It's gotta hurt. Does it? To be the only Vile Boy who doesn't get to be present for every big reveal and all the dramatic moments because you're off lurking somewhere in the dark to give us the intel we need. You do all the work, and we get all the credit." He laughs again, getting up onto his knees to lean over me. "Admit it hurts."

Never. My tongue is partially numb, but I say, "You just admitted I do all the work."

He's right, though. It fucking kills me, but I'll never admit it to him. Because I've learned to rationalize it within my mind. I tell myself that none of these assholes would be where they are if it weren't for me. I'm the one who accomplishes the most on our jobs, and without me, they wouldn't get their credit and their big dramatic moments. I'm the strength of Vile House. I'm the Ghost of Moros. I don't need the credit because I know I earned it.

But fucking hell, it grates when I don't get it. When I have to be silent and hidden while they get to be loud and powerful in the public eye. Every time I have to watch them get credit from our locals, be thanked by our citizens or applauded for their efforts, another piece of my well-glued-together puzzle chips away to stab at my pride and infect my already infected mind.

It's why I taunt Death. She's my most attentive audience member.

"Does it bruise your sensitive ego, Ghost?"

Despite all the numbness and the insecurities, I can still feel my face, so I morph it into the illusion of confidence. I'm a madman at my very core, and no one brings it to the surface like Riot does. I smile at him, forcing myself to laugh at how pathetic *he* is. He's the one with the inflated ego. He's the one who needs recognition without ever earning it.

"The fuck do you even do for Vile House?" I ask through choked laughter. "Cause some chaos? Fuck, that's easy. You think my ego is bruised? Look at yours, you sociopathic fuck." The root digs into my jaw, but I keep on laughing.

Harder and louder. Deeper and harsher. I can't feel my body, but I can feel my broken mind, and it's a goddamn master at deflection. He wants to hold a mirror in front of me? I'm gonna spin it until he can't stand to even look at himself. There's no time for introspection when I can tear someone else down first.

Riot laughs with me. He thinks I'm pathetic, and I think he is, and never, in the history of our feud, have either of us ever given in. It won't happen tonight, either. Straddling my body again, his toned legs press against my hips, and he brings my arms down and undoes the cuffs, letting my hands uselessly fall to my chest.

"Chaos, yeah," he agrees with me, dark hair flopping over his forehead. "Ready for a little more?" He lifts on his knees, opening his pants.

"The fuck are you doing?"

"You're dead, aren't you? This is what you wanted. A trip to Death's doorstep, and now I've brought you here with a deadened body and an awake mind. My turn to have a little fun with it. It's not quite necrophilia, but it's close enough. I've always wondered."

Reaching inside his pants, he brings his hard cock out, palming it above my still body. I watch for a second, transfixed by the bead of precum already on the tip, trying to figure out what his plan is and why I'm anticipatory over the unknown of it. But when I look up at his face, I see his thoughts. He's going to taunt me physically to fuck with me mentally just because he can. Because he somehow knows how flawed my mind is. Because he sees through the illusions I weave, peering into the mess of who I actually am.

Letting go of his dick, he grabs both of my wrists, holding them up above my chest. "Some guys sit on their hands to numb them so it feels like someone else is jerking them off." He laughs, looking at my slack hands. "Righty or lefty?" he asks.

"You stalk me enough to know the answer."

There is no way out of this—not until I get my control back. Whatever he has planned, I need to block it out and not let him invade my mind. Because I can take whatever he dishes out and not consider it a loss unless he gets in my head. He won't. I won't let him.

"True," he admits, dropping my left wrist. He moves forward, and when he wraps my right hand and fingers around the length of his thick cock, I hate myself just like he knew I would—taunting me physically to fuck with my mind, like I thought. Because it's not shame I'm feeling, it's regret, and he somehow knows it.

Regret that I can't feel him—can't taunt him back. Can't play the game because he's momentarily bested me.

I refuse to look at him. I won't let him see it in my eyes. Because there's a reason he's my biggest rival. My narcissism and his sociopathic personality aren't supposed to get along, and we don't, but fuck do we love goading one another. Taunting Riot is almost as alluring as taunting Death.

"Go ahead and try, Ghost. Try to block it out. But your

mind is online and your body is at my mercy, and when your cock gets hard, I'll let you know. You won't be able to feel it, but your blood knows exactly where it wants to go." He grins, tightening my fingers around him. "And tonight, with you dead in your grave, that's what dictates winning. You won't even have to admit it to me. Your dick will."

Oh, fuck him. "Why not just rape me? Hallows family tradition and all."

"You'd like that, wouldn't you? You'd finally get fucked by me and be able to use paralysis as an excuse." He slides my hand up and down, milking precum from his tip. "Nah, no excuses. I'll fuck you when you ask for it."

I laugh. "I never will."

"Your lies are so pretty, sweetheart." He leans down again, hair falling in front of his grey eyes now, shrouding him in something as sinister as this night. "Asphyxiation isn't your kink," he tells me, lips almost brushing mine while my dead hand jerks him off. "Restricted blood flow is. Don't worry. I know just where to apply pressure to give you that blood buzz in your head when you're ready." He licks the corner of my mouth before sitting upright again.

And I just have to watch it. Watch myself jerk him off without experiencing any of the sensations of it—having my mind experience it on behalf of my body.

I swallow thickly, my throat still able to feel, but my mind unsure of *how* I'm feeling. How does he know about the restricted blood flow? How could he possibly know that I'm into that?

"Stalker," I accuse.

"You already said that." He looks down at the show. My hand, his cock, my fingers twitching the odd time, a glistening tip. I swallow again, trying to hide that some sensation is already coming back a little. His deep V peeks out the bottom of his jacket, a dusting of dark hair where his pants are opened, and tanned skin covering toned muscles. It all heats my face because I don't appreciate finding him alluring. I don't enjoy the fact that he's winning and I find it hot. It's a contradiction my mind should loathe. "Like what you see?"

I close my eyes to block it out.

But then he's right there in front of me, breath fanning across my cheek. "What're you gonna do when you finally find her, Ghost?"

"Who?"

"Death. What're you gonna say to her?"

"I'm gonna laugh in her fucking face and turn my back on her."

"Keep going," he urges, his voice taking on a tone that brings tingly sensations back to my feet. Deep. Gravelly. Charged.

"I'm gonna spit in her face and tell her I'm better than she is!"

"More."

My eyes open, peering into his, up for the way he's enticing me. "I'm gonna tell her how fucking despicable I am, and despite it, she still failed to lure me into her trap."

"Fuck," he groans.

When he leans back, sitting on my lap, I feel myself shake. I'm gaining feeling back already, and fuck him for engaging my mind. Because my dick is hard. My eyes are glued to my hand, consciously trying to determine if he's still the one controlling it or if I am now. I feel it. Vaguely.

Hardly at all. But it's there—his hot, hard flesh in my deadened grip, giving me a sense of control.

"You didn't give me enough of the paralytic."

He grins, the master manipulator in him rising to the surface. "I gave you exactly as much as I wanted you to have."

Fuck, he knows I'm starting to feel. He planned it this way.

My heart picks up speed, gifting adrenaline to this dire experience. I'm dead, aren't I? Paralyzed in my plot in Moros Cemetery, living the feeling of what it'll be like when I'm put to rest here as an actual deceased man. But...

Epiphanies aren't fun when you don't want to have them.

Because the death that will land me here won't be near as appealing as the one I'm living now. Riot won't be here, taunting me like he always does, and there will be nothing left to fight for.

I look at him, finding his eyes already on mine. He knows what I've just realized. He knows that the chase with him is more appealing than the race to Death's precipice. He knows that I want to do it with him barking at my heels.

"There you are," he says. "You still tempting Death, Ghost? Or are you tempting me?"

My arm barely twitches. Not enough to rip this vine away from my neck, but enough to force my fingers tighter around his cock. "You think I'm at your mercy?" I ask, squeezing hard enough that his face tightens in pain. "Please. I just seduced you enough to drag you along for the ride. When this thing ends, we'll both be dead."

"Promise?" he asks, starting to sweat.

"Promise."

He buckles forward, his hand landing on my throat to press against the length of the root already wrapped there. He groans in my ear as his cock throbs in my fist, his orgasm as pained as my epiphany, painting my abs in warmth. "Game on, Sauder. Your cock is hard, so I win this round."

Fuck him, I'll win the next.

RIOT

3

NO EMPATHY

HIS MUSIC IS HIS MASK. A shield he hides behind. A way to feel without showing feelings. An emotion expressed without a word spoken—he's used this method so often that I've taken on the term.

Ghost keeps the house awake with his violin, but none of us have ever complained. He plays and plays, and the music gets stronger and more prominent, and as he lets go of everything trapped within the deep well of his seemingly shallow psyche, so do the rest of us. We settle in bed, close our eyes, and *feel*.

The strings of his violin make sense of our sensations. The tenor of his music pulls understanding from the locked boxes of our hearts. When Ghost plays his haunting harmonies into the dead of night, I start making sense to myself. I almost understand who I am and why I am the way I am. I understand it through the way he hurts, putting his pain into his music and ridding himself of the burden of it by creating something so deceptively dark. My self-understanding always fades away from my grasp as soon as the music ends.

Sometimes, Seven's guitar joins his violin, bleeding frustration and beauty into the music. Ransom's woodwinds sometimes join on nights Monster is having a particularly hard time. Oboe or clarinet, it doesn't matter, Ransom can play them all and make the melody hurt. Facts sometimes joins with his viola, deepening the tone until we're all entranced by it, but when he plays the organ at the asylum, I swear we all break a little. And when Monster adds himself to the music... it's so special it's hard to bear.

There's one piano in Vile House, and five of us can play it, but it's never me. I hardly even attempt to play in private, choosing to try to express myself in solitude because nothing about me makes sense and I forgot how to interpret my music. Nothing about how I feel, what I want, and who I am is meant for the outside world. They see my mask, what I manipulate them to see, and that's all they're allowed.

They don't even realize how fragile all my facades are.

Tonight, Ghost's music is full of desolation. Not pain. Not fear. Not even anger or rage. Just desolate longing, a feeling of emptiness and destruction. He's a broken boy who refuses to be broken; a destroyed man with no outer damage; a hunter whose prey is both too real and not real enough—a hunter who forgets to look over his shoulder and realize he is also prey.

Death. He seeks it. Not to die, but to broker a deal with it. To be better than it, more powerful than the allure of it. I used to think it was because he's a thrill seeker, and he still is, but he's also so fucking lost that he doesn't know where else to seek what he's after.

I'm going to be that thing. The thrill he chases. I'm going to be the emotion that finally fills him with something, overthrowing all that desolate emptiness to bring him back to life in a way he'll almost resent me for. I made a deal with my brother, but I'm not going to keep it like he thinks I am. I'm going to keep the one I made with Ghost instead, and when I win, everything will change.

Tonight in his grave was only the beginning, and I love that my actions have brought on this music. He's playing because of me. He's expressing himself because of me. He's broken because of me. My palm rubs my cock because of all of it combined. The way we both taunt something we won't name, and the game that brings a level of danger neither of us will admit to fearing. Our back and forth has always been exciting, but now... fuck, I grab my cock harder. I wonder if my cum is still painted on his abs along with the dirt from his grave?

As Ghost plays, filling Vile House with the relief we all need, giving us the comfort to do it in the privacy of our own rooms, I smile with my eyes closed and feel everything he feels.

Because without even knowing it, his violin playing is a cry for help.

I'm going to answer the call.

Dreaming of ways to do just that, I drift into a level of rest without ever falling asleep. My dick hard because of his music, my chest settled because of my pride, and my mind busy because of its dark ideas.

But when the emergency light in the corner of my room flashes red through my eyelids, I wait, my eyes wide open now. Waiting to see if it stays red to indicate an actual emergency or turns magenta to signal exactly what I need. Wide awake, I grin devilishly when the first tone from the alarm signals and the red light turns magenta.

Some little lamb has come to Vile House to make a bargain.

I LOVE THIS PART. The deals and the bargains. The lost souls who swallow their pride and make their way to Vile House as their last resort. The locals who have tried everything within their power but still failed, and the tourists who get trapped here, still seeking a way out.

Bargains in the stone hall of Vile House are so vibrant. Fear leeches into the air, turning the cavernous room wicked, and power rumbles from the ten of us. The combination of fear *and* power turns me on because I'm not the one who's terrified. I'm the god, standing here in my favourite mask, arms crossed and my smile in place beneath the material over my face, watching this poor, pathetic rodent wring his hands together, building up the nerve to speak.

All ten of us are here tonight, ready to fight over a new bargain. It's not often we're all home when someone comes knocking, but when we are, it makes the newcomer sweat so much more.

He's shaking on his feet, looking at the stone floor instead of us. As the door closes behind him and the initiate —Selena—leaves to monitor the house, he whimpers. Took balls to come here, especially on Halloween night, but now he's cracking, and I love watching them break.

We don't say anything. Director once told us to demand that they speak to get things moving, but by some unspoken agreement, none of us ever do. It's more fun to wait them out, watch them panic, see them second-guess their decision to come here. But no one leaves Vile House alive unless they make a bargain or fight their way out, and this one doesn't look like he has much fight left in him.

Shame.

Kyd vibrates next to me, and Facts jitters on my other side. Krypt leans against the wall, seemingly bored, and Monster shifts his weight from foot to foot. Ransom, Glitch, Seven, and Ghost are all stark still. Menace is poised, drinking down this guy's pained fear, leaning forward like he wants to goad him into a new reaction.

"I... I... hi," he says, voice shaking. "I, um, heard about the bargains you make?"

As one, we all breathe out, shifting our weight, acting as a unit. It's never planned, but we've been a team for years now, and we've been through enough of these bargain meetings to know how to dictate the outcome. My arousal spikes when the guy looks behind him, tempted by the exit.

"How... how do I make a bargain?" he asks, looking at our feet.

Menace answers. "You tell us what you want and then you tell us what you're willing to give up to get it."

"Don't waste our time," Ransom adds harshly.

"Oh, okay," he says. "It's a matter of... an estate."

Pathetic.

He's not a street-smart guy, that much is obvious. He's wearing a hoodie from the university Selena attends. I don't recognize him from Moros, so how the fuck does he know about Vile House bargains?

"I have family here. My great aunt passed away and left her house to me, but my cousin won't move out of it."

"Who's your cousin?" Ghost asks.

"Willow Olenna."

My smile is so sinister I wish he could see it beneath my mask. Love when Willow plays her own games, and now I know how this guy found out about Vile House. This isn't his bargain, it's hers, and I'm excited to see what she's going to offer up. Information is Willow's game, and I'm eager to be the one to collect.

"So, in exchange for you getting her out of my house, I will offer you... uh, money?"

"Don't want money," Seven says.

"Why do you want the house then?" Kyd asks. "Gonna move in?"

"I want to sell it."

"Offer something better," Glitch snaps. "Not money."

"Like what?" he asks. "I can pay you. I don't have much more than money."

Then why's he want to sell the house? "How about your ass?" Menace suggests. "Bet you're an anal virgin."

"N-no," he stammers, backing towards the door. "Please, I just want her out of the house! It's not worth my... ass. I just don't want her to have it!" He gulps, and the ten of us step forward as he steps back.

"Why'd your cousin tell you about Vile House?" Krypt asks, baiting him.

"She didn't. I overheard her talking about it, saying she was going to come here to make a bargain."

I laugh with my whole body. "So you thought you'd beat her to it?"

"Yes..." He tries to open the door, but it's locked. "Look, maybe this is a bad idea."

"Oh, it's definitely a bad idea," Ghost says, his voice playfully dominant. "But here you are. Too late to back out now."

"What do you want from me?" he shrieks, skirting around the outside of the room. "I thought bargains were safe!"

Oh, he thought wrong. Especially because he thinks he's the one making the bargain. Willow beat him to it, offering herself up on a platter by sending her cousin here. She's an old friend from high school, and no one can access real, undiscovered information like she can. The ten of us look at one another, coming to a decision. This is gonna be fun. Perfect end to Halloween.

"Offer something better and maybe we'll take it," Facts says, and when the guy looks at him in his copper mask, he adds, "Hello," in a creepy as fuck voice.

Monster hasn't said anything, but that doesn't prevent him from circling the guy and herding him away from the wall. He's busy now, trying to think while watching his surroundings, too stupid to realize he's ringed by sharks.

"Please! My car? I'll give you my car. And money. More money. Please."

"We want your body. Your life," Glitch says.

"Your soul," Kyd adds.

"N-no!"

I step to his front, the others surrounding him, Monster at his back. "What'll it be?"

"Please, have some *empathy!* I lost my aunt!"

Boring. Reaching forward, my smile parting my lips, I grab the sides of his face and say, "I ain't got no empathy." I snap his neck.

GHOST

4

RAGE & CONFUSION

WE'RE LINED up in rank. Again. That's twice this week, and I don't mind one bit because I'm second from the front, and fuck everyone else. I'll knock Seven down eventually, and then it'll be me in first place where I goddamn belong.

With Menace between me and Riot, I give him a smug look, not at all fazed about what happened last night because here I am, ahead of him like I am in everything else.

"The hell happened to you?" Director asks me. "You look half dead."

Riot snorts, and everyone looks at me.

"Something I need to know about?" Director asks us.

Yeah, my dead hand jerked him off and he came on my abs… and I didn't wash it off right away.

We've already been punished one too many times for our spats. Director made a rule: Riot and Ghost are brothers, but Killian and Soren are allowed to fight. We don't always follow that rule, but we did last night, so I ignore Director.

"Why are we here? I have to get back to Misfit Hall

before they start wondering where I am." I shift from foot to foot, agitated and sore from being strangled and paralyzed. My fingers ache from playing violin for so long, the calluses more tender than my ego. He might think he won, but it won't happen a second time.

Director sighs, knowing something is going on, but he chooses not to press it for now. "Sit down, boys. We've got news from Axel."

Kyd's smile widens, and like the little shit he is, he steps right in front of Director at the head of the table. He slams his palms down, terribly imitating Director. "Boys!" he shouts, trying to be stern. "My boyfriend is batshit crazy with a lazy eyelid and a big dick. When I got that tarot card reading last year, I knew he was gonna show up. And guess what?!" He looks at us all expectantly as we sit down. "Nine inches." He holds his hands out, measuring about fourteen inches.

"Bullshit." I snort. "He's too skinny to have a nine-inch cock."

"He ain't skinny, bud. He's a man with stripes, and I can't wait to hunt him like a lion."

There's a pause around the table, and Director sighs yet again, knowing what's coming. Our favourite guessing game.

"Twenty bucks," Menace says. "The nickname will be Gazelle."

"Forty says it'll be Simba," Riot guesses.

"Fifty says it's Lioness." Seven laughs. "He'll wanna make Axel part of his pride."

"What's a lion's biggest prey?" Glitch asks. "It'll be that."

"Zebra," I say. "A hundred bucks."

"Two hundred says he nicknames the nickname," Ransom says as he sits. "If it's Zebra, it'll turn into Z."

"Zeebs." Facts places his bet. "Hello, three hundred dollars."

It's become fun to bet on what Kyd will call everyone. None of us saw *bestie* coming when Remi showed up, but Kyd claimed him, so it stuck. Krypt doesn't like it, but he hasn't said shit about it because Director sat him down and had a talk about how Remi needs friends. Krypt didn't like that either.

"Alright, sit the hell down, lover boy," Director says to Kyd, shoving him out of the way. "I told you not to sleep with the doctor."

"I haven't!" Kyd climbs onto the table, walking across it with his fingers up in the air, a scout's honour. "I promise, pops! I only know how big his dick is because he wears tight fancy pants. Mmmm."

"Don't call me that. Sit your crazy ass down."

Kyd does a flip off the table, barely executes the landing, and plops down in a chair. His outfit is pastels today, and his hair is freshly dyed a baby pink that makes his pale blue eyes stand out. Pretty sure he's wearing baby pink lip gloss too, because his smile is sparkly. So are his teeth.

I lean back in my chair and wait for this bullshit to be over. I love Vile House, and I don't even mind Director despite how often he bosses me around, but I hate meetings. My brain wasn't built for meetings. I'm a doer, not a thinker.

"Before we start. Riot, you're owed by Willow Olenna?"

"Oh, I'll collect."

"Good. No more unnecessary deaths, got it?" He nods, moving on before Riot confirms. "Axel thinks Reaper Corp has a contact in Moros. Someone is feeding them information." Director looks right at me like I'm about to be the star of the show. *About time.*

"Yates, I'm guessing?" I lean forward.

"Axel thinks so."

Yates is the current leader of The Misfits. He's a filthy, pompous douchebag who inhales more cigarette smoke than air, relies on his younger crew members to do the dirty work, and is too fucking stupid to see how *fucking stupid* his son is. The Misfits used to bring a ton of importance to Moros, but since Yates took over, they've gone downhill, especially because his son is second in command. Being a member of their gang as my real name and having Moros know I'm one of them is goddamn embarrassing. I don't do well with embarrassment.

"Dr. Graves is a smarty-pants, so I'd trust him. Plus, I've been creeping on his brain doctor research," Kyd says. Director gives us all a pointed look, maybe trying to convey that we can't fully trust Axel, but no one asks, so neither do I.

"Why not just kill Yates and be done with it?" Krypt asks.

"Hello," Facts cuts in. "Because if we control Yates, we control the narrative."

"Exactly," Director agrees. "But first, we need to plant some devices and get some proof."

"Get Kyd's boyfriend to plant one of his mind chip things in his head and start brainwashing him," Riot suggests. "Then we control everything. Even The Misfits."

"Get me close enough so we can," Director says to Riot. "Yates has asked for a Vile House contact, and I need you to be it. Create some chaos, Riot. I want his crew questioning him. Time they get new leadership."

Riot lifts a brow. "You have someone in mind?"

"I do," Director says, but he doesn't tell us who. Pretty sure I already know, though. "Ghost, I need you there. Eyes on Yates. You need to report everything going on, and if you can't get devices planted in Misfit Hall, you need to be the device. Listen, learn, get intel, figure out who he's in contact with and how they knew to contact him. Got it?"

Whatever. Easy. I nod.

"There's a catch."

Of fucking course there is. I hate being in their gang, and I'm the one who always has to pay for their fuckups.

"Riot's going to build you credit within the gang." Oh, fuck, my blood heats to ungodly temperatures. "He's going to demand you're there at the meeting."

"*The fuck?!* Why?" I stand while Riot grins.

"Because it'll piss off Yates, earn you status, get you in good with the rest of the crew so that when we flip their leadership and eventually team with The Misfits in this fight against Reaper Corp, you'll be our bridge. Suffer now and prosper later, Ghost. Problem?"

Major fucking problem, but I keep my mouth shut, ignore Riot, and leave the room. Always the same.

Suffer now, Ghost. Buckle under, Ghost. Take the heat, Ghost.

Yeah, fuck that. I'm at my wit's end with being the punching bag around here. I'm the biggest asset Vile House has, and fuck Director for using it and then denying me any of the glory. I'll be his ghost, but outside of my jobs, I refuse to be subtle any longer.

I climb the stairs and march down the hall, banging my fist on Krypt's door. I try the handle, but it's locked, and it grates on my already frayed nerves to be denied access to yet another thing.

"Remi!"

He unlocks the door and yanks it open. "What's wrong?" he asks, seeing the frustration written all over my face. I bury it.

Everything is wrong. Nothing is wrong. It's the same feeling I always have. Complete rage and confusion over something that doesn't make itself clear. I'm pissed off about being in The Misfits while everyone else here gets to shine as a Vile Boy. I'm jealous and envious of their fame while I lurk in the shadows. I'm even mad that Remi is so settled, so broken but whole because of the way Krypt made him see himself.

I'm broken... Why can't I be whole like he is? Why does no one want to fix me?

Because I'm not fucking broken! Not on the outside. My illusion is strong, and until the day I die, I'll make sure it stays intact.

"Selena is at home. Let's go check on her and Mom." When he hesitates, I growl at him. "Grow a fucking backbone, Remi. You don't need his permission to leave." I walk away.

"Soren, wait."

"Ghost," I snap, not waiting for him to lock Krypt's door.

There was a time when Remi relied on me, turned to me, and trusted me for everything. He used to look up to me, and together, we set our minds on fighting this curse and beating it side by side. He never knew I was actively taunting it, but I was in his corner. I was in his corner so hard that I herded him to Vile House that night Malone stalked him through the streets of Moros. He thought I was out to kill him to end the curse, but I wanted him to come here for protection. I just hadn't anticipated Krypt jumping on his bargain before I could.

But now he has Krypt... and I don't know how to feel about not being needed. I don't want the burden, I just want to be important. I *am* important and I want everyone to know how much.

Remi follows me down the stairs, silent, but emitting energy like he wants to say something. "I heard... I heard you play last night."

"You asking me something?" I head towards the basement to access the tunnels.

"No. I don't know. Are you okay?"

"Remiel!" Krypt shouts, storming towards us. Remi stops. Krypt grabs my brother by his tattooed throat, looks him straight in the eye, and lets all his monsters shine. *How dare Remi move without telling Krypt.* Fucking pathetic.

I roll my eyes and keep moving, only to be stopped at the entrance to the basement stairs by the fucking prick who is apparently going to 'build me credit' in my own gang. Yet another kick to the nuts.

I open my mouth, ready to rip into him, but he talks over me. "You never know when to shut your mouth, do you, sweetheart?"

"What'd I say if you called me that again?" I push past

him, once again thriving now that he's here to rile me—that perfect coupling of desire and despair.

"Didn't say shit, actually. Started the threat and never finished it." He follows me down the stairs. "You ready for tonight?"

I spin and grab *him* by the throat, pressing him back until his head clacks off the wall of the stairwell. I crowd him, my chest against his hard pecs, his abs shifting against mine.

"So twitchy to get your hands on me again?" he asks while suffocating.

"Listen, asshole. I don't need you to build me credit with The Misfits. Tonight will go off without a hitch because *I'll* make it go off without a hitch. You're there to deal with Yates. Not me. Got it?"

He only grins, his grey eyes full of unspoken taunts.

"Don't blow my fucking cover." I slam him back and shout, "Remi! Let's go!"

I STARE at Remi's arms while Mom makes lunch for the three of us. I don't trust her, but she's still alive, and Axel isn't controlling her anymore. She's still a zombie, but part of me thinks it's an act. She's up to something, and the amount of times she's asked me where Gregory Malone is sets off alarm bells in my mind. Why does she think I'd know?

"You two are fucking stupid for that." I nod at Remi's wrists. "Moros knows you're with Keegan, and if they see your wrists, they'll figure out who he is. You'll have to wear long sleeves forever."

Remi pulls his sleeves down to cover the tattoos and stares at Mom. "At least his mark is better than hers."

True, I guess. Krypt's brands are better than the slice Mom left on his wrist because he did them to save my brother, and Mom did them to harm him. I'll have to work my way past Kyd to confront the fuck out of Axel Graves for making her do that to Remi.

"How's she been?" Remi asks Selena.

She'll be finished with school in a few months, and now that she's initiating with Vile House, I doubt she'll go back for the next semester. Remi is safe under Krypt's watchful obsession, and she's never worried about me as much, so there's no point in killing herself studying psychology for our curse anymore.

"The same. Mostly absent but has lucid moments. Always asks about Malone or Graves."

Both of which are at the asylum—Axel as a scientist and Malone as a lab rat.

"What're we doing with her?" Selena asks, looking at both of us. "I say we just back off and let her be."

"You shouldn't stay here. Stay at Vile House or the Hallows' place. Anywhere but here." I look at my sister, proud of her for how she's been doing. "You still have months before you level up, but you can stay in the lower-ranking rooms."

"Yeah, yeah." She waves me off. "Again, I ask, what are we doing with her?"

"Back off and let her be," Remi agrees with Selena.

"Even if she gets her mind back, something isn't right with her."

Yeah, she's too focused on Gregory Malone. Krypt knows something, but he hasn't told me what, and I'm getting real sick of his shit lately. Fucker is too obsessed with my brother. I once threatened him that if he raped my brother, I'd rape his...

Maybe it's time to make good on that promise.

RIOT

5

SLIPPING

MISFIT HALL IS pathetic compared to Vile House. Our house has character, tunnels, and creepy old treatment rooms that speak to the sinister, evil-experimental side of me. Vile House is as alive as Moros herself, but Misfit Hall is a fucking joke. It used to be a fire station, but now it's uncared for, dirty, and trashy as hell.

The difference between a gang like The Misfits and us is that we don't publicly gloat. They throw parties, invite the town to their house, decorate the lawn with red plastic cups, cigarette butts, and beer cans, and generally have all sorts of lowlifes passed out in their numerous beds. We don't invite anyone but Vile members into our house, unless they're there to make a bargain.

We respect our space; they destroy their space.

No wonder Moros doesn't value The Misfits anymore.

I'm early for my meeting with Yates, but I'm here on purpose. Unmasked. Ghost has been slinking around this place for an hour, planting all the devices without anyone noticing him. He's bored here. The jobs don't require all his skills, and it's eating away at him to have to fake it as a member of the gang. So, when he walks into the room he uses as his own here, he sees me sitting on his bed and closes the door behind him.

He's easy to read if you catch him without his shields up, so before he can slam them into place, I catch the rage and the boredom on his face. He fucking loathes that I get to come here as a masked member of the ten while he'll have to stand at Yates' side as a lower-ranking member of a useless crew. It makes me grin, and that earns me a fist flying at my face.

I grab it and throw him down on his bed, climbing atop to straddle the feisty bastard. "Hey, sweetheart."

"The fuck are you doing here?" He bucks, trying to dislodge me. "If you blow my cover with Yates, I'll help Director kill you."

"No you won't." I smile at him just because he hates it. His blue eyes narrow on my mouth, and his body tenses beneath me, so fucking lithe and toned it gets me going. "What fun would a trip to Hell be if I'm not there herding you exactly where you want to go?"

"I have fun all on my own, thanks," he says, lifting his hands to throw me off. I pin them beside his dark blond head. "Get the fuck outta my space, Ri-Killian. Jesus. Why are you all up in my business lately?"

"A bargain," I deadpan, loving how this feels. When I straddled him in his grave, he was so pliant and still. I like the lively version of him even more. "Is this how you fuck people when you're here? On your back so they don't see your Vile House tats?"

"From behind," he snaps. "Want me to show you?"

I definitely do, but he's not riled up enough yet. I won't fuck him until he begs, and to be honest, I don't know if he'll drop his pride enough to do so. Not with words, anyway. He'll pull a move, try to overpower me, make true on his threat to rape me, and that'll be his begging. I'll know it when I see it. I'll expect it when I manipulate it out of him.

I hum from deep within my throat as the night sky makes an appearance outside. His face darkens, but his eyes light up because as much as he doesn't want to admit it, he loves this. A challenge. An opponent. A way to blow off steam and be fucking sick about it. There's a reason we've been fighting for years, but now that it's part of an actual deal we made, it's coming to a breaking point, and Soren Sauder loves the unknown of it.

I love the unknown of *him*.

I grin and he glares, but when someone knocks on the door, his eyes turn panicky.

"Sauder? You in there?"

Ghost tries to shove me off to hide, but I pin him down as the door opens. Lockan Tate, one of Moros' most deceptive men and a member of The Misfits, walks in, pausing when he catches me straddling Ghost. I'm unmasked, and Lock is about to make his own assumptions that'll piss Ghost off. Even better.

"Didn't know you two fucked," he says, closing the door behind him. "Killian."

"Lockan." I give him one of my charming smiles, but there's trouble etched into it. Lockan's bright green eyes stay on me a few extra seconds, like everyone's do when they aren't sure if I'm flirting with them or not, so I meld my smile into a grin and lick my lips. Most people melt, but

Lockan just grins back, combing his tattooed fingers through his flop of dark and gold hair to push it back.

Little does Lockan know, his adoptive brother—for lack of a better term—is also my Vile House brother. Glitch has kept the secret from his lifelong friend since he joined, and if it ever comes to light, I'm excited to see how the pieces fall.

When Ghost bucks and tries to throw me off again, I wrap my fingers around his throat and squeeze. Not against his windpipe this time, but against the arteries on either side of his neck, proving to him just how well I know how to restrict blood flow to give him a buzz. He takes the hint, eyes widening and lips parting. Ah, such a good boy.

"Am I interrupting?" Lock asks, walking into the room to take something off Ghost's dresser. "Because I'm not leaving. Give me a show. Better than being out there." He leans his ass against the edge of the dresser and lights a joint.

Looking down, I see Ghost's face turn red. I hate red skin. It's such a weakness not being able to mask your sweaty, flushed features to hide how you feel. Pathetic fools. It irks me to see he has this weakness. I grin, and when I lean my weight back to find his cock thickening beneath my ass, I grin wider.

"I win," I tell him. "Admit it."

"Fuck you," he pants.

"Admit it."

His hips buck and his knee cracks against my ribs. He throws me off his body and coughs, rubbing at his throat. I laugh, wincing a bit at my ribs, but when I look at him, the victory is in the way he's so fucking ruffled. *Yeah, sweetheart, keep thinking about it. Start begging.*

"Shit, you two are hot," Lock says. "How long has this been—"

"It's not. Ever." Ghost stands, taking the joint from Lock. "Don't comment on it, asshole."

Lock laughs, not at all fazed by Ghost's mood. "Thought you were best friends with Keegan? You been living a 'best friend's brother' fantasy behind his back?"

I chuckle, climbing off the bed. "Bet he creates some amazing fantasies in that dark head of his," I say, standing with Lock. "Bet I star in them all."

"Fuck you... Killian." Ghost inhales the joint. We don't often fuck up on names outside of our masks, but his temper has always made him stupid, so Lockan notices the hesitation.

To stop the topic, I say, "He usually calls me sweetheart, but he's embarrassed."

Ghost's exhale is shaky. "You need something?" he asks Lock.

"To get the fuck out of this building," Lock says. "Yates is all worked up about..." He glances at me because I'm the outsider here, and I shouldn't know about the meeting tonight.

"About me, right?" Ghost asks. "Because I'm requested at this meet-up?"

"Yeah." Lock nods. "This fucking crew, man. Not what it used to be..."

Ghost doesn't disagree. Now that I know Lockan hates it here as much as Ghost, it gives me an idea of who Director has in mind to take over The Misfits. Lockan is thirty, like me, and he's been a loyal member of this crew since he was fifteen. Back then, the leader was awesome and cared about

Moros, the locals, and his crew more than anything. Yates fucked everything up and turned them useless and lost them respect in town.

"Don't you have somewhere better to be?" Ghost asks me. "Fuck off."

I grin at Lock and then shift it into a smirk I create for Ghost only. "See you later, sweetheart."

I leave Misfit Hall and head back to the asylum to change and get ready to meet Yates. All the while, my mask slips off and I stop forcing my smile. The pressure fades away as I exhale, and every fake facade slips away, leaving me exhausted from holding everything in place for so long.

Alone, I don't have to act for anyone. My face can be blank enough to scare because no one is around to terrify. I've trained myself to be the perfect representation of whatever is needed in the moment, and without a mask in place... I'm blank. Because under all the pretend and the acting, I don't know who I am anymore. When I don't have a person or a situation to manipulate, I don't know what to do.

It eats at me, this need to be something but never knowing if it's the real me or a fake version of me. I've become so good at pretending that I don't know how to drop the act, to let it go and let my personality shine through. I don't even know if I have a personality or if every facet of me has been fabricated over the years, molding and shaping me into whatever version of myself is necessary to survive.

All I know is what I *need*. Not who I am.

I need attention. I need recognition. I need importance and power. I need superiority. To get all that, I charm and lie and piss people off to get the rise out of them I require. I manipulate and force with no respect for their feelings because fuck them, their feelings don't matter compared to mine. These are *my* needs, and it's a cutthroat world, so I'm going to be the most cutthroat of them all. I'll do whatever it takes to feed my ego, even if I don't understand why it craves such things.

I didn't save my brother as a kid.

I didn't do anything other than sit with him in the lonely darkness while our parents called him sick but forgot to call me sick because I learned to act better than he could. I never taught him to act. I didn't fucking help him until I was a teenager and we killed our parents in the span of half an hour. That night, I shed the skin of my former self and became this new, unclear, twisted version of myself. Because this version protected Krypt, the one and only person I give a fuck about in this dire world. I tell myself that I'm his hero and I did it for him, but...

I saved him to give myself the ego boost. I helped him to prove that I was stronger than him. I freed him so we could murder together, so I'd have someone to connect with over something so monumental. I do love him, and he's my brother...

But it's too late because he doesn't even need me anymore.

But Soren does. He can't chase Death on his own, and if I can aid him in any way, even if it's sinister and unethical, I'll do it because of that necessity within me that needs to be in control of everyone and everything. Because of the part of me that needs to shape him into a toy for my own amusement.

"What are you still doing here?" Director asks, coming

to stand where I've been zoned out, staring through the slats in the door to Gregory Malone's cell. "Meeting is—"

"I'm aware." I ball my fists, loathing that he's checking up on me. "Come to babysit me like you always do?"

Director steps up beside me, peering at Malone just sitting on the floor. He's staring at the wall, but his mind hasn't snapped yet. It will soon, especially now that Axel has permission to test some of his new methods on him.

"I'm not babysitting, but you have to admit, you're irresponsible sometimes."

Because *my* priorities are most important, but other people like to shove theirs down my throat. I want life to be on my agenda, not anyone else's. When I first became a Vile Boy and joined the ten, Director almost kicked me right back out because I didn't want to put the needs of a society before my own. I learned to act, and over the years, I got really good at it. Now I care. Not about anyone, but about belonging. I want to be a member of Vile House because this is the most powerful place for me to be. I want to save Moros because it's the only place I can imagine living. I want to harness the power that comes with wearing a white and black mask, and I want to continue living my agenda with the backing of a society that praises me for who I am instead of chaining me for it.

"I've been good," I remind him, hating that he hasn't noticed.

"Yeah, you have," he says, contradicting my thoughts. "But the past few days, you've been... I can tell when you're slipping, Riot."

"I'm not fucking slipping."

"What's going on with you and Ghost?"

I grin at Gregory Malone's back. "A bargain. You can't butt in."

"I can, and I will if things get out of hand. You're brethren first and foremost." He turns his back to the door, looking across the hall at another door, its occupant chattering to herself. "I need you. Both of you. Don't make me step in."

What would he even do if he stepped in? He's locked us up, put us through hell, tried to get us to break and bend to his will, but he either fails or doesn't try to actually succeed... because he never has. Part of me wonders if he just does it to show there are consequences because I've never actually gotten the impression that he wants to change us.

"What would you do?" I ask, goading him and letting my facades shift beneath my surface until he gives me a hint at which one he needs right now.

"Step in to make sure you're both okay."

"Okay?" I look at him, trying to decipher his meaning.

"I understand your need to rival one another, but the two of you aren't... your games are deadly, whether you mean for them to be or not. It would hurt me if you ever succeeded in hurting each other irreparably." He sighs, pinching the bridge of his nose. "So? Are you close to that yet?"

I look away. "I'm keeping him from his curse, if that's what you're asking."

"For him or for you? Who benefits from this?"

We both do. "You're the one who says I'm sociopathic, so who do you think benefits more?"

"I never... you have some of the traits, Riot. Just be

careful and remember that you're family." He bumps my shoulder to add ease to the conversation. "And don't lock me out if he needs help."

I'll be the one helping him, thanks.

Done with this conversation, I grab my bag with my change of clothes and my mask. "Have a meeting to get to. Want me to take Lockan Tate out of there?"

Director huffs, adding a smile. "I want you to get him kicked out."

"Done."

GHOST

6

PATHETIC & WEAK LOOKS GOOD ON YOU

WHEN THE POWER is imbalanced within Moros, the town becomes more dangerous. There's a settled, predictable, confident hierarchy of control here, and Vile House has always perched on top. But that's not to say we're the most prominent. No. We're the power source that comes from within, controlling from the depths of Moros' very bones, protecting as often as we are harming. We do it silently. Secretly. Discreetly. Because that's the way of us and has been for generations—since the creation of Vile House.

Over the years, new crews, cults, and gangs have tried to overthrow us. None of them have. Moros doesn't respond to obnoxious power. Our citizens like taking care of themselves, working through their own problems, and relishing in the power that comes with getting their own shit done. So when a powerhouse gang tries to take over and deal with issues on their behalf, the locals dispute it. Turn their noses up at it. Fight it and challenge it, refusing to accept that something or someone is more in control of their lives than they are. It's why gangs don't rise to power here like they do in other areas of the world.

But Vile House? Yeah, we're the silent partner. The open door—the last call. When a real problem arises, and they've exhausted their efforts, that's when they come to us. And when we help them handle their problems through favours, bargains, or deals, we keep the dealings private. That's why we stay on top. Mystery and strength. Secrecy and discretion. Support and guidance.

Yates, the current leader of The Misfits, hasn't learned the lesson of aiding someone in dealing with their problems and creating a level of camaraderie once it's over. Yates wants to swoop in, overpower the town as well as the threat, and boast about it while taking all the credit. You can be pretty much anything in Moros, but you can't be a fraud, and that's exactly what Moros thinks of Yates. It's dragging down the reputation of The Misfits, creating unease within the crew.

I love unease. Makes finger-pointing so easy.

"They demanded you be here for it," Yates tells me, losing his shit and failing to hide it. "Fuck knows why. What do you have to do with Vile House?"

"Nothing." I flick a cigarette free and bite it between my teeth. I'm not a smoker, but Yates is, and I've learned to smoke in order to have an excuse to be out here, listening to him vent without him noticing he's doing it to me.

"You better not be double-crossing us, Sauder. Vile House is a stain on this town." Yates tries to light his cig, but his lighter won't spark.

I strike a match and hold it up for him. "Then why set a meeting with them? Why ask for a contact?"

He inhales before blowing smoke to the sky. "I didn't ask for shit. I *demanded*. I need them thinking we're working together."

"We aren't?"

Yates looks at me, eyes narrowed. "What would we be working with them on?" he asks, trying to get me to misspeak and reveal something he thinks I know. All his act does is show me he has something to hide.

"What would we need them to *think* we're working with them on?" I counter, lighting my cigarette and letting the match burn down to my thumb and fingertip.

He ignores me, and as much as being ignored irks everything within me, I suck in chemicals and nicotine to prevent myself from stabbing the bastard right here on the front step of Misfit Hall. I turn my back on Yates and look through the front window, seeing Lockan chat with some of the other members who wish he was in charge. I'm Vile House loyal, through and through, but Lockan Tate, Yates' third in command, has wormed his way in, and I like the crazy bastard. He reminds me of Riot; they've both got the art of charming people down to a perfected science. I'm smart enough not to fall for their bullshit.

Lock runs his hand through a young guy's hair, attempting to console him while he cries about something that happened to his dad, but he looks over his shoulder and grins at me. Ain't nothing sincere about his grin, and because of it, I can't help but grin back. Submissive people are intriguing to men like us because we enjoy lording power, but our attention never lasts long. This nineteen-year-old showed up to demand answers about his missing dad, but honestly, if he wants the truth, he should go to Vile

House. His dad is dead, and Director has a good way of conveying that message.

"Tom!" Yates shouts through the door. "Get your ass out here. Lock, let's go!"

Tom is Yates' son, and he's as much of a lazy piece of shit as his dad. He comes outside with a gun and a beer, a loyal pup to his daddy.

Seeing me out here for this meeting has him envious. "You rise up in rank while I wasn't looking?" Tom asks me.

"You grow a set while I wasn't looking?" I fire back.

"Vile Boy has the hots for Sauder. Requested he be here," Lock says, reaching his hand out to me for a smoke. "You fucking a Vile Boy?"

I hand him the smokes, trying to read everything about him. It's not easy to hide a full back tattoo, and I've had my Vile House tat for over three years. When I fuck, I fuck them from behind. When I shower, I lock and barricade the door. When I sleep, I grip a knife in my hand and leave my shirt on. The only time I let my guard down is when I'm in Vile House. But Lock knows something about me. I don't know if he's seen my tattoo or if he just suspects something about my lack of nakedness when I have a body that deserves to be shown off. I'm not shy, and he knows it, so he's suspicious. Riot being here earlier doesn't help...

"Maybe." I shrug, sparking another match for him. "They're masked, so I wouldn't know if I was, would I?"

He leans in, inhaling while his smoke lights. His dark and gold hair tickles my jaw, and his deceptive pale green eyes swirl with playfulness. "But you just admitted you fuck guys?"

No. I lick my lips at him as an answer. He's curious about Killian, but I won't confirm or deny anything because Vile House has taught me the power of mystery and secrets.

"No funny business tonight," Yates says. "Let me do the talking. If he tries anything, fucking kill him."

Over my dead body. When Killian Hallows dies, it'll be either by my hand or when I drag him to Hell with me. He thinks he's my god, but he's just my hellhound, nipping at my heels as I taunt Death, my loyal little puppy who will follow me anywhere. I'll lead him straight to her door without him even realizing it.

Yates and Tom walk down the steps, and Lock nudges me to get me moving. One of these days, I'm going to blow this gang up from the inside. As soon as I get Director the information he's after, he'll give me the green light to unleash on this fucked up place. Being with them keeps me up at night, and I'm done playing this part.

When Lock's shoulder brushes mine as we walk across the dewy grass under the cover of nightfall, I look at him, and he looks at me. Yeah, I'll get him out before I demolish this place. He's hated it here ever since Yates took over, and I've never asked why he stays. On the other hand, the crew would do so much better under his rule. Maybe The Misfits can be salvaged.

Hades Park is surrounded by trees, with a small playground and a soccer field. It's where Krypt and Riot found that kid's dad's body, but so far, Yates is denying he knows anything about it. I know one of his guys killed the dad, but I don't know why he took the kid in. It's where Riot demanded to meet, requesting that Soren Sauder be there.

So here I fucking am. Loathing that he gets to play the Vile Boy while I have to be the idiot at Yates' side. My tether of restraint is fraying by the second.

"There he is," Yates says, tossing his smoke butt and immediately lighting another one. Tom gives him a light this time, and I stand next to Lock, watching Riot approach the park from the woods.

His Vile mask is in place, white and black, stark and ominous. The way he walks compliments his god complex, and the energy that rolls off him makes my molars grind. He's deranged because he's so charming about it, but when he wants to be deadly, he has no trouble slipping into that role, too. Sometimes, I think *serial killer* is his base layer and everything else about him is the mask, but he's hard to read when he doesn't want to be read. All I know is that he exudes power and sex, and I hate him for both.

Yates stiffens in front of me, and Tom looks at his dad for direction. Lock shuffles from foot to foot, but he seems more amused than anything, and I watch my Vile House brother command attention and instill fear just by walking towards us. Fucking pisses me off. If I was masked, I'd be on par with him.

Dressed in black from head to toe, his boots come to a stop and his hands slip into his pockets. Casually lethal and powerful about it. "Talk," is all he says, his voice deep and raspy, slightly modulated by a filter in his mask. I pay attention to Lock's reaction, wondering if he'll recognize the voice from earlier. If he does, he doesn't react.

"I'd rather have this meeting without them." Yates hooks his thumb towards me and Lock, making me plot an entirely new way to murder him. Lock is his third, so why doesn't he want him here?

"No," Riot says.

"Why him?" Yates asks, pointing at me. "He's low-ranking. He's nobody."

Holy fuck, I see red. There are four throwing knives in my jacket, and my fingers twitch to grab all of them and bury them in the back of Yates' head. *I'm fucking nobody?* I can't wait to show him how much of a *somebody* I really am.

"Which means he's not full of shit. Start talking or I'm gone."

"There's outside trouble," Yates says while Tom sets his beer down, reaching for a gun in his waistband. He grips the handle but doesn't pull it free, and I look at Riot to let him know it's there.

"Is there?" Riot asks like he doesn't give a shit.

"Yeah. Group of homicide detectives looking into a string of murders. Leading them right here."

He's such a fucking liar. The unknown kid Lock was just comforting came to Moros with his dad, and his dad wound up dead. According to Director, Yates reached out to the kid's dad—who happens to be a homicide detective—meaning he was the one that led them here. But why? To distract us while he lets Reaper Corp in the back door? Yates has never wanted a Vile House contact before, and this seems like such a small deal to finally make him reach out for one. He's playing us, which is obvious, but I don't know why, and I don't know why the dad had to die. I'm pretty sure the whole homicide detective thing is bullshit anyway.

Silently, I move around to Yates' other side, getting a

look at his side profile. "Thought you didn't know anything about the kid's dead dad," I say.

Yates looks at me for talking out of turn. "Couple locals found the kid and the body. The kid's hysterical, doesn't know what he's talking about, but his story lines up with a few issues we've had. Wasn't us who killed the guy." *Yes it was.*

It was Krypt and Riot who found the kid and his dad, not a couple locals, but Yates doesn't know that. Is this just some half-ass plan he let go unchecked and now he's cleaning up his own mess?

"Get to the point, old man," Riot says.

"Talk to my dad like that again and I'll—"

Lock disarms Tom before he even has the gun all the way out. "You'll what?"

"Get your fucking hands off me!" Tom shouts, but Yates' is already smacking his son, telling him to get the fuck back to the hall. "Give me my gun," he snaps at Lock.

Lock throws it into the woods with a smile on his face. "Slipped," he says.

Riot turns to leave, letting us know this is a waste of his time.

"Hold up," Yates says. "I got word that there's going to be an ambush in Moros on Saturday night. Wanted to, uh, work together to take care of the issue."

"Got word how?" Riot asks.

"Just did."

"Why would we work with you? You're useless."

Yates steps forward, but Riot flings a dagger. It embeds in Yates' shoulder, and then Riot grabs me, and I have to goddamn go along with it. He spins me, my back to his chest, his arm around my throat and his mask beside my head.

"Hey, sweetheart," he whispers. "I like this look on you. Pathetic and weak."

Reaching back, I snug a throwing knife up to his inner thigh and ask, "Pathetic and weak?"

He groans. "This is how it's going to go, Yates. You wanna work together, you'll send this one." He taps my chest with his palm. "Messages come through him. If he isn't available, I'll take that one." He points at Lock. "But if you ever fucking talk to me again, I won't miss your throat."

Yates leaves the dagger in his shoulder. "Fuck Vile House," he snarls. "This was a warning. But I'll make sure Moros knows you turned your back on it."

"Moros knows where to turn for help," Riot says. "And it sure as fuck isn't you. Why not put that one in charge?" he asks, nodding to Lock again. "I'll kill you and your pathetic son tonight and set the balance right in Moros when he takes over. How's that sound?"

Fuck, he's dumb. He's going to get Lock killed. I press my ass back to warn him to shut up, but all it does is draw another groan from his throat.

Yates looks at Lock. "You fucking betraying bastard." Lock hasn't betrayed anyone, but he doesn't deny it. He's done taking Yates' shit, just like I am. "Get the fuck out and don't come back."

Lock barely reacts to being thrown from the gang he's been in for fifteen years. Looking at me, he asks, "You good, Sauder?"

"Oh, he's good," Riot answers for me. "He's Yates' little bitch now, and with you gone, he just moved up in rank."

Riot presses his hard cock against my ass before pushing me away. “Next time you want Vile House to save your ass, send Sauder. I won’t look at you again.” Riot turns and strides out of the park. “Lockan Tate,” he calls. “Let’s go.”

Lock gives me a nod and a secretive smirk, and then he stalks off with Riot, turning to walk backwards long enough to give Yates the finger and a smile.

I’m trembling. With rage. Because Riot just fucked me over so hard.

RIOT

7

90 SECONDS

AFTER A MEETING about the kid's dead dad, the homicide detective bullshit, and this supposed ambush on Saturday night, we're all sitting around the cafeteria, eating dinner and decompressing. I've never truly felt Moros was threatened until now. Reaper Corp is rich, powerful, and merciless, and if they want our town, they have the means to take it. But we won't let them have it without a fight, and now that my home is being threatened for real, I'm realizing how loyal I am to it.

Moros is everything to me. It's the one place where I fit. It's powerful in its own right, has a history I've become attached to, and has given me the means and the comfort to be exactly who I am without needing to hide all the time. I might not know who I am at my base, but I do know that belonging to Vile House has given me the time and safety to bring forth my instinctual urges. Director watches over us, but he doesn't tamp us, and fuck, I hate him sometimes, but I appreciate him for recognizing and accepting all our traits.

The world would see us as criminally insane; Director sees us as crucial evil. It's the perfect balance.

Ghost has been gone ever since the meeting last night. After I made him important and pissed off Yates, Ghost will be suffering the downfall of that. I grin at my plate, my blood surging to life in anticipation of how he's going to take it out on me.

After I left with Lockan, we walked down Death Row in silence. He smoked, and I stayed quiet, but he knew. *He knows.* My voice was modulated, but he's a smart, perceptive man, and he wouldn't have walked away from his gang with a Vile Boy if he didn't have another plan up his sleeve. When we got to the dead centre of town, he stopped, looked at me in my mask, and said, "Assume you guys have a plan?"

I nodded, and with that, we parted ways. Guess we'll see how his plans mesh with Director's plans, but for now, I'm staying out of it.

The cafeteria door opens, and I look, immediately grumpy that it isn't Ghost. Director walks in with Psych and Media, the latter going to fill their plates and the former coming right at me.

"Where's Ghost?" Director asks.

I shrug, not even attempting to tame my grin.

"He's supposed to watch Lock for me tonight."

"Why?"

"Because Yates won't let him go freely. They'll be coming for him."

"Seems like he can handle his own shit," I comment.

"Yeah, but with Ghost not back, it falls on you to keep an eye on him tonight. I want to see how Yates reacts, but I also want intel on what Lockan does. If he's going to be our ally with The Misfits, I need to know he has the power to control them."

Oh, he has the power. I spied on them before making myself visible for the meeting, and inside the hall, the gang members all flocked to Lock for advice and guidance. In their minds, he's the rightful leader, and an overtaking isn't going to be hard. Yates is a shifty bastard, so he'll put up a fight, but if he has Reaper Corp in his pocket, that's a whole other issue.

"Monster?" Director asks, looking down the table. Monster looks at him but says nothing. Something triggered him a few days ago, and he hasn't spoken since. The only one who can even get near him right now is Ransom, but Director still tries. Psych hovers nearby, waiting to see if Monster will agree to meet with her. He glares at her instead. "I need you with Riot tonight."

Monster stares at Director for so long that the room goes hushed. Ransom is the only one who keeps eating dinner, not intimidated by the little one's virulent energy. Eventually, Monster nods and looks away.

Great, a night with the angry one in the throws of a manic nightmare. This'll be fun.

The cafeteria door bangs inward, and a second later Ghost rips me from my seat. We both fall backwards, and he lands on top of me, all fired up and pissed off—just how I like him.

"Hey, sweetheart." I smile at his scowl.

"You fucked me over so hard!" he snaps at me, his fist following. I turn my face, but it still lands against my jaw. "You know what shit I've had to deal with all night thanks to you?"

"I made you important." I laugh in his face. "You're welcome."

Oh, the rage. No one has a higher sense of self than Ghost does. Oh, wait. I do. But he doesn't like being unimportant, so he shakes on top of me, weighing the pros and cons of killing me right here, right now. I buck my hips to press my cock against him, just to get him moving. He snaps out of it, his hands wrapping around my throat.

"Can't chase me to death when you beat me there." He strangles me, and I grin. I grin harder when he slams my head against the floor.

"Get the hell up. Both of you!" Director rips us apart, and I growl at him for intruding. "Out. Now."

"Are you fucking kidding me?" Ghost snaps at him. "You made this fucking—"

"Out."

Director doesn't add much power behind his voice, but he doesn't have to. He's powerful because he's proven he can punish us. I hate being told what to do, so I push past Ghost, ignore everyone else, and leave the room. Not because he told me to, but because I can't stay in this room and not blow the fuck up. I don't want these assholes to witness my breaking point in such a pathetic way. I *don't* break. Not publicly. I don't crumble or shatter or fucking crack. I'm Riot, the man in charge of creating chaos, not the man full of it.

Vile House is empty as I walk through it. But I'm not empty. My head is full of voices telling me I have to do better, try harder, be the best, and take down anyone in my way to get to the top. My chest is full of pressure that won't release.

Anger because Director doesn't know what he's doing. When he steps in, butting in between me and Ghost to try to create some semblance of peace between us, he doesn't understand the dynamic of what works and what doesn't work around here. Because if he takes my rivalry games away, he'll find out real fucking fast where my attention goes.

Don't crack. Don't show them weakness. Don't present any front except the one that shows you as nonchalant and powerful. Hide the rest. Hide the broken parts. Hide. Hide. Hide. Put the mask back on.

Climbing the stairs in a daze, I make it to my room and slam the door behind me. This room is safe. No one is watching me here. I can unravel and unwind, letting the imperfect parts of me rise to the surface to sweat them from my foundation. There's no need for a charming smile or a double play. So, I stand in the middle of my room and drop all my guards.

Inhale power. Exhale weakness.

Inhale confidence. Exhale insecurity.

Inhale indifference. Exhale vulnerability.

Inhale. Exhale. Inhale. Exhale.

I'm no longer the weak, inferior boy who watched his brother get abused and did nothing about it. I'm not the teen who fucked and sucked and felt nothing. I'm not the kid who hid his sickness so well that it caused my parents to focus all their hatred on my brother.

I'm stronger. Faultless. Supreme. I stabbed my dad fourteen times and watched my brother kill our mom. I learned to fuck and create stories in my head, manipulating the rumours and turning myself into a god through the tales my partners weaved. I learned to mask my sickness and turn it into my source of power.

I'm not Killian, the boy. I'm Riot, the man.

I rip my shirt off and toss it across the room. Stepping in front of my mirror, I spin, looking at my back to get the visual reminder of who I am. Riot. Vile House. White and black; complete contrasts, just like me. The skull cracked but grinning like I do.

My blood flow slows, calming me. Krypt uses weed to tell his mind to settle down, and I use visuals. We all have methods to tame our madness, but they're never guaranteed.

It's taking me too long to settle, to sink into a sane mind space that can rationalize what the fuck just happened. A scolding from Director, who claims to understand us, but didn't today.

"Riot."

My name comes from his mouth in a voice that doesn't fit his anger. I turn to face him, making sure he sees how turbulent I feel right now, warning him away from warring with me until I'm more sane.

He doesn't listen. He steps into my room, closes the door, and looks at my torso. Naked and scarred, inked and marred, toned and godly. I work for this body, and since I decided to stop being that pathetic kid, I've turned myself into a weapon that charms. Deceit is the mask I wear.

"Ninety seconds," Ghost says.

It's both a relief and a trigger. I close my eyes so I don't have to look at him. Ninety seconds is our rule, but we barely use it. I like to tell Ghost he doesn't know when to keep his mouth shut, but over the years, he actually has learned how to bite his tongue when it matters. The ninety-second rule became a grace period we started living by last year when we honest to god almost killed each other, but right now, I don't want it. I don't want the minute and a half to get my shit together. I don't want to be careful around him. I don't want him to see me as anything other than the raw, real, ravaged man I am. Because he's the only person who looks back with the same level of hypocrisy.

Oh, we try, don't we? We try to be the deities we think we are, but there are cracks in our foundations that'll bring us down with the right pressure. I hide mine better than he does, but he always seems to show up right when I'm splitting in two. Maybe he causes it.

Vulnerabilities are a waste of time.

"Get out." I open my eyes.

"No," he says, stepping forward. Blond, brazen, bold. He's silent when he walks, but the air around him ripples with his moods, even when he doesn't want it to.

"Death wish?" I ask as a warning.

"You know it." He grins. The bruises around his throat sate me, slowing my blood flow even more. When he's right in front of me, his body heat radiating in my space, I subtly breathe in the smell of him. Cedar and spice. It's a common body wash scent, comes in half the men's choices at the shops uptown, so I don't know why it smells different on him. "We're not allowed to fight here. In this house." He's right in front of me now, a dangerous place to be while I'm so volatile. So vulnerable.

I look up, meeting his blue eyes, trying to peel them open to reveal what he's actually thinking. What's he doing here, so calm and calculated, when five minutes ago he was ready to kill me at dinner? Nothing about Ghost makes sense, and regrettably, that's half the reason I like goading him.

"You follow rules now?" I ask.

He smirks at me, and everything else settles. Because being tumultuous around him is exactly my comfort level. He's here, not to calm me down, but to rile me up so I don't have to think about anything other than beating him. To challenge me. To be pissed off one second and deceptively settled the next. The ninety seconds are ticking down, and when they're over, who knows what's going to happen. Because pitting his narcissism against my sociopathic personality is a war no one can win, but fuck do we love trying.

"You follow me, don't you?" he asks, voice lowering to a timbre that makes my bones rattle. "Following me straight to Hell."

"Not following. Pushing."

"Hmm," he hums, looking down again. I have a lot of scars, but the ones on my inner biceps are the only self-inflicted ones. There are two fresh lines there from last night. He wasn't around to take my troubles out on, so I bled them out instead. "Ninety seconds are up, Riot. Whose heart are we breaking? My brother's or yours?"

"Neither," Krypt says, standing in the doorway with Remi in front of him. I look, but Ghost doesn't turn around. He keeps his eyes on me, leaning in to grab something off the dresser behind me. "You fuck up my bargain, I'll fuck up your life. Brother or not."

I grin at my brother. "He's alive, isn't he?"

Remi groans, but my attention dips down to my arm when Ghost trails the sharp edge of a razor blade over my inner bicep, adding another line. Bleeding me. Playing god when he has no right to the role. I don't even tense or flinch because I've conditioned myself to associate the sting with pleasure and relief. The hardest part about Ghost cutting me is that he's making me feel good in a way he shouldn't be able to. I'm jarred by the audacity of the act, unsure why I'm not throwing him off, and mindfucked because he's so casual about something so personal. Does he know why I cut? Does he understand what he's bleeding me of? Is he doing it purposefully, or is he simply trying to get in my head?

Warm blood drips down my arm, and when the line is finished, he smears his thumb over it. Looking right at me, he wipes his thumb over his bottom lip, his tongue following in its wake to lick it up.

Fuck, it takes everything within me to withhold my anticipatory shudder.

He grins. I grin back. My cock gets hard, my thoughts turn dark, and the charm in my current smile isn't meant for anyone but Ghost. Because he sees through the top layer to the diabolical need it masks. There's a reason Ghost and I became competitors, and it has nothing to do with being in Vile House together.

It's because he knows exactly how to speak to the part of me I keep hidden.

MONSTER HASN'T SAID a word since we left to follow Lock. Honestly, it makes him good company tonight. Because I'm stuck in my head about the new slice on my inner bicep. Nobody marks that area of my body but me, and I don't know why I let Ghost do it.

"You ever cut?" I ask him as we sit on the rooftop of someone's house, watching Lock get laid through the window of the next house over. No idea who the person is, someone who came to visit a friend, but Lock picked her up at Neon Demon and brought her back here to Glitch's parents' place. His former childhood home, too.

Monster shoves up his sleeves and shows me the scars inside his wrists. They look old, like he used to cut but doesn't anymore. He usually wears cuffs, but tonight, his arms are bare. They aren't obvious, but he has dot scars around his mouth, too. Like it's been sewn shut, and selfishly, I'm glad for his mask so I don't have to see them right now.

I nod at his wrists, shifting my eyes back to the sex show through the window. "I cut. Makes me feel less crazy. Less... pressured. Someone else cut me there today, though, and I'm all fucked up about it."

Monster's black and yellow mask turns in my direction, up-nodding to get me to show him. I take off my jacket, lift the sleeve of my t-shirt, and show him all my scars. The fresh ones from last night stand out, but not as brightly as the one Ghost gave me today. He reaches out to touch it, and I go stark still. He's never touched me before, and I sure as shit haven't touched him. Monster doesn't like touch, just like Krypt, but Monster's aversion to it is so much more lethal. A nurse once tried to turn his arm over so she could take his blood, and he hadn't been expecting it. He bashed her face in with a clipboard, and Ransom had to finish her off before Director burned the body. Then we all got reamed out because we're apparently not supposed to kill without reason. Monster claimed he had a reason, but Director didn't feel it passed the test. That was years ago, and he's learned a little restraint since then. And he knows how to feel guilt, so that dead nurse haunts him because he's remorseful about it.

When his fingers fall away, I pull my jacket back on. "Why do you cut? To relieve anger?" I ask because he's a pretty angry guy. When he shakes his head, I guess again, "Pain?"

He nods. A lot. So much pain.

"Why aren't you talking?"

He shrugs.

"Monster."

He looks at me again, his eyes shining through his mask. He just shakes his head as if to say he simply can't. He just *can't* talk right now. I lived a shit life with my parents, but it wasn't because of how they treated me. I had to live with the inner shame that I watched my brother get neglected for so long before I learned to do anything about it—even my trauma is selfish. But Monster lived through true horror. From birth to eight he was used, abused, raped, sold, rented by the hour, and conditioned to believe the mentality of a serial rapist's ways. Until Vile House saved him from the situation, but not from himself. Not even Psych can get through to him after all this time. Only Ransom can, and to be honest, none of us are clear on their dynamic. It's none of our business, despite how badly I wish it was.

Monster holds out his phone, showing me a text from Ghost.

Yates on the move. I'm following him. Meet me at Janie's Woods.

Knowing Lock isn't in any danger he can't handle tonight, I leave him a Vile House calling card with my white trademark on the front as a form of contact before we head out to Janie's Woods. When we creep through the forest, I almost get nostalgic for the other night when I see the pond on Carnival Hill. Fuck, the way he drowned was glorious, but the way he came back was even better.

Why would Yates meet someone in Janie's Woods? It's out behind the asylum, the closest forest to Vile House, and the riskiest for him to be caught in because so many of us spend time in these woods, tempting the history of Carnival Hill—a sacrificial piece of land that is still used today.

When we arrive, I don't hear or see Ghost, but tonight, he's masked as a Vile Boy, so there's a high probability that we won't see him until he wants to be seen. Fuck, can he move silently.

GHOST

8

PROMISES PROMISES

THE RAIN BATHES my heated skin in relief, drawing a satisfied smile from behind my mask. I love the rain. I love the weather. I love the way it charges me, the webbed lightning in the air igniting my soul and turning me fiendish.

My feet are silent on the damp forest floor, the patter of the rain giving me cover and the rustle of the leaves providing kinship. Krypt met us here, so him and Monster are watching from the west, but I'm the Ghost of Moros, moving through Janie's Woods as swiftly as the breeze.

Riot is my target. He got the better of me out here the other night, and now it's my turn. He's supposed to be the one watching me—keeping track of me. Didn't he take over my brother's bargain, agreeing to keep me so well monitored I can't take another step in Death's direction? He's fucking failing. Miserably. Hard to keep tabs on a ghost, and I have no intention of making his job easier.

Yates and Tom are at the edge of the clearing, the glint of the moon reflecting off the surface of the pond Riot drowned me in not far from where they stand. Whoever they're waiting for isn't here yet, so I keep moving like a phantom, skirting around them until I come up behind Riot.

He doesn't hear me. Because I don't *let* him hear me. His back faces me, his black outfit blending in with the night, damp from the rain and sticking to his athletic body. He's leaning against a tree, his chest pressed to it while he watches Yates and Tom through the forest. His white and black mask is strapped to his head, but the hood of his jacket is pulled up to hide his hair from me. I like his hair, dark and wavy, and a little long at the back for the style he wears it in, but suitable all the same.

Krypt is out of sight, but I peer up, seeing Monster in the treetop to our left, watching, but not caring enough to listen to what I'm about to do. Their masks are covered with a black bandana to hide the glow, and their hoods are up to shield their eyes as they watch from above.

Keeping my movements fluid, I stalk closer to him without making a sound. There's hypocrisy in what I do. I like recognition and attention, so being a ghost is detrimental to my need for fame. But it's not all bad because no one can move like I do, and pride swells within me every time I get something done that no one else can do. I'm needed, prized, skilled, unlike the others, and I love throwing it in their faces.

When I'm right behind Riot, I slow my breathing, move in a way that doesn't make my jacket rustle, and press up behind him. My hand clamps over his masked mouth as he startles, pushing the firm material against his face, and the majority of my body presses against his, pinning him to the tree. He stiffens in my hold but doesn't try to break free. He sinks into me, as if he were the one who lured me here.

I don't appreciate being deceived, so I ignore that feeling and bring my mouth to the side of his head. "You're doing a shit job of keeping your side of the bargain. Remi will be so disappointed."

He hums against the mask in the palm of my hand, his body pressing back against mine. He bucks me, then whispers, "I know you, Ghost. You think I don't know when you're tempting death or just doing something for attention? You're the biggest attention whore I've ever met."

I am, but I don't like being called out on it. "Got your attention, didn't I?"

He presses his ass back to find my dick hard. "Sure did."

I debate pushing him away, but fuck it. My hard-on has nothing to do with him and everything to do with the adrenaline rush of being so casual in a dangerous situation. I'm a thrill-seeker by nature, and Riot always provides a savage thrill. Especially when he pisses me off.

"You think you made me hard?"

He huffs out a laugh, spinning in my grip. I press against him harder, unwilling to let him get the upper hand. I glance past him, making sure no one has shown up to meet with Yates and Tom, and when I look back at his face, his mask is up and he's giving me one of those bullshit smiles.

"I think you get hard for the most sinister shit. And you've been repressed. Can't find a fuck buddy who gets your level of depravity, and you have to be so careful because of your tats and The Misfits." His hand comes up between our bodies while my stomach jolts at the truth of his statement. His fingers curl around my throat and he pushes my mask up so he doesn't miss my facial expression. "Should I add another level to this deal we have, Ghost? See how close I can fuck you to death?"

My cock throbs against his hip, making him smirk. "Nah. I don't get off on being the one fucked to death."

His smile only widens at my lie. "Ah, you want the easy way out, yeah? Fuck a little doll to their death?"

No. "Yeah. Have my eyes on that sad guy with the dead dad. He seems like a nice, sexy little doll, don't you think?"

Riot's grey eyes storm. His smile never falters, though. The moment stalls, building in intensity as the rain picks up and thunder joins the lightning. A new game has just been declared, and I hate that I don't know what will win me my victory. Poor kid might become the rope between us, and when we're through, he'll be so frayed and strained he'll snap in half.

When thunder cracks, my sanity splits away from my personality, letting my true self shine. Because I *am* repressed. I do get hard for the sinister shit. I crave a level of depravity that has everything to do with the thrill of it, the danger of it, the sickening need to test myself and prove that I'm goddamn invincible. A suicide curse hasn't beaten me yet, and I'm desperate to know what else I can get away with.

Riot's charming smile morphs into something purely mephistophelian, enticing my jigsaw puzzle pieces that aren't glued down as tightly as I thought they were.

"When this thing ends," he starts, hand clamping tight around my throat to press against my arteries, "we're both going to be dead."

"Promise?" I taunt him again.

"Promise." He licks his lips, drawing my attention to his mouth. "Mask on, Ghost. And I don't mean this one." He looks straight into my eyes, telling me to be myself around him. For some reason, it sounds like a cry for help. Because Riot is the one who wears so many masks, I wonder if he knows his true face anymore. I glimpsed the real him when I cut him, but it was only a tease. A peek, something I hope to strip away bit by bit to leave him bare. "They'll be here any minute."

Inhaling desire, knowing it's full of depravity and death, I pull my mask down and become the Ghost of Moros again. We climb the tree, perch over Yates and Tom, and when the person they're meeting shows up, everything changes.

Because Benton Wentworth, the billionaire funding Axel's research and the man who tried to buy Moros, is back, meeting with Yates.

Greedy fucker didn't learn his lesson on Initiation Night.

DEATH ROW IS vacant by the time we walk down the centre of it just before dawn. The crows and ravens are barely awake, and the sky is darker than it was at midnight now that the moon is gone, no longer peeking through the clouds.

The owner of the Neon Demon walks out, throwing a trash bag in the dumpster between the club and The Midnight Diner. She gives us a nod, touches her fist to her heart, and lights a smoke as she walks home.

It's still drizzling, and the sky is webbed with the odd bolt of lightning, but otherwise, everything in Moros feels settled. Which is deceptive considering how much turmoil is coming our way.

Reaper Corp is a major threat. They're an organization that plays by no one's rules but their own. They breed their own people, basing their skill set on a gene pool they pluck from, and they hold so much power because they *actually are* stronger than everyone else.

"Why Moros?" I ask Riot during a rare moment of peace. It bothers me to ask because I don't like to look uneducated, but... he's broken, not perfect, making me feel less pressure to be perfect right now. If he calls me out on it, I'll just remind him how inferior he is to me.

He doesn't look at me. "Why does Reaper Corp want it?" he asks. I nod. "Secluded. Strong gene pool. Government and law enforcement don't touch this place. Perfect spot to build a new stronghold and gain more control."

"What control, though?" We turn down the street next to Cauldron, heading for Misfit Hall. "Like, what's their actual goal?"

Reaper Corp is well-known, but there's a lot of mystery surrounding them. Essentially, they're Vile House, but on a global scale instead of a town-sized scale. They took over a whole city down south, turned it into a walled-off community they run, and somehow either bullied or convinced the citizens to become part of them. But Reaper Corp doesn't just breed mercenaries and talented killers; they breed geniuses, scientists, mathematicians, soldiers, doctors, and leaders. They pick and choose the qualities in their new breeds through DNA sequencing, but I've never understood why.

"They breed the best, so they are the best. They're stronger than any government, and whoever tries to challenge them loses. They control laws and politics, the medical industry, and the tech industries, so they're greedy and just want more. Total domination is why," Riot answers. "That's their actual goal. They're like you. Just do shit to see if they can." He grins without looking at me.

It's all too much to think about, and this calmness between us isn't as settling as I hoped it'd be. "If Moros goes down, I'm going down with her."

"Oh, you're going down long before that," Riot says, laughing. "Hurry up. Let's get this shit done so I can go lure someone with a smile and fuck until I pass out."

I hate his laugh so much that I slip away from him and move through the streets like the ghost I am, planting the rest of the audio devices in Misfit Hall without his help. Because it's not his laugh I hated, it's what he said.

RIOT

9

WICKEDEST MASK

IT'S Saturday and everything hurts. Nostalgia hurts worse than pain because the agony of it is so blunt and unwanted. I hate this house, the memories of my parents, the life my brother lived, and the uncertainty of my life while I resided here. To stand here, in the place I allowed Krypt to go unloved and unwanted, clashes with the memory of the night we killed our parents in this same spot.

He went through hell, but more importantly, I embarrassed myself by not being the older brother. The shame of it is what fucks me up.

To the left, I see my parents whispering about sending Keegan away. To my right, I see their blood splattered all over the walls and carpet, our teenage selves coming to life for the first time. Such misery and relief mixed in such a small space. A house that never felt like a home, but a building that holds the only memories of our early lives.

Let it go or keep it?

Torture or reprieve?

Why the fuck does this house still have a hold on me?

Walking into the room that was mine on the second floor, I know why. It's not because I care about the walls and the plaster and the carpet. It's not even memories that hold me hostage. It's confusion and failure, self-loathing because I hate myself for being that weak. It was living a lie while my brother paid for the same lie because he didn't know how to act. It's the fact that I was someone here, learned to mask here, and lost myself here. A three-step process I never learned how to reverse.

I'm afraid to get rid of the house because... what if some clue about who I am under all my well-placed disguises still resides within these walls? Does the base version of me still exist here?

Safe up here to crack with no eyes on me, because I can hear Krypt and Remi's footsteps on the first floor, I allow myself a single moment to feel weak. More pathetic than anything. Because I long for someone to fucking recognize me without all my masks. How pathetic is that? I'm Killian Hallows, Riot of Vile House, and no one's opinion of me holds power over me.

To them, I am strength and sinister glee. I am the charmer, the chaos creator, the powerhouse, and the one with no morals getting in my way. I lack empathy and show no remorse, making me terrifying in their eyes, and I've come to enjoy being terrifying. I like my reputation, no matter whose perspective it's coming from. Whether they loathe me because I'm better than them, need me because I'm more skilled than them, or love me because I fake it better than them, it doesn't matter. All my smiles have a place and a purpose. Every look, mannerism, movement, and word packs a punch however I need it to, and I've become comfortable reading everyone so well that I know exactly how to charm or scare them.

I am power!

Internally, I'm powerless because I forget who I am. A thought I will never admit aloud. A thought I barely admit to myself. Because I learned to read people but lost the ability to read myself.

Some people have body dysmorphia. I have self-dysmorphia. I mask that, too. I'm buried under so many layers I'm suffocating while thriving, too chickenshit to start peeling them back to see what sits underneath the bottom one.

What if it's nothing? What if I'm no one?

My nape prickles a second later, alerting me that I'm not alone. It's not Krypt or Remi because I can still hear them downstairs. Only one person moves so silently, so I steel my nerves, tame my temper, and turn to face him.

"How long have you been standing there?"

Ghost leans against the doorframe to my former bedroom, arms crossed, not breathing hard enough to make a sound. Even his energy is quiet. He grins, blue eyes deep and bright, dark blond hair flopped over his forehead. I don't know what he sees when he looks into my eyes, but whatever it is, his grin falters and his eyes deepen. He doesn't move, but something about the way he's standing changes. Like he relaxes or shifts focus or something. I know the look for what it is, and it's not something that belongs on his face.

Fucking worry. Pity. Sympathy.

"Don't," I snarl at him. *Don't look for something that isn't there.*

"You're not as hard to read as you think you are," he says, voice calm. "You hate the quiet, don't you? If something isn't life-or-death or getting you off, you don't know how to function. You don't know how to be alone because you can't manipulate yourself." His grin comes back when I scowl. "So fucking transparent."

"And you're any better?" I scoff. "You taunt death because you can't stand to live normally."

His lashes feather his cheekbones when he looks down, pushing off the doorframe to step into my room. I only came here to ensure the house hadn't fallen down, not to have this confrontation. His feet still don't make a sound on the carpet, and instead of hearing his heartbeat, I *feel* it thudding in my chest. I clear my throat and shake my head to rid myself of the feeling, refusing to back up as he gets closer.

"Quite the pair we are to be in a bargain, yeah? Maybe Reaper Corp will do you a favour and kill me tonight when they come."

"If Yates can be believed."

He's right in front of me now, his heart beating even harder in *my* chest. Why the fuck can I feel it? I look at his chest, trying to see the thump of it through his shirt. His pecs are taut under the thin, long-sleeved shirt he wears, but there's no movement that I can see—not the expansion of an inhale or the beat of his heart. When I look up at his eyes, the blue of them sinks straight to my solar plexus, like a punch that hurts more than all this nostalgia.

Is he seeing through my masks?

"You know," he starts, steps casually coming to a stop in front of me, "you're not as tough as you think you are. I had all this faith in you, Riot."

"What faith?"

His throat rolls with a swallow, moving so much more

than his chest does. Something still beats in mine, and the feel of it is so overwhelming that my throat rolls to match his. To swallow this fucking pressure and the strange looks and the way he's seeing something about me that even I can't see.

"You've been my opponent for years now, haven't you?" He shifts his weight to the other foot, not making a sound. I stare at the carpet, wondering how he commands it to shut up. "And you've never cracked like this before."

"I'm not fucking cracking."

Ghost laughs, harsh but mellow. "Oh, you're already cracked wide open, *baby*." The pet name comes out with a mocking cackle that worsens the beat in my chest. "I see it all."

How? How does he see it all and how can I manipulate him into teaching me how without him knowing he's giving me the lesson?

"You wear a different face for me, right? It never used to be this see-through, but a few months ago, when I started toying with you even harder, you became transparent. Actually, no." He tips my chin up from staring at the quiet carpet. "You aren't transparent. You keep donning new masks, layering them on so thick, trying to find the one that works on me, but it's pointless now, Riot. Because I've figured out how to look beneath them."

His knuckles under my chin are driving me insane, but I'm rooted here, a prisoner to his words and the way he wields them. It only makes me loathe him more. Anyone with the ability to read me better than I can read myself isn't someone I want in this world. Ghost needs to die for real, because if he ever finds the very base layer of me, he'll realize I've never been the opponent he thinks I am.

He's jagged and put together beautifully. I'm covered and masked to perfection. His ugly has already been morphed into something so pretty it hurts, but my ugly is simply hidden, able to be revealed. Ghost isn't stupid. He'll figure out that unmasking me is the epitome of breaking me. Because when the ugliness beneath is laid bare, it will end me and all my meticulous lies, and I'll become the boy who sat in this bedroom and listened to his brother lose his mind, too pathetic to do anything about it.

I want to ask what he sees when he looks through the masks, but I fear the answer, so I don't. I jerk my chin away from his knuckles, looking straight into his eyes as I don one more mask. The god in control of his life. The demon chasing him to tempt the afterlife. The powerful Vile Boy who has no weaknesses or vulnerabilities.

As my transformation happens, Ghost's smile widens. "Mmm," he hums sensually. "This is my favourite mask."

"It's not a mask. It's your fate." I'm so close to demanding the ninety seconds. This feels like too much, and I need the reprieve.

"You're my fate," he counters, leaning in until his nose brushes mine. In a husky whisper, he says, "And I've always loved tempting my fate."

I close my eyes to feel his words in my chest. They beat and bang and thump so hard my skin prickles with goosebumps and the fine hairs on my arms stand up. It's a declaration of who we are and what our purpose is. It's his body so near mine, alive and thriving, taunting me into turning it dead and sombre. When the thump in my chest stops, it'll be when he's gone.

Because my heart beats maliciously for his—because of his. Spiteful and cruel. Honest and offbeat.

His phantom warmth still lingers, but he's no longer here when I open my eyes. Gone, just like the ghost he is.

"You okay?" Remi startles me from the doorway. He looks like his brother, but their vortexes are vastly different.

"Where's Soren?"

Remi's face scrunches. "Soren? He never came here."

I hate that it takes me a second to question my thoughts. Was he here, or was he a figment of my imagination?

When I look down and see the corner of a calling card peeking out of my jeans pocket, I know it was real. Teal splashes across the skeletal torso, and on the opposite side, Ghost's message.

How can I descend any further when you are my deepest pit in Hell?

SOMETHING ISN'T RIGHT.

Moros is unsettled. The streets are vacant and dark, illuminated only by shop signs and the moon, and the curtains are all pulled back, owners peering through to see what may or may not come. Remi's shop plays sad, melancholic music that drifts out onto Death Row in gloomy waves, setting the tone for a night we have yet to experience.

Is this ambush coming or is Yates a fucking liar?

Masked, I sit atop The Midnight Diner, watching Death

Row before me and a backstreet behind me. The asylum's tallest turrets are visible from this high up, and even it appears still, holding its breath in anticipation of the madness it might be tasked with unleashing. Axel sits in there somewhere, waiting for his opportunity to brainwash a member of Reaper Corp.

Most porch lights are unlit, not wanting to invite the kind of company promised on a night such as this. The shutters are drawn, the cars parked and locked, but no one is sleeping. It isn't a restful evening because our town is on the precipice of turmoil. Reaper Corp is coming, and tonight might be their first strike.

Yates only said 'something is coming' but we're not stupid.

Ransom paces behind me, his red mask as menacing as it always is. Across the street, Monster stands stonily while Menace shifts from foot to foot beside him. Scattered throughout town, the Vile Boys are on watch, guarding the areas most likely to be attacked. Death Row. Vile House. The Asylum. The Cemetery. But Ghost is at Misfit Hall, playing the part of a gang member to relay any information from Yates. It was Yates who warned of this ambush, so it's Yates we watch closest.

Menace climbs over to the roof of the tattoo shop, Death Mark, and then hits the street to do a ground-level sweep. My eyes track him, but he soon dips out of sight in his blue mask.

"Monster talk to you the other night?" Ransom asks.

"Not verbally."

"How'd he seem?"

"The same as he always is, but quieter." I shift my mask

to get a better view through the eyeholes. "What's the deal with you two? You fuck him to make it all better?"

"Watch your fucking mouth, Riot."

I grin behind my mask. Ransom isn't easy to rile, and since I've known him, the only time I've witnessed it has been when it has something to do with Monster. Sometimes, it's a threat to Monster, but most times, it's the little shit himself. He knows how to button push, and he's made a living out of pushing Ransom's. It's their dynamic, but I'm curious if it extends to the bedroom.

"Anything?" Ransom asks into his earpiece. "Ghost?"

"Nothing here," Seven says. He's at Vile House.

"Nada," Glitch adds from the asylum with Axel.

"Kyd?"

Kyd makes the radio sound before answering. "I found a stripped deer carcass. Think it's from my lion? Over."

We all look in the direction of the cemetery, wondering if that crazy fuck is wandering around amongst the lion he freed from the zoo.

"His name is Fabrizio, remember? Over." He makes another radio sound. "Not over. He gets his name because his mane is dark and wavy like a sexy Italian. Over."

"Take that as a no," Ransom says, moving on. "Ghost?"

"Comms have been cut off at Misfit Hall," Director says through our ears. "I can't access any of our audio or video."

My instincts all tumble over one another, unsure if that means Ghost is in trouble or not. While Glitch and Facts talk about trying to fix our planted devices, I pull my phone from my pocket, taking a risk Director won't like. I pull out my earpiece and press my phone to my ear while it rings.

"Who the fuck are you calling?" Ransom barks.

"Hey, Kill."

"Lock," I answer. "Where are you?"

"Home."

"Can you get to Misfit Hall?"

"Uh, yeah. What's up?" he asks, shuffling around in the background. "Soren alright?"

"I dunno. All our—I can't get a hold of him, but you were there when—" Fuck. I'm just straight up giving myself away tonight, and I've never even come close to being this reckless with my Vile identity. "He said Yates warned of an ambush, and now I can't get in touch with him."

Lock is silent for a bit, probably choosing not to call me out on who I am or how I know these things, and then his front door slams loud enough for me to hear it. "Heading over there now. You coming?"

I can't. My post is here until we get further instructions. As much as I want to go there, I won't leave my wingman either. We're a unit, and I need to be a reliable part of it for once. "Just call me when you find him. Let me know what's going on over there. Something ain't right."

"K." He hangs up on me, and I put my earpiece back in.

"Lockan Tate?" Ransom asks, and I nod. "Why?"

"He's got access to Misfit Hall. Why not?"

"He know you're Vile?"

Probably. "No." I stand when I spot someone walking down the middle of Death Row. My hackles rise, staring at a person walking through our town like they belong here. They don't.

"Menace?" Ransom asks through the comms because Menace is the closest, being at that end of the street.

"Woman," Menace says. "Robes. Can't tell if she's armed. Not a local."

She passes Menace's location, and he creeps out to follow her until she stops right in front of Death Mark, the ink shop he works at. She just stands there, not doing anything or saying anything. She's wearing a wide-brimmed hat, but I know she doesn't belong here. I've studied the people of Moros as much as I've studied myself, and her posture isn't one I recognize. She's not a tourist because we put the town on lockdown and sent them home or to their hotel.

The cello and piano music from The Ambient Raven becomes louder now that we've all held our breath and focused our ears. A recording of Remi and his dad playing together sets the tone for the unknown, and my fingers loop into the holed handles of my throwing knives. I don't care who she is, if she doesn't make her intentions clear in the next minute, I will throw a dagger between her eyes and not stick around for her corpse to hit the street.

Her hands rise above her head like she's going to cast a fucking spell or something, her billowing maroon robes flowing like flower petals as she does a spin.

"Menace," Ransom warns as he stalks closer to her.

Monster is above her now, looking down from the roof of Death Mark, having Menace's back as he approaches her from behind.

"Town's on lockdown, lady," Menace calls to her.

She stops spinning, pausing with her back to him. No one puts their back to a strange man in a mask, especially not in Moros, so I pull a dagger free from its holster and position my feet to throw it.

"What ever for?" she asks the empty street.

"Who are you?" Menace gets closer.

I can't see her face, but I swear to fuck I see her teeth flash through a sick smile before she twirls to face Menace. My dagger flies at the same time she pulls a gun free and a bang goes off. My second dagger flies as Menace clutches his stomach, and Ransom leaps over the side of the building, just like Monster is doing from his side of the street, when Menace hits the ground. The woman's gun clatters to the street, going off again all on its own.

"Reaper Corp is coming," the lady shouts as I climb over the front of The Midnight Diner. "And you can't stop us." Her robes open to reveal my daggers in her gut... and her hands. In both of them, a red light blinks, counting down time.

"Menace!" I shout, my feet hitting the ground painfully.

"Monster, get back!" Ransom shouts, running straight for him.

But Monster drops right on top of the woman, knocking the handheld explosives from her grip. He rips her hat off and his yellow mask looks down at her. A breath later, the yellow is splashed red, and this woman chortles as she dies.

"Any others?" I ask my earpiece and start running.

"Death Row is clear."

My breath dampens the inside of my mask as I run to Menace, sliding to his side as he bleeds out on the street. I see the frosty blue of his eyes through his mask, panicked, but mostly just pissed off.

"The explosives!" he chokes out in a ragged yell.

Both small explosives are just sitting on the pavement, still blinking. Their size doesn't matter; they're meant to cause chaos, and they will if we don't get off this street. I press my hands to the bullet hole in Menace's side, looking at Ransom as I do it. Glitch isn't here, and he's the only one of us who knows how to disarm a bomb. He shakes his head, knowing they're going to go off.

Right next to Menace.

"Let's go!" I shout.

Monster and Ransom grab Menace's legs and I grab his armpits. We drag him down Death Row, blood oozing from his abdomen and harsh, wheezing breaths panting through his lips.

"Leave me behind the dumpster and fucking run!" Menace demands. "Hurry up."

The first bomb clicks. Then explodes. My chest booms, harder than it did the night I felt Ghost's heartbeat. The echo of the explosion sends me flying down Death Row, my arms still hooked under Menace's armpits. Suspended in time, everything muffles and slows down. The sound doesn't register right away, the boom of it so powerful my ears ring without hearing, my lungs cease, and my eyes close at the heat. When I slam against the ground with Menace between my legs, the second explosion strikes, shattering glass, setting off car alarms, and making debris rain down on us.

I try to blink through it, to get my eyes to focus, but all I see is smoke and fire and blood. Dust and debris make them water and sting. Shit. I look down, watching Menace struggle to sit up, blood coating the street and making his black outfit appear wet. Dampness trickles from my ears, sticking the sides of my mask to my face as I look back, making sure no other explosions are going to shatter us further.

"Director! We need Medic," Ransom shouts. Monster is next to him, the two of them stumbling towards us. I press my hands to Menace's stomach again, making him hiss out in pain.

"Thought you liked pain?" I ask to distract him, my voice too far away from my lips.

He chokes out a laugh, grimacing as his breathing intensifies. "Only when my dick is hard."

Monster kneels next to me, yanking at Menace's shirt to find the bullet hole.

"I'm a nurse!" someone shouts, and for the first time in a while, Monster makes a sound. He growls at the nurse approaching us wearily, her hands lifted in innocence.

"Let her through," I tell Monster. "His face is covered."

Monster points at his torso, indicating that his many tattoos are distinguishable. I stand, approaching the nurse. Grabbing her by her slender throat, not to harm, but to get all her attention, I bend until my face is right in front of hers. "If you recognize a single thing about him, you will keep it to your fucking self, got it?"

"I p-promise. I-I only want to help."

I study her for a long few seconds, finding her sincere. She's friends with Glitch's parents, and I recognize her as a good Moros local. "Thank you."

I let her through, and Ransom grabs her hand to help her over the debris. Director tells us Medic is coming, and I stand here, looking at the carnage of *my* fucking street! *My* town does not deserve to suffer a scar like this. Death Mark is burning on one side, and the windows of The Ambient Raven are blown out. The Neon Demon's front windows are no better, shattered, leaking fluorescent purple neon light onto Death Row. Cars burn, the sidewalk is destroyed, and decorations from Halloween are strewn everywhere, catching fire.

No. Reaper Corp will not have my town.

"Riot!" Ransom shouts at me through my muffled hearing. "Your phone is ringing."

Fuck. With sticky hands, I pull it from my pocket and answer silently, still unsure if I can hear normally. Lockan.

"Get the fuck over here, Kill. Misfit Hall is under attack."

All the good parts of me fade away as I don my most wicked mask. Because I'm the only one who chases Soren Sauder to a death he secretly doesn't want.

Reaper Corp will not have him either.

GHOST

10

HIS MASKS & MY CRACKS

I DON'T KNOW where it comes from, but there's a power within me. It's a deep well of something dark and sinister, a tool I can call upon whenever needed because it's never too far from my surface. Maybe it's reachable because I have so many cracks in my puzzle and my hand reaches through unhindered, or maybe it's just who I am when I'm not trying to hold my mirage together. Whatever it is, it's kept me alive, out of the Sauder curse's clutches, and let me walk off Death's doorstep more times than should be allowed.

Right now, it's keeping Misfit Hall from falling.

Warm blood bathes me, soaking through my clothes to rest against my skin like war paint. My fight-or-flight instinct is firmly planted in fight, and every step I take is made with purpose. My knives are an extension of my hands, causing as much carnage as my body position does. Because I won't fucking let them through.

With Lockan Tate at my side, we defend the fortress. Not because I give a fuck about it, but because I don't want

Reaper Corp to have it. They can have Yates—that dumb fuck is the reason for all of this.

Lock hooks his leg over the porch railing, wrapping his arm around a man's neck. He hauls him over and throws him at me, my blade piercing his windpipe before I shove him back at Lock. With another stab to the heart, Lock throws him to the grass, and we stand our ground.

"I need to get in there and check on my guys!" Lock shouts, blades flashing.

I rip a dagger free from my belt and fling it at another man pointing a gun right at us. It hits his shoulder, making him falter for a second. Long enough for me to get to him, but before I can, a fucking lion comes out of goddamn nowhere and barrels him over.

"Fabrizio!" Kyd runs up the street in his pink mask, goddamn katanas criss-crossed on his back. "Thank you, Fabi!" He huffs, stopping right in front of the porch. "Hey, boys!"

I wish I could see his smile because it'd be stupidly beautiful right now. I'm unmasked, so I'm not allowed to know who he is, so I nod at him and point inside.

"Yates has had Reaper Corp members living in Misfit Hall for a week. Hidden."

"The fuck?" Kyd cackles, thinking that's funny. "And he thinks he's gonna live through it?"

He won't. Actually, he will. Because I'm going to ensure he does just so Lockan can have his way with the leader who ruined his gang. I've suffered through him enough, so maybe I'm the one who deserves to dish out vengeance.

"Oh, he'll live," Lock says, voicing my thoughts.

"Because I won't fucking let him die until he knows how big of a piece of shit he is."

"What're we waiting for?" Kyd asks, looking in the direction his lion ran. "I'm feeling extra-extra warrior fae tonight. In the mood for a little cosplay." He steps up, patting my chest before he roars loudly, ripping his swords free and charging into the hall.

Lock looks at me with a weird grin on his face. "You know that guy?"

"Nope." I laugh.

Inside is worse than outside. Reaper Corp found a weak point in Moros and this is how they plan to establish their first stronghold. Misfit Hall was the target. Yates let them right in the front door, and they've been biding their time to strike while Vile House is distracted.

Because they're studying us. Learning how we work. Witnessing how we respond to threats and work as a team, and tonight proved that we have no loyalty to The Misfits, because other than me in my real face, no Vile member was here to aid them.

"Kyd!" I shout, drawing a look from Lock, who is piecing everything together all on his own. "How'd you know to come?"

"Director," Kyd shouts, his katanas working together to behead someone. "Couple more are coming, too."

"Director?" Lock asks. "Director of what?"

Fucking fuck. His eyes narrow behind me, and then he pulls me back, his fist flying over my shoulder. I spin, grabbing the sides of a Reaper Corp's neck, and with Lock's help, we snap it.

"You belong to Vile House, Sauder?" he asks me.

"I'm a Misfit."

"Fucking *sure* you are. You know Killian called me to come here tonight?" He shakes his head, letting it go for now. "Where's Yates?"

Why the hell did Riot call him? Is he trying to give himself away? I nod upstairs, knowing Yates is probably locked in his office with Tom because they're both too pathetic to fight for their crew.

We head up the stairs, only having knives in what is turning into a gunfight. Some of the Misfits have guns, and all of Reaper Corp's first surge of soldiers do too, but I've always preferred a blade. I like the feel of blood running down my arms and working into the creases of my fingers.

"How many of them are there?" I ask one of the Misfits. "A number?"

He shakes his head, aiming at a man coming up the stairs behind us. His gun fires, but so does the other guy's, and the crew member accomplishes killing him, but he dies, too.

"At least thirty," Lock says. "We've taken out *maybe* half. Maybe."

Halfway there then.

I look up the stairs, ready to fight my way to Yates and his son. Reaper Corp is not getting this building or over-taking this gang, and when I'm through, there won't be anyone left standing. Their legs will be broken, and I'll haul their asses to Axel myself.

I'VE DIPPED into such brutal darkness that it feels enlightening. Closing my eyes to relish the blood soaking me, to listen to the fire of guns and the clash of blades, the screams of anguish paired with the war cries all around me, I sink into my shadowy self until it draws a curve to my lips. I'm happy here, as this bloodthirsty man, powerful in a building I've had to fake being weak in.

Misfit Hall is a mess of gore and bodies, but I'm finally the one haunting it. I'm unmasked, but I'm still the Ghost of Moros, and these halls are my playground. When I open my eyes, I see the playsets and the obstacle course, willing and eager to cut men in half to get to where I need to go.

Yates' office.

Kyd's twin katanas spin as he twirls, a severed hand flying my way. I dodge it as he laughs like a lunatic, caught in the same bloodlust as I am, but experiencing it differently. He laughs, and I delve deeper and deeper into the abyss inside me, hauling my evil parts to the surface freely.

"You don't belong here."

I spin, finding a Reaper Corp man at my back. My blood-red hands lift curved blades, and my legs crouch into a fighting stance. But my expression shifts into something that shows all my jigsaw pieces and how comfortable I am being so messily constructed.

"You're not one of them." He motions to The Misfits. "You're something stronger."

A swell of pride surges through me. Someone finally fucking noticed. "I am," I agree, smiling at him.

"Where's your mask?" he asks, not moving.

I take a page out of Riot's book, merging my inner self

with my outer self to don the mask I want him to see. Wicked. Unafraid. Ready to die if I get to fight my way there. Deranged.

"We doing this?" I ask, spinning my blades. "Or are we wasting time by chatting?"

His smile matches mine. "Reaper Corp has a message."

"Don't give it to me. I'm not a good middleman." Another severed body part flies by, and the guy shifts to the side to avoid it.

"Soren Sauder." He steps closer. "The Ghost of Moros."

I tense all over. *What the fuck?* If he knows that much, what else does Reaper Corp know, and how long have they been spying on us? "You mustn't be very high ranking if they sent you in with their first wave. They've gotta know you'll all die tonight." Pathetic crew of thirty isn't going to take us down, but the way he smiles puts me on edge, making me think there's way more than thirty, we just don't know who or where they are.

"Here's the message," he says, his fingers nimble at his sides, not even holding weapons yet. "If you surrender the town, your citizens live. If you don't..."

I laugh maniacally. "Really? A trailed-off threat before a duel? Where do you guys learn your battle tactics? Drama movies?"

He laughs with me like we're old friends. "Old Westerns," he teases. "We're bred for this. Don't underestimate us, *Ghost*." He lifts his jacket, showing me a few guns holstered there, but he doesn't reach for them. He pulls two knives that match mine from his lower back straps, fingers flexing around the hilts. "Shall we start this duel you speak of?"

"Gladly. What're we dueling for? This building?" I balance on the balls of my feet, eyes zeroed in on his every move.

"The town, eventually. Tonight, how about we duel for death. I hear it's quite the prize you seek."

I funnel all this information into my mind, reminding myself to recall it later when I can think clearly. Reaper Corp already knows too much, personal details and sinister games, and if they know, it means they have other spies within Moros. It means they might know all the Vile Boys' identities if he knows mine. They played Yates, making him think they'd ally with him if he allowed them access, even gave him the 'homicide detective, kid's dead dad' story to get things moving, but they aren't here for alliances—they're here to take the only place I've ever called home.

"I've told her to fuck off a time or two," I agree. "Deal."

With another smile, he crouches. He doesn't lunge for me right away, instead choosing to throw a dagger at me from where he stands. I shift my weight, listening to it thud into the wall behind me. I don't dare look at it, unwilling to be distracted by near-misses. Inhaling through my nose, I become Ghost, the man capable of murder and mayhem and deals pertaining to Death. She hasn't gotten me in her clutches yet, and tonight will be no different. This is yet another tango of ours.

His laugh is ugly and gorgeous, lighting me up from the inside. "Respect," he says, nodding at me.

His men are mostly dead, but he doesn't appear afraid. Well, neither am I. I smile at him, and then my body moves through the space like wind, morphing to the shape of the hall and the openings in the air. I lash out, impaling him on my blade before retracting it and moving behind him before he knows where I'm going to settle. He spins with me, and I lean back to avoid the arc of his knife. It slashes through my shirt, adding a warm, sticky trickle down my chest.

"Touché." I bounce.

He presses his hand to where I've stabbed him, and my eyes drop to follow the movement. A second later, I see it for what it is: a distraction. His hand thrusts forward, his left blade piercing through the skin of my shoulder and retracting just as fast. With blood fully drawn and pain blooming brilliantly, I drop the act and give grace to my anger.

Swiping his legs out with mine, I knock my elbow to his face and draw blood from his nose, but he flips me off and rolls to get out from under me, his knee connecting with my groin in the process. I tackle him back against the wall, making us spin and stab and snarl. He headbutts me in the bridge of my nose, making me leak, so I snarl at him, kicking my foot to his gut. When he thuds against the railing, I charge, but he puts up a blade to stop me.

"This is how our training is different," he rasps, circling me. "You give in to anger. I don't."

Anger gets me places a clear head won't, so yeah, I sink into it, letting it fuel me. The only way our training is different is that I don't have to get into knife fights as often as he does. I'm at a disadvantage because I'm rusty, but I'm advantageous because of my unwavering need to be the fucking best. To win. To get the credit and feed my pride.

He's trying to take something. I'm trying to protect something. Our motives are different, and mine is more powerful.

His shoulder rams into my gut, lifting me high enough to throw me onto my back. Knives slash and knees are thrown. My head rings out in dizziness and pain when he slams it against the ground, but it gives me a chance to stab my knife into his kidney. He cries out, eyes narrowing and body tensing. I attack again, stabbing him over and over until he backs off to gain his composure. I rip the guns from his holsters, sliding them down the hall.

But as I climb to my feet, I realize I've been stabbed again, too. His right blade sticks out of my thigh, blood leaking in heavy rivers. I know I should leave it where it is, but I can't risk the chance of him getting it back, so I rip it out and toss it over the railing.

The rest of Misfit Hall settles as the battle winds down, captives being taken. Reaper Corp lost, and this is their last standing man. He touches his eye, removing blood from his vision, but my head tilts to the side as his eyeball moves. He's wearing contacts, and anyone born and raised in a corporation that breeds perfection wouldn't wear contacts. He'd have perfect vision either through birth or laser eye surgery. They're a video device, and that's how they're learning so much about Moros.

"Draco," he tells me his name in a raspy breath. "Pleasure has been all mine."

His final dagger flies, but I'm already charging at him. It embeds in the fleshy part between my neck and shoulder, but it doesn't stop my hands from wrapping around his neck and holding him over the railing. He's already half dead, and my temper got me here, so I lean in, nose to nose with him, and watch the life filter out of his eyes as I strangle him.

"Soren," I tell him. "A cursed man has killed you. See

you in Hell, Draco." I drag my blade across his throat and hold his body over the railing to feel his blood coat my hands. It rains down on the first floor like a crimson shower, and Draco smiles as he dies, content to leave this world. I'm lost in a blood high, but there's a part of me that envies him at this moment. This is that second or two between life and death, and I've always wanted to experience it.

"What's it like?" I whisper the question at him.

His pupils move and I swear he looks at me, trying to show me what it feels like to straddle the line between here and there. As his blood soaks through my shirt sleeves, whatever spark I found in his eyes extinguishes, and I let him fall backwards over the railing.

Watching him fall, I see my Vile brothers. Ransom, Monster, Menace, Kyd, and Riot. They're all bloody, but they're also coated in black smudges and smoke. Menace is barely standing, and Riot... I swallow at the way he's staring at me.

I can't look away from him because he's the one who chases me to the afterlife, and right now, I feel too close but not close enough as pain rushes forward now that the madness has settled.

"His eyes," I rasp, gripping my shoulder. "Contacts. Take them. Where's Yates?"

"Not here," Lock says from beside me, blood dripping down his face. "Misfits! Outside, now!" His hand touches my shoulder. "You good, Sauder?"

Dying, but yeah. I nod.

"Get to a medic, yeah?"

I stumble back a step, but before Lock can steady me, Riot's hand wraps around my throat to hold me up.

"Leave," he tells everyone without looking away from me.

"Don't fucking touch me right now," I snap at him. Because I'm dying but so fucking alive. Every part of me feels something. Pain, pleasure, intrigue, wonder. I'm bleeding from so many places, but it feels rejuvenating, like a purging of this gang and the loathsome way I've had to fake it here. The fight with Draco drains out of me, but the fight within me only rises in temperature, burning me up from the inside as Riot stares at me wordlessly.

When the front door slams and Misfit Hall is silent, his hand loosens on my throat and he takes his mask off. His eyes sweep my body before he slides his fingers down the side of my neck, pressing them to the stab wound at the base. He trembles. In rage.

"Your blood belongs to me," he seethes before ripping the dagger out, fingers coming away from my neck coated in red. He drags them over his lips, leaving three slashes of *me* over the lower half of his face. My eyes focus on those three lines, my exhale coming out long and hard. I lick my lips while staring at his, salivating for something that doesn't make sense.

Pain radiates, but anticipation is worse. I'm on the precipice of snapping instead of dying, but I don't understand what my breaking point is. Him. Riot. Killian. He's my fucking breaking point, and I don't know how he gained that power. I bled for someone other than him, and now he's here, taking it back, consuming me because he owns some sick part of me.

We're not rivals because we're not competing for the same goal.

We're not enemies because we're on the same team.

We're not friends because friendships don't make sense.

We're not strangers or brothers or lovers.

We're something morphed by his masks and my cracks, forced together out of some obligation to have a sinister partner in a dire game that pushes death upon the victor.

When he licks my blood off his lips, mine part on a shaky breath. I'm humming with energy that has no point, lost in a vortex of blood and lust and darkness. Unable to move, locked in place because of three slashes of blood on his lips and a stiffness in my pants that proves I like it.

"Who do you bleed for, sweetheart?" he asks, his voice so daunting it makes me shake.

I don't want to submit. I don't want to say him. But because I don't want to, it makes me need to. To defy myself while toying with him. My nostrils flare with the strength of my demise, loving how it feels to break away from myself for him. Power thrums inside me, pushing out my chest to match his. I still have a blade in my hand, and I bring it up between our bodies, pressing the flat of it to his lips.

"Who do *you* bleed for?" I twist it, and when the sharp edge slices into his bottom lip, his blood trickles down to join mine.

Riot grabs my wrist, throws the knife, and licks his lips.

I try to stop myself. I really do. But my body vibrates and my mind snaps, and when his tongue swipes his lip again, I growl loudly as I press forward to taste the combination of us. Drawn to the way our blood mingles, enticed by the way we taste, enraptured in this game we play, and addicted to the way he chases me exactly where I want to go.

My lips slam against his, drawing more blood. Riot's grunt is savage, his hand grabbing the back of my neck to imprison me exactly where I am. The metallic taste of his blood mingled with mine assaults my taste buds and hardens my cock further. Teeth clack and tongues fight, our mouths not even kissing, but consuming. His breath goes down my throat, reminding me of the night he drowned me, but this time, I'm not refusing his air. I'm inhaling him like he's the sole thing glueing me together, holding me whole. He bites down on my lip, making me wince and moan simultaneously.

I don't need him to squeeze my neck to get a blood rush because it's happening all on its own. I'm bleeding out onto the floor of Misfit Hall, but I've never felt more alive. And angry about it.

"Fuck." I grab his hair and yank his head back, watching spit and blood glisten on his lips. His eyes are two storms, warring with each other, but warring with me most of all.

"You fucking bleed for me, Soren."

Soren.

Our chests heave together, breath fighting for space between our lips, hips pressed so close I can feel all of him. *All. Of. Him.* Hard and honed, aroused and toned. Bloody and warm. As affected by me as I am by him.

"This is never happening again," I snarl at him, firming my grip in his hair. "If you ever fucking—"

Riot takes control, slamming my back against the hallway wall. His mouth devours mine, and I fight it, but not to rid myself of it—to get more of it. His cock grinds against the stab wound in my thigh, sparking pain that makes my cock leak. My fingers weave into his hair and his wrap around my throat. Our bodies bump and grind, our mouths bleed, our souls fight for dominance, and the world as I know it tilts.

While locked in some purgatory with Killian Hallows, something shifts inside me. Because chasing a curse and a death wish no longer seems as appealing as taunting this exact devil. This one, right here—the version of him that snaps so easily but still somehow remains in control. The bloody, broken, layered man who kills easier than he feels and masks everything from the way he looks to the way he understands his surroundings. The charming bullshit is gone, and in its place is the raw, ravaged, bare Killian who hates himself but regards himself as a god. It's the confliction of him that makes him so turbulent and addicting.

Because I'm just as conflicted.

"Fuck," he groans, teeth sinking into my bottom lip. "Fuck, I knew you'd beg."

"Beg?" I bite him and then shove him back, glaring at him. "You think this is begging?"

The tension deepens into something so dark I don't even know how to cope with the light of the hallway. He glares, but there's a smile on his face while he does it. Angry and charming and disgusting because he can morph the two together so seamlessly. He runs his fingers through the blood and saliva coating his chin, sucking them into his mouth. He hums in agonized pleasure, and I push off the wall, ready to fucking do something about it.

The front door of Misfit Hall bangs open, and Krypt's purple mask walks inside, looking for both of us. His shoulders relax a bit when he finds us whole, but he shakes his head at whatever else he sees between us.

"Let's go. You need Medic, Ghost."

Riot licks his lips again, grinning at me like he's won something. I'm so out of sorts that I push by him and limp down the stairs, unsure of everything because it really does feel like he's won. I just don't know what.

When I step outside, Kyd's lion roars in the distance, the lunatic in pink roars back, and I finally feel pain.

RIOT

11

REVEAL FOR TRUST?

I'VE KNOWN the Reaper Corp threat is real, but it didn't fully click in until last night. They're coming for our town, and we still don't know exactly why or when, but last night won't be the only attack. It was a sacrificial offering, a way for them to infiltrate Moros and watch how we reacted to the ambush. It was an information gathering mission, and it fucks with my head to know they have that many skilled members that they felt thirty of them were disposable. Because it was a suicide mission, and they knew it before they ever sent them here.

"What kind of fucked-up organization sends that many people to die?" Glitch asks, hunched over against the wall, nursing a few broken ribs. "And what kind of members are eager to do it?"

"Brainwashed ones," Axel says from the head of the room. He's got three Reaper Corp patients now, taken from Misfit Hall last night, and the way his eyelid flutters in excitement isn't right. "Ones born and raised for a purpose. A cause."

Kyd smiles at his doctor, chin resting in the palms of his hands, elbows on the tabletop, and hearts in his crazy eyes.

"What cause?" Seven asks. "The fuck do they even want here?"

The stone and brick room in the asylum Axel has turned into his new lab is chilly, making my sensitive skin prickle. Exhaustion tries to drag me under, but I won't leave this damn building until I see Menace and Ghost standing on their own two feet again. Director couldn't keep us away from the medical ward, so he brought the meeting here to Axel's headquarters, putting us all at ease.

"Our people," Ransom says.

"Our location," Krypt adds.

"Hello," Facts says, sinking into a chair next to Kyd. "Our DNA. In all our research on Reaper Corp, we've found their bloodlines to be... diminishing. They're breeding within their ranks, and over time, that leads to a few too many crossovers between bloodlines. They're looking for new DNA, and Moros offers a gene pool of power and—"

"Fucked-up minds," Seven cuts in, giving Facts an apologetic look because he hates being interrupted. "Sorry, Facts. We're all a little messed up though, which makes me wonder why they want us. Why the hell do they want the kind of darkness we breed here?"

I've never seen it on him before, but Axel almost looks nervous. "Their goals are changing," he says. "They have power. They have control over so many industries. The medical and pharmaceutical industries are ruled by their companies. They hold sway with a lot of governments and military operations. Now they're looking for something to give them another edge. A... wanted evil, if you will. People with no morals. People who will do despicable things without losing sleep over it. Mix Moros with Reaper Corp, and that's exactly what you'll get."

I watch Axel study his unconscious patients, thinking that over. But why? None of it makes sense. If they already have all this power, what more do they want? And why do they need to take over our town in order to achieve it? Surely there are smarter, more infernal people somewhere else. I'm not the thinker of the group. Facts, Glitch, Seven, and Ransom are the smart ones, and everything is still so new and unknown that they're only speculating.

When Monster walks up beside Axel, getting a look at the Reaper Corp members along the front of the room, Kyd's teeth snap, but he's still smiling. "Don't make me bite you for getting too close to my intended, Monster."

Monster doesn't say anything, but he gives Kyd a challenging look. Kyd's teeth chomp again. They're the two youngest Vile Boys, and they have an odd friendship because of it. It comes with a lot of bickering, but I know Monster loves Kyd because Kyd teaches him things in a way he can accept.

"I certainly have not been intended for someone so young," Axel tells Kyd.

Kyd stands, pink baggy crop top lifting to show his abs as his arms go wide. "I'm out of my teens!"

"Barely."

"I will mature," Kyd declares. "For you."

I smile to myself. Kyd became a member of the ten younger than anyone else in Vile House. Even younger than the age Ransom became one of the ten. He's just turned twenty, we think—he picked his own birthday based on a tarot card reading—and Axel is the first love interest he's taken. Up until now, he's been all about friends, pets, hobbies, and himself. He's fucked a bunch, but I don't think he does it for sexual reasons. He just likes to perform and try everything he possibly can. Kyd is someone who takes joy in literally everything he does. Whether it be going to the zoo, murdering someone, getting his hair done, or eating breakfast, he does it all with such happiness that it baffles me. Somewhere around the age of eleven, his mind snapped. Director found him in the psych ward, and whatever caused him to snap away from himself, this is the perfection it left him as.

Crazy and happy about it.

I wish I could be as happy as he is.

"Alright everyone, listen up," Director says, calling the meeting. "We have plans to make."

As we all sit around the lab, the door bangs open. Menace walks in shirtless, tattooed torso wrapped in gauze and a pugnacious look on his face, ready to argue if anyone questions his presence. He walks a bit funny, obviously in pain, but when Ghost walks in behind him, he refuses to show weakness. He has multiple wounds all over his body, but he lifts his chin, moves as silently as he always does, and refuses to limp. Anger and frustration permeate from him, and his blue eyes are fierce as fuck. When he looks at me, I can't even muster a grin because... fuck. Look at him. So broken and defiant about it. So strong while feeling weak. So sexy while wounded.

"My hero!" Kyd bounces up, running circles around Ghost. "We cosplayed so good last night. I was the warrior fae, and you were the dark prince who defended the castle he's secretly hated to live in all his life. Wait until I write our ending. It's gonna be a cliffhanger because I wanna do a book two. No, a game two. This is more like a video game vibe. Maybe a graphic novel. I've got a buddy in the asylum art class who can draw for us." Kyd wraps his arm around Ghost's shoulder, leaning in to stage-whisper, "Wait until you find out who your smutty love interest is." His wink is so exaggerated his whole body gets involved in the action.

Ghost looks at me again, and now, I grin.

"You two are supposed to be resting!" Director barks at both of them.

"Sitting in a room listening to you drone on during a meeting is about as close to resting as I can get," Menace says with a smirk. "Put me to sleep, Director." His black hat is on, like it always is, turned backwards with his dark hair poking out.

"Fucking ungrateful assholes," Director mutters. "Sit down."

Ghost sits with Krypt, as far away from me as he can get. Kyd not-so-casually stands at Axel's side, making sure Monster isn't closer than he is, and the rest of us settle in around the lab.

Axel turns his attention to Ghost. "The contacts are being studied, thank you."

Ghost nods. "They knew really detailed shit about us, too. Details that aren't common knowledge. Knew I was Vile."

Director and Axel share a look. "Means there are more of them in town. They could be townsfolk, planted here years ago. We have no real idea when all this started."

"We'll uncover them," Glitch says. "I'm tracking everything and making a list of people who are new to town within the last two years."

"Make it five years," Axel suggests.

Director brings our attention back to him. "Death Row is damaged. Death Mark needs a lot of repairs. Remi's at his shop with the Carson boy right now, working to board up the windows."

Menace's eyes turn dark at the mention of Cain Carson.

"Neon Demon is better off, but still has a lot of damage, and that whole section of the street needs to be mended. The fire department was quick to ensure the fires didn't spread, but the damage is still extensive. We've got crews working on it, but Vile House needs to stand with Moros to show support and aid. We'll go in shifts, but at least one of us needs to be present to put everyone at ease. The locals know Reaper Corp came, but the state of Misfit Hall is unknown for now."

"What do they think?" Ghost asks.

"They think Reaper Corp took over Misfit Hall and Vile House was there to save them. The Misfits have a bad reputation now, and that won't do us any good in the coming months. We need to be united."

"Where's Yates and his dipshit kid?" Seven shakes his head. "They been found yet?"

"No," Director says. "Few neighbours saw them running through the streets after the explosions on Death Row, but don't know where they went. We'll find them."

"And the state of The Misfits?" I ask.

"Lockan Tate is rallying them," Director looks at Glitch because Lock is his... family. "A change is coming, boys. We need unification with the cults and crews in town, and step one is allying with The Misfits. We need to take a vote." He looks at Glitch still. "To reveal who we are or to not. The Misfits aren't going to trust us if we remain behind our masks."

Glitch looks away, not wanting to be the one to make that decision. He's the only one of us with good parents in town. They don't know he's Vile, but they're good people who own the only butcher shop here, and he still gets along with them well. Lock is his brother, in a sense, and they're friends, but Glitch has always had to keep the secret from his family.

"No," Ghost snaps. "We aren't revealing who we are to all of Moros. It's the secrecy that keeps us in power."

"Agreed," Ransom says. "It won't benefit us if the whole town finds out."

I nod. "The masks are a part of Vile House, and if we lift them now, everything will change."

Ghost scoffs at me, shaking his head. "Figures."

"The fuck does that mean?" I bark at him.

"Killian Hallows is a fucking nobody, so of course you want the mask. Can't fucking live without it."

I stand, ready to fuck him up and put him in his place. That's goddamn rich coming from him, the guy who weaves illusions and glues himself back together every time a new piece breaks off. Menace stands with me, eyes on mine as a reminder to calm down.

"Don't," he says, hand on my chest. "Riot."

I glare at Menace, trying to find my footing. Ghost laughs from across the room, and every part of me bristles. Menace grabs my jaw and forces me to focus on him, and right at that moment, Ghost's laugh dies and turns into a snarl. Yeah, fuck you, Ghost. You're just as twisted as I am. Possessive and fucking brutal, and a hypocrite like none other.

"My god, boys," Director sighs. "Settle down before I send you to solitary to settle down."

Menace smirks at me, pushing me back onto my chair.

"We won't reveal ourselves to the town," Director continues. "But if we're going to form an alliance with The Misfits, we need to think about unmasking as a show of trust."

"If Lockan takes over, we set a meeting with him and unmask only for him. And only those of us who are comfortable with it." Ransom looks at everyone. "I'll do it if no one else wants to. It only has to be one of us."

Pretty sure I've already given myself away to Lock, so I up-nod Ransom. "I'll do it, too. Only him, though, and he has to give us something in return. Trust goes both ways."

"I'll do it if he's sworn to secrecy. And threatened," Glitch says. "It's an act of trust, but it has to be respected as one."

Everyone nods to agree. Everyone except Monster, who shakes his head and leaves the room. Ransom twitches to go after him, but he forces himself to stay put, looking at Director.

"What's next?"

"Next, we find Yates, clean up our town, call a town-wide meeting to inform them of what's going on, and start fortifying for Reaper Corp's next attack. This won't be the only one." Director looks behind him at Axel. "And we let the doctor experiment on these three to see what he can pull from their minds. We need all the intel we can get."

Ransom leaves to follow Monster, and everyone else lingers for a bit, chatting and checking in. I'm not in the mood for people anymore, so I step into the hall to wait on my own, letting my facades simmer without having to try so hard to keep them in place. I zone out, go blank, because when I have nothing to exploit, I have nothing to do.

This area of the asylum is old and mostly vacant. It isn't modern or updated, and the halls are echoey and dark. Pretty sure my brother hunted Remi through these halls, and when he walks out of the lab room, he looks down the corridor, his eyes darkening.

"Fond memories?" I ask with a smirk.

"Something like that," Krypt says, nodding down the hall. I follow. "Before Remiel ever admitted he likes being afraid."

I wonder if Ghost has that in common with his brother. I don't think so. Remi might get a hard dick over being scared, but Ghost seems more like the type to get a stiff cock over being dangerous... or in danger.

"You find what you were looking for at the house the other day?" I ask him.

He lights a joint right in the hallway, inhaling long and hard. "Yeah. Remiel wanted to see all my files from the doctors *they* had me tested by."

"The fuck? Why?"

Krypt scoffs. "He thinks he's a hero. He wants to defy all those diagnoses and show me I'm perfect or something."

I laugh, taking the joint. "Perfectly fucking tainted."

He grins, which is rare for him. "Remiel says that." By the time I hand him back the joint, the grin is gone, and a serious expression takes over. "You fucking Ghost?"

I exhale the weed in my lungs. "What makes you ask that?"

"What'd I walk in on in Misfit Hall?"

I crack all my knuckles and look back towards the lab, wondering if Ghost is still in there or if he snuck out undetected. "Tension. A blood high."

"You're my brother," he says, not finishing the sentence. "But he's Remiel's brother."

"Yeah, yeah. I'll keep the bitch alive. Doesn't mean I can't have some fun with him while I do."

GHOST

12

GHOST OF THE TUNNELS

NO PART of me gives a single fuck about being injured. I've come closer to death in my sleep, so a few stab wounds and a night in the medical wing aren't going to be what slows me down. I hurt, but I won't admit it. Riot is the only one looking close enough to see through my cracks and witness the pain festering within me anyway, but fuck him.

At this point, I don't even know if it's physical pain or mental pain. Emotional pain? It doesn't matter because I refuse to grant it the ability to rise to my exterior. My facade always stays in place, no matter how fragile it is.

Remi's fussing over me like a little nurse, trying to force me to focus on changing my bandages and cleaning my wounds. They're mostly stitched up, and thankfully, nothing serious got damaged.

Stronger than the pain is pride. Because I fought that Reaper Corp prick and won. He tried to tempt me into the afterlife with him by granting me a few seconds' glimpse into that hanging moment between life and death, but I was stronger than him. I was stronger than them all. I killed at least ten men, took down the final one, kept Misfit Hall from falling into the clutches of Reaper Corp, and helped prove what a useless coward Yates is. Because of me, Lockan Tate gets to have his crew back, and I know he'll be a better leader than anyone else there.

Everyone should be fucking bowing to me.

"Stop," Remi says, smacking my hand away so he can apply the final strip of medical tape to the bandage on my thigh.

"Thought you weren't allowed to touch me?" I shake my head at him.

"Krypt isn't here. Just make sure you keep it clean, for fuck's sake."

"Yeah, yeah." I pull my sweatpants on, cringing just a little at the way it stings to move my leg. "It'll stay clean. Don't have time for an infection." I leave my shirt off and let my brother look. He's seen my Misfit tats, but up until he started 'dating' Krypt, he's never been allowed to see my Vile House tats, so this is the first time he's getting a look at them up close and personal. The skull on my back, Vile House at the top, my name at the bottom—every inked needle of it earned. "How's the shop?"

He stares at my sides, ribs, back, and arms, taking the whole picture of me in. Yeah, I'm such a well-constructed piece of art that even my brother can't see through the dark ink to what simmers just below my surface. He sees a thrill-seeker, not a broken bastard with a need to prove I am stronger than the only sure thing in life—death.

"The windows are boarded up, and I'm staying closed for a few days, but otherwise, no major damage. Cain is there making sure everything is in good shape, and I guess the window repair people will be there tomorrow."

"Director had to bribe them to come," I say, laughing. "No one wants to come here right now."

"Don't blame them. Moros is a mess."

"Yeah," I agree. "A beautiful mess, and that'll still draw in the right people."

"Hopefully not Reaper Corp." Remi looks at me, wide-eyed and showing all his fear. "The hell are we going to do if they take over, Soren?"

"Ghost."

"Sorry. But what happens if they win?"

"We won't fucking let them. And if, somehow, they do, we'll die trying to defend our town. Like fuck I'm gonna become a pawn in a game as big as theirs. Death can't have me, neither can they."

Remi narrows his eyes at me, trying to crack the code of my words. "Death can't have you? Did you break the curse?"

I'm not even sure I believe in the curse the same way he does. Remi has always been afraid of it, and I don't blame him. He's watched the men in our family fall like flies, one right after the other, feeling the curse creeping up on him next. It broke me when our dad died, and it fucking killed me when our brothers died because it made me feel inferior, like I'm not strong enough to stop this curse. We're all that's left, so I have to believe there's a way to end it. To prevent it. Remi has Krypt now, and he's taking the medication Axel suggested he try, and he's doing it all under the professional supervision of Psych, so I trust that he's in good hands.

But me? Yeah, I see the allure of a curse and believe that our bloodline is somehow tempted by the idea of suicide and choosing our own death, but I don't know if I'm tempted by it the same way they are. My brothers fought it and eventually succumbed to it, Remi's been trying to outrun it for as long as I can remember, but I seem to be running *for* it rather than away from it, and it has nothing to do with wanting to die. I just want to be the fucking best, the strongest, the smartest. Imagine the ego boost I'd get if I defied death on numerous occasions?

Riot thinks he can chase me there faster, but it only adds more fun to my game. I'm dragging him along with me, and when I finally knock on Death's door, I'll shove him through the threshold and slam it in *both* their faces. That brings a smile to my lips.

"I don't believe in the curse."

Remi scoffs. "Sure. You just tried to protect me from it all this time by stalking me."

Sure did. Gregory Malone stalked Remi, and I stalked Gregory Malone. I pushed Remi to Vile House that night, and I don't regret it, because look at him now. He's stronger, darker, better equipped, and has a whole powerful society at his back. He has a team of medical professionals overseeing his care, and he has a possessive as fuck boyfriend who won't let him hold his breath long enough to die. It's not the way I foresaw it going, but it worked out regardless. I did that. Me.

"Someone had to chase you here."

"What?!" He gapes at me. "I knew it! I thought you were there that night... I—fuck, Soren. Why?"

"You needed protection, and I got it for you. So, you're welcome. For Krypt." I grab him by the scruff of his shirt. "And for the hundredth time, while we're here, it's Ghost."

"Ghost," he corrects, smiling at me. "Thank you. For...

well, for leading me here, for always stalking Gregory Malone, and for having my back even while I thought you hated me. I honestly thought you were going to kill me just to end the curse. Turns out you were just lying to me. About everything."

"Not by choice, but it gave me a little kick to sneak around behind your back." I smirk.

"Of course it did." He throws a shirt at me. "Come on. Let's go eat before this town meeting."

AFTER EATING and leaving my brother to get to the town meeting on his own, I'm silent while I walk through the tunnels. I drop back without anyone noticing, content to be concealed in the shadows with my thoughts. My mind still isn't a safe place, but ever since my murder spree, it's been mostly peaceful.

Except for when I think about Riot. His damn mouth, three finger streaks of my blood across his lips, and the way his tongue tasted me. The power that came alive in me when he kissed me, savage and raw and fucking finite, is addicting. There was nothing timid about the way he crushed his mouth to mine, and even if the whole thing is confusing, I don't regret it, but I don't want it to happen again. Because I can't feel alive while pressed to him. I can't accept power from him. I need it on my own, to be able to create it and thrive in it. An external power source isn't enough for me, and it sure as fuck isn't acceptable coming from him.

I need him to push me so I can create my own power,

strengthen myself, prove to myself that I'm all it takes to get through this thrilling life. I'm the powerhouse of my own life, and there isn't a chance in hell I'll let him take that role.

The water at the base of the tunnel ripples, alerting me to someone's presence. It's dark along the edges, but my eyes are adjusted to it, so when the steps come closer, the water shifting ever so slightly, I hold my breath and give myself a moment to simply sense the approach.

Riot. He thinks he knows where I am, so I slow down again, moving backwards instead of forwards, throwing him off my trail. His feet stop, and the echo of everyone's voices changes to something duller, farther away. His breathing is loud in this chamber, and I swear to fuck I can hear his heart beating as he tries to listen for my whereabouts. The guy has no idea how to be quiet.

He won't hear me. I won't let him. He's already drowned me in a pond, paralyzed me in my grave, and kissed me while in the throes of a blood high—I won't allow him to get another one over on me. He's made my head even less of a safe space, and I can't stand him having that sort of control over me.

But... the way it felt to cut his inner bicep. I took that control and he let me have it, and the way his blood trickled down his skin has been on my mind since.

My eyes adjust more, my ears pick up everything, and my body relaxes to a point where my wounds don't even hurt. Anticipation swells inside me, my fingers all flexing at my side as he comes to a complete stop, trying to be silent to listen for my movement. Here in the dark, I don't have to hide the cracks in my illusion or the over-glued pieces of my jigsaw puzzle front. I use the darkness as a mask, but it's a different kind of mask from what he wears. He tries to please, to accommodate, to manipulate those around him, but I'm only trying to manipulate myself into believing I'm not as broken as the voice inside my head tells me I am.

He walks closer to where I am, water rippling against the soles of my boots. I feel it like it's a caress, a subtle warning, and I use it to aid my silence. While he disrupts the water, I step backwards, pressing my shoulder blades to the tunnel wall. He's right in front of me now, but he doesn't know it. He's looking back the way we came instead of looking to his side, and I love the way I deceive him. The way he thinks he's smarter than me, but moments like this prove that he's not.

"Hiding from me, sweetheart?" he asks the long tunnel. His voice is dark-tinged yet gleeful, which pisses me off because he isn't aware that he's losing this round yet.

I grin, but I bristle, too. I want the ability to hide from him because he's too stupid to know where to look, but I don't appreciate the insinuation that I'm cowardly for hiding. I almost react, which is exactly what he wants, but I flex my fingers again and force myself to be still.

"When I was in the shower last night, your blood was all over me," he says, turning his back to me to peer against the opposite wall. "Fucking dripped down my body, and guess what I did?"

Pressing my lips together to force a silent breath through my nose, I flex my fingers once more. This time, against my cock. It better not get hard. Because I'm imagining it. His busted knuckles turning white as his bloody hand wraps around his thick cock, stroking my blood to mix with his precum...

"Fuck, my dick looked good coated in your blood." He turns more, and if he steps a little closer, his adjusted eyes will see me. "The water diluted it, but I can't wait to make you bleed all over me and try not to get hard at the sight of it."

My palm presses to my dick, willing it to stay down.

"We gonna talk about it?" Riot asks, almost facing me now. "That kiss you forced on me?"

Fuck. Him. When he spins to face my spot, I move with him, keeping my body behind him without making a sound. He looks at the tunnel wall, his shoulders tensing when he doesn't find me where he thinks I am.

"Couldn't get enough, could you?" he asks, acting calm when we both know he's pissed he can't find me. "Fuck, you were a desperate little blood whore. All broken and bleeding and using me to get your strength—"

From behind, I wrap my forearm around his neck and use my other hand to tighten the hold. Riot wheezes, his body fighting to get free, but fuck him. Fuck all of this. Fuck the bargain with my brother and the way Riot thinks he can push me to an early death. Fuck him for everything he's done since he came into my life as my best challenger.

"*I* forced on *you*?" I growl in his ear. "I'm the whore?" I squeeze tighter. "You called Lock and made him come check on me."

His breath rattles and his voice is forced. "Keeping... my end of the... bargain."

"You came at me like you fucking owned me." My laugh is pure evil. "You demanded I only bleed for you. You fucking kissed me. You're the whore, Riot. You're the one who turned this sexual."

He coughs, and I feel his throat spasm against my arm. He tries to say something while his fingers grasp my wrist, but I don't loosen my hold. This shit ends now. He can push me all he wants as long as the destination is Hell and not his bed. He's the desperate one who can't fuck the same person twice because he never remembers what mask he wore with them to win them in the first place. I won't be his easy way out just because he doesn't have to wear a mask for me.

Riot struggles in my grip, making all my wounds ache fiercely. Holding him tighter and pressing my lips to the shell of his ear, I exhale slowly. "You don't fucking own me, Riot. I bleed for no one but myself. You think you're the one chasing me to my death?" I pause, gathering the strength of the dark tunnels and the sinister things that've happened down here. "Stop acting like you have any control here. We both know I'm the one dragging you to Hell, and like the little puppy you are, you're following along eagerly."

With one more blown breath against his nape, I shove him forward and disappear before he ever turns around. Our games have always been rooted in challenge, but whatever new sexual energy he's bringing to our dynamic isn't going to fly with me. Because I don't like the way he makes me feel unglued, ripped open, my pieces scattered around the board for him to put back together the way he sees fit.

RIOT

13

TOWN MEETING

I LOVE it when Director gets diabolical. Under the light of dusk, he's giving Moros a show, but they have no idea just how serious this show is yet.

Strung up to the iron gates of the cemetery, a Reaper Corp prisoner groans. He's fully clothed, somewhere in his late thirties or early forties, and he's dripping blood onto Moros soil while every eligible citizen watches from between the headstones. The cemetery is the biggest gathering place we have within town limits, and I doubt there's a Moros resident who feels uncomfortable here, so here we all are, having the first town-wide meeting in years.

Director hasn't said a word, but as the energy shifts to signify the start of the meeting, the locals press their fists to their hearts in acknowledgement, and the ten of us do the same for our people.

"The threat is real, Moros!" Director shouts from behind us, the crowd already silenced. He's standing on the platform of a stone garden, and we're all ground level in front of him. His gold and black mask is in place, and his voice is modulated, capturing everyone's attention. "Reaper Corp is coming for our town."

"Let them fucking try!" Gemma, who owns the Cauldron, shouts, and a bunch of cheers agree with her.

"We're not ready," Director says bluntly. "We lack a plan, training, and weapons. We're too broken after the attack."

"What happened?" Abigail, the leader of the Death For Life Cult, asks. "Misfits are over?"

The crowd gossips, whispering all the lies and secrets and truths they've gathered about the other night. The assembled residents range in age from the elderly to parents who brought their young kids because they don't believe in shielding the truth from them. Shop owners, business owners, musicians, teachers, and high school teens stand together with cult leaders, gang members, and psychos. We all work together while a Reaper Corp member bleeds out for us.

Remi stands with Cain, watching the crowd but letting his eyes come back to my brother every few seconds. Next to Cain is his girlfriend, Sadie, whose hand is linked with his tattooed hand. Probably the reason Menace is twitching. Axel is out there, too. If anyone in town has recognized him as the presumed dead doctor from four years ago, they haven't said anything, but maybe that's because he walked in with Vile House, and everyone just accepts that he's one of us now.

"Years ago, Vile House and The Misfits were united with all of you in Moros. We were a team, a singular unit with one sole interest: keeping outsiders from infiltrating our town." Director looks at his audience. "And then Yates became the new leader."

The crowd roars their outrage. No one has ever done anything to overthrow Yates because he's from a legacy bloodline around here, but they've never liked him. His grandfather and father were the creators of the gang, and when Yate's dad refused to pass it down to him, Yates killed the successor and took it for himself.

"He fled!" Director shouts to calm everyone down. "Yates and his son Tom are on the run. We don't know if they're still in Moros, but there will be rewards for anyone who captures and brings him to Vile House alive. We need information from him. He's been in contact with Reaper Corp for weeks, maybe months, letting them in and hiding their members in Misfit Hall." He waves his hand to silence the crowd's murmurs again. "He thought he could work his way into their good graces, but they used him like they'll try to use all of us. Thanks to these ten and the remaining Misfits, Reaper Corp lost the first round."

There is no applause, only another wave of fists to hearts.

"I say we burn Misfit Hall to the ground!" someone shouts. "Never let Yates back in!"

"Oh, Yates is never getting back in." Lockan Tate walks forward, parting the crowd. "But The Misfits' members are still Moros locals. Still good people who want to fight alongside you to win this war!"

Everyone watches Lock, but they look at Director to see what he's going to do about it. Director nods, and Ghost and I step apart to let Lock through. He climbs onto the stone ledge with Director, showing a united front for the first time in years.

"The Misfits will undergo a purging. Anyone found working with Yates to aid Reaper Corp will be marched down Death Row for all to see, their punishments decided by members. New leadership will take over, and like before, we'll restore Misfit Hall to the stronghold Moros relies on. Allied with our new partners." Lock looks at Director.

In a show of respect that Director has never done publicly, he presses his fist to his heart and nods his head at Lock. The town gasps, but it's awed instead of alarmed. Lock returns the gesture, and just like that, we've gained even more trust within Moros.

"We want to be transparent with you about everything we learn," Director keeps talking to the townsfolk. "As we learn information, we'll relay it to you, but it must be kept calm. We cannot risk mass hysteria right now, Moros. If you have skills that can help, we'll be setting up a recruitment centre. If you lack training and want to better yourself, we will offer it. If you need advice as to how to protect your family, your homes, and our town, please come to us. To any of us." He waves his hands over the ten of us, plus Lock. "If you require a safer place to stay, we have made arrangements with the asylum board of directors to open an unused wing for communal living to those who may need it. And if you wish to leave town or send your young ones away until the threat is over, we can aid you with that as well."

"What 'bout my bidness?" Auggie, the scary-looking woman who owns the Umbra Inn, the only hotel in town, shouts. "Am I meant to be shuttin'er down?"

Ransom steps forward and takes her scarred hand. She

steps forward with him, facing the crowd, and as one, everyone presses their fists to their hearts for her. If she's going to lose business because of this mess, we'll find a way to take care of her.

"Stay open and work with us. The music festival is coming, and I know you're booked, but it can help. Every tourist who comes through town gets reported to us, and we'll pay you for your effort and make up the difference if your capacity is low." Ransom nods at her. "You know how to protect yourself if any of your guests turn out to be someone other than who they say they are?"

Auggie snorts and scoffs at once. "I ain't no fair maiden."

"Go, Auggie!" Kyd shouts, making the town laugh.

When everyone calms down, Director shocks them for real. "Because of this threat, Vile House has made the decision to host an early, additional Initiation Night. We're looking to increase our members, the ones who work their way up to becoming the ten."

Gasps. My skin prickles.

"Anyone who wishes to initiate can do so. Information will be posted around town by the end of the month."

Fuck, I'm already buzzing for another Initiation Night.

LOCKAN TATE ISN'T someone who reacts normally to a threat. Like a Vile Boy through and through, he grins in the face of danger and sees a threat as a challenge. But he doesn't fight it. Yet.

With a knife pressed to his throat and nine other masked

men surrounding him in the foyer of Vile House, he nods to accept his fate. He's in our house, under our rules, and unless he follows orders and agrees to our terms, he won't walk out the front door again.

"An alliance makes us stronger together. What's it going to take for us to prove ourselves to you?" Ransom asks, being the voice tonight.

"Trust," Lock says without missing a beat. "I want to know who I'm working with."

"Our identities?" As we expected. It's bold of him to suggest it because no outsider, apart from Remi, has ever been granted this gift. Director respects boldness.

"At least one of you and your leader. Preferably all of you, but I'll settle for one. For now." He spins, looking at all our masks. "You work on rank or what?"

Our rank lineups are for us only. We don't operate on ranks outside of internal challenges and a need to best one another. We all have roles, work together, and get the jobs done however we can while Director puts us where he thinks we'll best shine. Ransom is the one we all naturally look up to, but he's earned that respect from all of us for different reasons.

"No," is all Ransom answers. "You have any other terms?"

Lock shakes his head for now.

"Here are our terms. You have to establish yourself as the leader of The Misfits, however you do that within your crew."

"A vote," Lock says.

"If they agree to ally with Vile House, they don't get to

know our identities. Only you do. Then you have to prove loyalty to us by being branded with our mark."

"What fucking mark?" Lock asks, throwing his very heavily tattooed arms wide. "Don't got much skin space left."

"We'll find space. If you agree to those terms, you'll become our partner, and at least one of us will reveal our identity to you. From there, we work together, not only to defeat Reaper Corp, but to better our town moving forward. Which means you give us all the information you possess, and we'll do the same. Moros is the focus."

"If we survive," Lock mutters.

"You'll be sworn to secrecy once you know who we are, and if you break that trust, there will be a rivalry between our members, and I promise you, The Misfits won't win."

"Fine," Lock agrees. "If I meet those terms, I want one more thing. For my crew."

"Say it," I blurt.

"Training. A lot of them only know how to fight and defend, not to think. They're soldiers, which is probably what you want, but I want better for them. I want them to be able to work as a unit. To trust one another again. I want you to help me establish that level of strength within them because right now, they're fucking lost. Yates beat them down and only used them as murderers. They deserve to be more than that."

Ghost doesn't say anything, but he's nodding. His teal mask agrees with everything Lock says. I know he wants to say more, to comment on their lack of status and ability to work as a unit, but until he's forced to reveal himself, he'll keep his mouth shut.

"We can do that," Director says. "We'll help *you* do that."

Lock nods again. "Alright, thank you. I'll gather my crew and put it to a vote. I'll be back when I know where I stand. How do I get in contact with you?"

"For now, we'll get in contact with you." Ransom pulls the front door open. "This is your only chance to leave without a fight or a bargain. Don't waste it, Tate."

Lock grins as he sweeps his eyes over the foyer one more time, taking it all in. Vile House is such a myth, built into the lore of Moros, and its mystery is what keeps it so powerful.

"Night, boys." He leaves, and Ransom closes the door behind him.

"Initiate," he calls, and Selena Sauder comes forth, masked in a plain black Purge mask. "You have any of your brother's skills?"

She looks over her shoulder at us, unsure which mask hides her brother's face, and I swear I can see her smile through her eyes. She nods at Ransom.

"Follow him. Report back on the vote."

When she looks back at us, proud of being given her first official job as a member of Vile House, we all fist our hands over our hearts at her.

"Careful, girl. Don't challenge my reputation too much," Ghost says, revealing his mask colour to her.

Selena gives him the finger and heads out the front door under the cover of a dark night.

With the door locked and the house ours again, we all take our masks off. I spin mine to let it sit at the back of my head, but almost everyone else pushes theirs to the top of their head.

"No other identities revealed to her until she moves up a rank," Ransom warns, his dark eyes meeting all of ours.

"She's making the ten. I know it. She'll be my girlie bestie," Kyd declares, looking at Seven. "She's doing awesome, right?!"

Seven runs the initiates the most, so he's always got the inside scoop on how they're all doing. He pushes his mask up and nods. "Yeah, she honestly fucking fits here. Won't be long until she's tested and named."

We all look to see what Ghost thinks of that, but he's not here. Everyone laughs. It's about time I go find him and remind him who is in control of this bargain we have.

GHOST

14

HUNG REVELATIONS

"THE FUCK ARE YOU DOING HERE?" Selena whispers when I join her on the roof of Misfit Hall. "I can handle it."

"I know." Which bothers me because I don't want her challenging my skills. I settle down beside her, the moon starting to peek out now that the clouds are clearing. "But I'm still a Misfit, so I gotta go in there and act like one. Just wanted to make sure you were good first."

"I'm fine," she says. "Actually feel like..."

I grin behind my mask. "Like what? Like you fit somewhere?"

"Yeah. That."

Same way I felt when I joined. I loved my dad and siblings, but home never felt like home. As soon as I became a member of Vile House, I got that family feeling, even if it wasn't in a healthy way. And now, if I were to say I have dreams, they're all coming true. Not only is my sister becoming a member of Vile House, but my brother lives there, too. We're together, at least the three of us who remain, living with the family I made for myself.

"What's up with you lately?" Selena asks. "You're... off."

"I'm always off. You worry about you, and I'll worry about me and Remi."

Selena huffs. "Oh, I'll worry about Remi, too. That idiot went and attached himself to the creepiest guy I've ever met. Keegan doesn't even know how to smile."

"Yeah, but Krypt knows how to protect Remi, so take him as he is." I laugh. "His creep level has its advantages."

"Gay?" she whispers at me. "Remi? You ever see that coming?"

I shrug. "Why not?"

"He never gave any indication," she says.

"Being fucked by a madman sounds slightly tempting." I grin at her and pull my mask off.

"Yeah? Which madman are you getting fucked by? His brother?" Does she know Killian is Riot?

I grind my teeth together and press my mask to her chest. "Hold this for me. I have a part to play." I walk across the shingles. "And the day his brother gets in my pants is the day I kill him."

AFTER CASTING my vote and getting a cocky grin from Lock, I leave Misfit Hall as Soren and walk through Moros well after midnight. Soon enough, I won't have to pretend to be in the gang because Lock will know my true identity. He probably already does, but fuck, it'll still be an ego boost to rip my mask off and prove it to him. I've been repressed in The Misfits for far too long, and I've earned my moment of victory. I don't get them often enough.

The streets are mostly empty, but the cemetery is full of nightcrawlers. Sadie and her Death For Life cult are gathered around their family crypt, doing whatever crazy shit they do to one another. I'd never stoop so low as to willingly die just to come back and protect the living. Fuck that. I protect the living while being a *living ghost*, and my brother and sister both have me to thank for their current level of safety.

Turning my back on the cemetery, I head down Death Row and see the damaged section. The Ambient Raven has a new front window, but the second one and the door both still need to be replaced. Across the street, I get nostalgic as I look at the place Krypt and I found that nurse dealer who sold Remi the suicide pill. What a deranged night that was—it ended with him eating his own dick and hanging from the front porch of Misfit Hall. I grin to myself, loving memory lane when it portrays me as the wicked hero.

Out the far end of the street, I see the house Willow Olenna kept from her cousin—the guy Riot killed in the bargain hall. I wonder who came to collect her payment. I wonder what it was. I wonder a lot of things, which makes my mind busy, and since it isn't a safe place, I find myself agitated and unhinged. I don't want to go back to Vile House to sleep. I'm craving something different, something darker and more volatile.

I'm craving a brush with death just to settle me down. There's no one here to push me over the edge this time, so instead of heading to Vile House, I head to The Ambient Raven and lock the temporary door behind me. A soft recording lulls the empty shop to sleep, my dad's piano, Remi's cello, Selena's guitar and... I swallow when I hear my violin. The music breaks me enough to get sentimental. I bet if I looked through all Remi's recordings, I'd find one with all of our instruments together—five siblings and their father, playing a brutal, melancholy theme because we've always been comfortable in our anguish together. Until three out of six of us died and we stopped making music.

I take a violin off a stand, inspecting it without touching the bow. If I play, does it mean I'm giving in to something? The only place I've created music in the past year is in my bedroom at Vile House in the dead of night, afraid to let my notes meet the light of day. This violin is shiny and new, and while I think I deserve new things, I'm afraid of them, too. This instrument has probably never been played. What if the type of music I force it to create taints it? What if my music befouls the shop Remi loves? What if I'm not glued together well enough to prevent my sinister disease from seeping out, bleeding myself through music into his sacred space? Because I respect this shop...

I miss it here. I miss being in love with music with my brother. I miss family time that isn't dire, and I miss memories I've refused to remember. Being here brings them all back, so I grab the bow and slide down behind the front counter, my back to the wooden cupboards and my ass on the floor, shrouded in shadows.

Closing my eyes, I bring the instrument into position, but I don't play it. I listen to the recording coming from the speakers around the shop, picking out the notes and the instruments and matching them to a memory of the day we played this piece together. It was after our brother died, and none of us knew how to talk about it, so we played. We played while Mom listened, but now that I think back on it, I don't think she listened well. She was distracted. Angry at us for ignoring her in favour of the music. But I remember the way my dad's eyes watered, how Selena kept her face blank but bled her emotions into her guitar, and how Remi stared at the ground the entire time he played his deeply unsettling sounds. I don't remember what I did or how I looked.

I don't even remember how I felt. Broken, I guess, but I don't know if I was broken for myself or for the loss of a sibling. I know I'm selfish, so I was probably more concerned with how it affected me, but as I listen to the recording of my violin, I hear the depth of the emotions I tried so hard to tamp down and hide away.

I'm so lost in the music surrounding me that I don't notice when I'm no longer alone. I haven't touched the bow to the strings, and before I can, a thick, heavy rope loops around my neck. The violin clatters to the floor so my fingers can wedge behind the rope, but it's pulled taut, unremorseful of my current pain.

"Riot!" I shout, knowing it's him. "Fuck off. Not right now." Every wound on my body sings out in pain.

"Yes, right now." His voice comes from behind the counter. I try to look up, the rope biting into my neck harder, and when I see where it leads, my stomach flips. Either in anticipation or fear, probably a combination of both. "Hold on tight, sweetheart."

I keep my fingers between the rope and my skin, creating as much space as I can while my body is hoisted up, the rope slung over a thick beam. Up and up, my head damn near hitting the beam on the high ceiling of the shop as I'm pulled up to hang. My toes barely touch the front counter, but it's enough to allow my throat to stay open to breathe a little. Behind me, Riot secures the rope to something, and I look around, wondering what I can reach to cut myself down before he does something disgusting to me.

There's a knife in my jacket...

"I need the ninety seconds," I rasp.

The music still plays, but my busy mind from the street is gone, lost to the vibrancy of something I craved—a brush with death. Riot delivers right when I need him to. He plucks nightmares straight from my head, turning them into a warped reality he controls. I don't like the power that gives him, but I can't write it all off as unwanted. Killian Hallows is the only man I know who speaks the same depraved language as me.

"Were you gonna play this?" he asks, walking around the counter and picking up the violin I dropped. His finger plucks the strings, agitating my nerves with the dissonant sound. Riot can play the piano almost as well as Krypt, but he hates music because he can't hide himself in it like I can. When he plays, everything he tries to hide bleeds out, and he refuses to show that weakness to anyone but himself. Fuck, he probably won't even show it to himself because in his twisted mind, he's perfect.

My toes dig into the counter, lifting myself as high as I can to get some relief on my throat. With a good grip on the rope, I suck in air and smile at him. Some switch flips in my mind, and instead of simply smiling at him to goad him, I start laughing, my madness showing. I don't know what it is about Death that I find so fucking funny, but every time I come close to dancing with her, such elation consumes me that joy spills from between my lips.

Because he's twisted, Riot laughs with me, his grey eyes bright with a lack of morality. "There you are, sweetheart. Batshit and hanging, just how I like you." He plucks another string, but it doesn't annoy me so much this time. "Came here to be sad, but instead I turned you mad."

Nah, he's wrong. I came here to lose myself to insanity because I'm a masochistic prick when I want to be. Pain, even the emotional kind brought on by sad memories, feels good. Good because it's so strong. It's an onslaught of emotions I can't hide from, and when everything in my life feels so pathetic because *I'm* the most powerful thing, I love losing myself to my weaknesses. My feelings, fears, and insecurities. I don't want the world to see them, but I want to buckle under their pressure, let them taunt me hard enough to drive me crazy, and then see how far they'll push me towards my deathly dance partner.

Except lately, Riot has been the thing pushing me to dance, not my own downfalls.

"Still want to play?" he asks, holding the instrument out to me. "I can hold it for you and you can use one hand for the bow."

"You don't wanna hear what kind of music I'd play right now." I choke when my Adam's apple presses against the rope, coughing while staring down at him.

"Of course I do," he says. "But I already know. You aren't hard to read."

"No? What am I feeling then?"

He sets the violin on the floor and hops up to join me. He turns my body until I'm sideways on the counter and he's right in front of me, eye to eye. "Weak. Weak and crazy about it."

He's not wrong...

"Delusional because you still think death is the thing you're chasing." His grin makes his eyes brighter, and the stubble along his jaw darkens, turning him into a living nightmare. With his hands on my hips, he sways me, spinning us like we're dancing to a tune that's austere to me but congenial to him. When he looks into my eyes, I stare, refusing to acknowledge his sweet, shy smile that doesn't at all match the calamitous situation. I'm choking, literally hanging from the ceiling, and he's slow-dancing with me like this is a wedding.

"What am I chasing?"

"That's not the right question." He looks down my body and back up again. "It's more about what's chasing you."

I scoff. Then cough. "You? You chasing me?"

"Always." He nods. "But what else? You think you're knocking on Death's door, right? Ready to laugh in her face and slam her fingers in it, but she's not even playing with you, Ghost. This is a one-man game. You pretending to chase her, her rolling her eyes because you never try hard enough to catch her. You think she takes you seriously when you're clinging to life so hard?" He spins me, catching me in an embrace I loathe.

What fucking part of me is clinging to life harder than I'm chasing death? I want to live, but I don't want to live *just* to be alive. I want to defy the concepts of life and trick the only sure thing that comes from being born. A monotonous life isn't for me. Not even a thrilling one in Vile House. It's not enough. I need more. More ways to be superior, ultimate, unlike anyone else because I'm Soren fucking Sauder, the man who has yet to succumb to a curse that's taken almost every male in my family. A living ghost. Dead while alive. I want to be alive in death, too.

"You aren't chasing shit," Riot tells me. "You're running from something."

I scoff again, my head getting light as I partially hang.

"Monotony. Being average. Fear."

"What fucking fear?" I kick out at him, ending our dance.

I regret it a second later when he grabs my leg, making me hang for real now that my toes won't touch the countertop.

"That no one will remember you. When the Ghost of Moros is dead, no one's going to know who he was. He was just that ghost. Not Soren."

I splutter, kicking. I want to turn away. Breathing is only second to hiding my face from him because he's right. I'm just that ghost. No one fucking knows who I am. Soren will be remembered as a temporary part of The Misfits. Not the leader. Not anyone of significance. No one but some guy who was part of some gang for some undisclosed period of time. I'm fucking important! But nobody knows.

Riot laughs, grabbing my other leg as my face turns red. He wraps them around his waist and lifts me up enough to suck in air. His nostrils flare at the redness of my face.

"I love it when you try to hide your insecurities from me. Don't bother. I see them all and then some." He laughs some more. I'm not laughing this time. He struck a chord, and now I'm the instrument shrieking through Remi's shop.

"When're you going to stop using this bargain as an

excuse to stalk me?" I rasp, digging my fingers in and trying to buck him off my legs. All it accomplishes is a moment of panic.

Because when I try to swing him off, he loses balance, almost falling off the counter, and if he falls, he'll drag me down with him. My neck will snap. I wrap my legs around him tighter to hold him up, my eyes wide—his smile wider.

"Ah, fuck you," I gasp. Looking up, I see the rope looped over the high beam, wondering how the fuck he got it up there. Was I so lost in listening to my family play music that I tuned everything else out, or was he already here, lurking in the dark, knowing I'd show up at the shop? I better not be that predictable.

"Not until you beg, remember?" His smile morphs into a terrible grin that, resentfully, looks good on him.

The moment pauses, the only sounds coming from me. The beat of my erratic heart, the raspiness of my breaths, and the blood rushing through my ears. The soft music comes through the waterfall a moment later, and when I hear it, I hurt all over again. Because now I'm thinking about my brother, the one who died this way. Hung in our house. A noose around his neck, his body grey but his face still reddish purple, like all the blood got trapped there and congealed after he died. My eyes meet Riot's, and his grin morphs yet again, this time into something akin to understanding. Not sympathetic or kind, but a thing that represents kinship in horror. Like he knows how to hurt but doesn't know how to express it, just like me.

I don't like that it makes us similar.

How'd he get this power over me? For as long as I've been a thrill-seeking junkie, I've held my own power. I've never been submissive, given in to anyone's dominance unless it's Director, or fallen short compared to someone else's power. But Riot keeps winning, and I don't know what it means. Maybe he's not winning when I'm the one getting what I want: a brush with death.

I look into his eyes, trying to decipher what he gets out of all this. Why's he chasing me? What's in it for him other than bragging rights and the continuation of a rivalry that started years ago? The fuck does he want? His eyes tell me nothing, guarded and masked just like he is. They don't house monsters like Krypt's do, nothing roiling or surging from the depths of their confines. Riot's eyes are deceptively calm and calculating, like he sees everything even if it's not obvious. But when they storm...

In a weak moment, I ask, "What do you want out of this?"

"Who says I want anything? Maybe I just like reminding you how fucking pathetic you are."

"Pathetic?"

"For lying to yourself."

"About what?" I struggle, trying to lower my feet. He grabs my thighs tighter, pulling our bodies close enough that I can feel the heat of his. The hardness of it. I flush with something new, something that took over my mind the night I kissed him in Misfit Hall. I swallow against the rope and keep my eyes on his. "Lying to myself about what?"

"You're scared of the curse."

I shake my head, tugging the rope away from my neck as far as it will go.

"You're scared of succumbing to it before you're anything noteworthy, which is why you're taunting it.

Because, at least then, you'll be remembered as the madman who danced with Death."

My jaw clenches and my fingers go numb.

"Do you want to die, Soren?"

Soren. "No."

"Then why are you tempting a curse?"

"You know why." That one or two second precipice. To prove that I'm superior.

"Yeah, I do. But it's not the same reason you tell yourself."

What the hell does he think he knows?

Riot leans back, arms spread wide, acting as a weight to hang me. I grip my legs around him as the rope cuts into my neck, cutting off oxygen. I try to heave him back up, but my legs are shaking, my mind is slowing down, and my fingers are being pinched between my skin and the noose, choking me as much as the rope is now.

Riot keeps leaning back, held up only by my legs around his waist. If I release my hold on him, my feet will touch the counter and I'll be able to breathe, but Riot is proving a point: that he's in control, so I don't even bother, wanting to prove I can take whatever he dishes out.

"Here's a new game. For every lie you tell, I'll force your body to admit a truth." His smirk is small but packs a punch.

My stomach sinks.

RIOT

15

TRUTH OR HANG

I HATE HIS RED SKIN. To the point that I almost want to let him down just to get rid of the flush to his cheeks. Something about how Ghost wears the colour isn't as harsh as everyone else, and instead of seeing it as a weakness, I'm admiring it as a form of my influence. His cheeks are pink and his lips are slick with spit, but it balances nicely with the vibrant, angry blue of his eyes and the sweaty blond hair brushing his forehead. It's a nice combination that speaks to his level of stirred thoughts; part of him likes this, but most of him hates it because I'm the puppeteer.

I'll take both as a win.

Leaning back a little more just to feel the clamp of his legs around me, I inhale his hypocritical thoughts and meet his eyes. "True or false? You don't want to break the curse on your family now that Remi is safe because you like the thrill of not knowing if you'll kill yourself or not."

"False."

I lean back as far as I can go, strangling him by doing nothing more than shifting my body weight and dragging him with me. The rope digs in under his chin, making his blue eyes bug out. "Don't lie to me, Sauder."

His mouth gapes open like a fish out of water. Funny, because the last time his mouth gaped open like this, he was drowning in the pond under the weight of my body. When his forehead turns red and his arms start to slacken, I let up, leaning forward.

"True. Maybe. I don't know." He sucks in air and coughs in my face.

Good enough. I let his legs down, and he sighs in relief when his toes can balance on the counter again. "True or false? You think you're perfect."

"True."

"Which parts of you are perfect?"

He hesitates, unsure about lying to me again so soon. He doesn't know what else I'll do, and my threat to make his body admit the truth is weighing heavily on his choices. That part will come soon enough.

"The parts I let the world see."

I smile at that. Aren't we the same that way? Perfectly prettied up for whoever looks at us, ugly as fuck behind our well-placed masks.

"True or false? You like the idea of being taken against your will because you've never known someone strong enough to do it."

He swallows hard, his throat echoing to join the lulling music. "False." When I tilt my head at him, he curses under his breath. "False."

"You sure?"

"Yes."

I reach forward, watching him try to tip-toe away from

me. He doesn't get far enough before the noose cuts in, making him stop. I pop the button of his pants open and look straight into his eyes as a threat that I won't stop here if he doesn't admit the truth.

"Fuck! Not taken against my will," he seethes at me. "But maybe like... someone who can handle my roughness."

I undo the zipper.

"The fuck?! That was the truth." His knee comes up, but I back away before it connects with my thigh. "Someone who can handle my level of rough and pushes it even harder. Who doesn't stop when I say no."

There. That's better. Taken against his will, just like I said. I grin at him, offering myself up on a silver platter if he wants to be bold enough to fucking beg for it. "Wasn't too long ago you threatened to rape me if my brother raped yours again, right?"

"Maybe I'll make good on that promise."

"Love to see you try, sweetheart."

"Stop fucking calling me that!" He kicks out, knocking a display case off the counter. Pamphlets for music lessons and brochures for Moros' townwide music festival scatter across the floor. "I'm not your fucking sweetheart."

He is, so I smile at him. My charming one. He falters for a second, almost falling for it, but he fortifies his illusion, seals his cracks, and continues to glare at me with all the rage he wants to expel but doesn't have the power to right now. Because I took his power away, and I'll continue taking it away until he learns to fight differently. Until he learns that his power comes from somewhere else.

"True or false?" I push on his chest, making him swing a bit. When he drifts back to me, I fist his shirt in my hand and bring us nose to nose. "Your pride is the only thing preventing you from admitting you want me."

He laughs in my face, and there he is, my fucking sweetheart. I love when he laughs because it means he's at his most deranged. When he laughs, he's there, on that precipice of sanity and insanity, eager to tip the scales and let himself loose upon me.

"The only thing I want from you," he coughs, "is for you to keep fucking trying so I can keep fucking winning. You think you're in control here?"

"Mhm." I grin at him.

He matches my grin, and then, faster than I can react, he brings his leg up and kicks. I fly off the counter, my back slamming against the wall behind the desk, toppling Remi's stool. The wind knocks out of me, and, crumpled on the floor, unable to breathe, it's my turn to laugh.

"Fucking finally!" I roar, adrenaline surging. "Took you long enough to drop the pretense and start acting like you. Like Ghost. Like Soren fucking Sauder." I press my palms to the floor and stand up. "The crazed Ghost of Moros who shines so fucking bright in the dark."

He's trembling, though I don't know what with. Energy. Vitality. Pride because he's finally getting recognition for who he is. No one is telling him to grin and bear it. No one is warning him that he'll have to put up with some shit before he gets his reward. He's not listening to Director's rules or bowing down to play a part in a gang. He's hanging from the beam of his brother's music shop, being praised for how fucking unhinged he is. Because he likes it. He enjoys the thrill of being trussed up and weak because it tests his mental prowess. He wants to outwit me, and that's the game we're both too stubborn to lose.

His cock gets hard.

I knew it would.

"You're the fucking curse, Soren."

"Ghost."

I shake my head. "Not right now." This time, I move fast. With his pants already undone, I rip them down his legs, seeing his stab wound. When he tries to kick out again, I take the slack of his pants between his ankles and press my hand downward, choking him as his body is dragged down. "True or false? Your cock is hard right now because I recognize the parts of you that don't get recognized enough."

He fights it for all of ten seconds before he nods, completely unable to breathe. I let up, letting him press his toes to the counter again. He coughs, hacking out laughs that go straight to my dick.

"True or false? You hated not being able to feel my dick in your hand when I paralyzed you in your grave."

He's mostly delusional with dark power now, embellishing the game. "True," he says, laughing harshly. "But not because I wanted to jerk you off. I crave a level playing field. I wanted to rip your cock off and shove it up your own ass."

"I told you not to lie to me." I pull down on his legs and wait.

"It's not a lie. It's the truth."

"Not the whole truth."

He glares, but his smile somehow stays on his face, his eyes flaring with the challenge of the game. "I wanted the satisfaction of saying I made you come *before* I ripped it off and shoved it up your ass," he amends.

"Better." I let his legs go and step back before he can kick me. I walk around to where I tied the rope off, letting him have some slack. He finally removes his fingers from behind the rope, flexing and stretching them as I give him enough length to sit his ass on the counter. His legs give out, and he practically falls to his ass, his feet dangling over the edge. When he reaches to loosen the noose and remove it from his neck, I yank, firming it back up. "Leave it. I dare you."

His hands pause and he stops trying to free himself. I secure the rope just tight enough to restrain him. He's no longer choking, but he's not free either. He can't bend forward and lift his pants, and he can't hop off the counter without strangling himself.

I walk back around, face to face with him now. "You listened."

"I like a dare," he taunts. "What's next? My dick is hard, your dick is hard, you're insane and twisted, and I'm even more insane. Gonna rape me?"

"Would it really be rape if you're begging for it like this?"

He snarls at me, but it's all for show. "Never been begged before, have you?"

I have, but not by anyone who actually wants me to unleash on them. I always have to tamp myself down, be safe, play it smart, and tone down my baser needs. Ghost craves a rough fuck and someone who can match him... I crave a power exchange that has no boundaries and no clear successor. I want to let loose, and when he realizes my level of degeneracy, I want him to let himself loose just as hard. I want to *trust* him enough to be who I think I am around him.

"Restricted blood flow, right?"

He narrows his eyes at me, unsure where I'm going with this.

Grabbing a pair of headphones off the opposite wall, I loosen the noose enough to slip them under the rope. The head part leaves the rope off his throat, and when I tighten it again, it presses the ear parts against his pulse points.

"Oh," he mumbles, almost in disbelief.

"You let me do it."

He looks at me, unsure what to do with his hands. He's not reaching for the noose anymore, and he's not fighting me off because he likes the prospect of where this might go. But he's still Soren, and he won't submit to this without a little resistance. "It's funny that you think you're winning. That you can make me admit a bunch of things, get my cock hard with a few words, cut off my blood flow, and pretend that it's all about you. It's not."

"No?" I brace my arms on the counter, on either side of his thighs. "What's it about? What's making you hard?"

His hands come up, almost like he's going to touch me. When he rips a dagger from inside his jacket and presses it to my neck, my cock jerks and his eyes smile. "I have a fucking rope around my neck and I'm still more powerful than you. You want me to beg?" He huffs a laugh. "How about I threaten?" He looks down, a clear signal. "Or do you only want this while I'm paralyzed?"

I smirk at him, the bob of my throat pressing against his blade as I swallow.

"Your brother throat fucked mine. Time I repay that favour, *sweetheart.*"

His other hand lands on the back of my head. Forcefully, he fists my hair and pushes my face down until it hits the bulge in his teal boxer-briefs. I inhale the scent of him, revel in how hard he is, close my eyes at the feel of his cock against my lips, and exhale eager anticipation at the knife against the side of my neck.

Fuck yeah. Here he is, and I'm the one who goaded him out of his box.

"Now," he demands.

Hiding my grin, I pull back just enough to yank his boxers down. His cock slaps my chin as it bounces free, but he doesn't give me time to concoct a plan. He presses the knife in harder, lifts his hips, and rams his cock against my lips until they open. He fills my mouth before I suck in a breath, the dry stretch of my lips painful, but not as painful as his cock hitting the back of my throat. I gag around him, every muscle in my torso tensing with a dry heave. When he pulls out, saliva stretches from my lips to his tip as I suck in breaths. I try to push up, using my hands for strength, but Soren slices my neck and pushes on my head simultaneously, forcing himself to the back of my throat again.

I fucking hate to love it. While he takes what he thinks he's owed, a wildness stirs within me. My blood drips down the side of my neck, soaking into my shirt while my drool soaks his cock and mixes with the taste of his precum. I'm not quiet, but neither is he. While I gag and choke, he groans and moans, and it's the perfect prize. I knew it. I fucking knew he wanted me, and he might call this a threat, but I call it desperate begging. If he thinks he needs to stay in control and press a dagger to my pulse just to get what he wants, so be it. I'll play the game until he comes back for more because this is only the fucking start. This is training, and he's such a good little mutt.

"Fuck," he groans, voice strained.

My knees bend and I take a breath around him, allowing spit to coat my lips. The feel of his full, hard cock in my mouth is more satisfying than all my fantasies portrayed. It's an owning, and he's the one claiming me. He'll deny it, but I will remind him how fucking bad he wanted this every time he tries to dispute it.

I suck him all on my own, letting his hand on my head control the pace, fucking with his mind because he doesn't know what to do when he isn't fighting me on something. Tongue sweeping under the head of his cock, I listen to him gurgle out a moan above me, fist tightening in my hair. My body heats up, a mix of pain, pleasure, and an unhinged need to win this game. I'm so into it—into the feeling of being aggressively throat fucked; into the sensation of him so desperate—that I lift my hand, eager to rub myself through my pants.

I cry out in pain a second later.

"No," Ghost snarls at me, lifting my head by my hair and forcing me to look at him. "You don't get to touch yourself."

Shifting my eyes to my left, I look at my fingers, wiggling them to make sure they still work. The dagger that was pressed to my throat now sticks out of the top of my hand, the tip buried in the counter. With my hand pinned to the surface and blood oozing out, I breathe harder, unsure if I'm pissed off, pleased, or a mix of both. All I know is that I'm impatient, unable to stand here and do nothing. I have to fucking move, to fight back, to make him eat his words. Because he's going to come, and when he does, it will be because of me! Because I got him here, lured him in, trapped him, and goaded him until he took what he wanted. He'll take all the credit, but we'll both know it's my credit to revel in.

I baited him; he bit.

He's not laughing anymore, but he's even more depraved. He grabs my nape with both hands and forces me to bend back over. I swallow his cock and gag even harder than the first time. I have no control. His hands move my head at the pace he commands, every jerky thrust of his hips making the knife in my hand shift. Pain sings, but I don't care. I want more. Because he's close, his groans are anguished and full of dark pleasure. His body melds into a rhythm that suits his needs and his needs only. He doesn't care about me. He just wants to use me, abuse me, and take pleasure in the rope around his neck, pressing perfectly against his pulse points.

Use me all you want, sweetheart. This is step one to making you crave me.

"Fuck. Fuck," he seethes between clenched teeth. He pushes my head all the way down, suffocating me on his cock. I don't even have enough control to properly gag this time. "Swallow. Right now. Make me feel it."

With his cock halfway down my throat, I force a swallow, constricting my throat around him because I have no other choice.

"Ahhhhh, fuck," he moans loudly, the musical lilt to his

pleasure-drenched voice fitting in so perfectly with the sad lullaby playing through the speakers.

He curses me on his next breath, his cock throbbing in my throat. I'm losing feeling in my body, gaining pressure in my head, unable to breathe. I don't even know if I swallow his cum or if he forces it down my throat by sheer will and power, but either way, I sense it sliding down my esophagus. I feel his legs tremble, his body shake, his abs tense. I hear him moan in formidable delectation, and I sense his shame under the surface. Stronger than that, I sense his power. Because he thinks he won.

He pulls back, cum still leaking from his cock. I get the first taste of it when it hits my tongue, able to breathe in through my nose and savour the flavour longer. I swallow again, choking him down, a little addicted to the taste, extremely addicted to the force emanating from him.

"Jesus," he groans, pushing my head away. He rips the knife from my hand, making me flinch and grit my teeth. When he kicks me away, I hold the wound in my hand, lick my lips, and watch him become transfixed by the sight of his cum on my wet mouth.

He opens his mouth to comment on it, thinks better of it, and finally loosens the noose to free himself from my trap. He's breathing hard, cheeks red for a new reason—a better reason that looks hotter than it did when he was being hung —and shakes his head at me.

"Still think you won?" he asks, climbing off the counter and rubbing at his neck.

Oh, I know I won. So, I grin at him.

He barks out a pathetic laugh. "Seriously? You're *that* fucking deluded that me fucking your throat and spinning your trap on you counts as a win?" He swipes blood from his thigh, the stab wound open again.

Yeah, because he took what he wanted, and I didn't even have to beg him to. I shrug. "You had a knife this whole time and never cut yourself down." I straighten my jacket while his eyes widen and his cheeks get redder. "Counts as winning to me." I pick up the violin he was holding before I hung him, setting it on the counter.

I leave him in the shop and whistle the whole way back to Vile House.

GHOST

16

TO SHARE AN AWKWARD LAUGH

GREGORY MALONE IS SCREAMING because Axel Graves is making him relive the day we threw him in his cell at the asylum. He flinches, remembering the daggers and throwing knives that embedded in his body as we caught him in Neon Demon, and then he's verbally begging his wife to reconsider his punishment. He's telling her his pension isn't worth letting him rot for two years, and then he's crying when she makes that choice anyway.

"Isn't he a sexy thing?" Kyd asks.

"He's a piece of shit stalker who is nothing more than Axel's plaything and Remiel's punching bag," Krypt answers, not great at picking up social cues.

"Not him, Krypty. My boyfriend." Kyd's eyes scan the length of Axel's impeccably dressed body. Who the hell wears a suit by choice? Especially in a place as dark and dank as this? Who sees him for him to want to look good?

I've been watching the doctor long enough now to realize his eye isn't lazy. It's focused and alert, the same as his other eye. It's just his eyelid that flutters sometimes, especially when he tries to make eye contact. When he's watching his research, looking through scans or scopes, it's as sturdy as anyone else's. Maybe he's just awkward and used to being alone with his brain-dead patients instead of interacting with rational-ish people.

"What's the plan for Malone?" I ask.

"Better be death in two years," Krypt says, never taking his eyes off Malone.

Remi is in front of him, back to his chest, with Krypt's arms wrapped around him, but not in a loving way. More a possessive, don't fucking move, kind of way.

"He's practice," Kyd answers. "Dr. Hottie gets to test new techniques on him, and then he throws him back in his cell to try those techniques on the Reaper Corp captives. Fun on fun on fun!"

"Your idea of fun impresses me, Kyd."

We all turn when Riot walks up. Dressed in black tactical pants, an open black jacket, and a white t-shirt, he slips into his casual, sexy persona—the one that draws him all sorts of wanted attention, gets him invites, and charms the pants of anyone he sets his sights on. His hair isn't as long as Krypt's, but it's just as unruly, slightly wavy, and hangs haphazardly over his forehead, framing his steely eyes and masking them when he needs it to. His lips, pulled into his trademark grin, draw my eyes. Because fuck, those lips have been wrapped around my cock and coated in my cum...

Riot's grin widens when he catches me looking. I look away... because I won, right? Whatever sick fucking game that was last night, I won. I got the blowjob. I got free. I took power. That means I won. Though the smugness flowing from him doesn't come across as defeat.

"What happened?" Remi asks, nodding at Riot's bandaged hand and the slight cut on his neck.

Riot's eyes shift to mine, and something weird happens. A pause. A temporary truce that feels a lot like an inside joke. A lightness from the memory of the way he swallowed around my cock while his hand stayed fastened to the countertop.

"Someone pinned me exactly where they wanted me," Riot answers.

Now my blood burns. Fuck him. That's not where I wanted him, but it was the only place to put him when I needed to win the round. Krypt and Remi look between the two of us, but Kyd keeps his eyes on Axel's ass. I sense their attention, but I don't look. I'm too busy having a malevolent stare-down with Riot. He's challenging me to dispute what he said, and a part of me wants to, but... I still fucking won, and maybe that's enough to make me match his grin. As soon as I do, his widens into something genuine, and the two of us laugh.

"The fuck?" Krypt asks.

I stop laughing right away because it feels weird. I don't have jokes with Riot. I don't have anything but dares, challenges, and twisted games with him. This is just another one of those games, but lately, instead of them being exciting and dangerous, they're thrilling and sexy. Like, who the fuck paralyzes a guy in his future gravesite and then uses his dead hand to jerk off? Riot, that's who, and I'm a little impressed by his creativity for the dead arm handy.

Gregory Malone screams, shattering the moment. Well, their moment. Riot is still looking at me, and for whatever reason, I'm still looking at him.

You had a knife this whole time and never cut yourself down.

Fuck, does that mean he won?

"Hey, sweetheart," he purrs, stepping closer. The definition of his chest and abs is obvious through his white t-shirt, and because the fabric is so light, I can see the outlines of his tattoos through the material. "How's your neck?"

"How's your throat?"

"Barely raw." He tilts my chin, looking at the red, abrasive line under my jaw from his noose. "Can't say the same for yours."

I smack his hand away but butt my chest up to his. His masks fall away, and the real, mostly raw Killian comes out to play. "True or false, Riot?" I whisper. "You spit whatever was left of my cum on your cock and jerked off with it as soon as you left, didn't you?"

"True. True or false, Ghost? You jerked off again when you got back."

My grin is wicked and it makes me feel more alive than I was a second ago. "True." I reach up and pull down on his bottom lip, watching the corners of his mouth open. It pleases me to see they're a bit bloody and cracked, like I forced my cock down his throat so hard his lips split in the corners. I smile about it before I drag my thumb over his lip and let it go. "Maybe you'll be the one who begs."

"Maybe," he agrees. "But I have a feeling whatever front you're putting on right now is gonna crack in half soon."

"Guess we'll see."

"Guess we will."

He grins. I grin. The atmosphere changes and the game becomes darker.

"Vile House!" Menace shouts down the corridor. "Director wants a meeting. Lock got voted in!"

TODAY, we aren't in rank. We're in the theatre room, spread out through the seats with the lower-ranking members behind us. We're unmasked, at ease, and Director stands at the podium. Axel isn't here with him. Neither is Psych, Medic, or Media, and Lock hasn't been allowed in yet.

"Few things," Director starts, his exhaustion showing. He's gotta be in his mid-fifties—I've never cared to ask—but he looks younger. He's well-kept, well-dressed most of the time, and has good genes because his hair is barely salting and his skin only wrinkles on the rare occasion that he smiles. But this threat is real, and I can tell he carries the burden of it heavily on his shoulders. "First thing, Death Row maintenance."

We all groan, but he goes on.

"Shifts. I want at least two of you there at all times to help out. Kyd, you're going first because you need to get the hell out of the asylum and let Axel work."

"But he likes being distracted by me. Look how fun I am!"

"You're going to Death Row. Facts and Glitch, you go with him. Krypt and Menace, I need you two to head out to Carnival Hill."

Menace groans. "Ah, man! Come on, Director. You know The Harpy hates me!"

I snort. "More than hates you. Actively tried to kill you."

"Failed." Menace grins like he's King Shit. "Let the old hag try again."

"That old hag is twice the person you are, so keep your shit together and don't piss her off," Director says, dishing out more tasks.

The Harpy is an old woman who lives in a rotting cabin in Janie's Woods. It's close to Carnival Hill, and it's said that she haunts the forest—Janie was her granddaughter, so the name is fairly new, but the locals have taken to it. She's a crusty old bitch who never comes to town, instead sending her son-in-law to run her errands for her. She's alone out there, but she's probably the most lethal resident in Moros. I've been afraid of her since I was a kid, and she's the only level of death I haven't tempted. Her dark skill? Poisons. And she'll poison whoever the fuck she wants if they disrespect her, Carnival Hill, or Janie's Woods. She's like a witch, haggard and weathered, strong and wise, feared because of lore that terrifies children, but powered by gossip that is true. She really did try to kill Menace a few years ago because he walked into Janie's Woods and shouted her name seven times.

That's a no-no. The only person who can evoke Janie's spirit is The Harpy herself. She showed up out of thin air, spoke a weird language to Menace, and then blew a powder in his face. He passed out right then and there and got trapped in a nightmare for almost a whole week until Director brokered a bargain with The Harpy to get the antidote. He wasn't allowed to know what it was, so instead of giving him the antidote, she made us bring Menace to her. We dropped him on the decaying wooden floorboards of her cabin and watched as she covered him in some potion, blew something up his nose, and smacked him across the face.

Menace had sprung up, terrified, but he looked right at The Harpy and smiled. "Touché," he had said to her, and she gave him a single-tooth smile. It's been touch and go ever since.

"Ghost!" Seven smacks my thigh, dragging my attention out of that fun memory. He nods at Director, who is apparently speaking to me.

"What?"

"Anyone in The Misfits we need to be wary of?"

"Nah. Other than Yates and Tom, they're all just a bunch of gangsters in need of a better leader. They'll be good with Lock in charge and some structure, so no. They're fine. Everyone hated Yates."

"Alright. Let me know if you change your mind on that." Director bends down and grabs his mask from his bag. Motioning at the back wall of hanging black funeral robes, he says, "Throw on your masks and put on a robe if your clothes can be recognized. Auggie is coming in."

I haven't been seen in this outfit today, so I don't put on a robe, but I pull my teal mask over my face, secure it around the back of my head, and pull my hood up to hide my hair. When everyone is ready, an initiate escorts Auggie into the theatre room. She looks around, gawks a bit, fists her hand over her heart, and we do the same.

"Welcome," Director says to her. This is new. We don't let outsiders into Vile House, but we're trying to secure a bit more trust with some of the locals who will be beneficial during this oncoming war. "Welcome to Vile House."

"Thank ya," she says. "Not much for talkin'."

"That's alright. You said you had a few names you wanted us to watch for?"

Auggie, who owns the Umbra Inn, pulls out a few sheets of printer paper. Holding them up one at a time, she starts telling us who checked in over the past few days.

"This one's a twat. Frat boy but looks too old. This one's his boyfriend. This one's got somethin' bad in his room 'cause he ain't lettin' housekeepin' in." She holds photocopies of their driver's licences up one at a time. "This one say he got family in town, but won't say who. This one is lookin' for his missin' buddy."

"What's the buddy's name?" Riot asks.

"Wrote it down," Auggie says, fishing through her bag. She pulls out a small notebook, the pages all torn and tattered. "Rick Olenna."

Riot grins. The guy he killed in the bargain hall.

"This one says he knows his uncle and cousin are here but hadn't heard from 'em." Probably the kid from Mistfit Hall with the dead dad. "This one," Auggie goes on, "got that evil in'im. I know it." The last photo is of a guy, somewhere in his twenties, but she's right. His eyes are his biggest tell because he looks nuts, even in his driver's photo. Not the good kind of nuts, either. Trained to be nuts, born and bred to be morally inept and criminally insane. A sweet All-American lookalike who can't hide his wicked bits.

"Reaper Corp," Ransom says. "I'm sure of it."

Auggie gives him a curt nod like she agrees and then asks, "That all. Can I go?"

Selena escorts her out, and when the door closes, we lift our masks.

"Ghost, I need you on this one." Director holds up the last photo. "Brady Milton."

Bullshit name, but I nod. "Now?"

"Soon. Riot, you go with him. Monster, you're their backup. Got it?"

We all nod. I look at Monster instead of Riot, giving him a grin he returns. He still hasn't said anything, but he's coming back around to his wildly angry, bloodthirsty self.

"Next thing," Director goes on. "Lockan Tate is waiting in the bargain hall. Time to brand him and reveal ourselves. We're all going to go, but you don't have to remove your mask if you don't want to. I will, and Ransom will, and the rest is up to you."

Oh, I've been waiting to showcase my status to Lockan Tate for years.

ON THE INSIDE of Lock's bicep, Monster takes great pride in pressing a Vile House brand. The design is basic, just a skull like our tattoos, and the words 'Vile House' and 'ally' in block lettering. Medic, Psych, and Media all have these brands instead of the tats, and when we're initiates who make it past the first few rounds, we get a brand almost exactly like it, without the word ally at the bottom. It's not very big, but his skin sizzles enough to make his eyes water and his jaw lock.

"You enjoyed that too much," Lock says to Monster.

Monster tilts his yellow mask, not denying it. He steps back, and Lock holds up his burned arm so we can all see it.

Monster throws some salve and gauze to Director, unwilling to touch Lock with his hands. While Director tapes him up, Ransom starts the rules.

"You understand that revealing our identities is a crime we'll kill you for?" Ransom asks.

"Yeah," Lock says. "I won't. I just want Moros ours again."

"We'll make your execution public, boiiii," Kyd says, but it doesn't sound very threatening. "Just sayin'."

Lock laughs. "I'm aware. Trust me, I don't want to be like that nurse from a few months ago. I ain't eating my own cock."

"What makes you think that was us?" Seven asks.

"Well, it wasn't The Misfits, yet his body was hung from our porch, so..."

I grin. That was my idea, and to this day, I don't regret it. Yates had to put out a lot of fires for that body.

"Our trust starts now, Lockan Tate. Don't betray us and we'll be your best allies." Director turns off the voice modulator. "Ready?"

"Ready."

We're in the bargain hall, the stone chamber cold and mostly dark. Lamplight gives us enough to see by but keeps the corners hidden. The ten of us are standing in a line like we do for bargains, and Director is a few steps ahead of us. He's the first to take his gold mask off.

Lock's eyes widen when he sees our fearless leader. "Doctor fucking Cooper?"

"Vile House has been passed down through my family for generations, and this is the first time a director has revealed himself. Welcome to our world." He reaches out to shake Lock's hand.

Lock takes it, nodding, looking proud. "Thank you. Thank you for trusting me."

Director smiles. It's small, but it shows his crow's feet. "I've been watching you for years. This trust isn't impulsive. Don't let me down now."

"I won't," Lock declares.

Ransom goes next. His hood lowers and his red mask lifts to rest on the top of his head. Seven lifts his orange mask, winking at Lock because they know each other from high school. When Kyd lifts his, his smile is so fucking big his eyes are squinted.

"Hi, Lockey! I'm Kyd!"

Lock laughs again, taking Kyd's outstretched hands and letting the lunatic spin him in a circle. "Hey, Kid."

"With a Y."

"Right."

Facts removes his copper mask, nodding at Lock with a quick hello. Krypt takes his purple mask off, almost glaring at Lock.

Lock is more and more shocked with each face. He knows all of us, except Kyd and Monster, in some form or another. Moros isn't that big of a town, so we all have history. When Lock's eyes get to Monster, the smallest one of us shakes his head. He's not ready yet. Lock nods to accept that.

Glitch steps forward, chest to chest with his 'brother.' "Told you I'm more badass than you," he says.

Lock barks out a laugh. "Makoa?" He rips the mask off, and Glitch is already smirking.

"Glitch here, you dick."

"You fucking liar. How long?!"

"Long enough," Glitch answers. They bro-hug, and then Glitch tugs Riot forward.

When Riot lifts his mask, his eyes are as riotous as his name, and his smirk is sexy.

"I fucking knew it!" Lock shouts. "No way you knew all that shit the night of the attack. You called me! Wait, you were the one Yates met with. You fucked with Sauder..."

"He fucks with me daily." I shove Riot to the side and pull my mask off. "But I fuck with him right back."

Lock's smile is genuine. He tugs me into a hug, whispering in my ear, "You two totally fuck, right?"

"Hell no."

When I pull back, there's admiration in Lock's eyes. That's the exact look I've been waiting for since I joined The Misfits. It's appreciation, respect, and awe, and I'm fucking drinking it in. Finally, I'm not Soren Sauder, the lame as fuck Misfits prick. I'm Ghost, the Vile Boy.

"Meet the Ghost of Moros," Glitch tells Lock. "This fucker can move anywhere without being seen or heard."

"Not even sensed," Ransom adds. "Prick."

Knew my boys would pump my tires. "Finally don't have to fake it in your gang anymore."

"Ah, you were never good enough anyway," Lock jokes. "You been spying on us all this time?"

"Just since Yates."

Director steps forward again. "That's Ransom, Seven, Ghost, Menace, Krypt, Facts, Riot, Glitch, Kyd, and this one..." He pauses in front of Monster, waiting for permission to give his name. There's a pause, and then...

"Monster." His chin lifts, his voice shocking us all, but it's none of Lock's business, so we hide our shock and show pride instead.

Director nods at Monster. "And you can call me Director. Welcome to Vile House."

It's not required that he do it, but Lock fists his hand over his heart and gives us all a nod. He gives Monster an extra nod, as if to say he respects his choice.

"Thank you for letting me in. I won't fuck up. Now, what the hell are we doing about Reaper Corp?"

RIOT

17

GAME OF CHICKEN

THIS GUY AUGGIE brought to our attention, Brady, is a fucking douche. Not the frat bro kind of douche he tries to appear as, but the fake, pretending to be a tourist kind of douche who can't hide the creep in his eyes. He's smug and obvious about it, which makes him stupid, and I already want to kill him. I'm not sure if he's Reaper Corp, but he's up to something. Maybe someone they trained and sent in. We've been following him around Moros for two hours now. He's done nothing except tour the city and take pictures of random shit, plotting out the lay of *our* land. He's been with a friend, but not even the friend seems to understand why they're just walking around.

Now it's almost midnight, and instead of heading back to the Umbra Inn for the night, he stops for a change of clothes, fancies himself up a bit, ditches his buddy, and heads straight for Neon Demon.

... Because Ghost left him a calling card, inviting him out, and he was dumb enough to take the offer. Which means he either knows what Vile House calling cards are or he's just an idiot.

We walk in unmasked. Tonight, we're just three local boys out to have some fun with the tourists who came to town early for next weekend's music festival. We were going to cancel it, but Director thinks it's a good idea to keep it going because he wants to see who tries to sneak into town under the ruse of music. Remi and Cain help run the festival, and we'll be around to keep an eye on everything. Plus, the entirety of Moros knows to be alert now, so our bases are covered.

Monster points up, indicating that he's going to the balcony to watch from above. I head straight for the bar to order a drink because fuck, I've earned one.

Soren looks good tonight. Dark outfit in case his wounds bleed, top buttons of his shirt undone, tattooed chest hinted at, and a wild head of hair that sticks up in all directions like he purposefully commanded it to. He pairs the look with slip-on matte black boots and rolled-up sleeves, showing off the veins in his forearms that bulge through his tattoos—tattoos he's already asked Menace to cover because some are associated with The Misfits. His blue eyes strobe with the lights, and I know because he's looking at me. He never gives me his back, not trusting what I'll do if he turns away from me for a second.

But he's Ghost. He never gives his back to anyone.

"Gotta say," I shout over the thumping electric music, "your necklace is the best part of your outfit."

"What neck—" He rubs the red skin created by my noose and glares at me. "You look like a fucking wannabe biker."

Dark jeans over black boots with a band t-shirt and a thin leather jacket, sure, I can see it. My hand is bandaged, and I've been trying to grow my hair out long enough to tie it back, too, but it's not there yet. "Thanks."

"Wasn't a compliment."

"Sure." I grin, giving my attention to the redhead behind the bar. "Hey, pretty. Whiskey, please." My charming smile works wonders because she smiles back, and Soren rolls his eyes. "Make that two." I wonder if she'd smile back if my true self showed. Would she recognize me, or am I too disfigured from all these masks I've perfected?

Soren slaps a few bills on the counter and takes both drinks, leaving me with nothing. The bartender laughs, whipping up a double in a glass, winking at me as I hand her the money. With my back to the bar, I scan the club. Since it's the pre-music festival, tonight's theme is instrumental dubstep or something. I can make out the instruments, but there's a thick distortion, a lot of bass, and heavy drops layered in with them, all matched with a horror vibe. Horror dubstep, maybe. Haunted EDM. I don't hate it.

Monster is stoically watching from above, looking miserable about it, but Soren is in the middle of the dance floor, both whiskey shots already gone. He grins at me and starts dancing, and I'm so transfixed by it that I forget I'm supposed to be keeping tabs on this Brady guy until I see him bump and grind against Soren's body.

Oh, fuck no. That ghostly fuck is mine.

I don't hate the way rage feels, so I keep watching, letting myself become consumed by jealousy and anger. They swirl within me, morphing into something that turns me impious but also boosts my ego. Because I'm fucking hotter than that guy. That prick can't read Soren like I can. He can't give him what he needs, push his buttons the right way, or goad him into reactions his reasonable self would never make. Soren has one red button, and I'm the only one capable of pushing it.

He looks at me, eyes on fire, tempting me from across the club. His smirk is so subtle that I almost miss it, but I see it. I see it when he grabs Brady and pulls him against his chest. I see that smirk widen when he drapes his arms over Brady's shoulders, grinding his hips in time with the music. He winces slightly when his injured shoulder moves painfully, but he won't let something like pain stop him from starting this game.

And now I'm smirking for my own reason. This is the first time he's initiated anything. My training is already paying off. I've got him right where I want him, and the best part about it is that he thinks it's all his idea. Gaslighting is usually his forte, but fuck, I've got it in the bag.

I feel my phone vibrate in my pocket. The thing never rings because no one ever calls people in Moros. You wanna talk, you go find the person you wanna say something to. That's how it works. But I pull it from my pocket and see Monster's name flash across the screen. I look up at him as I answer it.

"You gonna speak?" I say, surprised he didn't just text me or walk down here.

He simply glares at me, breathing through the static to convey his message before hanging up.

Laughing, I nod at him. Yeah, yeah, I know. We're here on a mission, and that mission is to keep tabs on Brady and take him back to Axel once we've gotten everything we can out of him. *Alive.* Director's orders.

Soren's way ahead of the game because Brady, that city fuckboy, is whispering sweet nothings in his ear, and my *sweetheart* is playing along. Well, two's company but three's a party. I slam my drink, toss my jacket over the bar, and head to the dance floor.

The haunted dance music is pounding in my chest, amping me up, filling my blood with adrenaline that promises no good outcomes for the clubgoers. The bodies on the dance floor are jumping up and down, the club turning into a rave as the lights strobe in time with the bass. Faces morph into nightmares and inhibitions are left on the floor as the magic of the music takes effect.

It's the start of a horror story in here, and I'm fucking brimming with the need to be the villain. Soren's eyes are on mine as I make my way through the sea of nobodies, heading straight for him with one goal: Look. At. Me.

My eyes shift with his hands as they weave into Brady's hair, giving the guy's head a little tug. Brady throws his head back, clearly into it, revelling in how it feels to be a pawn in a game that makes him feel so deceitfully powerful. He's the prey tonight. The bait in a game of chicken. He just doesn't know it yet. His toned body is shorter than both of us, so it's not hard to look over his head and mock the hell out of Soren for being so predictable.

The crowd barely gets in my way, knowing I'm stronger and more dangerous than they are. They bounce, jump, bump, and grind, but they do it in a way that leaves a path straight to Soren, like they just fucking know that's where I'm headed.

I come up behind Brady, the idiot having no idea he's a sheep between two wolves. Soren's body might be bumping against his, but his attention is all mine. His eyes dare me to try, and my grin meets his dare with a challenge of my own. I've never been afraid of a game of chicken.

I grab the back of Brady's neck and spin him around. His face is drunk and shocked, but as soon as he sees me, he licks his lips and runs his hands down my chest. He says something to me, but I don't hear it and don't care enough to ask. Especially because Soren's hand comes in from behind, forcefully removing his palms from my chest. He pulls Brady's hands above his head, hips moving, grinding into the guy's ass in beat with the music. I sway with the vibe of the club, the dance floor one big wave of movement. Dragging Brady with me, I grab his hips and press against him, firm enough to feel how hard he is in his pants.

Is he Reaper Corp or just another drunk asshole? Is he aware Soren wears the teal mask and left him the calling card? How much do they know about us?

The music changes from fast to slow with a heavy undertone of sex, and with it, the atmosphere morphs from jumping rave-goers to horny sex-drunk dancers who only want to rub against one another. Someone bumps into me from behind, trying to grab me, but Soren's hand fists in my shirt to keep me where I am.

So predictable, sweetheart.

With his eyes on mine, he leans down, lips landing on the side of Brady's neck. I watch the guy's eyes roll back in pleasure, his hands coming down to snake into Soren's hair. I rip them free and wrap them around my shoulders, leaning in to bite the other side of his neck, hating the game but wanting the prize. My head bumps Soren's as we wedge Brady between us, using him to hide the truth he's still not ready to act on.

Brady moans loud enough to hear over the music, and he's wedged between us so tightly that when Soren grinds against his ass, I feel the motion of it when Brady's hips grind against mine. Soren leans back, drunk on lust and sexy because of it. He looks at me, not even a smirk left on his face. No, he's lost to need and turning hostile because of it, and this is right where I want him.

He spins Brady to face him, pressing his ass back against my cock and leaning in to grind our bodies together. All three of us groan, and Soren's lips meet my ear, panting so deeply the sound travels down my neck and spine, making my fists tighten on Brady's hips. Soren's fingers dig into mine, his forehead rolling against my temple. Fuck, my hard cock digs into Brady's ass, wishing it was Soren's.

But then he shifts the game. He takes his attention away from me and gives it all to Brady. As blood red as my vision goes, I'm up for the challenge. Because I'm ready and fucking willing to call his bluff. He might be a sneaky ghost in his day to day, but his intentions don't lie, and his eyes can't hide secrets from me.

He grabs Brady by his hips, grinding their bodies together and pressing their foreheads tight. Every speck of his interest appears to be on Brady, *but I know.* I know what he's really doing. He's goading me, just like I've been goading him. He's received my not-so-subtle messages, and now he's attempting to take control of it, to flip the script and be the one to tease me. Fuck, I've trained him so well.

He's the perfect little pup, calling out to his master in such a desperate way.

The song morphs into something creepy and deep. *Armageddon* by 13 fills the club, and Soren's body knows exactly how to move to it. It's not exactly dance music, but his hips roll, then bump, grinding against Brady, who is greedy for this. Whether it's a show or real, it doesn't matter, because he's in my way, nothing more than a prop for Soren to play with, to dangle in front of me like a carrot. But I don't want to bite this carrot; I want to fucking annihilate it.

I watch.

I watch Soren.

I watch the way he takes control of Brady, morphs his body into whatever position he wants it in, and teases the kid like I tease him. I watch the way Brady becomes putty in his hands, pliable to every motion and reactive to every touch. While I watch, I drop my masks. I drop the charm, replacing it with sex appeal. I drop hesitation and replace it with anticipation. I drop the concept of being the nice guy, letting the darkest parts of me rise to my surface until they're right there, within reach, ready to do my bidding.

My vibrations change with the switch in music. The people near me back away, but I draw the attention of other dark souls. Like Soren. His blue eyes hit mine, and with a grin that holds nothing beautiful or charming, I snatch Brady away from him and spin my back to him like he doesn't fucking matter. Dismissal.

Soren's body bristles behind me, but Brady gasps. "Oh, God," he moans, looking up at me. He's shorter and smaller, his big eyes wide with fear he finds arousing. He bites his lip between his teeth, and I rub my thumb over it to free it, making him tremble just to piss Soren off. "Please," he begs.

I tilt my head. *Please, what?*

Brady puts his hands on my chest hesitantly, like I'm going to snap his wrists for touching me. Slowly, he drags them down my torso, over my pecs and intercostals, feeling every ridge of my abs, until he gets to the bottom of my t-shirt. Innocently, he looks up at me as his fingers hook into my pants, knuckles brushing my skin. Our bodies sway with the depth of the song, his touch not near enough for me.

Come on, you ghostly fuck, make your move.

Underneath my shirt, Brady's fingers start moving, tracing my lower abs, the light trail of hair coming from my pants, up to my—

"Ah, ah, ah." Soren's hands land on Brady's, his eyes on mine as he chastises the blond for touching what he thinks is his. "You don't get to touch him unless I say you can."

Brady looks between us, but our eyes are caught in a war we both think we're winning. "Are you two together?" he asks.

I keep my mouth shut, tilting my head at Soren this time. *Well? Are we, you possessive liar?* He thinks I don't know what he's doing, but I do. He'll brush it off as a game, but I know it's obsession—possession.

Soren's fingertips graze my abs, bringing me to fucking life. "Want us to be?" Soren speaks into Brady's ear, starting to dance with him again as their hands stay on my abs. "Think you can handle us both?"

Brady's ass presses back, making Soren's eyes snap to mine again. He grins, grinding against him and touching me, controlling this guy's hands on my body. Brady nods too eagerly, rubbing his cock over my leg. "Yes," he moans. "Yes, fuck yes."

"Where are you staying?" Soren asks him.

"Umbra."

"Do you know anyone in town?" I ask.

He shakes his head, lying since he had a friend earlier. "I'm here for work. Let's get out of here."

Work. "What work?"

"T-the music festival. Please, take me somewhere." He digs his fingers into my abs, and Soren tugs his hands away. "I can handle you both."

He's lying. I know he is because he's too drunk to hide his tells. His answers are too quick, rehearsed, and he's either too horny and really does want to get out of here, or he's using it as an excuse to change the subject. With my eyes on Soren, my hands roam all over Brady. Soren's teeth grind and his jaw clenches, but when I search the guy, he has no weapons on him. Soren bends to check his ankles, distracting him with lips against his inner wrist.

We're luring him away from the club, but if he's Reaper Corp, he might have the same goal.

He's clear. Looking up at Monster, I nod at the exit so he knows we're leaving with the guy. Honestly, I want nothing to do with this preppy fuck, but he's the ticket to getting Soren to snap, so playing along is in my best interest, and nothing is more important to me than my best interest. Monster shakes his head at me like I'm exhausting him, and then he slips out of my sight and my mind.

As we leave the Neon Demon, Death Row greets us, dark and mostly empty, but that doesn't mean we're alone. It'd be smart to take this guy to Vile House so he's where we want him come morning, but I'm not ready to share this game of sex-chicken with my Vile House brethren. I want somewhere more private. Glancing at Soren, whose eyes are already on me, I nod towards the street my parents' house sits on, and he tilts his head at me in answer. It's a challenge, though I don't know what it means, so I grab Brady just to piss Soren off and wrap my arm around his neck.

"You have no idea what you're in for, little lamb. You sure you wanna disappear in Moros with two strangers?" I grab his ass to give my warning a playful tone, and Brady can't fight the urge any longer. He wraps his arms around my neck, grabs my hair, and tries to steer my mouth to his for a kiss.

Soren gets there first. He rips Brady's head away from mine, picks him up, and throws him over his shoulder. "Don't tempt me, tourist. I told you not to touch him without my permission." He ignores Brady's whining and takes off towards my house. I walk behind and grin the entire way.

Fucking checkmate.

GHOST

18

KNOCK HARDER

I'M A SURE PERSON. I know what I want and how to get it. I trust my instincts, even if my mind isn't a safe place, and I trust my body to know how to achieve what I'm after.

Right now, I have no fucking clue what I'm doing or why I'm doing it. I taunt devils on the daily, but Riot has never been the devil I'm most interested in riling—not sexually. The second his eyes leave me, no longer paying attention, a flood of shame and anger swells within me and I find myself doing whatever it takes to get his attention back. Why? Because he fucking infuriates me, and I like how it feels. Because he steps up to the plate just by being a dick, and he tempts the parts of me that don't get to mingle with daylight too often.

There's nothing safe about Riot, but he's turning into my safe *outlet* because I know he can deliver what I need.

Rapture in the form of ruin.

Pleasure in the ritual of danger.

Enlightenment in the task of unmasking.

A mutual destruction that strips us bare and unveils the

true parts we're after. He's looking for himself, and I'm looking for someone to appreciate who the fuck I am.

The tension hasn't died on the walk across town. Carrying Brady while Riot's eyes are on me has only built it to the point that I'm agitated and deadly. My needs are screaming at me in guttural voices that make no sense. I'm aware that I'm goading Riot into giving me what I need, but I'm still unclear on the details of what exactly I'm after.

I want him to be the one to crack.

I want him to be the one to snap and dictate the night.

I want him to take what he's been teasing for months.

... But I don't know how to force control on him when I've never willingly given it up.

I drop Brady to his feet when we get to the front porch of the Hallows' house. Riot unlocks the door, but he looks back at me while he does it, a challenge in his grey eyes that I'm eager and willing to accept. But I don't show him that. I set my eyes on Brady instead, looking at the kid like *he's* the challenge. Riot tenses, and then he pushes the door open and forces Brady inside.

The little fuck's hands are all over Riot, groping at his shirt to tear it off and fumbling with his pants to get things moving faster. I watch, letting my rage build, wondering who the hell this guy is. Isn't he here for Reaper Corp? Does he know we're Vile House? Is he setting us up because we're too lost in our challenge to see the signs, or are we the ones about to ruin him?

In the front entrance of the house, Riot flicks on a lamp to illuminate my anger, looking at me over the top of Brady's head as if to ask, 'game on?' I lick my lips and close the door behind me.

When Brady takes Riot's shirt off, I track the tattoos on his chest, following them down his ribs and sides, lost in a sea of scars and muscle definition. As I'm getting hard from the sight of the man who turns me into a new version of myself, Brady finally remembers my rule. He looks back at me for permission to touch Riot, and I'm tempted to say no. I *want* to say no. I want to deny him access to what is mine and throw him from this house so we can tear it down ourselves. But Riot hasn't broken free from his leash yet, and I need him crazy with power before I throw Brady out the front door.

Brady is an idiot. He must know about Moros if he's here for work—Reaper Corp or the music festival—which means he knows how troublesome the town is. He's almost as dumb as the girl Krypt killed in the cemetery, but instead of reminding him of that, I step up to him and grab his wrists. I place his hands on Riot's hips, sliding them down to cup his hardening cock.

"You sure you know what you're getting yourself into?" I ask him while looking at Riot. "You know nothing about us."

Brady whimpers. "I know chemistry. We have it."

We sure as fuck do. I'm one chemical and Riot is another; Brady is simply the ignition that will spark our first explosion.

He's too needy for my tastes. Too compliant and amenable. "Please," he begs. Too polite and submissive. *Fucking take what you want, man. Stop begging.*

"Please what?" Riot asks him. "So many manners and not enough demands."

I've said it before, and I'll say it again: guys like us are intrigued by the submissive type because we enjoy lording our power over them, but they never keep our interest for long. So, when Brady opens his mouth to demand something specific, I beat him to it.

"Get on your knees for him, tourist," I snap, shoving him down whether or not he likes it. His knees hit the wooden floors, and Riot's eyes hit mine, half hidden behind his unruly dark hair and whatever persona he's hiding behind. "Hurry up and suck him."

I demand it, but I don't want it to happen. Riot catches the confliction on my face, but I don't hide it from him. Because I have one more trick up my sleeve, and when I play it, it'll be the thing to break Riot's well-crafted control. His charm will vanish, and in its place, the true Killian Hallows will come forth.

He's the one I'm thirsting for.

Riot is still looking at me when I shift my focus downward, watching Brady undo his pants too slowly for my liking. I tug on his hair and smack his cheek, demanding he get on with it and show me the cock that belongs to *me*. When he pulls Riot's pants down his thighs, the bulge in his tight boxers has me licking my lips again, but when his hard cock bounces free in front of Brady's face, I clench my jaw in both restraint and admiration. I'm not ready to make my move yet, but since no part of Brady will act as anything more than a body to use and our ignition switch, I grab hold of the sides of his head so that I'm the one bringing pleasure to Riot.

At the first brush of Brady's fingers on his cock, Riot's hand snaps forward and cinches my throat, bruising my already bruised neckline. His grey eyes become as tumultuous as his brother's, and the way he's watching me is akin to that one or two second precipice between life and death—he's half mad with want and half sane with the game, unsure which direction he'll shift first.

But I'm the one in charge here, and with his hand on me, eyes on mine, I force Brady's face forward and watch Riot's eyes narrow as I fuck his cock with a city boy's mouth. I hate it. I loathe that this kid's mouth is touching him. I'm fucking raging inside, but I'm Ghost of Vile House, and I've become familiar with enduring the bullshit before getting the reward.

Riot's snapped tether will be my reward.

Brady chokes, gagging around Riot, and I push his face forward with no mercy. Riot's hand tightens on my throat, and I grin before looking down to watch the way his dick disappears inside Brady's mouth. When I pull Brady back, he gasps, sucking in air as his hands grab my wrists.

"Not so hard," he says breathlessly. "Give me a minute to—"

I dig my thumbs into his jaw joints and force him forward again. When his nose hits Riot's lower stomach, Riot buckles forward, using his hand around my neck for balance. His forehead almost hits mine, and his groan is so anguished that it fills me with diabolical pleasure. Oh, fuck yeah. He's almost there. Almost ready to buckle. Almost ready to be the puppet attached to my skilled strings.

"Fuck," he groans. "Think you're winning, sweetheart?"

I grin, knowing I am. With my lips brushing his ear, I whisper, "Game point."

Then I pull Brady back, force him to his feet, and let Riot look at him for a single second before I spin him to face me. His lips are slick with spit, but that's about all I notice about him. I don't give a single fuck about the guy, but I lure him with a sexy smile and nod downward, demanding for him to kneel. Because it's my turn now. He left the club with two devils, and if he thinks any part of this night is going to be about his pleasure, he has no idea what kind of town Moros is.

Luckily, he's still turned on enough—hopeful enough to think his turn is coming—that he kneels in front of me. His hands make fast work of undoing my pants, and when I look at Riot, the hand he had wrapped around my throat is balled into a tight fist, straining in the air because he hasn't figured out what to do with it yet.

"Oh, god," Brady moans, pulling my dick free. "I want you both inside me."

"Get me wet, tourist. You'll get your turn."

Riot's eyes snap to mine, and there he is. He's shifting his focus, ready to snap for good. Because this is it. There are no more moves left on the board. He either lets this happen, or he shows me just how possessive he's demanding himself not to be.

I go tense when Brady's hand wraps around me, letting Riot know what's happening. Because I'm acting for him and only him, and I'll always be the star of his show. Brady pumps his fist up and down the length of my cock a few times, yet I hardly feel it because every part of me is focused on Riot. When he leans forward to suck me between his lips, Riot's hands latch onto the side of his head, stopping him.

Brady moans because he thinks Riot is about to do exactly what I did, but I smile so fucking wide because I know better. This is the exact moment I win our game.

"Please," Brady begs while Riot wages an internal war

with himself. Is his pride more important than losing this game? Time will tell. A split second of hesitation and he'll drop his masks and show me his genuine self. "Please, let me taste him."

Brady fights his hold, leaning forward, and that's when I know I've won for certain. Because Riot's eyes are thrashing with an entirely new kind of power. I smile at him, goading him into doing it. I'm so pent up I don't even know if I'm breathing, but it doesn't matter because looking into his eyes, watching them swirl with turpitude and a level of need I've only ever known myself to feel, I pause to drink in the power coming from this very moment in time. Not life. Not death. Something better because it's so strong but so unknown.

His smile isn't charming when he gives it to me. It's broken and beautiful, and I want it forever. Because it's mine. Only mine. Meant for me and him and this moment that defies time and warps the orbit of our lives.

"Please!" Brady whines.

Looking at me, Riot says, "Drop the manners when you get to Hell, lamb."

"Wha—"

The crack is loud in the foyer, bouncing off the walls. When Brady's hands go limp and fall away from my cock, my chest heaves with adrenaline and a straight shot of arousal. Because here he is. Killian Hallows. Unleashed, unhinged, cracked in fucking half and bringing my omen of death. *This.* This is the thrill I chase whenever I tempt death. Riot brings it better and stronger.

It's about goddamn time.

Brady's body slumps to the floor, and as soon as his head thumps off the floorboards, it's like the starting gun of a race has gone off. With a dead body between us—the ignition switch flipped—our chemical reaction takes a moment to build, and when it combusts, it feels like the violin sounds.

It's angry harmony and contrasting notes of emotion, and I drink it down, breathe it in, and brace for madness.

With one twitch of his jaw, it happens. We combust. I lunge for him and he lunges for me, a clash of pain and pleasure over a body that does nothing but get in the way after serving its purpose. Riot's hand wraps around my throat again, but I'm already coming at him with a trajectory that won't be stopped. Our mouths slam together in a bloody mess of teeth and tongue, snarling lips and ragged groans that add to our music.

I come alive.

And now it's time to force him to control it.

His teeth cut into my bottom lip, drawing more blood, but his wolfish moan breathes vitality into my very core. Every part of me surges with a current so forceful I don't know how to contain myself. It doesn't matter. Because Killian does it for me.

Killian. The real him.

His fingers squeeze the pulse points in my neck and mine tug at his hair. Brady's arm and hand bones snap beneath our feet, and when Killian trips over his half-down pants, he does it with purpose, using his trajectory to move me.

"You fucking cheater," he snarls at me, pushing me backwards until I stumble over Brady's torso. My back slams against the wall of the foyer, the plaster and drywall too weak to hold up against Killian's assault, and when he comes at me, I swear he pushes me *through* the wall.

"Don't be a sore loser."

"The only one who's gonna be sore out of all this, sweetheart, is *you* when I bloody up that tight hole." He slams my head back, and I see stars as drywall dust floats around. "Someone who won't stop when you say no, right?"

Oh fuck. He remembers. I knew he would, but I don't want him knowing I'm pleased by this because it'll convince him he's winning when I'm the one who's in the lead. I laugh against his mouth, hysterical and heinous, but my laugh dies when he grabs my cock and squeezes so hard I cry out in pain.

My eyes water. When he leans back to look at me, he notices, and I enjoy the way he admires me while water leaks through all my over-glued cracks. Power rises, and I shove at his chest, unwilling to just succumb to this like some little bitch. I want him to fucking *take* it. Because it isn't in me to surrender on purpose.

He squeezes my cock harder as he stumbles backwards, but when he loses his grip, his pants and Brady's body take him down. He lands on top of the dead city boy, kicking his shoes and pants all the way off as I stalk towards him with my hard dick in my fist.

"You can do better," I step forward. "I didn't pick you only for you to give up once the final play has been made."

With his pants off, he sweeps his leg in an arc and takes me out at the ankles. I crash to my knees, and he climbs atop me, pushing me back and pinning me down with Brady's shoulder digging into my spine.

"You think the final play has been made?" He rips the buttons of my shirt open, finding blood leaking down my chest from my shoulder stab wound. "We're barely past round one."

When he leans down, I expect him to bite me. Hurt me. Push me. Something volatile and dangerous, but instead, he swipes his tongue through my blood until it coats his lips and mouth. Sitting upright with my wrists pinned to the floor, he smiles at me with bloody teeth, looking beautifully disjointed and hot because of it.

My lips part, panting through this swell of need, unsure what to do. I'm tempted to ask for the ninety seconds because I feel so out of sorts, but this level of discomfort is so wanted that I suck in air and concoct my next move. Getting off my back is number one because no one, not even Killian fucking Hallows, gets me on my back.

I buck my hips, but he only laughs, drawing my attention to his mouth again. Gathered on his tongue are spit and blood, and I hesitate, watching it drip down his lips. I bite mine in anticipation, and then Killian leans back, spitting that bloody mixture straight onto my cock. Then his own. Like he's washing Brady's saliva away with my blood and his spit.

I don't moan or groan, but a harsh inhale that is equal parts arousal and rage comes from between my lips. Killian crushes his mouth to mine to devour the sound while his hand spreads the bloody spit down my cock. I buck again, fucking his fist because *I'm* the one in charge. The glide is smooth, but his grip is tight, and every ounce of pleasure is met with an equal part of pain.

Everything disappears. The house and the foyer and the dead body I'm crushing. My attention fine-tunes to his hand on me and my mouth on his. Biting his tongue and drawing a rush of copper, I stop fortifying my cracks and let them come apart. My glue dissolves, my puzzle pieces scatter, and my foundation splits deeper than it ever has before. When I snap my wrist free from his hold, I use all my strength to push him away until I can get a knee up. The sole of my foot hits his sternum, and he flies backwards.

"Soren!" he screams at me, chest heaving. "Don't fucking push me right now."

"Why?" I crunch more of Brady as I get my pants off. "Thought round one was barely over?"

"You don't want to know what happens in round two."

I do. Because it brings that same sensation I get when I'm toying with Death. The night he drowned me in the pond on Carnival Hill, the way I swung from his noose at Remi's shop, and the devastatingly comfortable way it felt to be paralyzed in my grave. The thrill I seek that makes me so diabolically joyous I can't help but laugh. I laugh now, enlightened while so dark.

"Round two can't happen until you take it off."

He climbs to his feet to be level with me as I stand, looking down at his masterfully naked body. "Take what off? I'm fucking bare."

And harshly handsome. Killian is the embodiment of cynical strength. He's beauty in an unnatural way and a trap so well disguised no one ever knows they're falling into it. He's sexy because of his looks, but he's sexier because of his ambiance. He doesn't back up as I step over the body, and he doesn't flinch when my palm cracks off his cheek.

"This."

"No." He grits his teeth.

"Take it off."

"No."

I smack him again, making him stumble backwards. The hallway table slams against the wall, and when I smack him a third time, it breaks as his body hits it. He grabs my wrist so I can't do it again. The lamp he flicked on crashes to the hardwood, but the bulb doesn't shatter, illuminating us from a different vantage point.

"Take the fucking mask off, *Killian*, or you can't have me."

He snorts. "You think you get a say in this?"

I study him. Broken, bloody, almost panicked, but too powerful to give in to it. It clicks, and I tilt my head at him. "You don't know how, do you?"

"Fuck you."

"You've worn the masks and fake personas for so long that you don't know how to take them all off."

"Without a mask, I'm *more* than Death's door. You sure you want to knock on me?"

I've never knocked harder. My laugh is vicious. Because I'm goading a devil, and masks or not, I'm still going to win.

"Knock fucking knock."

RIOT

19

DEATH'S DOOR

NARCISSISTS ARE SO WARPED. It doesn't matter that I won't drop my final mask like he's demanding, and it doesn't matter that I'll be the one fucking him harder than he's ever been fucked before. Because Soren Sauder is the perfect narcissist. He has an uncanny ability to convince *himself* that, no matter the outcome or how much he has to suffer to get it, he wins. It doesn't matter that I'm the clear victor. That I'm taking control. That I'm the one who is going to put him on his back and use him like a sex toy. He'll still convince himself he's won because he got me to kill Brady.

Fortunately, my god complex rivals his narcissism, and I don't need to convince myself I'm winning. I've already won, and I'm done fucking around.

He opens his mouth to spit more venom, but I have no more patience to listen to him. I push off the broken table, grab him by his swallowing throat, and spin him. His face cracks off the wall, and his feet crunch the table and Brady's forearm.

"You never know when to shut your mouth, sweetheart."

I rip his open shirt off, discarding it like I want to discard my masks. I wish they were as easy to rip off. Soren fights me, but I'm too volatile to be moved now, so I pin him in place and spit on his ass crack. "Need me to gag you?"

When he bucks his ass back, trying to break free, it makes my cock hit his hole, sliding that spit all over his rim. "You'd miss my mouth as soon as you—"

Reaching around his neck, I shove my fingers between his lips, pressing down on his tongue until he gags around them. "Better get 'em wet if you don't want to bleed. I'm over this stalling bullshit. You're finally begging."

"Like fuck!"

I gag him harder, pressing them all the way back to his throat. He slobbers all over my fingers, his body fighting mine at every turn. The sound he makes while he gags is better than his violin. My body bristles with need, eager and willing to take everything I can get from him now that we're at a crossroads in our game. He's no longer taunting the curse; he's taunting me, just like I knew he would.

Ripping my fingers free, he coughs and starts to mouth me off. It switches to a harsh gasp when I shove two fingers in his ass with no warning. I don't care if he bleeds. I *want* him to bleed. I need the evidence that I've ruined him, marked him, made him mine. I pump them hard, making him hiss and writhe in my grip.

His gasp turns into a disgusting laugh, and I love it even more than his gag. When he laughs, that's when he's most deranged, and a fucked-up Soren Sauder is my favourite kind of prize. "Ah, fuck you! Prep? I thought you wanted my hole bloody?"

My smile isn't controllable. It's messed up and distorted

because, fuck yeah, I love it when he calls me out. No one matches my level of depravity like Soren does. When he laughs harder, I pull my fingers free, spread bloody spit all over my cock, and grip his hips so he can't turn around. I don't want him seeing whatever mask I'm wearing right now.

"Who knew Killian Hallows was a fucking pu—"

I thrust once. Hard. Abrupt. All the way inside his tight hole. He spasms around me as his laugh temporarily dies off to make way for a pained groan. Power swells in my chest, travelling all the way down to my toes. It mingles with pleasure and a horrible satisfaction I don't want to get used to.

"Where'd your laugh go?" I press in harder without ever having pulled out, the pressure on my cock so tight I crave the constriction. His body crumples forward, and my hands on his hips and his on the wall are all that hold him up. His legs shake, his forehead thumps forward, and he breathes through his teeth.

Time to bring him back to life.

I let go of his hips and wrap my fingers around his throat from behind. Pulling him off the wall until his back is against my chest, I graze my teeth over the shell of his ear. "Where are you, Soren? One foot in Hell or head in the clouds?"

He coughs to clear his throat, making his ass clench around my cock, his body moving to take some control back. His hips move forward, and I look down to watch my cock slide out of his ass all the way to the tip. Not bloody yet...

"With you at my back?" he asks, bracing his hands against the wall to get more leverage. "I'm in the goddamn gutter. Never sank so low before."

Atta boy. I smirk behind him.

"Maybe you'll end up with Brady."

"Dare you to try."

When I thrust forward, his laugh comes back. When I fuck him hard and fast, his laugh transcends into something like vile music, and when I growl against his nape, letting possession wash through me, he laughs to call me out on it. Then he breaks my fucking dick by slamming his ass back so hard I'm shoved backwards. My heel catches on Brady's skull, and I fall to my ass, agitated and riotous to do something about it.

Soren doesn't let me.

He plants his foot on my chest to pin me down. When I look up at him, I see everything about him that gave him his narcissist diagnosis. His unreasonably high sense of self, his attention-seeking behaviour, his lack of remorse, his gaslighting skills, and his need for admiration. He's doing such a good job of hiding his vulnerabilities that I slump down, giving him control just to see what he'll do with it.

"You don't get to be behind me," he snaps, straddling my body and lowering until his ass hits my thighs. "No one does." He looks at my cock, slick and shiny. "You'll fucking look at me while I fuck you. No more hiding." He spits, but he doesn't rub it in. He lifts up, lines up, and shakes his head at me as he lowers down. "It's funny that you still think you're winning."

Goddammit. When I'm all the way inside him, on my back like a submissive bastard, I shake all over for three different reasons. One, because it feels so empowering to have him fuck himself on my cock. Two, because his eyes are on mine, degrading me and fucking me, using me and wanting me. Three, because this is the first time in my life I've been ridden. I'm so much of a control freak that I can't even give it up in the bedroom with docile partners, but something about how he's fucking my cock doesn't feel like I'm losing the control. More like I'm taking it without him realizing it. It's deceptive, which makes it sexy, and when I remember to breathe, it comes out as a raspy moan. I don't want him to see my thought process, so I smirk at him, plant my hands beside Brady's outstretched knee, and lift my ass off the floor to fuck him from the bottom.

Even the race to come is a competition. I'm conflicted about winning because I want to take pleasure from him without giving it in return, but I want to be able to gloat about getting him off. The tightness around my cock and the slick glide from so much spit is pushing me close to the edge, but it's when he looks down at me with pure authority in his eyes that I have to clench all my muscles to prevent myself from ending this too early.

I'm on my back. He's above me. It's a power exchange I never thought I'd enjoy... but fuck, he looks good up there. He *feels* good there. So good I'm afraid I'm going to want it again and again. Can't have that, so I sit up abruptly, wrap my arm around his back, and flip our positions until he's flat on top of Brady's thighs. Jesus Christ, this dead fucker is everywhere!

He laughs again, but it's cynical this time. "I'm not fucking close enough," he screams at me. "Take me closer!"

To death.

His legs wrap around my hips like he can force me to fuck him half to death. I grin and revel in it, thrusting into him and bringing my hands up between our bodies. Looking him straight in his energized blue eyes, I cinch his throat with both hands, press my thumbs to his windpipe, and dig my fingertips into his pulse points.

His face turns red almost immediately, but it's not bothering me now. With his lips popped open and his hands clutching at my wrists, he smirks through his suffocation, eyes rolling back. A subtle nod accompanies his pleasure, and I nudge forward until he's right between my legs.

"Tell me when you get close enough to knock."

Using my grip on his neck, I fuck him for real. For the first time. Because everything before this exact moment has been a game. We're not playing anymore; we're chasing—a high, a darkness, a level of madness that only comes from glimpsing the afterlife. I thought I'd be his Grim Reaper, but instead, I'm his hellhound.

Everything about his body is tight. His muscles are clenched, making his ass squeeze my cock hard and unforgiving. I rock into him, barely noticing the dead kid's shin bones beneath my own. When Soren's fingers dig into my wrists even harder, I let up my thumbs to give him a single breath of air.

"Not yet," he rasps. "Not close enough."

The urge to kiss him whips through me ferociously. His slick lips and red cheeks are tempting, but his wide and almost afraid eyes are ecstasy. I slow my hips but deepen my thrusts, making Soren's body slide over Brady every time I fuck into him. He moans, the sound coming out gagged and strained, and when I look at him again, he gives me the nod I've been waiting for. He's there, ready to knock on Death's door and slam it back in her face, and that's a moment I want to taste.

I bend forward in a rush and slam my mouth against his as he ruptures into agonized bliss. He groans straight into my mouth, the taste of deliverance and desperation so potent it makes me shiver.

"Holy fuck. Holy fuck. Ahhh." He lets go of my wrists to let me choke him harder, grabbing my ass to keep me buried deep inside him and gripping his own cock with the other hand. He strangles my cock like my hands are strangling him, and pleasure shoots up my spine to give me a head rush. "Fuck..." Between our bodies, his cum coats our abs. "I'm knocking," he pants. "Don't stop."

I won't stop, but my cock has no respect for his brush with Death. As he holds me still, only the constriction of his spasming ass adding a firm massage, I can't hold myself back any longer. This is it, the moment he dreams about. Death and pleasure, the mingling of danger and desire, a desperate need so strong he's been chasing it for half his life. Soren's stifled moan sets me off, and I thrust my hips once, twice, and deepen the messy kiss as I fill his ass with cum. Because this is my moment, too. The one I dream about. The ability to leash a madman to my control and be the one to dictate his dance with mortality. It's the power my ego craves and the authority I need to feel in charge.

"Oh, fuck," I moan against his open lips as he nears death. I shiver and hold my breath, pumping my release into him so deep that he'll be full of me for the rest of the night and all of tomorrow.

"Kill..." He bites my lip, and I'm barely coherent enough to release my grip on his throat. As soon as I do, he sucks in air, coughs right against my mouth, and then pulls my face to his to drag out the moment and take the air straight from my lungs.

This is different. It's almost gratitude. Him thanking me for taking him to her door, and me thanking him for granting me this level of power. It's so honest and raw that my cock pulses one more time, a trembling aftershock to my already explosive orgasm. It's a fragile moment because it's softness in a sense we don't often show—it's emotion expressed without a word spoken, like his music.

With one final kiss, I brace for it. The end.

He pauses, lips against mine and his eyelashes hitting my cheeks as he closes his eyes for a beat. One. Two. Three...

"Fuck off. You ruined it. You let go too early. I was knocking, but she hadn't opened the door yet." He pushes on my chest, but his sated eyes meet mine, and a split second of admiration beams at me from the depths of them. He wipes it away, secures his rickety cracks, and hides himself away for another day. Scrambling out from underneath me, my cock hangs wet and heavy over Brady's dead body. Soren notices and kicks at my ribs, not wanting my cock that close to the kid I already killed for the same reason.

I slump back against the hall wall, and his legs give out, making him shuffle into a sitting position a foot away from me, leaning against the same wall. The house comes back into focus, the broken railing and hallway table, the gouges and holes in the drywall, and the lamp shining its bright light to illuminate the evidence of our cracked omens. We did this. Together. A game, a battle, sex. I'm almost too confused to feel proud. Until Soren opens his mouth...

"Fuck," he laughs, elbows on his knees, Vile House

tattoo rising with fast breaths as he leans over his legs. "Guess I win this round."

My head snaps in his direction. "The fuck are you talking about? I clearly won."

"How so? I got a dance with Death, and you gave it to me."

"I fucked you."

"I fucked you back."

"My cum is in your ass."

Soren grins. "And mine is coating your skin. I won, Riot. Admit it. Blink!" His smirk is so cocky it makes me want to smack him for using my words against me.

I'm Riot again, not Killian. I don't know why that pisses me off. I didn't purposefully put on any of my facades, but he noticed, and now he refuses to use my name. "Fuck, you *are* delusional if you think this means you won."

Before he can say anything else, the front door opens and we both brace for... something. Monster walks in, looks at the two of us, naked, with no expression on his face, and then sighs when he sees the dead guy on the floor. The guy we were supposed to bring back to Director... Alive.

Monster shakes his head, grabs Brady's ankle, and drags him back out the front door, slamming it and barely missing Brady's head.

Director is going to be so pissed. But I laugh because of it. "I'll win double when Director sends you to bottom rank for this. Worked so hard for second in line and now it's gone with a good fuck and a brush with the devil." I climb to my feet, my bare ass right in his face. "Knew you'd finally beg for it."

"I didn't fucking beg!" he screams at me.

Oh, he did. And he will again.

GHOST

20

WORTH IT?

MY ASS IS ON FIRE, but it isn't burning as fiercely as my mood.

Because I'm being a coward, and I'm *never* a coward. Director called the meeting twenty minutes ago, and I'm still pacing the rug in my bedroom, trying to work up the balls to go near Riot. See him. Look him in the eye and act like I'm not fazed by the way he fucked me.

Because he did. Fucked me straight to Death's door, and I *am* affected by it. It's the closest I've ever come to blending that 'one or two second' precipice with real pleasure, and I'm fucking jonesing for it again. And it didn't take as much brutality as I thought it would to get me there. I mean, he was harsh, and blood was drawn, but it was... missionary style fucking with some strangulation, and holy shit, did it hit the mark.

I'm chalking it up to being a new and dangerous experience. I've never been fucked in the ass before, so that added a level of appeal, and I've never given in to Killian's goading, so that added the dangerous element. That's all it was, I hope. A one-time thrill that won't hit the same a second time. If I go for it again, it'll probably be a letdown. There won't be a dead guy in the middle to add to the scene.

So, there's no use hiding out in my room any longer. Fuck him, and fuck everyone else if Monster told them what he walked in on. I'm done being a coward.

I pull my door open, lock it behind me, and run into my brother on the way down the stairs. "Aren't you supposed to be in a meeting?" Remi asks, waiting for me to catch up.

"I'm going. Are you coming?"

"I'm not invited."

He could come if he wanted to. Director knows Krypt tells him pretty much everything anyway, but I kind of respect that he doesn't want to. He's not attempting to be a Vile member, and I doubt all the guys would be okay with him trying to be. He knows where his strength lies, and it's not as a ruthless stalker or murderous hunter.

"I'm meeting Cain," Remi says, grabbing his cello case from the bottom of the stairs. "Windows are finally fixed at the shop, and now we have a whole day of work to do for the music festival. It's coming up fast."

Exhausted, I smile. Because through it all, he still loves music as much as he always has. I hope to get back to that someday. Maybe even play with him again for old time's sake. "I'll come by and help out later when everything around here is done," I tell him. "Let me know what you need."

He narrows his eyes at me. "Why you being so amicable?"

"Fuck you, Remi." It's definitely not because I got banged into oblivion last night, and it's certainly not because

I'm the caring type, so I have no idea why I offered. I'm all messed up, so I leave him to it, pick up my pace so I can't turn around, and ball my fists before pushing open the con room door.

Everyone is just standing around listening to Kyd tell a story, but I watch all their heads turn in my direction when I close the door. Riot's eyes most of all. I can practically feel his smug grin as I avoid looking at him, choosing to lock eyes with Monster instead. He stares back at me with a blank face, so I look at everyone else.

"What?"

Riot laughs, but Kyd breaks the tension. "Lil Baby Ghosty, I was just telling the boys about the progression of my love match with the good doctor. Basically, he's having a really hard time resisting me, just like that psychic said he would. So, what do you think? Should I ask him out?"

"You haven't already?"

"Not in so many words. I'm trying to be subtle."

"Not a subtle bone in your body, Kyd." Glitch laughs. "Pretty sure you asked him out when you held a knife to his femoral."

Kyd sighs dreamily. "Yeah. Good times. I already wrote that part of our story."

Since I don't want Riot to think I'm being a chicken, I look right at him, daring him to say something. Knowing him, he'll ask me how my ass is in front of all the guys, and then I'll have to fight him just to keep my ego happy. But he doesn't say anything. He bites his lip before running his tongue over it, eyes moving up and down my body. My fists ball harder, but my stomach flutters, too. Fuck, I don't like that he has the ability to influence my physical reactions now. Maybe he always has... but not like this. Before, he riled me in a way that brought a challenge and a level of rage that felt motivating.

Now he riles me in a way that brings a challenge with the prospect of pleasure, and that pisses me off. *A goddamn flutter?* God...

The door bangs open. Director walks in, clearly in a mood, and I roll my eyes at the predictability of what's about to happen next. Fucking rank. I'm about to get grounded by Daddy. I turn my back to him, but he won't let me get away with it.

"Can't even face your mistakes, can you?" Director snaps at my back. "Line the fuck up."

My teeth clench hard enough to pop my jaw, but it brings me a level of pride to go stand in second position. I'll probably lose it today, like Riot said, but whatever. It's mine for now and I'll hold it as long as I can. Because humiliation is eating me alive now that he's confirmed that I'm being a coward by avoiding my mistakes. Yeah, I got the kid killed and that wasn't the job, but fuck him. My needs were more important in the moment, and he should know me well enough by now to understand how selfish I am. Not my fault he tries to put me in a box I don't belong in.

In the rank line, I shove my hands into my pants pockets like I have no shits to give. Seven nudges me to ask if I'm alright, but I shrug him off without a word. I'm sure he's about to find out what happened, and I'm banking on Monster still being mute so he can't shout about what I did with Riot. Still can't believe I did that. Let him fuck me.

I was so convinced I won that round because I got exactly what I wanted, but as I lay in bed all morning, it got all churned up in my head. Because he accused me of begging.

Did I?

Not verbally, but maybe... no. Fuck that. I didn't do shit other than push all his buttons and get him to crack. He's the one who admitted how he felt by snapping Brady's neck and taking what he wanted. He's the one who kissed me. He's the one who has wanted this for as long as we've been feuding, and he's the one who took it to the final level.

Wordlessly, Director paces our line. He rubs at his temples, clearly sick of our bullshit, building the moment until he's ready to snap. He doesn't often lash out at us publicly, but we're a bunch of degenerates with personality disorders who thrive on our egos and let embarrassment control us, so it's in his best interest to humiliate us in front of one another. A lesson he learned a long time ago and hasn't stopped utilizing since he first started offering up the rank line as an incentive to outdo each other.

Still looking at the floor, his arm snaps out and he points at Kyd. "You find your lion?"

He gasps and presses a hand to his chest in mock outrage. "Fabrizio is an ally. He helped us take down Reaper Corp that night. I leave steaks out for him. Only the best cuts."

Director groans. His arm moves to point at Glitch. "You get the cameras at Misfit Hall back up and running?"

"Yeah, but Lockan keeps taking them down."

Director groans again. "Fix it." He points at Seven. "You have a plan for new initiates once we do the early Initiation Night?"

From beside me, at the head of the line, Seven says,

"Training plans, yeah, but no plans for what to do with the existing initiates. The ones who have made it this far are set to move into the dorms soon, but none of them want to live with new initiates and have their identities revealed yet. We need a new house. Somewhere to put the new ones temporarily."

"New ones can live at their houses like all new initiates do, can't they?" Director asks.

"Yeah, most of them. But a lot of families have young kids, and people are trying to put separation between kids and danger, so there's already an interest in a new boarding house."

"Hallows house," Riot offers, looking at his brother. "No point in it just sitting there empty. Use it."

"Yeah?" Seven asks, looking at Krypt for his approval.

Everything that lives inside Krypt's eyes rebels as he thinks about that house, but he blinks it away and nods at Seven.

"Make it happen. New recruits can move into the Hallows' house if they need a place, and our loyal initiates can use the dorms here." Director sighs and takes a few steps down the line. Pointing at Facts, he asks, "Security check-points set up for the music festival?"

"Yes, hello. We have video and audio devices planted, and we've worked out a schedule for us to take stations at certain times. Road is being monitored to scan all incoming vehicles."

"And run facial recognition," Glitch adds.

"Yes," Facts agrees. "And Auggie gave us a room at the Umbra Inn so we can monitor guests from there. It's booked solid."

"Good. Thank you," Director says, finger swinging to Ransom towards the end. "I need you to run Initiation Night next month, so start prepping. I won't be there."

"Why?"

"I'll be away with Axel. Benton Wentworth is still funding his research, and he's getting suspicious about Axel's new affiliations in Moros. I'm going to... meet with him to appease the billionaire bastard."

"Why?" Ransom asks again.

"Because we're one small town going up against a multi-billion-dollar ruthless corporation, and we need his fucking money!" Director shouts, losing his cool. Wow, this threat is really weighing on his shoulders, and it makes me feel slightly guilty for fucking up the job last night. "We need his money. His funding. He's been in bed with Yates, and it's time we utilize him for our own needs. Axel is in good standing with him, so we're going to build that bridge until we can burn it down later." Which means Director will have to apologize and make up for the fact that we kept Benton Wentworth in the basement cells and chased him through town on our last Initiation Night. Oops.

"You want me to be you?" Ransom clarifies. "As in, run the night?"

"Stay at Vile House. You play my role during this one. You aren't to leave and join the rest on the streets. You need to be here, welcoming the initiates who return. It's good practice for you."

"Practice for what?" Ransom scoffs.

Director only shakes his head and moves on to Krypt. "Remi is all set up with security for the music festival?"

"Yes." Krypt looks at Menace. "And his tattooed friend."

Too many Cs in Cain Carson for him to call the prick by name, apparently.

Menace smirks. He must be the protection. "We've got plans in place for all the business owners. Don't worry, Director. We're watching out for our people."

"Good. And as far as town-wide training goes, what are your plans?" he asks Menace.

"We've set up a spot out on Carnival Hill for combat training. The Harpy isn't happy about it, but as long as we stay the hell away from her place, don't disrespect Janie's Woods, and leave her the fuck alone, she's granted her permission. She has a request, though."

Director finally looks up, meeting eyes with Menace. "What request?"

"She wants to be hired."

"For what?"

"Poison. She wants a failsafe in place. If Reaper Corp takes over Moros, she wants to... uh, well, she wants a failsafe."

"What fucking failsafe?"

"Poison. Ready to be released into the water supply. She won't let Reaper Corp take over. If it goes down, they go down. She wants to kill everyone with poison. She claims she'll ensure the town residents know before it happens so they can avoid drinking the water."

Director inhales through his nose, nostrils wide and jaw clenched. "I'll talk to her." Gathering himself, he looks right at me, then Monster, and Riot after. "Weird thing happened early this morning. That mark you were supposed to track and bring back *alive* showed up in the morgue. Dead.

Snapped neck. Bunch of broken bones, almost like he got trampled. Weird, right?"

This is the calmest I've ever seen him confront one of our fuckups. I almost grin, wanting to lay claim to that particular mistake. "Neon Demon was pretty rowdy last night," I say instead.

"Must have been," Director says, looking at Monster. "Though, I got reports of Brady walking out of there very much alive. With the two of you." He whips his gaze to me and Riot. "So, oddly, I'm asking myself, where the hell did this guy get so many broken bones and a snapped neck?"

Kyd 'ooohs' like this is a suspenseful mystery story he can't wait to find the answers to.

"Monster?" Director asks. "Any information?"

Monster just stares, stoic and calm.

"Riot?"

"Haven't got a clue," he says.

Director's smile is almost as chilling as mine. "Ghost? Any insight?"

"He probably did something to deserve a snapped neck." I shrug.

Staring at me, Director says, "Everyone is dismissed. Get to work and report back tonight. Ghost and Riot, you're with me."

Fuck.

"And you're both at the end of the line."

Double fuck.

"Walk there. Now. Before everyone leaves."

Humiliation burns through me, but I go fast, wanting to beat Riot there so I'm not dead last. Everyone watches, a few smug grins are shared, and Menace actually laughs.

"You two finally break?" he asks.

"Fuck you," Riot and I say at the same time, fighting for the second to last position.

"I'll let you have it, sweetheart," he whispers. "Since I ruined your ass and all."

I punch him square in the eye.

RANK:

1. Seven
2. Menace
3. Glitch
4. Facts
5. Monster
6. Krypt
7. Ransom
8. Kyd
9. Ghost
10. Riot

IN THE MORGUE with Brady's mangled body laid out on a table, Director squares off with us, still calmer than I expected him to be. Riot's eye starts to swell and turn red, but he acts like it doesn't bother him. I should have hit him harder.

"After examining the body, we found this," he says,

holding up a tiny chip with a pair of tweezers. "It's different from the other Reaper Corp chips, and it's nothing like Axel's tracking chip. This is an implant from Reaper Corp, which basically tells us that Brady here was a low member. He was born from their breeding program, batch FV4027, according to this chip, but he never made it far. Axel can't find anything useful on the chip, but Glitch had a look at it. He plugged it into his computer, and from there, he got a detailed history of how this kid was bred, what his traits should have been, and where he fell flat. To summarize, he was bred for deception and coercion, but somewhere around the age of sixteen, according to the file attached to this chip, he was released from the program and sent to the general population of their ranks. He's a nobody, which means Reaper Corp sent a nobody into Moros."

Which means there are probably other nobodies already planted in Moros. That's what he's getting at.

"Think of all the names and faces Axel could have pulled from his head had he been brought here alive like you were supposed to do." He drops the chip. "We could uncover the moles in our town, maybe save lives. But no, you two couldn't play nice. Once again."

"Then stop putting us on fucking jobs together," Riot snaps.

"I will," Director says, inhaling deeply. "But first I'm sending you on one more together. Right now. And if you fuck this one up, you'll both be dead. Time to start learning to work together, boys. Complete this job as a team or die. And if you come back alive and still won't cooperate, then I'll be forced to remove you from Vile House. You're assets to this society, but you aren't acting like it." He steps closer to us as our rage builds. "I want you both here, but it's time you start making decisions. Is your feud more important than being Vile or do you put your society first?" He holds up a slip of paper. "Here's the job. Good luck. I do hope you both make it back."

With that, he leaves us in the morgue with Brady's body, the slip of paper fluttering to the floor. We both look at it, but I'm too pissed off to move, and Riot is trying not to breathe too hard.

"He doesn't know shit. He can't prove we did anything to Brady."

"He can, actually," Axel says as he walks in. "Found all sorts of things on his body, and semen was one of them. Guess whose DNA it didn't match?" His eyelid flutters when he watches us. "And guess whose DNA is already on record for Vile House? Your semen showed up on this boy, and the rest isn't a hard guess. Some daredevil games, bluff calling, a snapped neck, sex on top of his dead body. It's all very cliché for the two of you." He bends down to pick up the slip of paper. "He's not joking. If you don't work together for this job, you won't get out of there alive."

"Where?" Riot asks. "Where are we going?"

He holds out the paper. A flight schedule. "You're flying down south to infiltrate Reaper Corp Headquarters to get a very vital bit of information."

My stomach sinks and actual dread fills me. I'm not someone who fears death and danger, but this...

"All these chips and implants we've found require a keycode. Glitch has been able to crack a few of them, but they self-destruct within a few minutes. We need the master key, and you're going to get it."

RIOT

21

KING COBRA

WHEN KRYPT WENT to infiltrate Axel's lab, he got to say goodbye to me. It was awkward and unfocused because we're both terrible at anything deep, but at least it happened. It was a moment that ensured neither of us would regret anything if the worst happened.

I didn't get the same chance. Director put us on a plane immediately after getting us in shit, and I'm pretty sure he did it just to motivate us to come back. I didn't get to talk to my brother, and Ghost didn't get to talk to his. It means we have unfinished business, and I don't like how it feels.

The small plane from Moros was quick as it took us to the city. Waiting around in the city's airport was bullshit. I haven't left Moros in years, let alone gone to a goddamn airport with business fuckups and excited travellers. All those people frayed my already tattered nerves, but now? Holy fucking hell. This is the closest I've come to the underworld. Sitting in economy class with hundreds of normies going about their filthy lives is the worst kind of punishment.

Babies are babbling, parents are coddling, kids are not

complying, and couples are all... romantic and lovey as they set their screens to play the same movie at the exact same time. Fucking gag. It's all so light and monotonous and I don't understand how people enjoy this kind of life. I forgot how prevalent cell phones are. Pictures are being snapped every time I look up, and I can't fathom the reason to document so many boring moments. Why not live it? Why see it through a screen? Why not make it memorable by actions rather than captions? I don't understand it, and to be honest, I forget I have a phone most of the time.

My captions are written on calling cards, and my memories are documented in history through the tales Moros locals will eternally tell about me. Not social media and ten-second snaps.

I sigh, leaning back in my seat, thinking about why Axel would want us to find a research file while we're in Reaper City. I've got a file name written on a slip of paper in my pocket, and he told me not to mention it to Director. The fuck is that crazy doc up to? My head is too busy to think about it, and Ghost doesn't want to acknowledge it because he's nervous, despite how hard he's trying not to let it show.

Ghost didn't want to sit with me, so I'm stuck next to some kid in a frilly tutu, wearing a literal tiara. I suck at kids, but she's probably six or so, and I wanna ask her what kind of happy life she's living to make her confident enough to dress like a sparkly little shit and be so excited about it. But her mom is across the aisle and keeps side-eyeing me like I'm gonna snatch her daughter or something. Slipping into a mask I've perfected well, I offer the mother a charming smile to put her at ease, tell her she has a cute kid, and keep my elbows inside my armrests just in case.

Unfortunately, my charm doesn't just put her at ease, it offers her a window to chat. I'm just sitting here listening to how she's travelling alone with her two kids for the first time because her husband is meeting them at their vacation destination in a few days, and I have to pretend like I give a shit. Vacation? The fuck you wanna go to some stuffy hotel on a crowded beach for when you could go to Moros and get a real thrill? Maybe the girl's sparkly dress would liven up Death Row a bit.

"Where are you going?" the six-year-old asks me. "To see your family? To visit your friend? To the zoo?"

"The zoo," I agree. Probably going to be a zoo in Reaper City, and I need to be the lion instead of the monkey.

"What's your favourite animal? Mine's a king cobra."

There she is. Little Miss Sparkly Tutu hasn't been tainted enough by bullshit fears to be afraid of snakes yet, and it earns her a tidbit of my respect. "Why a king cobra?" I ask her, a little peeved at myself for indulging her.

"Because they can kill you with their spit," she deadpans, kicking her ballet-flippered feet. "And when they get all angry, they look like they're wearing cool hair."

Fair enough.

I don't know how to act around kids who aren't born and bred in Moros, so I try to come up with a cute answer, like an otter or something, but instead, her purple-painted fingernails drag over my bare forearm, tracing the lines of my tattoos. I stiffen.

"Mom won't let me get one," she tells me. "I want a tattoo of a parrot so I can say something and then hold up my arm and my arm can say something." She laughs super hard, but that sounds dumb to me. Why not just say it twice if that's her thing? "Do they hurt?"

'I like pain' might not be a suitable response to a child, so I shrug. "Yeah."

Never, not even once in my whole life, have I been touched like this. Like she doesn't give a shit about who I am or what boundaries are or what touch means. She's just... petting my arm like it's precious to her, looking at my art like it's a pretty picture, not expecting or insinuating anything or trying to taunt or hurt or manipulate me.

"Maybe when you're older, Leigh," Mom says, smiling at me. Guess she's not afraid of me near her kid anymore.

"Girls look stupid with tattoos," her asshole older brother says from the other side of their mom. "You have to be goth to get tattoos."

As their mom gives him a talking-to about something, Leigh looks up at me and says, "I'm goth."

Yeah, about as goth as she can get in that getup. "Damn right," I tell her with a grin. "Get a king cobra someday. Cool hair and killer spit and all."

Her smile is more devious than her outfit suggests, but just like that, I like her even more. Not all kids are so bad, I guess. When I glance back to check on Ghost, I find him watching me, a strange look in his usually closed-off eyes. He meets my gaze, blinks, and then looks away.

When we land, the girl holds my hand as we leave the plane, and I catch Ghost looking again. I'm trying not to be weird, but I've never held hands with a person before, let alone a kid, so when her mom whisks her away through the line, I breathe out in relief and wave back at her as she does a snake-fangs sign to me with her fingers.

We make it through security with fabricated IDs, find the rental car, and don't talk as I drive us towards Reaper City. There are five days until the music festival, and if I'm not back by then, I won't be coming back at all. That's my goal.

About an hour in, I say, "You're nervous."

"I'm not fucking—yeah, I am nervous. We're about to break into a lab in the middle of a walled-off city, owned and operated by the most powerful, dangerous organization in this part of the world, maybe even the whole world. You'd be stupid not to be nervous."

I look at my eyes in the rearview mirror, needing that visual reminder of who I am. Riot, not Killian, and today, I'm not going to buckle under pressure like I did when I was a kid. I'm gonna be fierce like that girl on the plane, confident like her, too. I'll be the goddamn king cobra instead of the lion, because if anyone from Reaper Corp comes for us—comes for Soren—I won't hesitate to bite. His death is mine to grant, and until I do, he's mine to have. No one else gets him unless they take me down first.

"Drop the fucking masks, Riot."

"I am," I admit. "Scared. So, let's make a bulletproof plan." Director was right. If we don't work together on this one, we aren't getting out alive.

IN A HOTEL ROOM several kilometers outside of Reaper City, we took down the decorative art on the wall to project our screen. Director, Glitch, Facts, and Ransom are all on the line, and Axel is available for questions if we need him. We've spent the last twelve hours plotting out the lay of the city, monitoring the security and guard routes, planning our paths and anything that might hold us up along the way, and arguing about variables. We have plans and backup plans, and we have instructions for what to do if we're captured, caught, or can't get out of the city undetected. Most importantly, we know what we're looking for and where to find it.

"Time to get some sleep, boys," Director says through the tablet's speaker. "Less than six hours until you move. Ransom is on standby, and Glitch is here with him. Rest up, and good luck."

"Tell Krypt—"

Ghost glares at me, hanging up before I get the rest of the sentence out. "No," he tosses the tablet onto the bed. "None of that. No lame goodbyes or *take care of my goldfish* bullshit. Six hours from now, we're going in, we're getting that key, and we're getting out."

For someone so skilled at silence and the art of moving without detection, he's shaking an awful lot. His fingers are trembling, and his eyes are twitchy, but I can't tell if it's from exhaustion, fear, or worry. Maybe all three. Maybe more than that. He never got to say goodbye to Remi either.

Ghost is still looking at me, and I'm not even sure if I want to call him Ghost or if he's Soren right now, so I turn away to look in the mirror, grounding myself in my own eyes.

"Riot."

"I need the ninety seconds." It kills me to say it, but he doesn't do anything other than nod in the mirror. He gives me a minute, sitting on the edge of the bed to gather our supplies and weapons for tonight.

This is different for me. I *am* scared. I've hardly been outside of Moros, and now I'm expected to survive this? The real world is hard for me, but the fact that I'm just a fuckup with antisocial personality disorder who belongs to a society doesn't buy me as much clout outside of Moros' limits. Reaper Corp is a powerhouse, and we're just two guys who can barely trust each other. I'm unfamiliar with feeling inferior to anyone or anything, and I'm definitely not used to feeling intimidated. I got comfortable being a king in Moros and forgot I'm only a spider outside—I can be squished and stepped on, but I'm still feared, so that's what I need to focus on.

I don't have much empathy or remorse for the things I do, and I see myself as the highest form of authority, so it's really fucking me up something fierce to doubt all that. I'm cowardly enough to admit that if I had the choice, I wouldn't take this mission. Not because I'm terrified of it, but because it will fucking kill me worse if I get captured and have to live in the proof that I failed. I don't fucking fail, and I don't let anyone beat me. Not unless I allow them to because it suits my needs. This whole mission is rocking me to my core because it goes against everything I've ever thought of myself.

There's one small part that can't wait to succeed so I have a new bragging right, but for once, it's hard to focus on that when the chill of doom is so real and different from what I'm used to. I'm too agitated to even fuck with him when he goes to shower, choosing to shower after him instead.

We're both on our backs, the curtains drawn to block the sun, in separate beds, unable to sleep. He doesn't make a sound, but I must sigh because he scolds me a few times before he climbs out of bed and rips the blanket back on mine. I look at him, baffled and confused.

He curses as he slips in beside me. "I don't trust that window or the door. There's nowhere safe to put my back, so for one time only..."

He'll give me his back, and I can give him mine. For protection and safety. Wow... never thought... just never thought.

It's unsettling to feel so comfortable next to him. Nearly naked without the thought of sex entering my mind, tired and unguarded without worry about what he'll try to pull, unmasked and unsure of what part of me is showing through. It's a breath in time, that silent second between heartbeats. Nothing really exists here because we never spend time here, but we're here now, breathing and existing in that pause between lightning and thunder.

"Why'd you do it?" Ghost—Soren?—asks the silent room, his voice breathy like he had to push it out.

"Do what?"

"Hold that girl's hand."

I feel myself go tense but I don't know what it means. I don't dare look at him, not because I'm intimidated by the question, but because I'm unsure what the question insinuates. "She held mine."

"But you held it back."

Where's he going with this? Is he pissed that I held her hand, or is he merely baffled by the fact that I'm capable of doing something pure? I don't want a kid, but I don't despise them and see them as vulnerable weak points like Monster does, so I am competent enough at communicating with them, even if my way was different from her mom's. Sometimes I feel like I relate better to kids because we all see life through a lens that society hasn't tainted. Their looking glass is pure magic and mine is dark magic, but it's all still magic.

"I've just never seen you touch someone like that," he whispers.

Meaning I've never touched *him* like that? Does Soren Sauder have a soft side that comes out to play when he isn't taunting death and his family curse? Does he crave sentiment as much as he craves danger? I'm not about to try it now because it might spook me as much as it spooks him, and neither of us can afford to have our minds out of focus right now.

"Anyway," he says, clearing his throat and rolling onto his side, facing away from me. "You got the door and I got the window?"

It's an odd thing for me to give my back to someone, but I turn over and face the door. "Yeah." I don't know if he does it or I do it, or maybe we both do, but sometime later, my ass hits his and our backs flatten together.

And we sleep.

I dream of King Cobras.

GHOST

22

INFILTRATION WITH NO INVITATION

AFTER THROWING up in the hotel bathroom for the second time, I brace my hands on the sink and stare into my haunted eyes in the mirror. I'm not weak! I'm fully fucking capable of doing this job. I'm skilled, honed, trained, and mentally prepared, but there's a level of risk to it that I'm unfamiliar with.

Because we're outside of Moros, have no backup, and if we get caught, we're dead—tortured *and then* dead. I trust myself, but I don't know if I trust my partner. What'll I do if he gets caught?

He's the variable making me sick. It's the conflicting strategies about Riot that are warring with themselves inside my mind, making my jigsaw puzzle come unglued. My eyes are as crazed as my mind is, doing a terrible job of hiding my irrational worries. He's Riot—Killian Hallows. He's just as capable as I am, despite how badly I don't want to admit that. He can handle this, so I don't know why I'm freaking out about what's going to happen to him.

Maybe it's because our plan involves me doing the

sneaking and him taking all the heat. Maybe it's because he's going to be the charmer, the one talking and distracting and steering the attention away from me as I slink through the compound to get the key we're after. I'll be concealed in the shadows while he'll be spotlighted to keep me hidden. Our risks are different, which means our outcomes and downfalls will be different if shit goes south. I already know what I'm supposed to do if I get caught, and I know what he's supposed to do if he gets caught, but I don't know what *I'm* supposed to do if *he* gets caught. That's a lie I'm trying to make myself believe, because I do know what I'm supposed to do, I just don't know what I *want* to do.

He's my Vile House brethren, but he's also... Killian Hallows. That never used to mean anything to me, but it does now. Because he fucked me. Because he sees me. Because he knows what goes through my mind when I taunt a curse that has set out to ruin me since birth.

Because I slept with my back to him for safety, and I've never sought safety in another person before.

I shower and brush my teeth, and when I open the bathroom door, he's standing at the window, looking out over the city in the distance we're about to infiltrate.

"No masks," is all he says.

No Vile House masks. No Vile House power. No Vile House status. We're two men going into enemy territory under a cover that might be moot. They could have our faces on recognition software and blow our cover as soon as we step foot in Reaper City. Draco, the man I fought and killed, knew exactly who I was. Maybe the entire organization does, too.

My stomach tightens, but I refuse to let it churn. The

time for nerves has passed, and now I need to focus on what comes next. This plan has merit, but it also leaves room for spontaneity. We have a target and a goal, but the rest will be a series of 'what comes next?' questions as we pass through each stage of the plan.

It's late evening, the sun almost hidden behind the tall buildings in the distance. With hats on our heads and the cover of darkness, we'll penetrate Reaper City with no invitation. The only intention we have is to walk back out. With or without the key.

He's not wearing a shirt, so his Vile House tattoo steals all my focus. Another thing to identify us by if we get captured, but right now, it doesn't feel like a bad thing. The tattoo suits his body, looks good on his back, and grounds me because it reminds me who we are. Ghost and Riot, two ruthless assholes who never let anyone else take us down. Tonight will be no different. I refuse to let it be.

Standing beside him, reluctantly feeling his warm and stoic energy, I look at Reaper City in the distance and narrow my eyes at it like I do everything else. It's just one more conquest to conquer. It's an obstacle, and I love puzzle-solving. It's a useless fucking game that I'll enjoy winning.

"We got this?" I ask the window.

Riot is an egotistical prick, so he grins at the pane of glass. "We got this."

I don't want to ask, but I do. "How can you be so sure?"

Riot's grey eyes meet mine, and his grin only widens. "I love showing up where I'm not invited. This is just another chance to shine." He steps up to me, making me lift my chin with the confidence I'm still trying to convince myself to feel. "Reaper Corp is about to meet the Ghost of Moros."

Replacing my nerves, a thrill runs through me, heating my skin and fuelling my adrenaline. "Nah," I correct him. "They're about to meet the many masks you wear and get caught up in the riot you start. Me? I'll go undetected because *I am* the fucking Ghost of Moros."

Riot smiles at me, and trust me, there's nothing charming about it. He hasn't slipped into that mask yet, and maybe this is the first time I'm seeing his base layer. "You're goddamn right you are."

The thrill intensifies, and just like that, my mind goes delightfully dark and the job becomes a challenge to win. Riot has always been my best competitor. He notices my shift in mood, commenting on it with the glint in his eyes and the tilt of his lips.

"Come on, sweetheart. Let's fuck over Reaper Corp."

IT ALL STARTS HERE.

It was surprisingly easy to enter the city with a group of tourists. We were on a bus, snapping photos of a place people come to visit for its architecture and history. Once an old sacred city, Reaper Corp overtook it twenty years ago, and since then, they've brainwashed the country into believing they did it for the preservation of history, claiming the government and tourism industry would ruin it. Which means people respect Reaper Corp and what they've done to protect a sacred city.

Bullshit

They aren't protecting it. They're utilizing it, mind-controlling the citizens, and bringing in tourists to spread their gospel far and wide. Facts said that statistically, a hundred thousand people a year put in a request to move to Reaper City because they believe it to be a safe and wonderful place to raise children. The school system is its own, renowned, and the proof is in the pudding of how many geniuses Reaper City produces. Little do they know, those geniuses are bred in a lab with genetic modifiers for those exact traits, skewing the statistics to further brainwash the continent.

Whatever. None of my business, and seriously, I couldn't care less about this place. If Reaper Corp wasn't actively trying to do the same thing in Moros, I'd even respect them for it. But since they are, they're my enemy, and the only thing I care about is stopping them because Moros is mine. Ours. And no one, not even this corporation that wields power like we wield darkness, is going to take it from us unless they kill us all first.

We got the tour, and towards the end, we slipped away from the crowd near the centre of town. Ransom is in my ear, directing us where to go, and Glitch is remotely bypassing doors for us as we sneak through the lower levels of their research facility. The late evening tour ends a few blocks from here at a cathedral-style building that used to be a church; now, it's still a place of devotion, but to Reaper Corp. Our plan is to get in, get the keycode, and join up with the tour in no less than forty-five minutes so we can take the same bus back out of the city walls.

You know what they say about well-crafted plans...

"This is it," Riot says, closing a door behind us.

"Ten minutes before guard shift rotation," Ransom says through the earpiece. "Get ready."

Ten minutes. My nerves come back because ten minutes isn't enough time to… I don't know, think things I'll never say aloud. What happens if we don't make it out of this mission? What will I do if Remi has to live without me? If Selena has to deal with Mom all on her own? If my family loses another brother…

Maybe it'd be a good thing. It wouldn't be suicide, so it'd break the family curse. I'm too selfish to willingly die to save my family, but if it's forced upon me, I'll go down as the hero who ended the infamous Sauder curse, right?

"Get your shit together," Riot snaps at me, pulling on my wrist until I sink down beneath the glass windows of the room we're in. It's an empty meeting room, and right outside the door is the elevator bank that'll lead to the lab we need. "Stop thinking."

"I'm not." I pull my pack off my back.

"You are. Remi and Selena will be fine. Wanna know why?" He kneels in front of me, pulling shit from his own bag. "Because we're getting out of this fucking place, got it? I don't give a shit what it takes, Reaper Corp won't beat us."

They might…

"I'll make ya a deal," Riot says as he pulls on a pair of black gloves, reminding me to do the same. "If we both make it out of here alive, I'll give you something you want."

"The fuck do you know about what I want?" I snap, watching him slip a vial of something into his pants pocket. "I have everything I want."

"Almost," he grins, pocketing devices. "You want me to hold your hand like I held that little girl's hand."

My whole face flushes and I shove against his chest, needing him out of my space while insecurity eats me alive. "You're fucked." But he's not wrong, and I hate that he's not wrong. I hate that he caught me looking, watching, baffled by the simplicity of hand-holding that comes with no danger and no deception. No one has ever held my hand, and I don't understand why I want it. It's a pointless gesture that does nothing but confuse, and I refuse to accept that it means something to me. "I thought our deal was about curses and death chasing?"

He simply grins, and I resent him for masking it in something innocently challenging. "It was."

"It still is."

"Okay," he says like he's coddling me. "But plans can change. Hurry up and put the contacts in."

I set my gloves on my lap and use the small mirror he's holding to place a pair of blue contacts in my eyes. They burn, making my eyes water until I blink enough that they settle in. They're only a back-up plan if Glitch can't get me through doors with retinal scanners. I'm going to be a ghost tonight, but there are cameras that will register my body, so I need to look like I fit in. I throw on a blazer to go with my black pants, appearing more business casual than I ever have before.

"Mmm," Riot hums, eye-fucking me in his utility outfit that looks so damn good on him it only makes me begrudge him more. Since when does he appeal to me so intensely? He's always been... but now he's...

"Two minutes," I remind him, putting the gloves on and

making sure all my weapons are in place. "We ride up to the seventeenth floor, and as soon as those doors open, you gotta put on a show so I can walk down the hall unseen."

"Figures you'd need me to put on a show to make your job easier," he mocks, smirking. "You got it."

Call me sweetheart.

The one-minute alarm beeps, and we both stand, hiding behind the door we'll need to open quickly and quietly to enter the elevator across the hall. Glitch has control of them, and he'll open the doors for us as soon as the guard rotation switches.

"Ready?" Ransom asks.

"Set," Riot says.

"Go," I whisper.

But before I can pull the door open, Riot spins me to face him, lightly grasps my chin, and presses his lips to mine. Simple, quick, entirely jarring, and... overwhelming because it feels so wanted. His lips move against mine, igniting my insides with something sweet and powerful. I'm breathing harder than I want to be when he pulls back, licking his lips.

"The fuck was that for?"

His fingers trace my jaw before falling away, the black eye I gave him staring at me. "Just in case it's my last chance," he says. Then he changes into someone new right before my eyes, getting into character for the role he's about to play.

"Move!" Ransom and Glitch both shout in our ears.

"You got this, sweetheart."

Sweetheart.

He pulls open the door and, rejuvenated, we dart

straight into the elevator, the doors closing a split second before the guard comes back.

GHOST

23

I BLINK, SWEETHEART. YOU WIN

I DON'T KNOW if he's smug enough to have kissed me as a distraction or if he simply did it because he wanted to, but either way, it's distracting me. Almost in a good way. Because instead of worrying about what I'm doing, I'm feeling the way my lips tingle and my neck flushes as I slip down the hallway unnoticed. He's causing a ruckus with the guards, using his charm to manipulate their reaction to him, and I'm becoming a ghost who blushes.

Blushes!

Fucking bullshit if you ask me. My mind is on that simple kiss as I use a stolen security card to enter labs, and it's still on that kiss when I slip past three guards and a medical professional to enter the secure area I need to be in. My tongue roams over my bottom lip as I bend down to let the sensor scan my contacts, and I taste something that isn't *me* as the red light turns green and beeps me into the research office.

It's Riot. Killian is on my lips and against my tastebuds,

but mostly, he's in my head. Normally, he fucks with my mind in a way that agitates me, but tonight, it's calming. I settle into the feeling instead of fighting it, slipping into a shadowed corner of the room as the door beeps open again.

"Fucking focus, Ghost," Ransom says in my ear. "There are only two of them. No one else in the hallway."

Director says I'm not allowed to kill them, but...

Quietly, I pull a syringe from my blazer jacket, grab the first woman, and stick it in her neck. I set her down quietly, stepping over her body as the second syringe slips into position between my thumb and fingers.

He kissed me. Softly... Just in case it was his last chance. The fuck?

"I can't believe they're letting us in this file," says the second one as she opens something on the computer. "We don't even have this security clearance, but something must be coming if they're granting us access. The hell is Project Doom?"

I pause behind her. Right behind her. Not making a sound and not emitting energy enough for even the hairs on her arms to stand at attention. Project Doom? Moros is the word for the personification of impending doom, so my interest is piqued.

"Claire?"

When she spins, I cover her mouth, prick her with the needle, and plunge the cool liquid into her neck before her eyes see me. Just in case she wakes up from this, I don't want her knowing my face.

"Director said no deaths," Ransom says, not in a chiding way.

"They aren't dead."

"Yet," Glitch adds. "Plug in to that computer before the screen locks. I'll get whatever I can from it while you look for the key. It'll be a program or device somewhere near a chip reader. Look for it."

I plug in the first device I was sent with, letting Glitch hack into the computer from back in Moros. Glancing around the room, I'm met with so many different kinds of technology that I barely know what to do with any of it. Glitch had to send me a video on how to plug the devices into the right holes. Moros isn't like this. We're caught in the past, reliant on word of mouth and paper products rather than technology, except for the select few people who know their way around it. Director, Facts, and Glitch being three of those people.

"Riot?" I ask as I search.

"His big mouth is still running," Ransom says.

"Show me footage of the room so I can help you locate the right machine," Glitch says. "Hurry up. Riot's going to need to get out of there soon."

I click on the camera and slowly spin around the room until Glitch tells me where to go. With the second device inserted, a screen pops up that says I'm denied.

"Fuck," Glitch mutters. "This is gonna take me a bit to crack."

While he cracks the passcode, I aim the camera away and search the computer next to it. I type in the file number Axel gave us, download it to a USB, and shove it in my pocket while Glitch and Ransom are busy. That creepy doctor owes me for this, and I'll definitely collect.

"Riot?" I ask again, lips still warm.

"Listen in," Ransom says.

I turn on my audio for Riot and listen to him argue about human rights with a growing number of people. He's in a full-blown debate about being a Reaper City resident and wanting to know more about what their research entails, claiming that, as a resident, he has a right to know what goes on in his city. Says it'll make him feel safer. Weirdly, some people in the background are agreeing with him, which pumps his ego so hard that he goes off on a whole new tangent.

Yeah, he's fine. I smile to myself.

I wonder if he's been manipulating me, and I've been too stupid to notice? I've been caught up in our bargain and enjoying the thrill of it, but suddenly he's kissing me and I'm hopping into bed with him for safety and security, and I don't fucking know where shit went so wrong. How did taunting a curse turn into this, and why the hell aren't I more pissed off about it?

Psych says I'm a narcissist, or that I have narcissistic traits at the very least. I never really gave a fuck about the diagnosis because it didn't mean anything to me other than being a fancy word for *superiority*. Now I'm all mystified by it. I don't handle humiliation or embarrassment well, and if anyone else tricked me like Riot did, I'd fucking murder them with a justifiable reason. My mind is all warped and mixed up now because I don't want to kill Riot. I want to study him, figure out why the hell he's treating me like this, and then ask him a question I've never asked anyone.

Why me?

I've never been loved in the way other people are loved. I've never been seen, gotten the recognition I deserve, or been prioritized the way I should be. I'm the one with the most skill when it comes to getting the jobs done. Like, fuck, you think any other Vile Boy could be here in the midst of the enemy's lab without getting caught? Fuck no. They need me, so they use me. But maybe Riot needs me, and instead of just using me, he's giving me something in return. Something I didn't know I needed. Something less thrilling than chasing death but more fulfilling because it's honest and terrifying.

Riot looks at me like he knows I'm a mirage, but instead of trying to fix my illusion, he wants to hold my pieces together so I don't have to try so hard. Why? Why the fuck would he want that?

"Ghost." Glitch's voice refocuses my attention. "I'm in. I've got the keycode, but I'm gonna download as much as I can in the next ninety seconds. This is going to trigger alarms, so be ready to leave. Riot, you hear me?"

Riot doesn't verbally answer since he's in the middle of a monologue, but he must signal them because they confirm it to me. Our exit strategy is the riskiest part of the job because we have no idea what their response time is once we're detected in their computers. I look at the women on the floor, not bothering to check if they're alive or dead.

"Get the devices and get out. We got what we need, but I need those in our hands, Ghost. Don't ditch them."

I nod and grab them from the computers, shoving them into the inside pocket of my blazer. Time to get Riot and get the hell out of here. Without getting caught. Without getting caught *with these devices on me.*

"Hall is clear," Glitch tells me. "Go now."

Silently, I leave the research lab and turn left, heading

down the corridor with soundless steps and fluid motions. My heart thunders in my chest, a mix of adrenaline and premature hope that'll get me killed if I don't staunch it. Through one door and out another, I steady my steps and listen to staff chat and machines beep. The overhead comm system calls for Dr. Thali, and my ears split with the abruptness of it.

Exhaling slowly, I round the final corner, the sound of Riot's voice and his many enthusiastic listeners finally greeting me. He's here, alive, distracting the staff and causing just enough of a scene to keep the guards where they are. I swallow that bit of hope and replace it with determination, grounding myself in my self-confidence.

"Coming," I tell Riot through the earpiece. "Right around the corner. Be ready to move."

Kneeling behind an unmonitored security desk, I let him rile the crowd just enough to make the noise needed to cover the sound of my small electric screwdriver. One, two, three, and four screws come off the grate that leads into the ventilation system under the desk, disappearing into my pocket.

"I'm here. Vent cover is off."

Riot smiles at his audience. "As much as I love the sound of my own voice, it's time I—"

An overhead alarm sounds, followed by, "Security breach. Main console. Seventeenth floor, west wing. Lockdown initiated."

Fuck. *Fuck!*

I stand from behind the desk, peering around the corner at Riot as guards swarm and green lights on doors turn red. The crowd he had entertained is panicked now, but not as panicked as I am.

"Riot!" I whisper-shout through the mic. "Get the fuck over here. Now!"

I duck when security comes around the corner, grabbing at members of the gathered crowd. Most of them are staff with badges and reasons to be in the building. All except Riot.

"Riot!"

He looks over at me, his grey eyes as stormy as they've always been. He's telling me something I don't want to hear, so I fucking tune him out and demand him with my eyes. Goddammit, Riot, if you've ever given a single fuck about anything, give it now.

"Let's go. Now. Riot, please."

Panic creeps into my whisper, grating at my throat and burning my eyes. It worsens when three guards step up to him, pulling his hands behind his back.

"Where's your staff identification?"

"In my pocket," he says calmly. "Let my hands go and I'll gladly grab it for you."

"Someone in a black suit jacket and dark grey pants left the main console. Male. Dark blond to light brown hair. Six foot two or three. Suspect is considered armed and dangerous." The guards' radios all echo my description.

We fucking planned for this! But he's not here. We're not side by side, ready to dip into the ventilation system for our quickest escape. My heart picks up its pace, barking in my chest while my mind whirls through our plans, merging every strategy together to get him out of this mess.

"Don't," Glitch says in my ear, but I ignore him.

I crawl around the desk, ready to take Riot out of here by force. We're outnumbered and overpowered, but like hell

I'm leaving him here while I run to safety—the selfish part of me would, but my ego can't handle leaving my partner behind.

Peeking around the side of the desk, I see him with his hands behind his back, guards all around him and more coming. He looks at me again, eyes full of confessions and a grin fighting its way through his fear. But Killian Hallows is too cocky to admit to fear, let alone show it, so he smiles at me fully, and in my ear, I hear his voice.

"I'll hold your hand when you meet me in Hell, sweetheart. Race ya there." He smiles at me as I start to stand, but he ruins it by shouting, "Fuck Reaper Corp! I've got a bomb!"

I rush out, but Glitch, Ransom, and Director are in my ear. "Don't! If you go after him, you're both dead and Reaper Corp will know for sure it was us. Get out of there, Ghost. Now. That's a fucking order."

I grit my teeth, my brain warring with my heart, and my morals coming to life in a way they never have before. Anger is the easiest way to feel my feelings, so I allow rage to consume me, filling me with power and adrenaline that convinces me I can still get us out of this. I fucking refuse to let him sacrifice himself for me. Not a fucking chance. He doesn't get that right, and he sure as fuck doesn't have the right to put his death on my conscience.

My jaw aches and my eyes sting, refusing to look away from him. He's grabbed from all directions, thrown to the ground and pinned down. When multiple guns point at his head, I barely contain myself from stepping out of cover.

"Ghost!" Director yells at me. "Go!"

"I can't fucking leave him!"

"You can," Riot says. "Tell Krypt—"

"Fuck you, Riot. Fight harder. We can get out of this." I watch him as he's cuffed and restrained, knowing it'll only be a few seconds before his comms are discovered and ripped out. "Please, Killian."

He laughs, struggling to look backwards at me. "I blink, sweetheart. You win. Now go."

"Killian!"

His earpiece is taken out, and he's forced to his feet, my anger building as I track every man who touches him, vowing their death by my hands.

"Ghost, you have to move. Right fucking now," Ransom shouts. "Now. Think of Remi and Selena. Get moving before they lock every other floor down."

"I can't."

"You can."

"No." I'm stuck, rooted to the damn floor behind a desk, watching Riot's body be dragged down the hall as he laughs ominously for my benefit. "No. I'm not leaving without him. They'll kill him."

"Then get out of there so we can make a plan before they do," Ransom says. "I fucking promise you, Ghost. We will go back for him. I need you to trust me."

I silently scream in a fit of rage. Ransom said the same thing to Krypt the night Remi took the suicide pill. He asked Krypt to trust him, and now I'm the one who needs to put my faith in him. I loathe myself for it, but I slip into the vent, pull the grate against the opening, and force myself not to feel a single fucking thing but redemption as I escape Reaper City with the stolen devices.

But not my partner.

My cracks have never been split so wide open. My puzzle pieces no longer fit together to create one perfect picture.

I'm a different man now. A truly vile one. Because Killian somehow became mine, and I'm not fucking done with him.

GHOST

24

CLOSE TO THE CURSE

MY EYES HAVE NOT LEFT the hotel room window since the moment I walked through the door. I haven't slept, taken a piss, or eaten because there's something inside me that won't allow me to move from this spot until I get him back.

It might be unfamiliar to me because it's failure. It might be resentment that he gave himself up for me when I never wanted him to. It might be pain because it fucking hurts that he's gone. It might be fear because I don't know if he's still alive. Whatever it is, it blocks everything else, turning me into a single-minded missile, aimed where I want to be but with no lit fuse to take me there.

But the most fucked up part is that this is the closest I've ever come to succumbing to my family curse. Never, not even once, has suicide crossed my mind with such ferocity. Killian said he'd hold my hand in Hell when I got there, and for the first time, I'm planning my way to Death's door with the intention of breaking in. If he's there, I don't want to slam the door in her face. I want to step over the threshold and find him so I can kill him all over again for getting us into this mess.

Because I don't understand how this happened to me! I don't fall for people, and I sure as fuck don't get attached. I'm loyal to my siblings, my town, and my Vile Boys, but this is something beyond that. I never considered following my two brothers or my dad to the afterlife, and one invitation from Killian has me avoiding the dagger in my pocket just in case the temptation is too strong.

Truthfully, I don't know what it is I feel for him. It's not love. It's not anything with a name. It just *is*. It's this thing that happened over the course of a bunch of ruthless months and challenges with no clear winner. Somehow, he got what he wanted, and I got what I wanted, and neither of us ever gave up any power for it. It's a dynamic of intensity that blends us together, his masks and my cracks, pulling and pushing until our bits meld into something that brought us both up short because we never expected to feel anything from it. Nothing beyond a need to win and out-maneuver one another, a competitive edge that became a need for more.

Now I'm all fucked up because thinking about going back to Moros without him isn't sitting well in my head. I can't do it. I don't know why I can't do it, but I can't. I won't. Remi and Selena will have to accept it and move on, because if Riot is dead, I'll burn Reaper City to the ground and let the fire guide me to Hell.

The two devices I smuggled out are on the floor; I refuse to look at them because they tricked me. They became more important than Riot in the moment, and I'll never forgive myself for being so easily deceived. I don't look at the bed we slept in together, back-to-back for safety, showing trust when we never have before. I don't look at anything other than the city in the distance, as if I can peer through the lights and the buildings to see him there, laughing in the face of his captors.

He has to be laughing. *He better be fucking laughing.*

With a knock and a beep, the hotel room door opens, and Ransom and Krypt announce themselves when I don't turn around. Krypt's hands land on my shoulders, touching me when he hates touch. He forces my face away from the window, looking at me with all his monsters on display. For the first time, my eyes water, blinking away dryness and brokenness and unfamiliar guilt.

His hands press on my jaw, thumbs on my cheeks and fingers at my nape. "We're getting him," is all he says.

"Yes," is all I say.

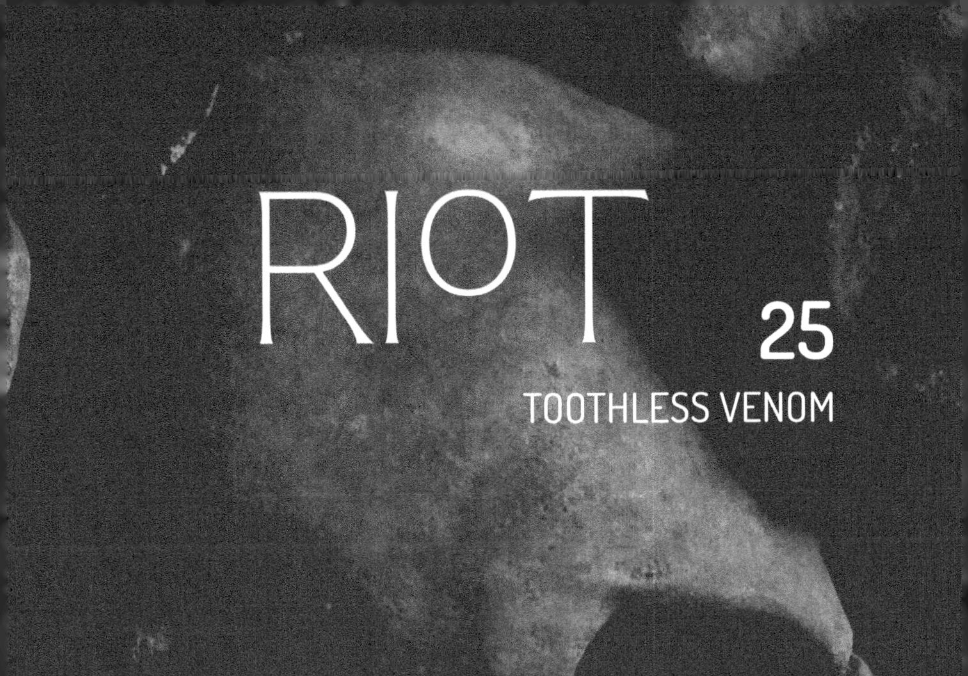

RIOT

25

TOOTHLESS VENOM

MY MIND IS NOT Krypt's. It's not a vault, impenetrable and fortified. It's weak, full of insecurities and buttons that are easily pushed when my authority is questioned. It's a burning pit of shame. Knowing I'm here, captured and useless, is the biggest letdown of my life. What will the boys think? What will Director say? *I told you so.* I can almost hear him laughing at me.

But Soren got out. So I smile to myself, knowing I'll at least be his hero. He'll fucking remember me now, long after I'm dead, eternally suffering through his gratitude for my sacrifice. The thought makes me smile wider, knowing he'll hate me for it as much as he'll thank me for it. *Well, fuck you, sweetheart. If I can't be there to taunt you in the flesh, let my actions taunt you forever.*

"Why get it?" the man who has been with me since yesterday asks, nodding at my naked body. "A tattoo that signifies exactly who you are. Seems stupid to me."

I won't go out silently. I'm not a ghost, and I really do love the sound of my own voice, so as long as I have the wherewithal to use it, I will. "You'd get it if you knew what it was like to be a part of something. You fucks are all just brainwashed, inbred fools. Following the big guy's lead just because he told ya to. Fucking rats in a lab, man."

The back of his hand cracks across my face. It stings like a bitch, but I laugh harder, spitting blood at his feet. "Sore spot?" I ask, licking my bloody lips, wishing I could still taste Soren there. "It's alright. You can admit it to me. I won't tell anyone."

I'm naked, hanging from a chain attached to the ceiling. My arms are above my head, long gone numb, and my toes are barely touching the ground. It's not as fun to hang when Soren isn't around to be beautiful while dying. They've asked and asked questions, but I've managed to keep my replies sarcastic and witty despite how dark my mind is turning. The torture methods will intensify soon, so I might as well have my fun while I still can.

"Riot," he reads my name from the base of my tattoo, walking a circle around my body. "You pick it because it sounded cool?"

"Earned it because of who I fucking am." I grin wide. "Imma call you Puppy."

"Why?" he indulges me.

"Because you pace around in a damn circle like a dog trying to find a comfy position to sleep." I cough, spitting more blood. "We getting on with this, or do you just like staring at me naked?"

His smile is almost as cocky as mine, far less charming, though. "Very well." He releases the chain holding me up, giving me enough slack to stand properly. My ankles haven't held my weight for the better part of a day, so they give out as soon as I plant my feet on the ground. The man catches me, sliding a wooden chair behind me and pushing me to sit on it. Breathing a little harder, I shake my head to relieve the dizzy spell, trying not to show how badly my arms hurt as the blood rushes through them.

"Ever been tortured before?" he asks as a second man wheels in a trolley of goodies. "Something tells me you have."

I have in training, but I'm still scared. I slap a smile on my face and admire all his tools. "Oh, that one looks fun. What's it do?"

He picks up a pair of long tongs, snapping them in front of my face. "Just a basic pair of surgical tongs. They're usually used up the nose, down the throat, or, in your case, on the teeth."

Fucking awesome. Just what I need, a few dental extractions. This'll be fun. "Don't fuck up my face, man. It's my panty dropper."

"I'm sure it is." He nods, snapping the tongs again. "Who were you working with?"

"Not a very good team player. I work alone."

"Where is your partner?"

"My fuck buddy, you mean? Probably back home, fucking someone else." The thought brings a bit of jealousy to my mind, fortifying some of my strength.

"Your work partner. Where is the blond man in the blazer?"

Hopefully back in Moros resenting me for saving him. "I'd never work with a guy in a blazer."

"Why are you in our city? What did you come here for?"

"Took the tour. Nice place ya have here if dictatorship and a bunch of sheep are your thing. Though, I gotta say, not near enough nightclubs."

"Or cemeteries," he adds, proving he knows all about Moros.

"Exactly." I wink at him. "Cemeteries are fun."

From behind, my head is strapped to the back of the tall chair, and I'm so out of it that I didn't even realize someone else was here. A second later, as I'm struggling, a device enters my mouth, and I scream through the pain when it's cranked open, forcing my mouth wide.

"These are fun, too," he says, snapping the tongs one more time.

I'm pinned back as they enter my mouth. I'm afraid. I like pain, but not this kind of pain. I don't want him to see my fear, so I close my eyes and breathe through my nose, reminding myself that it's worth it. Soren got out. Soren got out. Soren got out. I'm the hero of his life. That's all I need to know.

"We'll start with the back ones. They bleed the most."

I shake all over when the tongs scrape against my molars, and I hyperventilate as anticipation builds. Squeezing my eyes closed, I recall the way it felt to kiss Soren yesterday. Timid and soft and vulnerable, I just had to fucking kiss him one last time, and I've never been so grateful that I gave in to my impulse. He kissed me back so hesitantly, so sweetly, I never thought him capable of it.

I scream and feel my eyes roll back, head buzzing and dizzy when he yanks a tooth out. Blood fills my mouth and drips down my throat, my eyes doing the same down my cheeks. Breathing hurts, the air too much for my exposed nerves, and my body wobbles on the chair, light-headedness abrupt and overwhelming. When he removes the device keeping my mouth open, my jaw already aches as it closes.

I force myself to laugh, despite how weak and pathetic it comes out. "Thanks. Been having trouble with that tooth." My words are slurred and garbled by blood and pain, but they're audible, and that's all that matters.

"You're welcome," he says calmly, setting down the tongs. His smile is as pretty as Axel's, but his face is nowhere near as ethereal and defined. He's a rugged man with a soft voice, deceptive because of how he looks and sounds. His timbre doesn't match his rigidity, and his smile doesn't match his morals. Maybe we have that in common. "Anything else giving you trouble, Riot?" he asks. "I'm more than willing to play doctor."

Blood floods down my chin when the strap releases and my head falls forward, the dizziness slowly fading. "Fit as a fiddle."

"Hmm," he muses, pulling up a second chair to sit in front of me. "What did you steal?"

"My pockets were empty, weren't they?"

"Indeed. Who were you working with?"

"Lone wolf."

"Do you have a diagnosis?" he asks instead.

"ASPD, I'm told, but doesn't always fit now, does it?" I swallow blood and wince when I press my tongue to the hollow in my mouth.

"How so? Your superiority is showing even now, despite how inferior you currently are."

My superiority will always show because that's who I am, but I did something selfless when I'm notoriously selfish.

Sure, I did it to have something to hold over Soren for the rest of his life, but I still did it. Psych told me that I'm manipulative because I have a gnawing need to always get my way, no matter the consequences or morality of it, but when I took the fall to let Soren escape, it didn't feel manipulative. It felt right, and I've never had a good sense of right and wrong.

"I'm still superior," I tell him through ragged breaths. "You think you're gonna get something out of me, but all it'll accomplish is wasted time. Which means I'll still win, even if you kill me. Might as well get it out of the way now so you can go back to your suburban lifestyle under your Reaper Corp rule. Fucking pathetic, all of you. You know you have no power in this place, right?"

"Power comes from where we wield it," he says. "And I'm currently wielding it over you, so I do, in fact, have power."

When I clench my jaw, my mouth sings out in pain. "Good luck holding onto it." This is all just a new game. One where he'll try to get me to crack, and I'll win by resisting him. I might not have my brother's vault-like mind, but I do have a god complex that refuses to let another man get the better of me. If I can live through torture, it'll give me one more thing to brag about.

Sounds almost perfect.

NOT SO PERFECT ANYMORE.

I'm down three more teeth, lost a few fingernails, and

my lungs gurgle every time I try to use them, full of water that hurts to cough up. My eyes don't see much anymore, and my bodily functions are no longer under my control. But the worst part is my mind.

It's gone.

Not because he's broken it, but because he poisoned it. Somewhere between the loss of the third tooth and the slices all over my chest and back, he placed something on my tongue. The taste of it barely registered through all the blood, but it didn't take long for my mind to wander off, hallucinating a whole world that scares the fuck out of me. The music is so loud and the lights are so bright that I can't even escape into my mind, and my eyes are being pried open by a device I already ripped out once and regretted immediately.

"How's the zoo?" Leigh, the girl from the plane, asks.

Her tutu is black now, but she's wearing rainbow unicorn ears and a horn, king cobras tattooed all over her tiny body. Her eyes are three times as big as they were the first time I saw her, but she's still the same curious kid.

"I think I'm one of the animals," I tell her.

"Which one? A velociraptor?"

This isn't a dinosaur zoo, but I wish it was. At least a raptor would kill me faster. "An ostrich. Head's all buried in the sand."

"Well, pull it out," Leigh says. "He needs you to be alive when he gets here."

"Who?"

"Your boyfriend. He wants to hold your hand." Her giant eyes turn speculative, like she's listening to something I can't hear. "And kill you."

"He's not coming," I tell her while something burns behind me. On me? The pain registers, but my mind never rights itself. I think my back is on fire. "He got out."

Leigh laughs really hard. Almost like Soren laughs when he's on the brink of death, except her laugh is higher-pitched and twinkly.

"What did he steal?"

I tune that voice out and watch Leigh's cobra tattoos slither up her arms and shoulders. "Told you I'm goth."

"Yeah."

"Who were you working with?"

I wince at the man's voice, knowing it doesn't belong in my colourful world with the goth girl.

"He is coming," she tells me, her voice visual as sound-waves. "And he's angry. Like that scared kind of angry that makes him look like poison."

Poison. A thought finally registers, a failsafe I actually put into place. How long has it been since I dropped that gifted vial into the water system? The Harpy has ideas, and she wanted to test them before implementing them in Moros. I smile, clearly remembering Menace slipping me the vial before we boarded the plane to Reaper City. At least I did something right.

I straighten in my... midair. There is no chair anymore. No floor or sky or walls either. Just empty space with sound-waves in colourful echoes and a goth girl covered in tattoos. "I'm the king cobra," I tell her instead. "My bite can kill."

"I know," she says, looking at me like she knows what I did and is gleeful about it. "But be careful. Your hair is pretty, but it's not king cobra pretty, so they can still chop off your head. Your poisonous bite might kill you instead."

I frown, not liking that she doesn't think my hair is as pretty as the cobra's crown. I'm better looking than a fucking cobra.

"Tell me what he took, or you'll no longer be Vile House!" The man's words are punctuated by more burning, a scorching heat eating at my back.

"I got the tattoos," Leigh says, showing me. "But yours are disappearing."

"No," I mutter, infuriated in my colourful world. My Vile House tat? Gone? Burned off? "No!"

"Tell me what he stole, and I'll let you keep the tattoo!" he shouts right in front of my face. But I can't see him. All I see is Leigh as she twirls, dancing with cobras and unicorn horns.

"Lie," Leigh says, giggling. "Lie. Lie. Lie! Buy time."

"Your breeding program records," my mouth says, even though Leigh's lips are the ones moving.

There's a pause in time. Pain goes away and my head clears, but nothing clear comes of it. Leigh waves at me like she's going somewhere, and I reach out to stop her.

"Please, don't go. Stay."

"I don't like the zoo. Too many animals in cages. You need to break out."

"I'm trying! Help me!"

"He'll help you. The scared angry one. He's almost here."

"Leigh?"

"Ostrich?"

"Show me your purple tutu. Let me see it one more time. My brother..."

Her tutu turns the purple of Krypt's mask, and with the

change comes clarity. Calmness. A visual reminder of what I have to live for. I might be selfish, egotistical, and cruel, but Krypt is an exception to all my instincts. Unfortunately, the scared, angry one is, too.

"Bite!" Leigh shouts at me. "Your venom is working!" She vanishes into the nothingness, and with her disappearance, the brightly lit room with blaring jazz music comes back.

"Breeding program records? Why?"

His hard face and pretty smile are right in front of my swollen, pried-open eyes, demanding answers to lies. Somewhere deep inside me, there remains a well of pure entitlement. I knew it never went anywhere, but I couldn't fucking find it. Now I smile because of it. Toothless and mostly dead, I show him my bloody remaining teeth and laugh in his fucking face.

"My venom is running through your city now, asshole. Game fucking on."

He leans back. "What? What venom."

I hiss through the gaps in my teeth, letting my hair go wild, real king cobra style. Thanks, Leigh.

GHOST

26

ICE COLD MURDER HIGH

I DON'T HAVE time for this. Every minute we waste arguing is a minute Killian could die. I don't give a fuck if I get caught so long as I get in there to see him alive.

"Think about it," Ransom says, stepping between me and Krypt. "He's got the mind for this. Let Krypt get caught to be thrown in with Riot. You're the only one of us who can move around their compound undetected. We need you out here, Ghost."

Logically, I know that, but I'm not a very logical guy right now. I'm trying to hide it because I don't want them knowing there's something going on, but I fucking suck at hiding it because I'm pissed off and scared about it.

"I'm going in there. I don't give a fuck what you two do." I shove Ransom and butt my chest up to Krypt's. "He's my responsibility."

"He's my brother."

"I'm the one who left him in there, so I'm the one getting him out!"

"Yeah," Krypt snorts. "Wouldn't fucking be in there if it weren't for you."

"He blew his own cover!"

"Boys," Ransom says again. "Shut up and listen." He shoves us apart and points at the wall where the screen is being cast.

Glitch clears his throat through the speaker while I simmer in a mix of guilt, worry, and honest-to-god fear. I don't even know which part is scaring me the most, but not knowing makes it more intense and I need to use it to my advantage. Killian has already been in there for twenty-four hours, and the longer we wait, the less our chances are of getting him out alive.

"He'll be here." A part of the map lights up.

"If they haven't killed him already," I snap.

"He's alive," Director says. "They'll know he's from Moros, and they'll be interrogating him. Especially because they still don't know what was taken from their labs. Riot can withstand torture."

Yeah, but for how long? What if he took his suicide pill and really does plan to meet me in Hell?

"Hello," Facts says through the line. "We have audio and video to these parts of the compound. Twenty-three hours ago, we watched him being dragged through these doors. We've been monitoring the compound ever since, and he hasn't come back out. He's in there."

"Alive," Krypt says.

"Right," says Glitch. "So, our best bet is to create a diversion while Ghost goes in undetected. It means one of you has to get captured, and the other two need to carry out the rescue. Ghost, don't cut me off," Glitch stops me when I start to speak. I throw the lamp across the room, pacing. "You know you're the only one who can do this, so stop fucking fighting it. You want him back? This is how."

"Think about it," I tell them. "It's me on their security cameras, so they're already looking for me. If they capture me and throw me in some cell, they'll stop torturing Riot and stop the lockdown, making it easier for us to get out."

"Ghost, you're—"

"Hello. Actually, that's not a bad idea," Facts cuts in. "If they think they have both of you, they'll drop their guards, leaving more room for Ransom and Krypt to get in and out."

I throw my arms wide. "Fucking *thank you*. Finally. Can we go now?"

"No. We have no masks and no power here. We need your stealth outside of a cell," Ransom tells me. "If you get captured, we're all fucked."

To finally get my recognition at a time like this is torture in its own form. Finally, they realize how essential to the team I am, but it's coming at a time when I don't want my skills to be the deciding factor. I want in that fucking cell with Riot to kill his tormentor and get him the hell out of there so he can follow through on his deal to hold my hand. Like fuck I'm gonna let that bitchy little girl be the only one to experience the feeling of his hand in hers. Fuck her, fuck him, fuck Vile House, and fuck Reaper Corp. That asshole is mine, and if I don't get him back, the goddamn world is gonna burn anyway, so fuck it all.

"I'm sick of arguing about this. Fuck it! Tell me where the hell to go and let's fucking go. We're wasting time."

Ransom nods, but Facts speaks. "Statistically, torture victims are killed between forty-eight hours and seventy-two hours after capture, either by their tormentor or from sustained injuries. That gives us less than twenty-four hours to plan and complete our rescue."

My teeth chatter and my jigsaw scatters even more. I try so hard to steady my breathing that I start hyperventilating. Krypt notices but doesn't call me out on it while we develop a new plan. Yeah, I threatened to rape his brother, and here I am, panicking over the guy like he means something to me. I'm not a person who struggles with a guilty conscience, but if this is the way Riot goes out, sacrificing himself for me like some noble asshole, I'll kill myself just so I don't have to live with the shame of it.

BENEATH THE SECURE compound with Ransom and Krypt, I shake my limbs out, mentally and physically preparing to be silent and stealthy. To be the Ghost of Reaper City.

"What's happening?" Krypt asks me while Ransom talks to Glitch and Facts. "Why do you suddenly give a fuck about him?"

"I don't." I pace. "Just don't want the stain on my record."

"What fucking record, Ghost?" Krypt grabs my wrist and hauls me forward. "Your conscience?"

"What conscience?" I rip my wrist free. "Fuck off and

let me focus. If you shit the bed on this mission, Remi'll go back to being suicidal."

Krypt snarls under his breath. "And if Riot dies on this mission, so will you."

I glare at him, unafraid of his monsters. "Fuck you."

"Fuck you back. You care."

"About the job!"

"About Kill."

I shake my head, all the death games mingling with the last-chance kiss and the promise of a held hand. "He's Riot. Not Kill. Not Killian. This is a Vile House job, and I'm not gonna fucking fail it. So piss off and let me focus." Because he might already be dead, and I'm trying way too hard not to believe that. "And be fucking careful, Krypt. I can't deal with Remi like you can."

He grunts at me, and with that, I nod at Ransom and leave the utility room through yet another vent, this one a service shaft that runs alongside the elevator. It should take me eleven minutes to climb down to the floor Riot is being kept on, and from there, another seven to fifteen to get into position in the hallway we believe his room is attached to. That's eighteen to twenty-six minutes of thinking I don't want to endure.

The 'what if' questions have never been my thing. I don't care enough about anything to worry about multiple outcomes. Even when Remi was struggling with the curse, I never questioned what I was gonna do about it. I didn't ask a million 'what if' questions then, so I hate that I am now.

Because what if Killian is dead? What if he's damaged beyond repair? What if that kiss really was the last chance?

And what if that little bitch is the only one who ever holds his hand?

The service shaft has a ladder, and as I descend, I try to decide if I have any regrets. Remi, I guess. If me and Krypt both die here, he'll join us in death by choice. Selena is stronger, and she'll work her way through the ranks of Vile House with my brothers at her side. But when it comes to Riot... Killian, fuck, I might have some regrets.

Like not pushing him as hard as he pushed me. For letting him tempt a curse with me instead of appreciating him for doing it. For loving the harshness so much that I forgot to ask for the softer side of things.

For wanting him to kiss me just like *that* again. For being too cowardly to admit it, too broken to know I wanted it, and too stubborn to see it as anything but weakness. Somewhere along the course of my life, I started viewing gentleness as a weakness. Moros is a ruthless place to live, but it isn't unkind to me. No, my faults are entirely my own making because my mind doesn't think like anyone else's, and I started viewing power as invincibility. I mean, I chase a fucking curse just to prove my power, for fuck's sake.

If—*when*—I get the chance again, I won't let it go. We can chase a curse and taunt death, but in those moments in between, the ones that are more terrifying than the dangerous thrills we seek, I want something else. Something exposed and pure. Because Killian Hallows is the only person I know who can see me as powerful even while vulnerable.

"It's two floors down, Ghost," Glitch tells me, my earpiece coming to life. "Don't leave the shaft until I signal."

Two floors between us. The 'what if' questions swirling

in my mind take a back seat, letting sheer determination and a thirst for blood lead the way. I'm loaded down with throwing knives, daggers, and even a gun that I hope not to use. Not a single fucking thing is going to get in my way, and if it tries, it'll meet the coldest parts of me, a cursed man with a purpose.

Pausing outside the hatch to the floor I need to be on, I settle my breathing while I wait for Ransom and Krypt to get into position at the main security checkpoint. This is it, my defining moment. The one where I refuse to let anyone else be my hero and instead take the hero role for myself. The stakes are higher than ever before, and if that bastard isn't alive when I get to his room, something inside me will break. I'm a well-crafted mirage, a master illusionist, and a perfectly presented puzzle, but I know something about my presentation is about to change.

Because I have what it takes to rescue him, but does he have what it takes to survive this long?

"Everyone in position. Hall is clear. Ghost, you are good to move. Signal your location when you find his room. All clear?"

"Clear," I say, climbing through the hatch while Ransom and Krypt both call their status. If Krypt does his job right, he'll get caught and thrown in with his brother as a bargaining chip, and Ransom and I will be the escape plan while they're busy using Riot's brother against him.

The underground bunker hallway is brightly lit but empty, lined with plexiglass windows that spotlight the rooms and the people inside them. Quickly and quietly, I peer into each window, finding men and women who aren't Riot. Most of them are bloody or battered, some of them insane and snapped away from their minds, and all of them are awake and staring back at me. I don't give a fuck about any of them. Barely even a spare glance, only long enough to confirm they aren't Riot.

When I pass the second to last window, I look inside to see a man being tortured by a Reaper Corp member. A blow torch blazes, and the man screams so loud it rattles the plexiglass. I move on, hoping to fucking hell he's in the last room. If some fucker has a blowtorch against Riot's skin, I'll break protocol and find a way in before Krypt gets a chance to get caught.

Before I get there, the door at the end of the hall beeps, and I only have a split second to duck behind a medical cart in the hallway. A lone woman walks through, weirdly professional looking considering we're in a torture chamber. She's on the phone, dressed in a lab coat, looking at a tablet as she walks past me. When she's just past, I snatch her ID card, move around the cart, and duck on the other side. Hopefully Glitch is in control of the security cameras for now.

"He's still in Moros. Reporting back every three days," she says to whoever is on the phone. "Their gang is under new leadership."

The Misfits? Does Lock have a mole in his midst?

"We're keeping him in place. He had to kill Reaper members the night of the raid, but it gained him loyalty and respect, so it was a worthy—"

Whatever else she's about to say is halted when she tries to leave the hall, realizing she doesn't have a keycard. *Fuck.* As she's checking her pockets, I sneak up behind her, grab both sides of her head, and snap her neck. The blood rush starts as I drag her to the nearest door, using her card to open it. I shove her into the prisoner's room, press end on her phone call, and close the door with a soft click. Because I'm me, I don't spare a second thought for what that prisoner will do to her.

"Lockdown the hall," I tell Glitch.

"I can't yet. You have to confirm his location first or you'll be trapped there."

Slinking across the hall in a crouch, I peek into the last window. What I see shatters the remnants of my glass illusion and turns me to nothing but ice.

Because Riot is about to die.

Hanging from a chain in the middle of the room, his arms above his head, he smiles at his torturer, a toothless thing full of blood and anguish. I know that's not a smile he's perfected because it shows all his pain, and Riot never willingly shows pain. His one eye doesn't open, and the other is barely a slit, his eyelashes crusted with dried blood and his nostrils freshly trickling. He's naked, every part of him dirty and painted red, and if I'm not mistaken, either his fingertips or fingernails are missing.

The part that scares me the most is the device pressed to his temple. The kind of device that releases a metal bolt that kills instantly when it pierces the brain. The man's finger is on the release, but Riot's pathetic, unhinged smile and the gargling laugh he lets out makes him pause.

"Riot is about to die," I say, eyes on Riot's mouth. "I'm going to break this plan." I tremble in restraint, hastily trying to make a split-second decision. If I use the card to open the door, will that force the man to release the bolt, or will it distract him enough to pause?

"Ghost," Ransom warns, but there isn't much heat behind it.

"Go," Krypt demands. "Do not let him fucking die."

"We're almost there. Break the plan."

When Riot says something that makes the man angry and panicked, I lose my common sense and act on instinct. An instinct to keep him alive.

I open the door.

RIOT

27

LUNG FULL OF POISON

KRYPT AND REMI have a joke about the moment of death. Remi says it's regret that goes through your mind when you're about to die, but not for me. It's vengeance. Because if this asshole is going to nail a bolt through my brain, I'm going to ensure he knows I'm the reason for the many people who are about to die from an illness that'll show up anytime now.

He was stupid enough to bring me down from the LSD trip, and now that my mind is my own again, I'm going to use it until it no longer works. I laugh in his face, the air hurting my mouth and my vision almost entirely gone. One sliver is all I need.

"What could possibly be funny right now?"

My smile feels good. Better than it should. It's my omen, the little thing I leave behind to haunt Reaper Corp. "Anyone sick?" I ask, a new lisp in my voice from my missing teeth.

The device next to my head shifts as his interest is piqued. "Sick how?"

I simply laugh harder. So hard that I throw up from pain and damn near pass out with the effort it takes. Vomit drips down my chin, nothing but spit, blood, and bile, and when he smacks me across the face before grabbing my chin to press the bolt to my head, I choke on my next laugh.

Fuck, I feel like Ghost right now. No wonder he laughs so hard in the face of death. There's nothing more satisfying than pretending you don't give a fuck!

"Sick how?!"

"Drink the water lately?" I ask, tears leaking down my cheeks. "Hospitals full?"

"What'd you do?" he barks at me while I laugh more. "How? You've been in captivity this whole time!"

Yeah, but while Ghost was stealing those devices and the keycodes we came for, I got up to no good before putting on my show. Never thought I'd be sticking around to see the results, but here we are, and I'm not too mad about it. The Harpy is a crazy old bitch, but she cooks up some lethal things in her cabin in Janie's woods, and I was more than happy to test her newest creation when Menace handed it to me before we boarded the plane. Undetectable through security, and tiny enough that the small vial fit in my pocket.

The guy is on his phone, telling someone to investigate it and get back to him, but I can tell he doesn't fully believe me. Which only pisses him off. I understand that. When people get one over on me, it sends me into a rage that's so consuming I can't think straight. So, when he firms up the bolt to my head and finally looks me straight in my one remaining open eye, I know this is it. He isn't going to let me hang around long enough to watch Reaper City reap the benefits of The Harpy.

"Any last words?" he asks like this is a fucking movie.

"See ya in Hell." I smile as wide as my busted jaw will allow. Like fuck I'm closing my only open eye, so I stare right at his, breathing in the last seconds of my life, waiting for that precipice between that Soren is always after. Maybe I'll be able to tell him what it feels like.

I'm barely coherent, but right as the bolt presses to my temple, a commotion outside the room draws his attention, and at the same time, his phone rings again. When I look over, I see *my* omen of death. The one I'm chasing to the afterlife but almost beat him to.

Stalking into the room like the phantom of pure rage, his ice-blue eyes glow at me, bringing back my hallucinations from the other day. Fuck me, has he always been so pretty while lethal? He doesn't spare me another glance. Soren moves in like he commands the air in the room, grabs the man's wrist, and snaps it. The bolt device clangs to the floor, and right in front of me, Soren grabs the man's hair, forces him to his knees, and makes sure I have the best seat in the house to the knife he drags across his throat.

Instead of looking at that, I look up, meeting his eyes. While the man who has been torturing me gurgles and bleeds out, I take stock of reality. Because, admittedly, it takes me a few extra seconds to ensure this is real and not a hallucination from the drugs. Soren is here, killing my enemy, staring at me with an intensity so abrupt my hot skin breaks out in goosebumps, and a few thumps of my heart remind me I'm not dead yet.

Because of him.

"Is this our new game?" I ask, hoping he can understand my slurred and lispy words. "No longer chasing death, just competing to be the hero? Because if so, I think I won, sweetheart. You aren't supposed to be here."

"Couldn't live knowing you fucked me over by being the hero." He looks at my chains. "Can you stand?"

Gunfire echoes outside the room, making all the other prisoners scream for their freedom. Through the window, a blurry man moves by, and when that man grabs another man by the throat, breaking his neck and throwing a dagger at the third man, I laugh. I'd recognize my brother anywhere.

"Fuck, you're all so dumb."

"Thank you works too," Soren says. "Key?"

I have no idea if there is a key for the lock on the chains, so I tell him to leave me and get the hell out. He's Soren Sauder, so of course he doesn't listen.

"We gotta move," Krypt shouts from the hall, throwing more daggers. "They overrode the lockdown. Ransom! Left!"

Gang's all here then, yeah?

Krypt disappears, and the hall fills with more bodies.

"Ghost!" Krypt and Ransom shout at the same time from down the hall.

Ghost spins, watching the door fill with armed men. His back is to me, but I watch his shoulders relax, his body crouch into a fighting stance, and I just fucking know there's a smile on his face.

"Try not to get hard, baby," he tells me. "I know I'm sexy when I kill, but you're naked right now and I don't need anyone getting jealous of me."

Baby. I scoff, but it hurts my throat. I have confidence in him, but as the hall and doorway fill with more and more men, fear prickles my nape like it hasn't in the few days I've been in here. I'm self-entitled, so I hold my life above others, but right now, my brother and my... Soren are putting their lives on the line for me. And while I think I'm worth it, I never considered that they did, too.

Beneath all my masks and charming smiles lies an insecure boy who never did anything right. I hate that he's showing.

Twin blades twirl in Soren's nimble fingers. No. He's not Soren right now, he's Ghost, and he's about to shine in a spotlight he doesn't often get to have. I force my eye open, ready to call out his enemies as they come, but faster than my fuzzy head can follow, he moves. As silent as an asp and as fluid as a river, forging his way through men as if they're ghosts themselves. His knives dance, and blood shoots up like fireworks to paint the walls. Disarming them one by one, he cuts, slashes, and stabs fluently, guns only going off to misfire once they hit the floor.

Adrenaline surges within me, finally giving me the strength to do more than just laugh. When one guy gets by Ghost, I kick off the floor with all my remaining energy. My weak legs wrap around his neck, holding him in place as all my wounds reopen.

"Ghost."

He throws a dagger, and it embeds in the man's forehead. When I release my legs, he slumps to the floor, face down, impaling himself deeper. Ghost smirks at me, a subtle glance going down to my naked crotch. Not hard yet, which of course he sees as a challenge.

Good luck, sweetheart. I'm barely coherent enough to even know if I'm pissing myself.

A second wave of Reaper Corp soldiers come in,

bringing Krypt and Ransom with them. My Vile House brothers fight like they've been trained to for years, and my only regret is that I don't get to fight alongside them. Krypt breaks bones and stomps on faces. Ransom's accuracy with a knife is unmatched, and when he runs out of knives, he fires his clip until it's empty, leaving ten more men on the floor.

But Ghost. He moves from person to person, barely making a sound as he kills one before the previous one even hits the floor. When he's cut by their blades or grazed by their bullets, he doesn't react, fuelled only by the blood high he's soaring in.

"We gotta move! Someone get him down!" Ransom shouts as he rushes another man.

Krypt runs up behind me, swaying my chains to get me out of a knife's path. "Family bonding?" he asks, pushing down on my head as he rips a gun from his pants to shoot the lock.

"Something like that." Talking hurts and doesn't sound right, and a vain part of me wants to close my mouth and hide it from all of them. My looks have always been part of my charm, and without them, I feel as though half my masks have been ripped to shreds.

"Try to stand," he says just before his gun goes off.

My feet land flat on the floor and my arms drop uselessly to my sides. I manage to get my balance for all of two seconds before my legs give out and I fall forward. Agony tears through me as blood rushes into my bloodless arms, the pain akin to a billion tiny needles hitting every nerve. I can't even get them out in front of me to brace for my fall. When my knees hit the hard floor, I buckle forward, ready to faceplant.

My face hits a chest instead. Ghost's arms hold me up. Looking at him, coated in blood and handsome with death all over him, I hate him a little more and a little less simultaneously. Fuck him for being the hero.

He grins, pushing me upright. "Don't worry. You can hate me for it later. Right now, we gotta get the fuck outta here."

Ransom comes back, nodding at me. "Hall is clear. Riot, can you walk?"

I want to lie, but it'll only slow them down. "Not much."

Ransom looks at Ghost. "You still have the keycard?" Ghost nods. "Then we're taking the elevator. Glitch, we need evac on the roof."

Krypt shoves an earpiece into my bloody ear, and I catch the end of Glitch's response. "—some sort of chaos downtown and at the hospital. No idea what's going on, but the mayhem might work in our favour."

Krypt and Ghost get me to my unsteady feet, but I'm smiling because I finally have something to bring to the party. "That might be my doing."

We're on our way to the elevator, each of us looking in prisoner rooms and doing nothing about it. "What'd you do?"

I gag, vomiting a little before I answer. "Remember The Harpy wanted poison for Moros? Well, she gave some to Menace, and he gave it to me. I poisoned Reaper Corp."

Glitch laughs in our ears, but Krypt shakes his head. "You get captured and manage to poison their water? How?"

"Not all the water, but they hosed me down and cavity-searched me in the basement decontamination room. Right next to this building's water filtration system. Half went there, and half went before I even got caught."

"Kinda like the lisp," Ghost says, ignoring my heroics. "Gums might be beneficial, too."

"Fuck you."

"What the fuck?" Ransom asks us, stabbing the elevator door and shoving the key card in the slot. "You two finally crack?"

I grin at Ransom and Ghost glares at me. Krypt curses us all.

"Helicopter is seven minutes out, heading to the roof. They aren't going to let it in easy, so you're gonna have to be fast."

"Did you get what you needed?" I ask Glitch, hoping Soren was at least smart enough to get the devices out.

"We got it all and then some. Now we just need you, so don't fucking die, yeah?"

Pretty sure I'm already three-quarters dead, but I laugh. "Workin' on it."

As we ride to the top floor, I lose a bit of the adrenaline I had. My arms are in excruciating pain, my legs can't hold me up, my head is swimming in space, and my second eye is starting to swell shut with the extra movement. I'm weak and starved, coming down from an LSD high where I saw a goth girl in unicorn ears, and I refused every bit of water they offered me, but...

"Look, there might be a bit of a problem," I force the words out as my lungs rattle. "I might have been water-boarded."

All three of them snap their eyes to me. Yeah, I'm totally

dying of the poison I administered, so this rescue mission is pointless anyway.

Ghost grabs my chin, forcing my one eye open. "Glitch, get Menace to The Harpy for an antidote. Fucking now!"

"Better be ready when we get back," Krypt growls. "Hurry up!"

But it's Ransom's eyes I latch on to. "Trust me," is all he says, and for whatever reason, I do.

When we get to the top floor, Ghost gets right in my battered face. "I'm the one who chases death, *sweetheart.* Don't change our dynamic now. You made me a deal."

My smile is weak and pathetic because it feels so soft. Soren still wants me to hold his hand. Let's hope this lungful of poison lets me live long enough to grant his mushy wish.

The outside air hits me with jarring authority. It wakes me up, making me more alert, but with that alertness comes more pain. Devastating pain that crumples my body and blacks out my fevered mind. I hear the helicopter, the boys shouting all around me, Glitch and Facts in my ear, but I'm floating through it without experiencing any of it. Listening to bullets whiz by and stationary guns fire at the helicopter, I'm thrown into it, and that's when I pass out, the voice of Facts shouting hello echoing as I slumber.

Guess it's up to fate now.

I smile when I glimpse Soren's muse. Death herself, smiling back at me.

Hey, Bitch.

GHOST

28

SOLITUDE SAFETY

REAPER CITY IS in utter chaos, but I can't focus on it. Mass hysteria breaks out on the street, sirens and announcements about the drinking water not being safe ringing through the downtown core as I shove Riot into the helicopter and cover his body with mine. Bullets hit the exterior and fly through the open doors, and Krypt is barely inside when the pilot lifts off the roof. He rolls into me, helping me cover his brother, and our eyes meet, a silent exchange of truths being admitted. Never out loud.

Yeah, I care about his brother, but I still don't know what it means. I'm smart enough to know it means something, but I don't have the energy for introspection right now.

As the adrenaline from the situation fades the further we get from Reaper City, the shakes take over and my fingers tremble, digging into Riot's hair just for something to hold onto. Ransom throws a blanket over him and grabs my chin.

"Breathe."

I can't.

"Menace is getting the antidote. Trust me, Ghost."

I can't.

Why isn't he reassuring Krypt instead of me? I don't want to know the answer or what my face is revealing, so I bury it against the floor of the helicopter and keep my hands in Riot's hair as Krypt adjusts the blanket over his naked and broken body.

"Wait." I shove the blanket aside, wiping away a bit of blood on Riot's back. He winces in his slumber, and my rage reignites. "They fucking burned his Vile House tattoo!"

Krypt is the one to grab my shoulder this time. "Look at what he fucking did, Ghost. He caused a riot while he was being tortured. You think he needs the tat to prove he's Vile? He's fucking Riot."

Exhaling, I look back towards the city he managed to fuck over. He didn't get his name for nothing, and I smile, shaking my head at how smug he's gonna be about it.

Fucking asshole outdoes me even as he's dying.

When we get back to Moros, I don't take a full breath until we meet The Harpy at the asylum and she administers the antidote. I lose my shit when he bubbles from the mouth and has a seizure that won't stop, and I lash out at everyone who fucking touches him while he's dying. Death is my thing, and he can't beat me there!

I hold two blades to The Harpy's neck, making sure she stays right where she is until the antidote works and he's in the clear.

"Why is he seizing?" I snarl at her.

"It's how it works."

"He's not fucking breathing." I press the tip against her carotid.

"Give him a minute."

"If his heart stops, yours will, too."

The Harpy doesn't look away from me.

Not until his heart starts and he breathes again.

And when he is in the clear, no longer dying from the poison he unintentionally ingested, I stare at his busted body while ignoring everything I feel.

I don't move a muscle until Medic and Psych are working on Killian, and I don't step aside until they tell me his damages are severe but not life-threatening. I listen to them plan his treatment, talk about dental surgery, and confirm that he's going to pull through before I even blink. When I know Krypt is fine with Remi in his grasp, I sneak out of Riot's room, leave the asylum, and don't come back.

Because feeling my feelings isn't something I'm good at, and I'm not too narcissistic to know that. Music is my expression, and I never do it while anyone can see me. I shower, change, and grab my violin from my room, leaving Vile House. Time to be alone so I don't go to The Harpy's cabin and murder her for inadvertently putting his life at risk. I need to stop trying so hard to hold my pieces together. To let myself break in the safety of solitude. For once, I don't want to be the star of this broken show.

IT'S the second to last day of the music festival, and both the cemetery and Death Row are crowded with tourists and musicians. Creeping through the shadows of buildings, I pause to listen unseen, searching for a sound that reflects how I feel. The musicians are skilled, and the choirs are beautiful, but nothing hits me where it should. The melancholy mood is matched with upbeat voices that are too light for the way I'm feeling.

Because there is a new well of darkness inside me, and I'm not sure where it came from. It's different from the playful way I felt dark before. I'm not craving a chase that leads me to Death's door because I'm not sure I want to slam it in her face anymore. I'm craving pain, the emotional kind. The sort of anguish that's cleansing because it hurts so ferociously. An exorcism of my jagged bits and a rearranging of my jigsaw pieces. I need to become a new mirage, a different illusion that reflects the unwanted changes in me.

I need musical expression and a new foundation.

I need to hide while expressing myself.

Behind the Ambient Raven, I put on my Vile House mask, concealing my face in the safest cover I have. With my hood up and my hands bare, I pick up my violin and make my way down the dead centre of Death Row, drawing attention to the mystery of who I am and what I'm doing. Riot had his dental surgery last night, but I haven't been to see him. I don't know *how* to go see him. What would I say? What would I do? I don't know, so I'm going to let the instrument find my words for me.

I haven't been back to Vile House or the asylum in two days. I've been staying with Lockan, warning him about what I overheard about a rat in his crew, working through the prospects of who it could be. But all that was just a distraction, a way for me to avoid my own head and evade my emotions. It's time to face my reality.

Groups of musicians perform along the road, shops and sponsors show off their products, and Moros citizens mingle with tourists to listen and take it all in. We're a musical town, but the kind of music we create has become the soundtrack of how we live. Morose, melancholy, dark, and deceptive, a community of people who speak better with notes than we do with words. As I walk through them, the locals fist their hands over their hearts, respecting my mask, but the tourists stop to admire me because of how the locals are reacting. To them, I'm someone with power, but they don't understand why or how yet.

I'm about to show them.

In the centre of Death Row, right in the middle of the closed street, I sit on a wooden chair, bowing my head to my violin and closing my eyes behind my mask. From that new well of darkness within me, I pull forth the true reasoning for it, letting it infiltrate my mind and weave through my limbs until I'm born of it. One with it. A new man hiding behind the same mask.

The fog shrouds me in more comfort and the ravens and crows perch on lamp posts and power lines for a front-row seat to my misery. Misery because of change; change I don't want to accept but can no longer fight. I always thought it'd be my own life that flashed before my eyes, but it was his. A fear I've never felt and a sense of surrender I almost succumbed to.

I've always been one to build off the weather, and according to Lock, it's been a beautiful weekend with clear skies and mild temperatures to make the music festival enjoyable. I didn't even notice. But as I sit and bring my violin into position, placing the bow across the strings, the skies cloud over and I revel in my ability to influence the weather as much as it influences me.

Here I fucking am. The Ghost of Moros. Hurt with me.

Alone in a crowd but with all eyes on me, I sink and rise at once. My bow moves, and the first note of music is brutally magnificent, tinged with a slow, deep tone that resonates my fragmented anger as the strings vibrate. I let it play out, not rushing the single note, allowing it to cause its harm and set the weather on edge. When the first crack of thunder booms, I become the sentiment of my music.

I become a man who thinks of another man above himself.

I become resentful because of the power he wields over me.

I become irritated at the world for forcing me to live in it, but grateful to Moros for giving me a place to fit.

I lose my mind to feelings that conflict, my narcissistic tendencies mingling with selfless thoughts about a man who wears many masks and doesn't know how to take them off. I hurt for him because he's lost himself, and I hurt for myself because I suddenly care. My music picks up tempo, showing my temper, overpowering the thunder. And when lightning strikes to spotlight me on Death Row, I ignore my gathered audience and play for me and only me.

He'll hold my hand.

He'll kiss me, not for the last time. Just in case...

He'll chase me towards death and always pull me back because he knows the end is not what I seek.

It's my undoing, this music. A mile marker of a new kind

of *here* and *there*. Instead of that one-or-two-second precipice, I'm on the ledge between the me who taunted a curse and the me who now fears that curse. My violin shows how terrified I am—it shows that fear will not undo me. The notes mingle with the atmosphere, the thunder my percussive backup and the lightning my webbed truth. And when our harmony is so well perfected that I'm sick with how sincere it is, I stop playing and breathe in petrichor and fog.

The drizzly mist turns into a steady rain, soothing the heat of my music and cooling it into understanding and admittance.

When I pick up playing again, slower and softer this time, a cello joins me.

I cry.

Hidden and secretive, I cry behind my mask of power and play terrible beauty with my brother, clad in a black mask. For whatever reason, it hurts worse than everything else. It's been so long, this thing I refused to do because I didn't know what my music would say if I started playing with Remi again. I should have known not to fear it because Remi is stronger than I've ever given him credit for. He gets it. Understands it. Knows what it's like to break in half and reassemble the pieces. He knows what love feels like, tainted yet pure, and he knows the same fear I know. The curse that has threatened us since birth.

He admitted he feared it.

I refused to fear it.

In the end, we're in the same place. Mixed with Hallows boys who sew our sanity to theirs in a way neither of us ever asked for but cling so hard to that it's impossible to talk about. It can't be explained. He never expected to need Krypt. I never expected to want Riot. So, here we play, two Sauder brothers, living the same lie and turning it into a truth.

His cello adds depth to my violin, the instruments harmonizing like soulmates. Our music awes me, but it awes the town even more. Men weep and women reminisce. Children don't know what it means but feel it deep in their innocent souls, knowing it's something, but not what. They build off us as we build off each other, the weather witness to it all, accompanying our melody and adding mood to our sound.

It's all made worse when Selena joins, clad in black with her black-faced mask, playing the violin today. Her mood fits into our stringed instruments, and the three of us mourn together for lives lost and pain unspoken.

We play until there's nothing left to say. Until the emotions and the pain are bled from our souls. And then we stop. Still. Instruments dropping but positions never moving. Moros takes a breath, and the rumbling thunder plays us out, finalizing our song. Soaked through from the rain, I allow it to blanket me, protect me, until I breathe enough times to look at my siblings. I can't speak, or talk, or discuss any of it, and they don't expect me to. We nod at each other, and then we all go our separate ways through the crowd—every person with their hand over their heart. Even those who don't know what it means.

If any locals recognize us as siblings, they don't mention it, giving me a reprieve from discovery for now.

Something leaves me as I walk away. I don't know what it is, but when I look up at where I'm walking, I wonder if it's resistance. That dark well no longer feels new. It feels like me. The very essence of who I am, and I'm not fighting it as much anymore. The resistance to this new thing is gone.

RIOT

29

BACK TO BACK

I LOATHE him for making me try so hard to hold everything in. The pressure building inside my chest and head is too much for my injuries to bear. With my legs hanging over the side of Death Mark's roof, I listen to Soren play his emotions through four strings while I break all over again, weak from so much healing. Afraid because of his music and what it means. Proud of him without wanting to admit it. Feeling everything he feels as it slips into the rain and reverberates in my chest.

Krypt doesn't comment or touch me, but when Remi joins his brother in the middle of Death Row, he becomes stoic and full, just like I am. We used to play piano together, too, but in the years since I joined Vile House, and him shortly after, we forgot how to express ourselves and turned only to violence instead. Violence and power and manipulations. For so long, I've forgotten that there's another way.

"Are you going to tell me about it?" Krypt asks, staring at the Sauder brothers as Selena joins them.

My new teeth implants hurt enough to use as an excuse

not to speak, so I don't. I don't know what to tell him. Everyone knows Ghost and I have issues with each other, but we're doing a shit job of hiding how drastically they've changed. Krypt thinks he knows something, but how can he know when we don't even know? How is it possible to explain a shift in dynamic that isn't yet properly defined?

If I had to tell him anything, it'd be the truth. That somewhere along the way, I stopped manipulating Soren and started letting him lead. That I don't know how to manipulate him anymore because he doesn't make sense to me. When he was chasing a curse, I got it. That made sense because a thrill-seeker respects another thrill-seeker. But he's not chasing it anymore. He's chasing me, just as I planned. Now that he is, I don't have to manipulate his actions anymore, so I don't know what else to fucking do.

I look down at my healing hands, a few fingernails gone. When I shrug, the burned parts of my back scream in pain, but Krypt never looks at me. He doesn't have to. Because I think he gets it. He never meant to feel anything for Remi either.

My eyes stay locked on Soren and how his instrument becomes a part of him, listening to the way he sends me a message without knowing I'm hearing it. *I hear it, sweetheart, and I wish I knew how to say it back.*

When Menace climbs up to sit with us, he doesn't speak until the Sauders stop playing, each of them heading their own way. "I can fix it," he says to me. "When the burns are healed. We can make something work."

The Vile House tat is still there. Still obvious but warped, and I'm not ashamed of it. I *am* ashamed of ruining it, like I didn't do it justice—didn't protect it. Instead, I say, "I want a king cobra." My mouth aches.

He laughs but doesn't ask why. "Alright."

I met a kid on a plane, and she saved my mind when it wasn't mine. I've never really been grateful to anyone before, but I am to her. I'll never get to tell her, so I'll honour her on my skin.

It takes a lot of energy that I don't have to push myself up to stand, the rain feeling nice on my overheated skin.

"Leave him," Krypt warns me. "He's never pleasant after he plays."

I don't care how unpleasant he is, but I nod to take his advice. I don't have the energy to deal with Soren's emotions anyway. Mostly because I don't know how to convey mine.

IT MAKES me uncomfortable that his presence is calming. I haven't even limped my way out of the bathroom yet, but I know he's in my room. He used to be able to sneak up on me, but ever since I sucked his cock after hanging him at the music shop, I'm sensing him more and more.

Wrapped in a towel, I leave the ensuite bathroom and enter my dimly lit room. I love Vile House, but I've been in this bed for too long, and I'm itching to get out. To get back to Vile business and put that goddamn Reaper City job in the past.

I poisoned their city... they're going to retaliate, and I need to be ready. Especially because they know my identity now. Krypt and Ransom were masked, but Soren wasn't, and with our faces known, I'm certain we'll be targeted.

"Hey, sweetheart," I say to the dark corner as I drop my towel and step into a pair of white boxer-briefs. There's a small part of me that is insecure about all my wounds and scarring, but I'm not going to let him see that. At least I have a full mouth of teeth again, even if they hurt like a motherfucker. "Couldn't keep avoiding me?"

Sitting on the edge of my bed to work up the strength to complete the monumental task of pants, I hold my sweats in my hand and blink away my fatigue. How the hell am I still so tired when all I've been doing is sleeping?

Before I work up the energy to put my pants on, something cold presses against my fist. I open my hand to grab it, the coldness of a plastic cup feeling nice against my stiff fingers. "What's this?"

"Smoothie."

I grin. "Aw."

"Fuck you."

I laugh, wrapping my lips around the straw. "Aren't you sweet." Creamy, tropical and coconut coolness fills my mouth, easing the pain in my teeth and coating my throat in a soothing sensation. I drop my pants and inch backwards to sit comfortably, legs dangling. "You gonna stand there like a creep or...?"

He heads for the door without a word.

"Soren."

"Ghost," he snaps at me.

Guess we're both feeling vulnerable again. "Stay."

"Why?"

"Because you brought me a fucking smoothie."

He huffs. "Doesn't mean shit."

"Okay."

He sits on the other side of my bed, facing the opposite direction. It's strange to be calm around him without requesting the ninety seconds. I sense him, but other than vulnerability and a bit of irritation, there's nothing dire or dangerous about him. His energy has shifted, and maybe that means mine has, too.

"Are you—"

"Don't turn around," he demands.

I stay where I am and face my bedroom door, sipping the smoothie for long moments of silence. Back-to-back with Soren Sauder.

"You scared me."

"I'm—"

"Don't talk."

My insides tingle, knowing something rare is coming.

"Don't ever do that again. Don't fucking... sacrifice yourself for me."

I ignore his rule. "It wasn't for you. It was for the job."

"Liar."

I am a liar. Clearly, I don't give many fucks about jobs. I killed Brady that night when the job was undoubtedly to bring him back alive, and I didn't even feel sorry for it.

"You fucked me over so hard," he goes on. "You gave yourself away when we could have gotten out. You made my job harder, kept me away from Moros for longer, and put me in more danger than you would have if we'd just fought our way out of there. So fuck you for doing that, and if you ever do it again, I'll fucking... just don't."

I take a long drink to buy myself time. I don't know if

he's expecting a reply or not, but I feel obligated to give him one. Because he's lying, too. He doesn't give a fuck about being put in danger. Hell, the guy chases it for a thrill. He's pissed off because it scared him in a way he's not been scared before.

"I never expected you to come back."

I feel the bed jostle, but it doesn't seem like he's moved. "No? Are you fucking stupid? You think I could be friends with Krypt after letting you die? You think I could live with the fact that you played the hero... for me? Fuck you, Kill. Fuck you for putting me in that situation, and fuck you for scaring me." He sighs, the sound coming out heavy and drained. "You scared me."

He's never called me Kill so emotionally before, and he's never shown me this level of timid exposure. I'm someone whose natural instinct is to poke at it and use it against him, but... I can't. "I needed you to get out."

"Why?"

"Because it scared me too, okay? Fuck." I hang my head, fiddling with the straw. "I pictured you getting..."

"Talk faster."

"Bit fucking hard right now, asshole." I wince as my mouth flares in pain, but my surge of anger helps ease it. "I just needed you to get out. And next time, don't fucking come back for me."

"Don't tell me what to do."

"What are you, eight? Jesus." I shake my head.

"Killian," he snarls, and I sense him turning around. He touches my shoulder, pulls his hand back quickly, and then sighs. "I brought you things," he snaps at me like it's my fault he did something nice.

"What things?"

"Soup, pudding, Jello, soft food. I brought fucking ice packs and heat packs and salve, and all this medical bullshit *because you fucking scared me!*"

I twist to look at him, seeing his blue eyes lit up with the reflection of the bathroom light. He's scared, even now, for admitting that he did all this because he doesn't know what it means. He's so insistent that it means nothing, but it does, and we both know it. Because I, a selfish fucking sociopath, gave up my life for his, and it scared him enough to bring me a care package. Neither of us has ever been the giving type, and here we are, caught in a strange situation that wants to go somewhere, but neither of us will step on the gas.

"Turn around!" he shouts. "Would have been easier if that poison killed you."

Prick. Back-to-back so we don't have to face our feeble declarations head-on, I try to get comfortable in a role that is so out of character for me—submission. It's real and horrifying and kind of weak, but I don't feel unsafe being... me.

"Are... are your fingers still fucked?"

I try to see them in the dark, but it's hard to tell. They hurt, but my nail beds are bandaged and only one finger is broken, so I shake my head. "They're fine."

"You, uh, we had a deal."

It takes me a second, but when I realize what he's saying, my smile is entirely genuine. It's not a smirk, a grin, or a charming mask across my lips. It's happiness and shyness because Soren wants me to hold his hand.

"That girl really fucked you up, eh?"

"Fuck this. I'm leaving. This was a mistake."

When he moves, I grab his fingers and pull him back

down. "Just sit with me. My god." We start back-to-back, our shoulders twisted so our fingers can wind together in the middle of the bed. Back-to-back feels safe, but slowly, my body turns, and so does his. We don't look at each other, but we slide to the headboard to sit side by side. One hand on my smoothie and the other in his, sweating because I'm nervous, I ease my bandaged back against the smooth wood, trying not to lean too hard on any of the burns.

"You're in my head, Sauder."

He snorts like that's an understatement. "But why?"

I take a sip and offer him the cup. He denies me and then takes it, so I say, "We're just all twisted together when we shouldn't be."

"Why not?"

"You're *apparently* a narcissist and I've *apparently* got ASPD. You think our mental situations are gonna be anything but destructive together? We can't even manage friendship, let alone whatever the fuck this is." I laugh because, even though it's true, it doesn't seem so daunting. "So, what is it?"

"Sex and curses."

"Doesn't sound half bad when you put it that way."

He hands the cup back. Soren's palm presses against mine, and then he lifts our hands, playing with my fingers while he watches them together. He makes sure all my bandages stay on, entranced by the way we look touching each other.

"Psych tells me that our kinds of diagnoses aren't exact," he says.

Yeah, she tells me that, too, but... why is he saying it? "And?"

"I don't know." He sighs, like he wants to justify that we're allowed to feel new things for each other despite what our medical records say.

"You know what's messed up? I've fucked and fought a lot of people, but you touch me in two ways I've never been touched before, and it's all weird in my head because they're opposite ways." He stares at our hands while I watch his side profile. "At first, you touched me like you knew I could handle it. You're probably the only person who's ever given me all their strength and not doubted if I'd live through it. But you're also the first person to touch me like this." He links our fingers. "Like... it means something, but nothing malicious."

"Wow."

"Don't fucking make fun of me."

"I'm not." I chuckle. "I thought that too when that kid touched my hand. But this is different. She was innocent, but you're..."

"What?"

I want to say *mine*, but our bubble is too thin to risk breaking it yet. "Intentional." I hold his hand harder. "You know, this is the first conversation we've ever had that hasn't had a death threat in it."

"Pretty sure I threatened to kill you if you ever sacrificed yourself for me again."

He didn't, but maybe he thought it. Chatting isn't easy between us, and I don't overly want to talk anymore, but I also don't want him to leave. It's the middle of the night, and I have no idea who he conned into making me a smoothie, but despite how tired I am, I'm content to spend the rest of the night sitting just like this.

"What kind of soup?"

"I don't know. Just soup."

I smile. "Thanks."

"Fuck you." He bends, resting his temple on my shoulder. We both stiffen, even though we want it, and it takes a second or two to remember to be comfortable with it. "Terrorize me, Killian, but not like that."

I lean my head against his and close my eyes. "Okay."

GHOST

30

HOW DO YOU KNOW?

DIRECTOR CALLED a meeting that starts in thirty minutes, but I still haven't left Killian's room. I wouldn't say I slept, but I drifted in and out, and when I came to, we were back-to-back like we were at the hotel. It's not my natural instinct, but I offer to change his bandages and help him clean his wounds, but when he denies me, claiming he's going to see Medic right after the meeting, my teeth clench.

I'm not the fucking caregiver type! So why does it piss me off that he won't let me fix him?

He smiles at me, his new teeth even prettier than his old ones. Only a few of them are implants, but they give his charming smile a whole new edge that sets me off. "Oh, come on, sweetheart. You've never given a shit about anyone else a day in your life."

I have. But only Remi and Selena, and to be honest, when Remi almost died, I didn't want to be the one to take care of him. I wanted to ensure Krypt did it, or Director. Anyone other than me. I'd be a terrible pet owner. The thing would die in three days because I'm too self-absorbed to remember to feed it.

But I fed Killian last night...

"Whatever. I'm going to this meeting." I grab the doorknob.

Killian's fingers wrap around my other wrist and turn me back. Just like in that room before we started the Reaper City job, his lips softly land against mine. My stomach gets warm, swelling with pride or something, and his long fingers wrap around the side of my neck. I close my eyes and let him kiss me, unsure if I'm kissing him back because it's so quick and soft.

"Just in case," he whispers. Then he opens his door, pushes me into the hallway, and grins at me with a bruised face before shutting it.

I'm just standing here, my lips alight and my mind blown, staring at his closed door. What the hell is happening? Back-to-back sleeping, smoothies, handholding, and now these gentle kisses that mean so much more than a forced dick down the throat? I shake my head, trying to stabilize my thoughts.

"Hello."

I'm usually the silent one, so it startles me to realize I'm not alone. Shirtless, Facts leans against the wall at the end of the hall. His chest is tattooed with Latin words and ancient runes, and he's glistening with sweat because he's an avid morning exerciser. He dances, too. Ballroom style, and he's damn good at it. His lithe body is his temple; his brain is his power.

"You didn't see anything," I warn him.

"I did," he corrects, because everything has to be fucking

accurate with him. He pushes off the wall and follows me into my own room. "But I won't say anything about it if you help me with something."

I strip down and don't give a shit that he's here. He never looks anyway. Stepping into my shower, he stands outside the glass wall to chat with me. "Help with what?"

"A personal matter." He jitters.

I close my eyes and lather shampoo. "Get on with it."

"Well," he starts, "I seem to have found myself in a predicament."

"Facts, my patience level is at an all-time low. Get to the point."

"I'm sexually attracted to a strange man."

I drop the body wash bottle. "What?" I gasp. If anyone is less sexual than Krypt, it's Facts. He's never, not even once, shown interest in another person. Not romantically, not sexually, not even at all, really. He's selfish, but it doesn't come from his ego. It comes from his inability to slow himself down enough for anyone else and his weird relationship with what is real and what isn't. He cares about us, but only in the sense that we're some sort of family he's never had, so he understands what loyalty is, but he's not interested in friendship or comradeship in the same way the rest of us are. He likes belonging, cares about our wellbeing, and that's about it.

"Yes," is all he adds, a jerky nod following with another, "Hello."

"What strange man?"

The screen of his phone slaps against the glass wall of the shower. I look, seeing a man I sort of recognize but can't name. He's a Ransom type, by the looks of him. Authoritative, sorta calm, and masculine. He's older than Facts, judging by the photo, and I've seen him around town but never talked to him.

"Why's he strange?"

"He talks slowly," Facts says, turning his phone around to look at his crush. "Walks slowly. Keeps eye contact. Listens to people chat without interrupting."

I snort, picking up the bottle. "Yeah, he sounds like a real wacko. You love people who don't interrupt."

"I know. So, what do I do?"

"This is what you need help with?"

"I want you to spy on him. I need to know more, if only to appease my curiosity. I'm not going to talk to him, but... I must know more."

I grin. "Was that a pause in your sentence? Jesus, Facts. Never heard you pause before."

"Temporary lapse in focus."

Rinsing, I turn off the shower and take the towel he holds out for me. He doesn't look anywhere but at my eyes, and I know he's getting impatient because I'm not immediately agreeing to spy on his boyfriend.

"Talk to him."

Facts tilts his head at me in his method of getting annoyed. "No."

I roll my eyes and push past him, drying off as I go. He follows as I grab dark pants and a white t-shirt, covering it with a dark grey hoodie. I have a few wounds from the job, but none of them hurt too badly. "Fine. I'll check him out, but if you wanna make a move, that's on you."

"Deal." He holds his hand out, and I laugh as I shake it. "Are you dating Riot?"

My laugh fades and I feel my face flush. "No."

"Okay. Goodbye." He leaves my room and doesn't look back.

When I get to the con room, Director is in a mood, but it's not his typical 'frustrated with us' mood. It's more of a 'weight of the world on his shoulders' mood, and it makes me feel guilty for making shit harder for him. I wasn't exactly... sane over the past few days, especially before we got Riot out of there. Fortunately, he doesn't make us line up in rank. He probably figures the two of us have been through enough lately and wounding our already wounded pride by making us stand at the end of the line isn't worth the hassle it'll cause him.

We all sit around the table, and Kyd rubs Director's back in an attempt to ease his woes. "There there, Pops" Kyd croons, making us all grin. He tries so damn hard.

"Nice chomps, Riot." Menace whistles.

Riot, despite being battered, beaten, and bruised, flashes his new smile at everyone. His confidence hasn't faded, and his ego is just as mighty as ever, but I swear there was a flash of embarrassment in his eyes when I first saw him without teeth in that torture room.

"Has Lockan found anything in The Misfits?" Director asks, and it takes Monster nudging my knee to realize he's talking to me. I rip my eyes away from Riot.

"Uh, no. Not yet." I glance at Riot, trying not to make it obvious. "He's looking."

Director nods. "I want you to be the go-between. Help him find his traitor. They'll all be in Janie's Woods for training today, so go join in."

Whatever. It's a bullshit job, but I don't care.

"Riot, you're benched until—"

"No," Riot snarls. "Get fucked. I did your job, played nice with Sauder, and lived through it. Don't you dare fucking bench me."

No one laughs at his outburst, not even me. Because I'd react the exact same way. He put his life on the line, endured almost three days of torture, kept his wits about him, and managed to poison the research building in downtown Reaper City. If anyone deserves their time to shine, it's him. Well, it's me, for getting him out of there in one piece. I probably killed more people than his poison did anyway, but I get where he's coming from. It doesn't matter that he's injured and healing, he won't sit this one out because now he knows exactly what our enemy looks like. Reaper Corp is coming for Moros, and none of us will sit on the sidelines and let it happen.

Respectfully, Director nods. "Don't you have a bargain to close up and collect on then?"

Riot grins. Willow Olenna, the cousin of the guy Riot killed by snapping his neck—the first one—still hasn't paid up. "On it."

Before I head out to meet up with Lockan, I leave my first calling card for Riot.

"HEY, SOREN," Cain says as he leaves The Ambient Raven for the evening. He closes the door behind him and pulls his hood up to block the rain. "You going in?"

I'm too combustible to go in. After a day of thinking and

dreading and trying to work out the puzzle that is my mind, I'm not stable enough to stand in Remi's shop and respect it like I should. "I'll wait for him out here. He almost done?"

Cain is cute. He's a weird mix of adorable and harsh, artsy and tough, and I know he has a kinky side because Menace has run his mouth about it. I wonder if Cain will ever know Mason is a Vile Boy or if he'll continue to cheat on his girlfriend on the side. He's too good for Sadie, but I don't know if he deserves the torment Menace will put him through if he ever decides to take Cain as his own.

"He's just locking the back door."

"Thanks. You all set at home if anything... comes to town?"

He tilts his head at me, wondering why I'm asking, but the whole town knows about the threat, so I'm not giving myself away. "Yeah, and I'm gonna go to some of those training sessions in Janie's Woods. To hell with anyone who tries to take Moros."

I grin at that. "Night."

"Night." Just like the Moros local he is, he walks down Death Row while the Ravens watch his back.

After another five minutes of the drizzle soaking through my jacket, my brother comes out. "Hey." He locks the door and smiles at me. "How was your smoothie last night?" He grins.

Fuck him. "Good."

"What flavour was it?"

"Strawberry."

Remi laughs, and we start walking towards the house we grew up in. "Killian liked it?"

"Just fuck off about it, Remi."

"Okay." He holds his hands up. "Someone came to the shop today to ask if I'd sell my… house. Or, uh, the property it sat on."

The ravens join our walk. "Who?"

"I don't know. Some rich guy. Not local."

"So, you said no?"

"Yeah, I said no. But he gave me a bad vibe." He pulls his phone from his pocket and shows me the screen. "I snapped this. Recognize him?"

I take his phone. "Yeah, I do. Send that to me so I can show Director. Or send it to Kr-Keegan."

Remi looks around like I'm speaking dark secrets out in the open. "Who is he?"

A slimy fucking billionaire. "Benton Wentworth."

As he texts it to both me and Krypt, his sleeves slide up, showing a peek of his burns. Still hate them. Still think they're stupid. Still think Krypt is a fucking possessive maniac. Kind of love the reason he marked my brother's body, though.

"You love him?" I ask, startling myself. Love isn't a topic we chat about. Sure, their relationship a bit, but never love.

Remi's blue eyes meet mine without any shame or judgement. "Yeah."

"How do you know? Don't you just feel like he owns you?"

"In the beginning, yeah. He did own me. It's different now, and I'm different from you."

"How?"

He pockets his phone as we turn down the side street. "You want to control everything, be the man in charge, and never let anyone see your vulnerabilities. I didn't have that choice. Keegan saw all my vulnerabilities without me even wanting to show them to him. I got comfortable being exposed to him, and I don't crave the same kind of control you do. I give him power because I want him to have it, but that doesn't make me powerless. Think about it, Soren." He shrugs. "I have the power to love him, even though he doesn't know how to be loved."

Do I know how to be loved? Does anyone love me? I want to ask Remi, but I can't make myself sacrifice the pride it will take to voice the question.

"Loving someone doesn't make you weak. You know that, right?"

"Maybe not, but it's one more *point* of weakness. Someone could use him against you, and you'd do anything to save him."

"Like Killian gave up his life to save you?"

I walk faster, resisting the urge to disappear into our surroundings and give Remi the slip. "Why the fuck did I bring him a smoothie, Remi?!"

"Welcome to giving a shit," Remi says with a laugh.

"I don't give a shit, though."

"Deny it all you want. You still ordered me to make a smoothie and brought it to him. And soup. You care."

"I've never cared before. Not about anything but myself."

"Not true. You care about me and Selena, and you care about Moros. You care about Keegan."

"You know, he told me he raped you and I got mad because it felt like he got one over on me. I was pissed on my own behalf, not yours."

"I've lived with you my whole life, Soren. I know who you are."

"That doesn't bother you?"

He shrugs, feet scuffing on the sidewalk. "Sometimes, yeah, but you're my brother and I still love you for who you are." *He still loves me for who I am...* My brother loves me? "You might not have cared that he assaulted me, but you herded me to Vile House to protect me. Dad always said you were a bad narcissist."

"What? He did?"

Remi snorts. "Yeah. I mean, don't get me wrong, you're vain as fuck and only give a shit about yourself, but the odd time, you get super loyal to something or someone and you give them everything you can, even if you do it in your own way. You led me to the most dangerous place in town, but it saved me. You got Selena in to protect her. You left the music shop so you wouldn't ruin it. Your protection methods are insane and borderline deadly, but you still protect us." He looks at me, adding, "You brought Killian a smoothie."

"And soup," I mutter. "Fuck, Remi! What is happening to me?"

Simply, and with a smile, he says, "You met your match."

"But I've known him forever."

"Timing is right then. Have you...?"

"We fucked," I blurt out fast. "Once. I hated it." I swallow. "So much that I want it again."

"I have a fear kink," he admits, not dwelling on my confession because he knows I can't handle it.

"Don't overly wanna hear about it."

He ignores me. "How does that make sense? I've been

afraid all my life, and suddenly he comes along and makes it arousing? My point is, not everything makes sense. Just because you like him doesn't mean you have to stop challenging him. Sex with him doesn't make you submissive or weak. Wanting him doesn't mean you have to be romantic. Krypt can't even say the word love, but I know he loves me in the way he can, so... try that. Figure out how *you* care about someone, and then... show him."

"What if I don't know?"

"We hardly ever do."

"What if I hate him more than I, uh, like him?"

"That'd suit you." Remi laughs. "I don't know Killian all that well, but from the outside, it seems like you both try ridiculously hard to be the best, and maybe it'd be nice to just... not try so hard around each other all the time."

That does sound relaxing, in a sense. I don't often let my guard down, but holding his hand last night, falling asleep in his bed with his fingers between mine, felt oddly comfortable. I think I like those parts of him, but if he ever stops goading me like he has been for years, everything soft will shatter. Because I can't take the soft without the harsh, and I don't want the innocence without the evil.

In front of the house, we stare at the lit-up living room window. Mom is in there, watching TV like a zombie. I should probably care that she's brain-dead and messed up, but I don't. Remi and Selena are fine, and that's all I have left to care about in my family.

"You sure you wanna be here for this?" I ask him.

"Yeah," Remi says. "We're all gonna be here for this." He points to the front porch. Selena, that mini ghost in training, slips out of the shadows to stand with us.

"Let's go kidnap Mom and bring her to the mad doctor."

Axel is going to help us deal with our 'mother' problem. Either get her brain right or just lock her up in a cozy cell so she's not a liability during this upcoming war. Gregory Malone is in there, and she keeps asking about him, so it's time we learn the real reason why.

"Wait," Remi shouts before we step forward. "I feel like this is one for the scrapbook." He holds out his phone, the camera app open. And because it's so fucking ridiculous, we all laugh as he snaps a few photos.

"First family kidnapping," Selena laughs. "Here we go."

Ah, there is still joy in the unexpected things.

RIOT

31

MAKE ME UNAFRAID

THIS TIME, I'm the one lurking in the shadows. Soren is listening to Axel tell him the details about his mom and Gregory Malone being high school sweethearts or something, and I'm busy concocting my own plan for him tonight. My energy level is better after an easy day, and I'm up for this task.

"That's... she killed my fucking dad?!" Soren shouts.

"If she did, the curse would have broken," Axel reminds him, pretending to buy into the curse. "She pushed him to take his own life."

Soren scowls. "To get him out of the way so she could be with Malone? That's why that nasty fuck always stalked my brothers? They were offing my family for their second shot at love?" He paces the hallway between the new room his mom is being kept in and Axel's lab, steam brewing and his dark side coming out. "I'm gonna fucking kill that bitch."

"That bitch is your mumsie," Kyd says when he bounces into the lab, making Axel sigh in frustration. "Which just means I'll help." He smiles wide. "I've been building a guillotine in arts and crafts. Wanna try it out?"

I barely hold back my chuckle. Kyd is technically a patient at the asylum. He has a file here, even though he's never read it, and he's part of a lot of patient clubs. He's in the asylum orchestra, joins, and sometimes leads, the arts and crafts class, and he's been practicing to audition for a stage play they're putting on next year. He goes on field trips with the other patients, sits in on family visits, and has a bunch of friends who are also patients. The guy takes joy in everything, even being a live-in patient, and honestly, if it weren't for him, the rest of us would forget to have fun so often.

"Would you please sit down and stop talking?" Axel says to Kyd, eye only fluttering a little. Kyd complies, for now, and Axel turns back to Soren. "Yes, she pushed him to suicide. It's why I picked her as one of my test subjects. If she didn't make it, well, I figured I'd be doing you a favour."

"Don't act like you give a fuck about me," Soren snaps at the doctor. Axel doesn't deny it. "I want her dead, but you can't tell my brother and sister."

"I'm not murdering your mother."

"I got you the fucking file you asked for. You owe me."

"Not the whole file," Axel grumbles.

"I'll do it!" Kyd shoots to his feet again, pink hair flopping into his eyes. Axel pushes him back down, and Kyd pouts while secretly loving being touched, leaning into it like a purring cat.

"Sleep on it. She's contained here, and you can make that choice tomorrow. Or another day. We have a lot more pressing matters at the moment."

Soren just grunts and leaves the lab. I don't have more than a second to react to him stepping into the hallway, so as soon as he does, I step in front of him and smile.

"Hey, sweetheart."

"The fuck do you want?" he barks, trying to push by me.

"Everything," I whisper, holding up the calling card he left me. Then I slam his head off the wall and catch him as he falls. "Got him! He's ready!" I shout to Axel.

Kyd wheels out a gurney, and the three of us get him on it.

"He's going to kill me for this," Axel reminds me.

"You're lucky I didn't kill you for taking my brother. Call us even if you do this."

"And if he comes for me?" Axel asks as we wheel Soren down the hall to an imaging room.

"I'll be your knight in pink armor." Kyd flashes his teeth.

"Don't worry, doc. I'll take the brunt of his fury." I grin, anticipating it.

"We'll put him under for now, but he's going to have to be awake for some of it. He'll need to undergo emotional trigger tests and stress tests so we can watch the connectivity signals."

I nod, promising I'll stay here for all of it so Soren doesn't kill anyone.

He puts Soren under general anesthetic, injects a dye into him, and for an hour, I watch screens and monitors and things I don't understand while Dr. Graves does the brain mapping thing Soren refused to get. Remi has been so much better since starting his medication, and even if Soren won't take meds, I want to know what we're working with. I'll help him chase death forever, but only if it's to slam the door in her face. When I saw him walk into my torture room, I didn't like the look in his eyes. Buried under his murder high was a scared, dark idea, hinting at his shift in need. He was closer to the curse than he'd ever been before, and I'm no longer taking the risk.

Because I've decided I don't want to live without him.

I think I can, but I don't want to. He suits my needs, and my needs are most important.

Before Axel wakes him up for the next portion of testing, I press my lips to his forehead, giving him a small kiss. "Just in case," I say to his unconscious mind.

I DUCK when a glass bottle flies by my head and smashes against the brick wall outside the asylum. I don't even care that he almost took off my head. To see him so alive and pissed off... fuck yeah, he's making my cock hard. I love him like this, pissed off and unremorseful about it.

"How fucking dare you!" he screams, stalking closer to me with menacing steps and a blue fire in his eyes that guarantees to burn. "It's my fucking head! My brain!"

I snort at his delusions. What part of himself does he still think he owns? The prick is mine, and the sooner he comes to terms with that, the easier it will be. Though he's never been one to take the easy path, and I do love a challenge, so he can resist it all he wants. He'll know eventually, and when he figures it out, it'll be a battle to go down in history.

The weather isn't on my side tonight. It's stormy and windy, adding strength to Soren's anger and amplifying his power. I don't care, though, because the calling card he left me caused me emotional discomfort all day, and I didn't appreciate that.

Last night, he told me I scared him. This morning, on the back of the card, he told me he's still scared.

Make me unafraid. Show me you're still you.

I will gladly remind him who I am, and I'll do it ruthlessly like I always do. I don't give a single fuck that he's pissed about the brain mapping, and I care even less that he's butthurt over being knocked out and studied against his will. What I do care about is keeping him on the living side of his curse, and if he's afraid, he's the wrong kind of unstable. We can't be having that.

Simply to entice another angry outburst out of him, I give him my charming smile, the one I use on everyone but him. His face goes red, and to be honest, I kind of like red on him now. When the pressure inside him gets to a boiling point, he whips another abandoned bottle at me, and I barely shift in time to avoid it. As it's shattering, he kicks over more bottles on his way to me.

Come here, sweetheart!

I laugh aloud as his body slams into mine, wincing a second later when we make contact with the brick wall. My burned back screams, but not as loud as he does. Right in my damn face, loud and unhinged.

"You had no fucking right, Riot!"

Riot. Back to having his shields up then—or maybe he sees that I'm back to donning my masks. He slams me harder, hands coming up to wrap around my throat, but he doesn't squeeze. He holds me right where he wants me, wedged between him and the asylum, stepping on broken bottles left by teens who snuck out here to get wasted. His eyes glare into mine, so much fury coming at me through his gaze, but there's something else hiding behind it. Something unsure, like he wants to know what the scans showed but he can't make himself ask.

"What makes you think I give a damn about rights?" I open my mouth to ease the tension on my teeth implants. He looks at my parted lips for a second, tempted by whatever he sees there. A memory? Blood? I don't know. "I've never asked your permission for anything before, why should I start now?"

A bolt of lightning streaks across the sky, immediately followed by a crack of thunder. The storm is right on top of us, maybe fuelled by Soren's mood. As he snarls at me, body coiled and holding me at his mercy, he opens his mouth to speak, but nothing comes out. The venom he wants to spew disintegrates on his tongue, and against his will, he asks, "Why?"

"Why what?"

"Why'd you do it?"

Because I want to know how to protect him from himself, but I don't know how to say that without making it seem like I care about him more than he cares about me. Because I understand what Krypt felt when he found out about Remi's mind, and those scars all over his body make a lot of sense now. Soren isn't the type to cut or take a pill, but he'll find his way to death eventually, and I've never felt so pathetic because I can't predict how. I can't protect him from what I don't understand, so I'll protect him from himself. I'll manipulate him for my own benefit, and maybe someday, it'll benefit him, too.

"The Sauder Curse isn't such a curse, is it? Just a fucked-up signal in the brain." I watch him listen, rapt attention warring with his desire to shut me up. Desire. Despair. Death. It's such a circular pattern for him. "I wanted to know how fucked up you are, sweetheart."

He snaps his teeth at me, and I see self-loathing etch into his features. "And?"

"What's it matter? You don't fear the curse anyway, right?"

"Riot."

"Hmm?" I tilt my head in his grip.

"Killian," he amends, the storm taking a recess as his anger pauses to let curiosity win out. "Tell me. I have a right to know since it's my fucking brain."

Sure he does, but I told him before that rights mean nothing to me. Breaking his hold on my throat, I spin us until his back hits the wall. Bracing him between my arms, I get right in his face.

"Want me to kill your cousin? End the curse with a murder and stop the suicide train?" I lean down, listening to him suck in a breath as I run my nose along the side of his neck. "We could do it together. If we murder a Sauder male, we'll protect your brother, which protects my brother. It's a win-win, and we're selfish enough to do it."

His hands grip my shoulders, fingers digging into my flesh to stop the shakes. "It won't help if it's all lies anyway."

I grin, refraining from shaking my head. Moros does crazy things to a person's perspective of the world if it's powerful enough to make people believe that suicide curses are real. I know Soren doesn't actually believe in it, but he's tempted by the idea because so many of his family members have yielded to it. He's intrigued by outrunning it just to be better than them, which means he doesn't really want to know what his scans showed. Because he can't outrun his own mind.

"Do you trust me?"

"Fuck no," he scoffs.

Grinning, I lift my head to look at him. I know my face is a mess, eyes barely visible through all the swelling and bruising, but he doesn't look at me any differently than he has before. We had a tender moment last night in my bed, and we're both a bit messed up about it, so I know tenderness isn't what he wants right now. He needs something volatile to justify the softness that'll come after.

"Are you sure?"

His lips press together, and he forces a breath out of his nose. Shifting his gaze to my mouth again, he speaks to it rather than to my eyes. "I can't. I can't trust you."

Above us, a patient screams bloody murder from a window high up, and when we both look, lightning illuminates the sky. Soren's breath shifts into something shaky and laboured, and then he grabs the back of my neck, forcing me to look at him again.

"I have so many questions about fucking everything," he says in frustration. Looking into my eyes, he adds, "Choke them out of me." It's a plea, and I'm finally hearing him beg.

It's not how I imagined it, but I can give him this one thing without sacrificing anything in return.

Nothing else needs to be said as adrenaline swells within me, amplifying my power over him and turning it into something I won't disrespect. I press on his shoulders, Soren only fighting me for a second before he lowers to his knees, breathing even harder. He won't undo my pants, but that's okay because I like capturing his attention. He watches my broken and busted fingers undo my button, lower the zipper, and palm my cock through the opening. His nostrils flare as I rub myself in front of him, the barrier of my boxers doing the trick to agitate him into action. With the wall at his back and the storm all around us, the patient screams again, and Soren's hands lift to bat mine away.

The glossy blue of his eyes flicks up to me once, and I'm so entirely enraptured by it that I miss his hand moving. He grips my cock hard and firm, squeezing the base to show dominance from his knees. I'm already hard, hardening impossibly further, my mind whirling with filthy, insane thoughts about what I want to do to him, but when the rain starts, he lets his own fantasies run rampant.

Soren's tongue swipes at the tip, dragging a hiss from between my new teeth. I brace my hand on the wall and look down, watching him tease me in a new way. There's nothing dangerous about this, but it still feels dangerous. There's nothing diabolical or unhinged about a blowjob, but he makes it intense because of what it means to him. A need, a want, a way to choke back questions he feels entitled to know the answers to, a mingling of what he desires and how much it despairs him, and a submissive act warped by delusional dominance. It's perfect because it's so simple *and* so complicated. It's my undoing, because seeing him like this has changed yet another fundamental part of me.

So, while he's not looking, I drop the first layer of disguises I'm wearing to let me, as mostly myself, enjoy Soren Sauder willingly on his knees for me.

The rain picks up when he runs his tongue down the side of my dick, familiarizing himself with the desires he has. It only takes him a few seconds before he gives in to temptation and sucks me into his mouth. My eyes close and my head hangs between my shoulders as his wet, warm mouth envelopes me, bringing to life everything that's been dead inside me since I started wearing so many masks. I feel him. His hesitation, but mostly his needs, and that's not something I'm familiar with feeling.

I'm never attuned to the needs of others. Never. Until him.

He wants the questions choked out of him, and I want to give it to him—to comply with his command. In one more minute...

My ass clenches in restraint when he takes me down as far as he can, gagging around the head of my cock. He coughs, but he doesn't stop, and the spasm of his throat one second and the caressing of his tongue the next are the most potent things I've ever felt. Pleasure shivers through me, scorching the raindrops into nothing as they meet the back of my neck. I sink into it, let myself experience it, and breathe through what it means. How it feels. How it changes me.

Then I take him at his word and shift the power dynamic.

I thrust my hips, and Soren's head smacks off the bricks.

He tries to lean forward, but I fuck his mouth hard enough to keep him pinned to the wall. His ass hits his heels, and his eyes look up at me in a slight panic that doesn't last long. They turn wicked, and it makes me smirk to see him so beautifully defiant while at my complete mercy. He opens his throat, taking a few tries to get it right, building off the weather and letting it build off him. Then I give him what he wants.

I choke every fucking question from his throat.

His teeth scrape my cock, but it only adds wreckage to my ruin. Fisting a hand in his wet hair, I hold him where I want him and don't stop thrusting until his tears mix with the rain and his gagging turns to actual gasping for air. When I pull out, he inhales harshly, but his hands land on my ass and he tugs me forward, gulping all of me down in one slobbery swallow.

"Fuck," I whisper to the skies, unsure if I'm fucking him or his mouth is fucking me. All I know is that I feel him everywhere, and I'm not familiar with someone consuming me so wholly. Sex acts are usually just that. Acts. This is something more.

Soren takes charge while I pretend I'm still in control. Every part of me comes rushing to the surface, and for the moment, I just enjoy it. Enjoy him. Him and whatever game we're playing but not admitting to. I have control, but I don't try to take more, letting him strangle himself on my dick because he fucking needs it. *He needs me.*

Shit, I think I need him, too.

His drool mixes with the rain, coating my dick and making every slide of his mouth euphoric. More of my facades fall away as pleasure takes over and I'm unable to put in any effort to keep them in place. I stare at the sky as he sucks me down, wondering if it's looking at me and seeing me for the first time since I was young. But when Soren's hand joins his mouth, my head snaps forward and I take in an even better view.

Him, ragged and breathless, using my body without a lick of shame for it. He's sexy when he takes what he wants, and I hope he never stops. This is trust. Even if he says he can't trust me, he's showing me that he's trying. Despite how ferociously I hope he doesn't look up at me, I'm also desperate for him to look at my face so I can gauge who I am by the expression on his.

Soren's free hand pushes on my hip so he can move me back enough to inhale. Saliva stretches between his lips and my cock, and he stares at it, transfixed by the strings that attach us. Or maybe by something else because when he looks up at me, I barely have time to feel self-conscious when he says, "Come here."

My healing jaw clenches.

"Killian."

I can't. I want to, but I can't go to my knees. I don't know why.

"Fucking pathetic." He bangs his fist on the back of my knee, making me buckle. When I fall forward, he catches me, and I try to fight him off, but then he grabs the sides of my face and pulls my mouth to his.

Oh.

Oh fuck.

His tongue pushes into my mouth, meeting mine, and even though I'd been so turned on before, it's amplified now. Because kissing, making out, is something more than everything else. I felt pleasure in my whole body before, but I feel it in my soul now. I taste my precum on his tongue, and it pulls a moan from my throat. My eyes close and my body feels his inability to stay still beneath me. He lifts his ass, straightening his legs out between mine and pulling me down to straddle him. My bare cock rubs against his shirt, grinding into his abs through the damp material, and I kiss him harder, devouring him because he tastes like smoke and salt—something hellish and refined.

"Why do you make me crazy?" he asks against my mouth, pushing and pulling my body until he gets his pants undone. "Who the fuck are you to do this to me?"

My forehead rolls against his when his cock ruts against mine, his hand fisting us together. *Mmm.* I can't tell if this moment is ignited by challenge or vulnerability. Maybe it's all mixed together and feels irregular because of it.

I love it.

I love it so much that I barely wince when his fingers scrape down my burned back. We're not chasing death anymore. We're chasing rapture, and holy fuck, the journey is even more unhinged.

"Fuck, keep going." I bite his lip as his hand jacks us off, my hips thrusting to fuck through his fist. He grips us harder, rolling us together in a way that lights sparks behind my eyes and makes my dick leak. "Holy shit."

He hums into my mouth, hips rising to meet my thrusts, hand never leaving. The thunder becomes nothing along-side his moans, and the lightning show doesn't hold a candle to how gorgeous he looks in pleasure.

"Killian," he rasps, forehead against mine. "I'm not afraid anymore."

"Fuck." It's my ruin. I brace my hand against the wall and the other on his neck as my body writhes against his and my lower stomach clenches so hard I can't breathe. I'm the one choking now. Choking on an orgasm so intense my eyes roll back. My cum coats his fists, making him groan, and when his cock throbs against mine, I cry out in bliss.

"Fuck," Soren groans, coming all over my dick. His legs bend beneath my ass as he squirms, but he grabs my hair and forces our open mouths together for a kiss that tastes like something I'm getting addicted to.

I'm still panting when we part, eyes closed, trying not to slip into my masks again. I keep my eyes closed and listen to his heart thunder louder than the rain and the screaming patient. As I focus, I realize I can feel it again. His heartbeat in my chest, pounding in my ribs like a war drum that means we're on the same side—the same team.

I brace for the moment to shatter, for him to push me away and pretend this never happened. I'm half tempted to ruin it myself just so he can't, but I'm glad I don't. Because Soren's lips twitch against mine, lifting into a half-smile.

"You don't have to tell me what the scans said. This proves my brain is fucked up." He nips my lip before pushing me back and holding out a hand for me to help him to his feet. He squeezes my sore fingers together, and we stare at each other as we do up our pants without cleaning up.

"Trust me, sweetheart, you've been fucked up since way before tonight."

He laughs, and it's almost camaraderie as he wipes his mouth and shakes his head at me. Looking up at the asylum tower, he says, "I'm gonna go make sure my mom is locked up."

I grab his wrist when he starts to leave, gently tugging him back. My lips meet his for the briefest of moments, and I hum my contentment against them. "Just in case," I whisper.

He rolls his eyes at me as he pulls back, but he's blushing, too.

GHOST

32

ONLY MASK YOU NEED

TOWNWIDE TRAINING IS underway in Janie's Woods, and now that I'm seeing them all here, I'm realizing it's the first time so many Sauders have been in the same place at the same time. My dad's side of the family is vast, most of them still living in Moros, but a few of them have moved to a smaller town not too far away—an escape from the darkness of Moros in order to save themselves from the curse. But here they all are, cousins and uncles, even some aunts, training to prepare themselves for the Reaper Corp war.

And I'm looking at them like they're weak, obviously. They're still alive, but how long until they succumb to the curse? Will this war be what tips them over the edge, or will they take training seriously and survive through it, only to be left with PTSD and an inclination to off themselves afterwards?

I want to roll my eyes at all of it, but who am I to judge when I've been battling the same curse as them? I see myself as better than them because I taunt my curse, but what the fuck are they doing about it? Just *getting through* it? What kind of life is that? Why is no one stronger? Why don't they fight harder? Why was moving to another town their main way of upping their chances?

Do I believe in the Sauder curse?

I thought I only believed in it when it came to *them*. Not myself. They'd always been inferior to me, so I assumed the rest of them died and I lived because I was stronger than them. But then Remi got his mind mapped, started medication, and is doing better, and I don't understand if that's because of the meds or because of Krypt. I don't overly want to know the answer because if both are the true reasons, then it means I need Killian and medication. It means my mind has slow connectivity or blood flow or whatever, just like my brother's. And wouldn't that just be the worst stab to my pride? To know I'm on the same level as them.

I've always been superior, and I'll remain superior. Fuck the brain map.

"Quicker on your feet, woman!" Menace shouts right before he lashes out and knocks Sadie to the ground. "I'm going slow, and if you don't work on your footwork, you'll be dead in three minutes."

Cain kneels to help his girlfriend to her feet, glaring at Menace for being a ruthless combat trainer. Menace's blue mask stays trained on Cain, and the two of them compete in a stare-down that Sadie is oblivious to. Then again, so is Cain because he has no idea who Menace is. Well, other than being the madman who put him through an unforgettable night during the last Initiation.

Menace is running a sparring and hand-to-hand combat

training session while Ransom and Seven have a group of trainees set up at the gun range, teaching them to work a pistol. Riot and Kyd are handing out security supplies to people who have come to fortify their houses, and Monster is prowling between it all, judging people for their weaknesses. He's always been sensitive to the vulnerability of others. He's smaller than everyone in Vile House, short and petite, but his dark hair clashes nicely with his bright yellow mask, and his energy is worse than a twister. He's constantly churned up, and when he gets manic, he's every deadly part of the tornado, never once being the eye of the storm.

"What do you wanna do with your mom's place?" Glitch asks, stepping up beside me to watch the training. "We can secure it and put up video surveillance if you want."

Honestly, I wouldn't care if it burned to the ground like Remi's house did. Mom has apparently been burning bridges for years, so even though she's locked up in the asylum for now and no one is missing her, they'll notice if her house is empty.

"Selena is gonna stay there, so talk to her about it." I look at my family members as they struggle through arming and disarming guns. "You're still close with your family, right? Like, all of them?" I ask him.

"My parents and Lockan, yeah."

Glitch's birth name is Makoa Kamaka. He spent the first ten years of his life living in Hawaii until his mom's best friend, Lockan's mom, talked them into moving to Moros. We're the same age, so even as a kid, I remember Makoa and his long dark hair coming to town. I thought he was a pussy, but one day out in the woods by the cemetery, I saw him shoot an arrow and pin an asshole kid to a tree for fucking with Lock. And when the time came for the beating, he let Lock do it and never tried to take any of the credit for himself. I liked them both right after that. I felt challenged by them both... and I enjoyed the sensation.

"You ever feel like they're a burden to you?" I ask.

Glitch snorts out a laugh. "Fuck, you're a dick."

Not arguing that.

"If anything, I'm the burden to them. They barely know shit about me anymore because I have to keep Vile House a secret. I go missing for weeks at a time and they don't know what I'm doing. Pretty sure they think I have a drug addiction or something. Having things open to Lockan makes it easier now. We're closer, so we've been going to visit my parents more."

Lock's parents are both dead, so Glitch's parents took him in as a pre-teen, and they basically grew up as brothers. They didn't like that Lock joined The Misfits, but they're perfectly fine with it now.

"Why?" Glitch asks.

I nod at the Sauder group, shaking my head at how pitiful and frail they are. "How the fuck did I come from that bloodline?"

"You think you're better than them?"

I glare at Glitch from behind my mask. "I know I am."

"Your ego tells you that you are," he agrees, pissing me off. "But you started like them."

"Yeah, when I was a kid. I haven't been that pathetic since I was eleven."

"Whatever," he snorts again. "What're you asking me?"

"If it'd be easier to just kill them all now so I don't have to protect them in the war."

"Fucking hell, Ghost. You're twisted as fuck." He steps in front of me to block my view of my family. "If you don't care if they're alive or dead, why bother killing them to save them from the war?"

"To end the curse."

"Oh." He nods, dropping his hands from my shoulders. "Why not get all their brains mapped and have Medic, Psych, and Axel start them on meds like Remi?"

Because that'll mean I need the same meds as those tragic losers. Riot won't tell me what my scans showed, and I'm too much of a hypocrite to ask. If I believe my mind is superior, then it is, and I won't have to deal with the utter disappointment of being the same as all these other idiots.

"Where's Lock?" I ask instead.

Glitch nods his head to Lock and The Misfits, going through their own training while also rebuilding their reputation with the townsfolk. I don't say goodbye, just walk over to Lock and tug him aside.

"You find your traitor?"

Lock turns his back on his crew to speak to me. "No, but out of everyone here, only three of them joined about two years ago. If that lady in Reaper City is to be believed, then those are the only ones it could be because everyone else comes from a known family in town."

"Director wants to test them. Feed them information that is different from what the other members know and see if any of it makes it back to Reaper Corp. Glitch has spyware all over that place now, so he can listen for trigger words."

"Glitch," Lock says with a laugh. "That's gonna take me a bit to get used to. But okay, what's the info I'm leaking?"

"Ransom will tell you." I nod at his red mask and strong body. "Let me know if you need help."

Unable to be near my extended family any longer, I disappear into the fog of Janie's Woods and end up at the pond on Carnival Hill—the one Riot drowned me in. I fucking hate myself for being here, getting nostalgic over something so ruinous. But I'm a puzzle, and I sense that one of my pieces got left behind here. Something chipped away from the foundation of who I am when he pushed me under the water and made a new deal with me, and I can't decide if I hate him or appreciate him for it.

Because I'm different now, and different isn't always good. Bending to look at my face, I lift my mask and study the murky water. I try to wrap my head around the way my illusion shifts, morphing my familiar reflection with these new parts of me, exposed only because old parts are missing. I think the piece I miss the most is the one that pushed my biggest button—the button that triggered me into becoming a madman who sought out Death like she was a dance partner.

Am I still looking for her? Am I obnoxiously flirting, screaming at her to pay attention to me so I can slam that door in her face, or am I tongue-tied, unsure what I'll say to her if I ever wind up on her doorstep again?

Uncertainty isn't my friend, and introspection is worse. I'm still the same person, and Riot—Killian—has gotten too many tricks over me. As I smile at the wobbly mirror reflecting my insanity back at me, I know exactly how to make myself feel better.

I'll use Riot.

HE'S NOT in his room, but I'm being patient. Facts told me he's with Medic, and that's all I needed to know. While I wait, I write out more calling cards, getting my vulnerable bits out onto paper to rid my physical body of them. I can't say it to his face, but I can write down the things that scare me and the softer things I enjoy and hide them around his room for him to find if he's ever inclined to look. I hope he never finds them.

It's another way to express emotion without having to verbally admit to this shit.

By the time he finally unlocks and opens his bedroom door at Vile House, I'm jittering with impatience and a need to expel everything morbid about myself straight onto him. I have a plan, and I'm ready to enact it, but when I step out of the shadowed corner and see his head hang, I pause. I don't even breathe.

Riot whips his shirt across the room, sighing in a way that sounds painful. With his back to me, I barely swallow my gasp. *His back...*

His Vile House tattoo...

It's burned and broken, the skull a grotesque mess and his name almost entirely gone. As the burns heal, peeling away skin to build new skin, the design changes into something deformed and nearly unrecognizable. For a man like Killian, who only found himself once he joined Vile House, I can understand how devastating this must be for him.

His dark wavy hair hits his shoulders now, hanging over his nape in rambunctious waves. When his shoulders slump and he braces his arms on his dresser, head hung, it falls to cover his side profile, blocking my view of his anguished face. He's hurting. Emotionally.

I don't know how to deal with that.

Especially because Riot is the kind of person who needs visual reminders of who he is, and his tattoo has always been his anchor. Now it's his downfall, and a part of me wants to make him feel better without knowing how to achieve that. I won't admit that I'm broken, but... he's fixed me before, and it's time I do more than bring him a fucking smoothie.

I pull my mask over my face and grab his off the hook by the bathroom door. Silently, I stand right behind him, barely emitting a signal as he keeps his head low, shoulders and back heaving while he self-regulates horribly. I look at myself in the mirror over the dresser. The glow-in-the-dark parts of my mask are lit up teal, and Killian's dark head of hair and tanned, scarred shoulders block my body. We're a sight together. An ominous one with a soft side I'm not yet ready to admit to.

I care about him in some sort of way that left me half dead while he was captured, and breaking on his behalf now that he's suffering. What does it all mean? I don't know, but the fight in me isn't against it. It's for it.

When his back rises with a deep breath, I spook him. "Unmasked and broken. That's your base layer, yeah?"

Killian whips around, hand on my throat, face right in

front of mine. He's seething, pissed off about being spied on while he was letting himself crack in solitude. He looks at my mask, wondering why I'm wearing it inside the house, but he doesn't ask because he's too busy trying to come up with excuses for what he was doing. To talk it away and pretend it doesn't exist. To put up a front that shows him as nothing but corrupted perfection. To manipulate the situation to his benefit.

His eyes are roiling with storms instead of Krypt's monsters, and in the grey of them, I see it buried under all his power. Weakness and fear. A lack of understanding. A need to prove himself *to himself*. "Get out."

"No."

"Soren, I swear to fucking god, if you don't back off right now, I can't be responsible for—"

"This is you? The real you without the masks?"

He falters for words but holds my throat tighter. I watch him try to reinforce every bit of charm and deception he's mastered over the years. Those masks don't come, though. He can't grasp one, which makes him try to hide even more. When he drops his hand and looks down to avoid my gaze, I tilt his chin and force him to look at me.

My knuckles brush his stubble, and his eyes narrow in another attempt to disappear. "You don't need them. Not with me."

His nostrils flare and his cheek muscles feather. "I need them. With myself."

I shake my head at him, holding up his Vile House mask. "This is Riot. You. Killian fucking Hallows." I show him the white and black, the opposing shades that mark him as who he is. "It's the only mask you need."

He looks at it, trying to accept my truthful words, but his eyes dip downward and he shakes his head in my grip. "I... fuck, I need the ninety seconds."

"No, you don't."

"Don't fucking look at me right now."

"Fine." I grab his wrist and twist, locking his arm behind his back and spinning him to face the mirror. "Then look at your fucking self. Look, Killian! Look at who you fucking are." I shove his face forward, almost nose to nose with the mirror. "Ruthless Vile Boy who wears the white mask and goes by Riot. The master manipulator. A protector of Moros because of the power you hold and the authority you demand. Killian Hallows, the man who helped his brother kill his parents to protect him." I lean in, lips brushing his hair. "The one and only man to ever fuck me."

He growls. The sound starts as a rumble that builds into a scream of freedom. He looks in the mirror, trying to see himself as I see him. He blinks and yells even more, choking fire straight from the depths of his throat, struggling in my grip.

"And when you need the visual reminder, you put this on." I release his arm but pin him with my body as I strap his mask over his face, securing it at the back of his head. "Because this is who you are. Doesn't fucking matter what your skin looks like. I. Fucking. See you."

He's trembling, but he doesn't stop me from grabbing the razor and slicing one fine line down his inner bicep. He needs a purging, and I'm the only one strong enough to handle the demons that leave him.

He pauses, time stopping as he lets the force of everything he is sink into his bones. I think all he's ever wanted was to be seen without all his masks. The moment is full, pregnant with purpose and painful because of it. And when it ends, Killian explodes.

His eruption is gorgeous.

His teeth snap beneath the mask, audibly setting us off the starting blocks. He spins, both hands coming out to pound against my chest. With the force of his shove, I fly backwards, slamming into his bed, and he keeps coming at me.

Ah, fuck yeah. Here he is. I grin beneath my mask and revel in the force he projects. When his hands slam against my chest again, I brace myself on the edge of his bed and kick out with my legs, making him buckle forward. I laugh loudly as he falls, head tilted back and throat bared, ready to go mad with him.

Killian screams louder when his sore back hits the hard floor, and I take the chance to kneel at his feet. When he kicks out, I grab his foot and rip his boots off, tossing them aside. Before I can tear his pants away, he tries to sit up and throw me onto my back. I don't let him. Pressing on his chest, I lean over him and push him back down. My hips open his legs, and my groin rubs against his.

"Who are you?" I ask, voice muffled behind my mask.

"Me," he says. "In fucking charge. Stronger than you."

Good story. I laugh, grinding against him to draw a groan from his lips. "Feel that?"

"Your cock? Yeah, always fucking ready for me, aren't you, sweetheart?"

"Your back," I correct. "Burned and broken against the floor. Feel it, Riot. Feel those burns and stop letting them control you."

He snarls, gaining strength. He sits up, making me fall backwards to my ass. When he stands, he grabs the back of my head and forces my face against the hardness in his pants. "Oh, I fucking feel it. Nothing controls me but myself."

I suffocate in his groin, not even mad about it because he's coming back to life. His shoulders are tense and straight, not slumped and sad, and his authority over absolutely every situation is rising to the surface. He's a master manipulator, and this time, I'm going to let him manipulate me for my own personal gain—him at his best.

I bite down on my lip, groaning against him. He smacks me, twisting my mask sideways with the force of it. When I reach up to straighten it, he grabs my wrists and pins them to the bed behind me, making my back press into the frame. Killian kneels, shirtless and masculine, empowered because of himself. He rights my mask and squeezes my wrists.

"Admit you want me. Fucking blink, Soren."

I do blink, but only because he can't see it. "There you are, you egotistical prick. Knew you'd rely on me to bring you back."

"I never fucking went anywhere." He unzips my hoodie, letting it hang open. "Admit I'm winning."

"Are you stalling?"

He groans, hauling me to my feet. Killian rips my clothes off angrily until I'm wearing nothing but my mask and a pair of black socks. On my own, I sit on the edge of his bed, stroking my cock to entice him. I track his nimble, still-bandaged fingers as they undo his pants and push them down his thighs. His boxers go next, and then I zero in on his hand wrapped around his cock, precum already pearling on the tip. This is a dick-measuring contest if I've ever seen one, but instead of it being about size, it's about who's going to reign as the dominant one.

Simply because he's having a shitty day, and I admittedly enjoyed his dick in my ass, I push back onto his bed and bring my feet flat to the mattress as an invitation to goddamn take what he wants. Look at me being selfless. And still dominant, because I'm the one in control of this.

His throat rolls with a swallow as he prowls towards me, grabbing lube from the bedside table on his way. The white face of his mask is glowing, so stark against the black, and I've never seen something fit him so well. He's every shade of grey there is, and between white and black is where he thrives.

Instead of popping the top, he drops the lube and pushes on my knees, folding me back to expose my ass to him. He pushes his mask up to free his mouth, and I gasp, ready to fight him off...

But then my asshole vibrates as he growls against it, his tongue pressing inside me. "Oh, holy fuck." I grip the sheets to avoid touching him, but I don't last. When he licks all around my hole, I go wild with a level of pleasure I've never experienced before. My hands end up on his shoulders, and I can't even look at him because it's too much.

I'm the one on my back, but he's the one servicing me, and I've never felt more conflicted about our power dynamic.

The inside of my mask dampens with my laboured breaths, and I sink into his bed without a clear thought. I'm not fighting for or against anything, and I'm not proving a point to shine in the spotlight. I'm just rendered useless because of pleasure. My cock is so hard that I reach for it, but Killian bats my hand away and lifts his mouth from my ass to glare at me.

I don't know where it comes from, and I hate that I say it, but I whisper, "Don't stop."

And he doesn't.

I hold one of my knees and he holds the other, the two of us spiralling into new territory. Worship and praise, a place that comes with pleasure without despair, and a level of trust-building that scares me because it's so natural. I lift my mask slightly so I can breathe easier, pressing my head to the mattress and barely refraining from moaning. His tongue delves into my hole, his stubble brushing against my skin, and the combination of rough and soft is so goddamn good I squeeze my eyes tighter.

"I knew you'd be needy, sweetheart. So fucking repressed."

I pull him up my body, wrapping my legs around his waist. I'm tempted to kiss him, but I can't. I can't start craving kisses now when I'm already so fucking pliable beneath him. He grins at me, seeing the hesitation. He pulls my mask down for me, settling it over my face before doing the same to his.

"Who are we right now?" He grabs the lube and reaches between our bodies to lube his dick and my ass. "Riot and Ghost or Killian and Soren?"

I want to say Killian and Soren because it feels more sentimental, but I'm not a sentimental person and I need some barrier between him and my sensitive feelings. I touch his mask to give him my answer.

"Thought so," he says, nudging my hole with his thick

cock. "Ghost and Riot can fuck, but when you're ready to admit how needy you are, Soren and Killian can have sex."

I start to argue. He fucks me instead. Abruptly and without enough prep. The stretch and pressure feel good because it's harsh amid gentleness, and I like the opposition.

Because we're masked and need this, the ability to remind ourselves of who we are and give in to something that feels so good is humiliating.

There's not much of a burn when he stretches me open this time, only a fullness that glues me back together and pulls me apart simultaneously. Every swivel of his hips sends a spark of fire through me, making me sweat and demand more. My fingers dig into his biceps, controlling him with a tight grip but wanting to give him free rein because, holy shit, he knows how to fuck.

Riot's abs rub my dick between our bodies, sliding me up and down the bed with each thrust. I hate how close I already am, especially when I ignite in passion when he tilts himself to hit me at the exact right angle.

"Jesus," I groan, eyes rolling.

"Riot," he corrects. "Killian, if you're honest."

I am honest... in my head. "Shut up and fuck me."

"Anything for you, sweetheart."

He's such a prick that I enjoy it. His sweaty body glides with mine, his wounds forgotten as bliss and darkness take over. I don't know what he's thinking or if he's remembering who he is, but I know I'm not thinking about anything other than taking everything he gives me. The absence of thought is almost peaceful.

I'm so close it's discomforting, but I want to erupt right now. Letting my hand fall down his arm, I grab his wrist and bring his hand to my throat. I don't want him to choke me or give me a head buzz by cutting off my blood flow, and somehow, he knows it because he doesn't squeeze. I just want to feel his hand on me, letting my pulse beat out of control against his fingertips. Needing him closer, I wrap my legs around him tightly, dragging him in. His cock hits deep inside me, and he holds himself there, rocking without pulling out.

Somehow, it gets hotter and harder to hold off. "Fuck. Fuck, I'm gonna..." I almost wish our masks weren't on so I could kiss him.

"Soren," he says as he pulls out. "I fucking see you, too." He thrusts back in.

I combust, grabbing my cock to jerk off as I come all over us. I moan louder than I ever have, unable to keep the music inside, releasing what feels like years of repression because... I finally found him. The person who is my match, like Remi said.

Killian Hallows.

Our masks clack together when he bows his head, grunting through his orgasm as his hips stutter and he fills me full. The old me would have felt defiled by his cum in my ass, but the new me feels cleansed. Of what, I don't know. I'm too high to understand. All I know is that we're wearing masks, but we aren't Ghost and Riot.

"Holy fuck, sweetheart," he gasps as he catches his breath.

Fuck my own rules. I rip his mask off and kiss him, but he laughs against mine. Goddammit. I push mine off, grab the back of his neck, and kiss him like I mean it. Mean... *it*.

"We gonna cuddle now?" he asks, pressing one more kiss to my lips.

A bite of embarrassment creeps up, but I don't even know what I'm embarrassed about. "I made you a fucking smoothie. What more do you want? Jesus."

Killian laughs as he rolls onto his back, his hand falling into mine and the world seeming alright.

RIOT

33

WINNER TAKES RANK

IT CHAPS my ass to stand at the end of the rank line. It chaps even more that everyone is laughing at us about it.

"Come on, Lil Baby Ghosty!" Kyd begs from further up the line. Any rank below Kyd is a fucking tragedy, and here I am. "Like this? About a nine?" Kyd holds his hands out, measuring fourteen again.

Just to be a dick, Ghost moves Kyd's hands apart more. "This kind of nine."

Kyd's smile is so wide I can see the red stains from his cherry slushie on his teeth. He leans forward, looking down the line at me, and gives me the world's most exaggerated wink. "Atta boy, smiles. I always knew you'd be blessed." He kisses his fingers and lifts them to the sky.

"Wait," Seven butts in.

"Yeah, fucking wait," Krypt butts in on him. "You two fucked?"

"Like you get a say, you hypocritical fuck," Ghost snorts.

I look at Director, who has the bridge of his nose pinched between his finger and thumb. "Remind me why

I'm at the end of rank when these children can't even focus?" I quirk a brow.

He sighs, but I can tell he's happy to see me on my feet again. "Because you put your ego ahead of a job and fucked us over."

Ugh. Dick.

"Let's sit," he says to all of us.

Kyd races everyone even though no one is competing, and the rest of us take our time. Ghost lingers, so I drop back to brush my fingers against his, teasing a hand he secretly wants held but won't admit to in front of everyone else. He snaps his narrowed blue eyes at me and shakes his head, taking a seat next to the one I sit in.

Director sits at the head of the table, his tablet open in front of him. "I can't believe I'm saying this," he starts, looking up at us, "but I'm proud of you all."

"Even me?!" Kyd stands, hand on his chest.

"Have you found the lion yet?"

"Maybe."

"Then less proud." Director hides a small smile as Kyd sits back down. "You've helped to bring Moros together. Death Row is mostly repaired after the explosions, training is going well, and more than half the locals have come to us for assistance. The alliance with The Misfits is working out well, and the locals are accepting it. It's a good sign, and I'm grateful to all of you for doing your part to unify the town. Thank you."

He doesn't thank us often, so it hits deep. We all nod or ignore him like he never said it, but I know we're all pleased.

"And, despite why they got the job, let's all recognize what Riot and Ghost accomplished in Reaper City."

We're praised, as we should be, and I drink it in, flashing a cocky smile at my boys. My knee nudges Soren's, and he raises his arms to accept the praise. He's finally getting recognition, and instead of mocking him for it, I'm praising him, too.

Director laughs. "Maybe a reward is deserved, yeah?" he asks, his grin growing. "I'm proposing a challenge. Yates is still in town. We've had at least four sighting reports in the last ten hours. So, whichever one of you finds Yates and brings him in will move to the head of rank."

Monster leans forward and Menace stands, itching to hunt. Ransom grins at the table, concocting a silent plan, and Seven and Glitch glance at one another, forming an alliance. Facts jitters, fingers tapping together, and Krypt barely reacts, but I know he's been craving something vicious. Ghost doesn't move, not even a twitch, but I can feel his mind working from here.

"Oh," Kyd pouts.

"Problem?" Director asks him.

"Nooo," he sighs dramatically. "I'm just working on a slow burn with my smarty-pants boyfriend. This puts a kink in my plan."

"Come on, Kyd. You love a hunt, and distance makes the heart grow darker." Menace laughs, and Kyd's grin turns playfully sinister.

"Fonder, dipshit." Krypt stands, eager to go. "When does this challenge start?"

Director meets all our eyes before grinning again. "Right now."

Everyone gets up, scrambling for the door. But *not so fucking fast*. I block everyone's way by pulling Soren against me, his chin between my fingers. When I press my lips to his and whisper, "Just in case," his cheeks turn red, he rolls his eyes, and he shoves me away to be the first one out the door as everyone else mocks the absolute fuck out of us.

Me, mostly. But I don't care. Sooner or later, Soren will admit he likes the gentle moments, too.

"Awwwww!" Kyd squeals.

"Fucking pathetic," Krypt snaps.

"I knew that tension would eventually snap." Seven laughs.

I look back at Director to see what he has to say about it, but he's just watching me with relief and some sort of fondness in his eyes. I don't like it, so I push my way out.

My smile is all charm as I leave the con room, but it turns to a feral smirk with bad intentions towards Yates when I grab my mask from my room.

TURNS out we have more competition in finding Yates than just each other. The Misfits are also on the hunt, and it seems as if half of Moros is out for him, too. The town is unified, everyone working together for one greater purpose: to catch the traitor who let the enemy into our home.

I'm still sore and injured, but I'm ready to get back to my roots. Fuck my ruined Vile House tattoo, and fuck my insecurity over my masks. Tonight, I'll prove to myself that the only thing that matters is the power within me. Because I'm a hunter at heart. A sinister mind with an even more sinister need, and Yates is about to become the dopamine hit I need.

Bonfires are lit all across town. The cemetery is flickering with torches and small fires, and the streets glow orange from lampposts. The vibe of the entire town is ominous and predatory, and fucking hell, it's building up inside me. Even the ravens refuse to slumber, sitting on tree branches and power lines to be our eyes and ears. I love it when every part of Moros comes together for one despicable purpose.

On this chilly, damp night, I'm prowling down Crucifix Street with a new blade in my grip. It's never met blood until I used it an hour ago to slice my inner bicep, bleeding all my second thoughts from my body to leave me with nothing but confidence and a capable mind. I spin it in my palm, the hilt warm from my hand and the sharp edge eager to meet flesh. The ravens *caw* above me, and two figures dressed in black slink up the street between parked cars and front yard bushes. It's not Tom and Yates. It's a husband and wife, close friends of Yates', and the reason I know where they are is because of that neck I snapped in the bargain hall.

Willow Olenna's cousin died by my hands, and the price she paid me was agreed upon a few days ago when I paid her a visit. Information. She's a shifty, smart woman who knows everyone's business and is wise enough to make her skills transactional. The first bit of information she gave me isn't up for grabs yet. I'll share it when I'm ready, but earlier, when I left her a calling card to call me, she delivered exactly what I needed.

Yates and Tom have been house-hopping between a few different sets of friends who are willing to protect them from the townsfolk. No surprise that none of them are members of The Misfits. This husband and wife are guilty of hiding those filthy traitors, and now they're on the run, smart enough not to take a car out of town because they know the road will be blocked.

Well, their footpath is also blocked, and when they meet Krypt up ahead, they'll turn back towards me, falling perfectly into our trap. I'm trembling with anticipation for it.

Our masks aren't battery-powered, but they are glow-in-the-dark. So when the husband and wife step out of cover, ready to sneak into the next yard to escape Crucifix Street, Krypt's glowing purple mask greets them. Their shrieks are audible from back here as they scramble over one another, grasping at each other's clothes to quickly turn around. Where they're met with my glowing white mask. If only they could see my smile. It's one of my best, only coming out on rare occasions when I know for absolute certainty that I'll get to lord my power over someone.

I don't stop walking as they scramble. Krypt is closing in on them from behind, and they're whimpering such beautiful sobs. Their fear leaches into the night, and if I don't get hard over this, I'll consider myself broken. I love scaring people!

"We didn't do anything!" the husband shouts, grasping at his wife's jacket. "I swear! We don't know nothing."

I tilt my head at them, a silent question, because they sure do know something, and we're going to get it out of them. The wife looks behind her and screams when she sees two knives glinting in the moonlight from between my brother's fingers. I don't care about their fear beyond enjoying it for myself, and I have no empathy for their situation. They chose to become friends with Yates, and they chose to hide him after he fucked Moros over. Whatever happens to them, they have it coming, and honestly, I take pride in being their deliverance.

"Please," she cries, clutching her husband's arm. "Just let us leave town. We won't come back. We don't know where he is."

The vein in my neck pounds with the drum of my heart. Adrenaline spikes as anticipation builds. This is where I'm most comfortable; behind my Vile House mask, armed with a weapon that feels natural in my hand, wielding power over those beneath me, and delivering justice to pathetic liars who believe themselves to be stronger than the full force of an unhinged town. In Moros, power is checked at the door, and if you don't have what it takes to hold onto it, you fucking lose it. Quick.

"Yates," is all I say, my voice projecting authority.

"We don't know!"

"Yates," I say again, this time letting the force of my manipulative instincts infiltrate the name.

"I swear!"

Stepping forward, I spin my new blade, letting it catch in the light. "Last time."

Krypt makes a sound behind them and they both jolt, damn near pissing themselves. They're past middle age, on the shitty side of life I hope I never make it to, and finally realizing they're worthless.

"Yates?" It's the third and final time I'll ask.

The question is punctuated by Krypt's knives. One for each throat. I laugh behind my mask, appalled at how easy this is. He doesn't even have to hold them in place because his blades do it for him. Mr. and Mrs. Newton are pin straight, afraid to even blink, all because they know, somewhere deep down in their souls, that we're the brothers who killed our own parents.

The ravens *caw* like they're cheering us on, amplifying my grin. In the middle of the rainy season, the night sits calmly as a backdrop, the moon unhindered by clouds. It spotlights me, shining down to give me centre stage, and I'm not one to turn down attention. Time to play a 'this or that' game.

"Lie to me and your husband loses his ability to see," I tell the wife. "Have Yates and Tom been staying with you?"

She trembles, crying hard enough for Krypt's sharp edge to dig into her pulse point. Without turning her head, her eyes shift to look at her husband, wanting his opinion on the question. I hate these types of couples. Why the fuck would you willingly get into a marriage with such an imbalanced power dynamic? Even Remi, as a fearful cursed man, holds innate power over Krypt, and a lot of it. Dominance and submission by choice is one thing, but these two are just ridiculous.

"Why're you looking at him?" I ask, keeping my stance casual. "You either answer with the truth and he's fine, or you lie to me and he loses his eyes. Are you so loyal to him that you need his permission to answer? Because I'll wager a bet that he wants you to tell the truth. Wanna know why?" I wish she could see my face and recognize me for who I am. "Because it saves his eyes, and when the next question comes his way, he'll throw you under the damn bus to save himself."

The husband spits, ready to weakly defend himself, but

Krypt is fed up. He shoves the wife to my chest, and I hold her around the waist as Krypt buries one dagger in Mr. Newton's eye. His right one. He screams. The wife screams louder. The ravens cheer and the moon winks.

I laugh like Soren.

"Oh my god!" she wails. "Oh my god!" She vomits down her chin, and I bend her forward so none of it gets on me.

"No time to delay, Mrs. Newton. He's only got one eye left. Where the fuck is Yates?" I haul her up by her hair. She smells putrid and brittle, nothing more than another lamb who can't avoid the slaughter. Her red face annoys the living fuck out of me. Learn to control your reactions, woman!

"He's escaping!" she screams down Crucifix Street. "He betrayed us! We were all supposed to get out together, but he locked us in our cellar and took all our weapons."

Krypt rips his knife free from the husband's eye, and blood pours down his face in pretty streams. Because there's time, I compliment my brother on his knife skills. Didn't even fuck up the guy's brain.

"Where?" Krypt asks.

She vomits again at the sight of all the blood coming from her husband's eye socket. Mr. Newton reaches for his eye to stop the flow, but Krypt twists his arm around his back, kicks him in the thigh, and forces him to kneel. When that same blade presses to the man's throat, he asks his question again.

"Where are they escaping?"

"Please," Mrs. Newton begs.

Krypt cuts.

"Please!"

He pauses, looking at her for his answer. Fuck, I love

him when he's ruthless. His purple mask is the best backdrop, but if only I could see all the monsters that writhe in his eyes.

"Janie's Woods! He's meeting Benton Wentworth!"

"How long ago?"

"Less than an hour." She slumps in my grip, and I shove her towards her kneeling husband. We have our answer, but it's up to Krypt what he wants to do with these two.

Krypt shrugs his shoulders at me, not giving a shit one way or the other. Murder isn't allowed when we don't have a justifiable reason, but... we have one. So...

"Axel?" Krypt asks. "See if he can find out what else they know about Wentworth?"

Logical, since the billionaire has shown interest in Remi's property, and he's meeting with Director soon to negotiate a new alliance. Might be a way to protect Director if we know more about Wentworth and whatever ties he has to Yates, and since I'm experimenting with this whole 'thinking of others' bullshit...

But... murder.

I almost pout. Instead, I bloody my brand-new blade by slicing both their Achilles tendons. "Wait here. Don't hobble too far. Someone will be by to pick you up soon."

Krypt laughs. "You're sick." Remi changed that word for him, and he now has it branded on his chest. I'm not great at gratitude, but I'll never be able to properly thank Remi for everything he's done for my brother.

"Oh?" I look at him. "We're cool with that word now?"

He turns his back to me, strolling down the raven-lined street, but I know he's grinning in that twisted way he does.

GHOST

34

JUST IN CASE

FUCK, they're dumb. I've been following Krypt and Riot since they left Willow Olenna with the information I wanted. And now I'm going to beat them to Janie's Woods and claim Yates for myself, earning my position at the head of the rank line.

Where I fucking belong.

Director never said how we had to find Yates, and while I don't like cheating, I don't consider this duplicitous. I have a fucking skill, and being a ghost is it. Like hell I'm not going to use that skill whenever it benefits me. I'm not as dumb as they are.

But we're all getting fucked over tonight. Because Lockan Tate is already here, and he's rabid.

"Are you fucking kidding me, Ghost?" he shouts with Yates in a chokehold while two other Misfits restrain Tom on the ground of Janie's Woods. Discarded weapons litter the forest floor, and Yates' mouth is duct-taped. "You know he's mine! After everything I put up with from him and all the shit he did to my crew, you think I'm gonna let you take him? Fuck off."

I can't say I blame him for feeling betrayed. We had a deal, and Yates was his to handle. Silently, I close the distance between us, making sure his crew members keep their hands where I can see them. We're allied, but there's still a traitor in his crew, and since we don't know who it is, I don't trust any of them.

"Where's Wentworth?"

He looks confused. "Not here."

I scan the forest, wondering if those two lied to Krypt and Riot or if Wentworth already fled.

"Don't fucking fight me on this. You know I deserve to punish him." Lock throws Yates to the ground while he spits and gags, trying to speak through the cloth gag under the tape.

I *do* know he deserves this. He made Moros a promise to punish Yates and march anyone found helping him down Death Row for the town to see. I've been in The Misfits' madness for years with Lock, so I see myself entitled to Yates' downfall, too. Plus, I want top spot in rank.

"I'm helping you."

"No."

"Lockan."

Lock steps over Yates and butts his firm chest to mine. He knows who I am under this mask and what I'm capable of. I respect him more for challenging me. "My crew needs this more than you do. You have Vile House. We're still pulling ourselves together."

Softly, so his two men don't hear, I say, "I put up with him, too."

"While always having Vile House at your back. We didn't have anyone at our backs." He fists his hand in the front of my jacket, tugging me forward so he can speak in my ear. "He's fucking mine, Sauder. I might act calm, but I've got years of rage built up and I need somewhere to fucking aim it."

"Hands off what's mine or I'll cut 'em off and force 'em up your ass, Tate."

I close my eyes behind my mask, unsure if I'm pissed at his protectiveness or if I'm even more pissed that it's possessiveness. His voice is calm, but it's that threatening kind of calm that comes before something unleashes. Lock must sense it because he drops my jacket and faces Killian.

"Riot," he greets through clenched teeth.

"Pleasure," Riot greets him back, nodding at how close he's standing to me. When Lock takes a single step back but otherwise does nothing to submit, Riot laughs. "You'd make a good Vile Boy."

"Even better Misfit. I'm taking Yates and Tom whether I gotta fight you for them or not." He squares up to both of us while Killian's hand touches mine, teasing a grip that has no fucking right to be appealing at a time like this. "What's it going to be?"

"What do ya think, sweetheart?" he asks me.

I smack his hand away and shove him off. "What're you going to do with him?" I ask Lock.

"Whatever the fuck I want, but he won't get off easy."

"Promise?" Riot asks.

"Promise," Lock agrees, nodding.

I tilt my head to let them go, unsure why I'm allowing it. Yeah, I get that Lock deserves this, and I even get that it's his crew's business, not ours, but I'm not someone who passes up opportunities to climb ladders. Yates gets me top rank, and as I watch Lock and his guys drag them out of the woods, I see my second-to-last spot become my reality for a lot longer.

I don't know what to think, so I take a silent step to leave this place, but Killian's fingers tighten around my wrist.

"Not a chance, sweetheart. No slipping into shadows tonight."

Am I letting him pull me back or am I playing a game? "Where's Krypt?"

"Gone. Looking for Wentworth. Everyone else will be stalking Lock now. Just you and me taking a walk down memory lane." He wraps his arm around my shoulders and turns me to face the pond. "Remember the night we made our first deal? I drowned you and you blinked."

"I got a brush with death and blinked to drag you down with me."

"It's like we're listening to the same song and hearing different lyrics," he muses.

"Same lyrics. Different meanings." I like the way his arm feels around me, so I pretend not to notice it there. "What song are we listening to now?"

"You could play us one," he suggests.

"We could play one together."

Killian goes tense. Music makes him uncomfortable because he doesn't know what his sounds mean. He can't manipulate, interpret, or influence it, so he steers clear of it because it's a better opponent than he is. It bests him every damn time, and he's sick of losing to it.

I pull him deeper into the woods, almost within sight of

The Harpy's cabin, and then I push my mask up. He doesn't, so I do it for him. "What're you scared of?"

"Nothing."

"Killian."

He scoffs, shoving at my chest. "The fuck is this? We don't talk. Not like this."

"We talked the other night."

"Yeah, about bullshit... *your* bullshit."

"Oh, so my bullshit is fair game, but yours isn't?" I grab his hip and force him to stop pacing. "You don't have anyone else you can talk to, so talk to me."

"Fuck you. I have my brother."

My turn to scoff. "Yeah? Like you'd ever willingly show weakness around him? Yeah, right. You have yourself built up as his hero because you feel like you failed him early on."

He punches me. Right in the gut. I buckle over, eyes watering, wind knocked out of me, eyes staring at the grassy forest floor.

"I *did* fail!" Killian seethes at me. "It's the last time I ever let myself fail, so fuck you for bringing it up. Like you've never failed."

"I failed two brothers and a dad already," I shout at him, standing upright despite the pain. "You think I'm too full of myself to know that?"

"Yeah, I did, actually."

We stare, unstable because we're supposed to be mad, but it's taking too much energy to stay that way. Embarrassment kills me, and failing my brothers is one of my greatest catastrophes. I've never said it aloud until tonight, and with Killian as the only one who heard it, I feel safe while insecure. Trapped in the truth but allied with him because he admitted fault, too. I failed my brothers, and that's my reality. But instead of it feeling terrible because I lost them, it feels terrible because I wasn't strong enough to save them. Failure is failure, and...

"I almost failed you," I whisper against the wind, hoping it carries that confession away. Straightening, I don't look at him until he breathes loudly. His eyes are soft but surprised, full of questions he doesn't want to ask.

"In Reaper City?"

"Yeah." I look away, trying to see the moon through the leaves.

"Soren." He grips my chin and turns me to face him. "You didn't fail me. I did that."

He told me he needed me to get out, but I've never asked why, and I don't know if I'm ready for the answer.

He answers anyway. "Just in case," he says. "Just in case you died trying to save me. Just in case it was your only chance to get out. Just in case it was the last thing you ever saw me do. Just in case."

Just in case...

The meaning of those three words pounds in my chest, and Killian grabs his like he can feel my heart pounding there. Our eye contact is as sketchy as it always is, but there's a new defiance to it. Something strong and feeble, like it's willing to be there if we let it. It's a connection, and I'm so goddamn desperate to latch onto it that I force myself to blink so that I don't. But blinking doesn't wash it away like it usually does.

Just in case...

What the fuck does it mean?

I know what it means...

Killian's hand drops from my chin to the side of my neck, fingers brushing my nape and his thumb playing with my jawline. His touch is so tender that I close my eyes to feel it. It's better than holding his hand, and it's more than when he held that girl's hand. It's a touch full of desire but mingled with feelings, and holy fuck, there are feelings here. Real ones. Harsh ones. Ones we don't want but can't deny. Because somewhere along the way he became my tormentor, turned into my safe space, and started glueing my foundation back together so my puzzle pieces have something to sit on.

When I open my eyes, Killian licks his lips, dampening them enticingly. Yet the rush of desire that washes through me isn't all heat and passion. It's comfort and conflict, a chance to shift our dynamic, and the realization that 'just in case' means something to me, too.

I meet his grey eyes, watching them swirl with the same confusing clarity I'm feeling. "Oh, for fuck's sake. It happened, didn't it?" he asks.

"What?" I narrow my eyes on him.

"This. We became a thing."

"We're not a fucking thing." But I don't pull back, and I think I might crumble if he takes his hand away. "We're just..."

"... in case? Just in fucking case, Soren." He leans in, lips brushing mine in his usual 'just in case' kiss. But I'm the one who doesn't allow it to be chaste. Not this time. Because we're alone in Janie's Woods where this whole thing started, and now he's mine.

My hand sinks into his hair, simply feeling the wavy strands between my fingers. When he drops his hand to my hip, pulling me closer, our kiss deepens differently. Lips together but mouths closed, never parting. And I'm changing...

Because it fucking hurts to kiss him like this. He's breaking through all my jagged bits, dissolving my glue, rearranging me in a way that suits *my* needs, not his. It's so selfless that I want to be more selfless, so I push my body against his, weave my other hand into his hair, and kiss him like I'm telling him what 'just in case' means to me.

He groans against my lips, body hard against mine, opening his mouth to take everything that I willingly give. Confessions, once again, without words spoken, but it fits us. And it's even better that tonight, two attention-seekers confess their feelings with no attention on them. No people, no birds, not even the moon can see us under all these leaves. We're alone. Real. Honest.

For once.

My tongue meets his in a way that isn't frantic—curious, instead. His breath fans against my wet lips, warming me, and his palms lay flat on my lower back, holding me against him without forcing me to be here. Lightly, I graze my teeth over his bottom lip and feel his smile tug into place, forcing me to smile, too. Simply breathing, our foreheads roll together, and his arms tighten around my back.

... My hands drop from his hair to wrap my arms around his neck, temples together. In a hug.

It's weird. So fucking weird I don't know how to end it. I don't know how to make it last forever. I don't know what to do other than to fight how much I enjoy it. Our chests are pressing together, transferring heartbeats and sharing breaths, and I look into the forest to see if anyone is looking back to spy on this glass moment.

"I am afraid," Killian says softly, holding me tighter to make sure I can't pull back to look at him. "I'm afraid of music because it's speaking a language I can't understand anymore. I lost the ability to interpret my own music when I layered on too many masks. I don't even know who the fuck I am anymore. You were right about that."

A snide comment wants to come out of my mouth. I swallow it. "Because you don't trust anyone enough to look at you without them on."

"No," he agrees. "Who the hell would even wanna—"

"Me, you dick. How many times have I told you to drop the masks?"

Again, I feel his lips pull into a smile against my cheek. "I just made you mine, sweetheart. Can't be chasing you off so soon."

I scoff.

I don't deny that I'm his.

"Trust me, asshole. You are the thing I fear least in this world. Masks or not, you're softer than I thought you were."

His fingertips dig into my back as a playful threat, and his dark hair brushes my temple when he laughs. "Balance then, yeah? We still chasing a curse on the weekends and being all 'just in case' on business days?"

"That's not balance," I say. "Death games on weekdays and 'just in case' on weekends. I can't handle you soft all the time."

He laughs again, releasing me just enough to bring his face in front of mine. "New deal, Sauder. We end your family curse and learn to play music together instead. What do ya say?"

"No masks?"

"I'll... try. If you admit you're afraid of the curse."

The moment almost shatters because he's fucking half-right and I don't want him to be. I scowl at him, and he huffs out a laugh, brushing his thumb between my brows to smooth it away.

"Admit it, sweetheart. I won't judge."

"Yes, you will." I shake my head at him. "I'm not afraid of the curse, okay?"

"Then what?"

I purse my lips together, but he just admitted to being afraid of his music, so... "Fuck, I'm afraid of being like them! My family."

Killian barks out a laugh, and this time, I sucker punch *him* in the gut, shoving him away. He buckles over, but he doesn't stop laughing. I don't know why I'm fighting a smile.

"Are you shitting me?" he barks with amusement. "Soren Fucking Sauder just *has* to be superior to his own family members? Oh, god. I should have known. It's so you."

I can't help it. I laugh with him. Because it is me. But it's Killian, too, and if our roles were reversed, he'd feel the same way. He's afraid to admit he fucked up with his brother and now his biggest fear is letting Krypt down again, and mine is being just as fragile as the rest of my family who fell prey to the curse. We're a mess of god complexes and insecurities that create superiority issues, but fuck it. We can't change who we are, and tonight, it's funny instead of embarrassing.

"Fuck you." I laugh with him. "I *am* superior to them! I bet my brain scan proves it."

"All hail King Soren, reigning supreme of the Sauder line!" He bows to me like a complete idiot.

But I like being bowed to, so I'm still smiling. "You're such a loser." I grab his hand and stand him up, letting our fingers twine all on their own. "Music lessons and staying superior to my family. That's our new deal. Death chasing every other day of the week, yeah?"

When he answers, it comes smiling against my lips. "Yeah, sweetheart."

I grin, kissing him back. "But tone it down on the soft shit, yeah? I'm fucking sick of it. And never kiss me in front of the Vile Boys again, you dick."

When he laughs again, I slip out of his hold and into Janie's Woods. This time, I let him catch me.

RIOT

35

LOST THE MUSIC

HE'S EVEN quiet in his sleep. Peaceful, like he isn't trying so hard to be above everyone else, letting himself relax into whatever he dreams about. While everyone else shouts throughout the house, complaining about Lockan Tate taking away their shot at Yates, Soren sleeps through it all like he doesn't give a single shit about it, like the closed bedroom door blocks out everything unimportant.

And I like that. I like him like this. I've never seen him at ease before. He's either insisting he's on a higher pedestal than everyone else, laughing in the face of danger, or quick to anger whenever his authority is questioned, but he's never calm. He's never willingly vulnerable.

But his back is to me like he trusts me enough to be safe, and his muscles are pliant under his tattooed skin. The Misfits tattoos are still on his arms, but Menace is working on a design to cover them, and I know he'll go right back to being a smug bastard as soon as the gang tats he's been embarrassed of get hidden under his true identity.

Soren's hair is a bit darker than Remi's, a bit shorter, too.

After he showered in my bathroom when we got back to Vile House, he went to bed with it wet, and it dried all fucked up. Short little sections sticking out at odd angles like a kid, adding an innocence to him I know he doesn't possess.

Maybe he does, though. Because the calling card I found in my sock drawer earlier is a dagger straight through my heart. The skeletal torso on the front splashed with teal is pretty, but his handwriting on the back is chicken scratch.

I like salty snacks. Crackers. Chips. Nuts.
I don't like being alone. My mind isn't safe.

His mind isn't safe, and he's telling me through a calling card because he thinks I don't already know that. It's cute, and it shows he's either delusional enough to believe his faults don't show, or he really is innocent, thinking he's hiding it better than he does. But the next calling card makes me laugh.

I like that Remi has Krypt and I respect how much he needs him.
I don't like thinking I'll need someone that much.

Oh, he already does, just in different ways. Soren doesn't need a controller like Remi does; he needs a follower. Someone who will go with him from mood to mood and understand that he shifts his needs on and off like a switch. I don't mind chasing him around because I know he'll take me right where I want to go. My pride can take the hit because, in the end, it's me steering him from behind.

I'm tempted to look for more cards hidden around my

room, but I don't want to wake him yet. I close my eyes, hold his cards on my chest, and let all my fragile facades fade away until I'm so empty I can finally start looking for myself.

Sinking deeper and deeper into the well of emptiness where my true self slumbers, I poke at the boy there and rile him into looking at me. His eyes are mine, but they're glassy instead of riotous, and I don't know what the look in them means. My mind whirrs, sorting through my history and coming up with nothing concrete. I don't fucking know who I am or why I ended up this way. I don't know when I started masking and manipulating, and I'm starting to wonder if I've done it from the very beginning.

Memories of Krypt, dejected in his room, his eyes turning into jail cells for the demons he started carrying. They come at me, and the longer I look at them, the more I realize I knew what was happening to him all along. I never did anything about it. I offered him company and a brother to talk to, but I didn't do anything noteworthy to change his situation. The word sick was thrown around in the hallway as I sat with him in his dark room. The way our mom's blond hair came into view every time her head whipped with the force of her hissed whispers.

No wonder he hates those things... Sick. Blonds.

Going deeper, I find the place where I lost music. No, I never lost it—I lost the ability to interpret it. In my early teens, I played with Krypt, and something about the song broke us. He split one way and I split the other, yet we remained tethered together in shared history and familial bonds. He kept playing, even after we killed our parents, but I never could. The notes came naturally, but they stopped making music. They were just sounds that expressed a feeling I could no longer name.

My masks got more detailed after that. If I could no longer control my music, I'd control my situations and surroundings. I learned the art of acting at a young age, but it wasn't until I lost the music that it turned into the art of pure, selfish manipulation.

I layered lies on top of secrets, dramatized it all with charm and a well-placed smile, and got my personas to do my bidding. Establishing the exact right kind of connection with someone would get me exactly what I wanted from them in the moment, and eventually, I developed so many different disguises that I could pluck them out at random and slip into the role and the power they gave me.

So, where did the real me disappear? Did I lose myself when I lost music?

Would anyone recognize me if I looked at them with a bare face? Under all this confidence I carry around, I'm too cowardly to find out.

The calling cards in my hands slip through my fingers, and I tighten my grip on them, snapping my eyes open. Soren is at the side of the bed—my side of the bed, and I never heard him wake up or get out. His blue eyes calm me, bringing me back to reality, but I latch onto his calling cards like I'm attached to them.

I am.

"I'm just setting them down," he assures me like it annoys him. I watch him set them on the bedside table and then look at him again when he climbs on top of me. I spread my legs so he can settle on his stomach between them, his hips on my thighs and his chest on my stomach. "Tell me," is all he says, his breath scented with toothpaste.

"Tell you what?"

What is this? He's just... on me. Settled. Like he belongs here and it isn't weird for him to be so touchy. Is this cuddling or is he pinning me down... gently? So baffled. So right. Soren crosses his arms on my chest and rests his chin on them, looking up at me all cute and sleepy. The fuck?

"Where'd you just go? Your mind was so busy you didn't even hear me call your name."

I shake my head to pretend I don't know what he's talking about. "Was asleep."

"Riot," he groans.

I glare.

"I'm not calling you Killian while you lie to me. This is my 'just in case' morning, and you're ruining it by being afraid of yourself."

"I'm not fucking afraid."

He turns his head and rests his cheek on my chest instead, and with his eyes no longer on me, the pressure is off. The pressure of what I must look like to him while so unguarded, grasping for masks but trying not to put any on.

"I, uh, was trying to remember when I stopped playing piano."

"And?" he asks, his chest expanding against my body with each breath.

"I don't know. It was the piano in Krypt's room. We played together one night, and I think we were both so lost that we, uh, like, left ourselves in that song. Or I did. He somehow kept playing, but I never could. Any time I tried after, the music sounded wrong."

"What made you play together that night?"

I recall the day, trying to remember why we sat at the piano together. "I'd had a good day. Krypt—Keegan, at the time—was all pissy because Gia was giving him a hard time about school. He sucked at it."

"I'm aware. Best friend, remember?"

Right. "I was good at it. So, while Gia praised me for doing well, I drank it in and was too selfish to notice her ripping him apart for not doing well. She called him sick, told him it wasn't his fault but that he'd never be like me because he was sick and I wasn't. Selfishly, I just fucking grinned that she knew I was the best."

Gia, our mom, was sicker than both of us. I hate that I used to beg for her attention and praise.

"He got angry. He got so angry that he scared her, and when Dad got home, they locked him in his room. I think it dawned on me that night that I should have been teaching him how to mask this whole time. I was too self-absorbed to even consider that before. I just went and spent time with him, got him out of the house, had his back, and made sure he wasn't alone, but I never actually did anything to help him."

"Yeah, you're a dick," Soren says, fingers drumming on my chest to soften that blow. "But so was he, and he probably didn't want your help anyway."

"I broke into his room that night, didn't know what to say, so I sat down at the piano with him. I think he realized how fucked his life was, and he was so caught up in being sick, as Gia said, and I finally clued in on how that was killing him, and we just started playing together. Like an agreement to do better. To change our situation. I mean we were old enough and big enough to fight them but, maybe because we didn't want to lose each other, we never did. We were both aware of what we were doing that night, but we didn't talk about it, and when the music ended, I don't know, I was different after."

"Different how?"

"Cracked. Like, I cracked in half. The old me stayed somewhere in that fucking house, and the new me built more personas that'd give us the power to change our lives. I forgot to be me and only focused on getting Krypt out."

"You never call him Keegan," he says.

"He asked me not to."

Soren nods, like Krypt maybe told him the same thing. My brother is more of a person as Krypt than he ever was as Keegan, and I respect him enough to abide by that.

"I don't even know if I did it because I wanted to protect him or if I did it to prove to myself that I could. Guess I lost music and myself."

Soren straightens his head, chin on my chest, eyes on mine. "Not lost. Set aside for when you're ready."

"What..." I blink at him. "What the fuck is this? Are you smart now? You speak this deeply? I thought you were a narcissist who only gave a shit about himself."

He grins, watching my throat swallow. "Yeah, well, back in Reaper City, you got put in that box Remi and Selena are in. I don't give a fuck about much other than my pride, but the few fucks I do have go there. And there you are."

And there I am. My throat gets tighter, and breathing seems hard. His heartbeat pounds in my chest again. "You capable of love, Soren?" I ask, a mocking tone to my voice to hide how serious the question is.

"Yeah," he says honestly. "I'm narcissistic, not a narcissist."

"The fuck does that mean?" He's delusional if he thinks he isn't a narcissist. But then again, no two brains are the same, and maybe he's not. Maybe he's just Soren Sauder.

"I can do whatever the fuck I want, which means I can love. Can you?"

I snort at that. Such a Soren answer.

Looking at the ceiling instead of him, I think about my appointments that studied my personality. "Psych says I use love as a strategic tool rather than an emotional connection. Like I use my brother to make myself feel better about his life now, instead of actually loving him. I don't know. I want to. Like I kind of crave it."

"Psych tells me my love is superficial and never lasts long. That I want love just to be worshipped." He moves his body, drawing my attention. "She's not always right, is she?"

She usually is, and he definitely wants to be worshipped, but I think he wants me to say no. He wants to hear that we can maybe love each other. "No."

His cheeks pinken, and he licks his lips as he lifts onto his elbows above me. "Well, just in case she is..."

When he kisses me, music fills my head, and I know exactly how to interpret it. Because he's the one playing it, but I'm the one orchestrating.

His lips are soft against mine, not playful, but honest. Gentle because he wants to be languid, and sincere because I'm kissing him back the same way and he doesn't have to take all the blame. Warmth spreads through my body. A wave of something so foreign yet so comfortable that my arms slide up his back, lifting his shirt so I can feel his skin.

His Vile House tattoo is intact, and I picture it on his smooth, muscled skin as my lips open and our tongues meet.

Soren licks my lips, smiling as he lifts his body to let me pull his shirt off. He's only in boxers, and as much as I want to see all of him, this mussed morning look is new to me, attractive because it's like seeing him from an angle I've never been allowed to look from before. I tug it over his head, tossing it aside and meeting his eyes. So blue in the early morning light and so wide with all his conflicting thoughts.

When he opens his mouth to potentially ruin the moment, I pull him back down and shut him up with my tongue. It's even better this time because neither of us are running our mouths to downplay the moment. We aren't fighting instinct, pretending we don't enjoy this because it's outside of our normal personalities, or trying to outdo one another. This time, we're working together, and fuck if that doesn't make our music pure harmony.

His fingers weave into my hair, and mine trail down his spine, feeling every inch of him as he subtly grinds against my body. Aligned, his cock hardens against mine, rutting together through our boxers so slowly that my breathing slows with his motions. I've never felt calm and aroused together like this, needy for something but in no rush to get to the finish line.

He deepens the kiss, his tongue diving into my mouth, and I cup his ass, rocking him between my legs so we're grinding together. Soren has a lithe, athletic body riddled with some gnarly scars, but he's sexier because of them. He's a bit leaner than I am, which makes him fit perfectly between my legs. When he lifts up to pull my shirt off, I pull him back down with my legs wrapped around his hips, letting him go through the motions of fucking me while we're still dressed where it counts.

Would I? Could I?

He feels good there. So good that I moan into his mouth when he humps me, our cocks rubbing blissfully.

"Still thinking about masks and music?" he rasps.

"Soren?"

"Yeah?"

I drag my teeth over his bottom lip. "Shut up."

He smiles, but it turns into a groan when my thighs open and I grab his ass to grind him against me. Because I'm not thinking about masks and music.

I'm already maskless...

I feel the music...

All without thinking about any of it, and before the moment shatters, cracking into shards I'll never find again, I want to live in it with him because he's the only one I've ever been able to experience it with.

When he quietly moans against my mouth, his hips pausing where he wants them to, I drink in the feeling of seeing him this way—hearing him this way. He's the one who said he couldn't handle softness all the time, but he initiated this by being *on* me, and there's something so euphoric about the gentleness of our bodies existing together. I never thought it possible that we'd forever be caught in a race to Death's doorstep, but we're not running towards anything but bliss and orgasms right now.

"Fuck," he moans, fingers tightening in my hair and lips

turning messy with distraction. "Shut up," he adds, embarrassed by how much he's enjoying this. He moans louder.

The gentle moment becomes overpowered by a desperate need to mark him as mine. As I rock my hips against his, grabbing his ass to grind us together, I nudge his head up so my mouth can get to his neck. Soren moans again, especially when I suck a mark into his skin, making his breathing pick up.

I suck his skin harder, and when he curses me out with a voice soaked in pleasure, I bite down on the side of his neck with my new teeth and make him come in his boxers.

"Oh, fuck you," he moans, long and drawn out. "Fuck you so hard."

I will fuck him so hard. Next time. Because this is hot as fuck, but he's most beautiful while laughing through his insanity, and I can't wait to bring him there again. I'm his god, and I have that power.

His cheeks are bright pink when he lifts his head to look at me, a perfect contrast to the purple mark blooming on his neck. I grin at him just to be a smug bastard, and Soren reaches between our bodies to cup my cock over my boxers.

"Shit." I clench my teeth when he squeezes, pulling a power move over me because he can't be alone in his orgasm. He's an even more smug bastard than I am, and he needs the bragging rights.

"Yeah," he says condescendingly, rubbing my cock perfectly. "Ninety seconds, Kill. Think you can last?"

Fuck him for turning our ninety seconds into a challenge. I clench every single one of my muscles to stave off an orgasm that's coming at me faster than I thought it was.

"Easy," I answer.

He cheats. He rubs me, grins at me, and then bites my jawline hard, adding his own teeth marks like art on my skin. It's hot, but when he says, "Tattoo those there. I fucking dare you," I come in my boxers without any warning.

GHOST

36

HE'S A GIANT DICK

MENACE GRINS at me over lunch a few hours later. Killian isn't one to back down from a dare, so my bitemark now sits in black ink under his ear, my top teeth on the side of his face, and my bottom under his chiselled jawline. Even had to shave to do it, and he looks just as good clean-shaven as he does with his stubble. Menace was up for it, and I loved every second of it because he never stopped mocking Killian once, and since Kill couldn't open his jaw without fucking up the tattoo, he couldn't even dish it back.

Killian isn't here. He left right after his tattoo but wouldn't tell me where he was going. I'm pretending like I don't care, but I do. He's mine now. I marked him, Menace tattooed it on his body, and with the hickey on my neck that won't be going anywhere for weeks, I'm fucking entitled to know where he is and who he's with at all times. I've been a jealous person all my life, but it's always been about status, recognition, and rank. This is a whole new beast, and I hate how consuming it is.

Ransom slides onto the bench across from me, setting his

lunch plate down on the table. The cafeteria is full, especially since the initiates who've made it into Vile House are allowed to be here with us now while we're unmasked, but I don't mind. Yet another place I can showcase my status as a Vile Boy.

"We leaked the info to those three in Lock's crew. Guess we'll see what happens," Ransom says, glancing over his shoulder at Monster. "You know what he did with Yates?"

I don't because I was busy with Killian, but I don't want Ransom to know that, so I shrug.

"Covered him in honey and birdseed and let the crows and ravens at him." Ransom laughs as he takes a bite, his dark brown hair freshly buzzed. "Chased them off every time they were close to ripping him open, made him think it was over, and then let them back in."

I smirk around my fork. "Is he dead?"

Ransom shakes his head. "Nah. Parade down Death Row tonight. Yates, everyone who helped him, Tom, and a few Misfits Lock has uncovered. He's keeping his word."

Good for him. "Still pissed he took Yates from me. I would have been head of rank if it weren't for that fucker."

"Maybe for a day, but the way you've been acting lately, you'd have ended up right back at the bottom by tomorrow. What's up with you and Riot?"

"Tension snapped," I admit with another shrug.

"Finally."

"Yeah, yeah." I nod at Monster. "He talking yet?"

Ransom wobbles his head. "One or two words every now and then."

I lean in, not wanting to be overheard. "You know why he goes mute sometimes?"

Ransom nods. When I widen my eyes at him, asking him to tell me, he shakes his head. "Not my story."

"No, but he sure as shit ain't gonna tell it, so fill me in so I know how to be there for him." Fuck, did that seriously just come out of my mouth? Why am I so selfless lately?

Ransom looks a little surprised, but he doesn't comment. "It's just because he spent so much time yelling and screaming and begging for help for the first eight years of his life that he can't stand the sound of his own voice sometimes. He was made mute when he screamed. They stitched his lips together or..." Ransom clears his throat, becoming furious on behalf of Monster.

"Fuck. Is he...?" I don't know, okay? It's a stupid question because, of course he's not, but he's strong, and if he needs to turn off his voice sometimes to stay strong, I'll support him in it.

"We've never been able to track that woman down. The one who had him all those years. I'd love nothing more than to help him get his vengeance." Ransom looks at me. "If we survive this shit with Reaper Corp, I wanna give him that. You think Vile House will have his back?"

"Fucking always, man. Always." I'd do anything for one of my Vile House brothers because I know what they mean to me and what I mean to them. "And *we will* survive this shit. We'll get Monster his monster."

Ransom nods, and with that, I get up and head over to Krypt. "Come on, asshole. We gotta chat."

KRYPT HAS BEEN my best friend for years. I mean, friendship is a loose term when it comes to the two of us because we aren't really the sentimental, companionable type, but whatever. The title sticks, and now that he's with my brother, there's one more layer of attachment.

But I'm nervous, and I fucking hate being nervous. Because he's looking at my neck like it pisses him off, but he's looking at *me* like I'm pissing him off more. Proven true when he lights a joint to calm himself down.

It's mid-afternoon and Remi is at The Ambient Raven, Killian is out doing god knows what, and it's the best time to catch Krypt undistracted and alone. I've got a million things to think about with my mom, my lame-ass cursed family members, the brain scan that was forced upon me, and this upcoming war with Reaper Corp, but... Krypt is my best friend, and I'm doing selfless things lately.

"Get the fuck on with it, Ghost."

"Your brother is *my* fucking asshole," I bark.

He smokes like I never said anything. Meanwhile, I'm sweating because I just confessed my biggest downfall. I'm roundabout dating his brother and trying to do the decent thing by giving him a heads-up. I'm not asking for permission because he sure as fuck didn't ask for permission to date mine, if that's what they're doing, so fuck him and fuck this whole situation.

I pace the hall of the asylum, ready to slink down the tunnel and escape him and this conversation forever. Instead, I get pissed off.

"You hear me?"

"Yeah."

"Nothing to say?" I get in his face, watching his monsters rile. "No threats? No warnings? Nothing?"

Krypt inhales weed and blows it to the side, watching me. "Think you meant to say, 'your brother is fucking my asshole.' Right?"

I shove him so hard his back slams against the wall. "Fuck you, Krypt!" I shout as he lets out a huff of laughter. "Maybe I fuck his asshole."

"Nah." He leans against the wall like this is no big deal and gives me the slowest once over. "You're bottom."

I glare at him, partway between offended and proud. "Like fuck." How dare he assume I'm the bottom. What makes me the bottom? How does he know? Bottoms are dominant as fuck, and so what if I like giving up a bit of control to Killian.

Krypt holds out his joint, and I snatch it from his fingers and keep pacing. "I wanna say he deserves better, but to be honest, you both sorta just deserve each other, so go for it. If you kill him, I'll kill you."

I face away from him and roll my eyes. "Yeah, I'm sure Remi will just love the fuck outta you if you kill his brother."

"He's mine no matter how much he hates me." God, they're pathetic. "I know."

I turn, walking back towards him. "You know what?"

"That you... I don't know, love him?"

What the fuck? "No." *Yes?*

"I saw it in Reaper City. I always knew you two would blow up. Just didn't think it'd be like this. Do me a favour, though."

"What?" I hand the joint back. "What favour?"

"The piano."

I look at Krypt, seeing something so rare in his eyes that it stops my lungs. He's not someone who thinks about how things feel for others, so it rattles me that he knows how deeply Killian struggles with his lost music. Krypt knows things. More than I thought he did, and he has a big heart under all those bars and cages. I don't know his point of view from when they were growing up, if he blames his brother for not protecting him like Killian blames himself, or if he sees things differently.

"He thinks he let you down," I say.

"He saved me."

"He doesn't know that."

"Because he has an ego the size of the Milky Way, and it isn't winning unless he's able to brag about it. He kept me sane, reminded me that I wasn't alone, and helped me kill our parents. He might have a god complex and take credit where it isn't due, but it's due here and he still won't take it because he doesn't think he did enough. So get him the piano back, yeah?"

"Yeah." I nod, feeling this promise deep in my chest. "Yeah."

The silence isn't awkward. It's safe and subtle, and there's a reason Krypt and I are friends. We're both dark-minded, but my energy never overwhelmed him, and his self-confliction always spoke to me. We're finding ourselves now, at the same time, dating each other's brothers, and it feels like we're growing together because of it.

"Remiel's mind is different from yours," he says to the cell door, watching my mom instead of me. "Riot told me he mapped your brain. Don't let him fool you into thinking the results were the same as your brother's."

I turn my face to look at him. "They weren't?"

Krypt shrugs. "Don't know, but knowing Riot, he'll make you believe the results were shitty just so he can play your god." He stubs out his joint and drops the roach to the dirty stone floor. "Just saying. He might be fucking your ass, but that's because he's a giant dick." He grins, leaving me in the asylum hall outside my mother's cell door.

Killian would do that...

Fuck.

RIOT

37

YOU COULD ASK ME

MOROS IS FUCKING THRIVING!

Under a blood moon, pitch black skies, and caressed by a haunting breeze from the north, Death Row has turned into a town party. Everyone is drinking, half drunk or on their way to being drunk, and those who don't drink are high on justice.

Because the town traitors are being marched down Death Row just like Lockan Tate promised. I'm humming with energy just being here, everyone else in a wicked mood to shame those who have betrayed their home.

I know the rest of the world runs on a 'don't sink to their level' mentality, but we have no such reservations. We sink lower, and we enjoy every sinister second of doling out justice and enacting revenge. Life is too short not to get a sick thrill out of the things that feed our devious joy.

Half the Vile Boys are here in masks, monitoring and joining the locals in their dark celebration, and the other half of us are here as ourselves, blending in and acting the part of Moros townsfolk. I love it because Soren is here, unmasked, drinking and letting loose. We barely get time to unwind, and seeing his face while he's dropping his guards is such a rarity that I'm staring at him more than I'm staring at the twisted parade.

As the husband and wife Krypt and I encountered are dragged down Death Row because their Achilles tendons are cut, I watch Soren down a can of beer before tossing the can at them. He laughs, and it's different from his insane laugh. This is joy; unhindered and needed, and his smile is so warped with his idea of fun that my dick firms up and my fists tighten, craving his throat in my grip.

I walk across the street, drawn like a goddamn moth to his flame, taking a swig of rum from the bottle as I step between the husband and wife, grinning at them like they should know who I am. They do. They know me as Killian Hallows, the guy who *most likely* killed his parents. But when they look into my eyes, they know. Deep down, they know I'm the Vile Boy who demanded the answers that led them to this exact shameful moment.

And you're goddamn right I take pride in that, laughing as I finish my walk to Soren. He's dressed in a pair of dark jeans and a white horror movie t-shirt, hair sticking up like it was the other morning, and cheeks pink from alcohol this time. The beer has him so flushed that his jacket is missing on this cool autumn night. His blue eyes are a fucking gut punch when they land on me, so full of trouble and fun that I'm eager to get up to more of it with him. With only a little stubble along his jaw, scratchy enough that I itch for my fingers against it, I instinctively rub my own jaw, his bite now tattooed there forever.

"Hey, *baby*," he goads, amping me up even more because I love this mood he's in. "Up for a little spying?"

I step right up to him, chest to chest, and rub my fingers over his stubble to appease my craving. "Who are we spying on?" I bite my lip and he looks, biting his to mirror me. *Atta boy. Even my actions get through to you subliminally.*

"Facts has a crush."

My eyes widen, and I look to the left where Soren nods. Facts, wearing his copper mask, stands creepily behind a guy in black pants and a Moros Township t-shirt. I've seen him around town. Pretty sure he moved here with his buddy a few years ago, and the two of them bought a fixer-upper place out by Cain Carson's house on Crucifix Street. The guy looks easygoing, laid back like he's having fun with the rest of the town, but also like he could fuck you up if you looked at him wrong. He's a fighter, that's for sure, but I can't tell if he's more soldier-trained or street-trained.

"Facts?" I look at Soren. "Facts finally figured out he has a dick?"

Soren laughs, not stepping back from me. "He accosted me in the shower and made me agree to spy on him."

I growl, my fingers tightening around his throat. "Naked?"

"Yeah, *sweetheart*. Naked." He licks his lips, and this time, I mirror him.

"Don't make me kill one of our own, Sauder. I'll do it." I love Facts, but he doesn't get a free pass to the body that belongs to me. "How long have you wanted to call me that?"

"Sweetheart?"

"Yeah."

"Never. I just want to take the power away from it so it doesn't piss me off every time you call me that."

I smile and tilt my head at him, fingers drumming on the side of his neck. "Try again. Don't lie this time."

Soren scowls, unwilling to admit he loves the nickname. "Are we spying or what?"

I glance to the left again. "Facts looks like he's got it under control." The guy has no idea a jittery, uptight man who can't understand sarcasm and can't spout a lie to save his life is watching him like a hawk.

"Facts can't talk around this guy. Let's go talk to him and let Facts eavesdrop." He steps back, but he grabs my hand, and yeah, I like that. I like it a lot.

Facts can talk ten miles a minute, so if he's tongue-tied, it must be something extra special.

Moros erupts into cheers as Tom is walked down the dead centre of Death Row, half of The Misfits trailing him. He's butt-ass naked, cock in a cage, a ball gag in his mouth, and a trail of anal beads hanging behind him. Ah, it's the least that cocky fuck deserves. Doesn't even surprise me that he's glancing behind him, looking for his daddy.

When we get close to the target, Facts shakes his head in agitation, trying to warn us off, but Soren isn't deterred.

"Can I bum one?" he asks the guy, who is lighting up a cigarette.

He passes us each a cigarette, offering the lighter to me first. "No problem. Killian, right?"

Soren scowls, not appreciating that my name is known but not his. "Yeah." I tilt my head at my needy man. "And Soren." I light my smoke and hand him the lighter.

"Novak," he says, taking his lighter back from Soren.

"I've seen you guys around. You own that music shop, right?"

"My brother does," Soren says, eyeing this guy up. He's got long blond hair and a scruffy short beard to match, real Viking or biker gang style, and I can't believe this is the guy who Facts finally decided to get hot over. The guy looks like Thor. Maybe a bit less bulky. "What about you? You do something?"

"Was in the NAVY for most of my life, but didn't take another tour when my mom got sick. When she died, I needed a change, and I'd been to Moros for trips. Bit of a true crime junkie, so this place spoke to me. I moved here with my cousin, and we're both in the fire department now, fixing up our house in our spare time." He shrugs, nodding at his cousin with a grin on his face. His cousin is throwing eggs at Tom, maniacally laughing as he does. "We fit in, I guess you could say."

I like them. I look at Facts to find him leaning forward, trying to hear as much of the conversation as possible. Probably clamping his lips to repress his greeting when his eyes meet mine.

"I don't wanna misspeak because you're in The Misfits," he says, looking at Soren, who is glaring, "but they really fucked up the old Fire Hall when they took it over."

"New one is better," I say before Soren blows his cover. "New leader of The Misfits is solid, though. He'll bring them back around."

Soren turns to Facts, ready to make sketchy introductions, but then the gathered crowd starts shouting, and we all look towards the street. Eggs fly, ravens squawk, citizens seethe, and bottles and cans whip across Death Row.

Yates. Torn and bloody, barely standing, beaten and tortured, finally doing the walk of shame he's deserved for years. And right behind him, Lockan Tate holds the chain around his neck. The new Misfits leader is shirtless and flecked with blood, looking powerful as fuck and appealing because of it.

Soren steps up behind me, lips by my ear, brushing my new tattoo. "Get hard right now and I'll cut it off."

I turn my face towards his, a grin on my lips. "Trust me, sweetheart. If I get hard, it'll be because you're so fucking possessive."

"I'm not possessive of shit," he says against my lips. Yet, he grabs my jaw and forces my head to turn even more, eye to eye. "But facts are facts. I fucking own you, Killian." He licks my healing tattoo to prove his point. Totally unsanitary, but yeah, that does it. My cock firms up, and like the egotistical prick he is, he pats it, knowing it's hard for him. "Mmm," he hums.

Time to knock him down a peg. I glance at Yates, pleased with how unified the town is now that the traitors have been caught, but it's time for us to go. Moros has all come together, and we're ready to face this war as a united front, so I can take the night off to face my own war with Soren Sauder, the man who became mine but doesn't always need softness. The night's vibe is diabolical, and it's affecting me just right.

I grab Soren's wrist to bring him in front of my chest, possessively wrapping my arms around his shoulders from behind. "Nice to meet ya, Novak, but we gotta go." I turn us around and steer him down the alley between The Ambient

Raven and Death Mark. "Did you forget about your family curse, sweetheart? Time you got a reminder."

I'M USED TO A LITTLE—OR a lot—of unrest in my life. There's always someone to deal with, a threat to abolish, a bargain to make, or a fight to be had. With Moros all on the same page, so 'together' that they're all training alongside one another, partying in the streets, and hosting a fucking sick parade for Lock and The Misfits to get their status back, I'm off-kilter. It's all good things, but I didn't get my name for nothing: I need a little chaos in my life.

And now I have the perfect man to unleash it on.

Holding up the same razor blade he used to cut my bicep the first time, I close the distance between us and hold his eyes. He doesn't look at the blade I pulled from my pocket, but he sees it, and for whatever reason, his heart rate accelerates. Excitement? Fear? Both? Doesn't matter because I feel it thumping in my chest again, and it's at this moment that I understand how to read music sheets. It's his heart acting as the drum, beating out music, but it's my actions orchestrating the notes and rhythms it pounds out. Fuck, that's powerful, and I'm ready to see how far I can push the beat.

"What're you gonna do, bleed me like Krypt tried to bleed the curse from Remi?" he backtalks, all attitude because he's still unsure where this is going.

No one has moved into Hallows House yet because we haven't had the additional Initiation Night, so tonight, we're alone here. The table in the foyer is still busted, and the drywall is still cracked, but we're upstairs this time. In the bedroom that used to be Krypt's, the piano is sitting in the corner without any intention of letting me play it. Not yet. First, I have to trust myself to play, and I'll gain that trust by reminding Soren of who I am. By reminding Soren that he's still a sorry man with a curse haunting him.

"You think it's fair that you got to mark me, but my mark isn't on you?" I ask, wetting my lips and pinching the razor blade.

Soren tilts his chin, showing me the purple bruise I left on his neck. "You marked me. Against my will."

"What will, sweetheart?"

He retreats, back hitting the wall. He doesn't like that he backed away from me, so he pushes off it to butt his chest against mine. "You wanna mark me, baby?" he goads, lifting my hand and holding the blade to his jawline. "Start cutting."

"So compliant." I grin at him. "No fight left in you?"

Soren is a beautiful man because he's so savage about it. Every expression he wears is finite, like he can't do anything half-assed. If he's mad, his face tells you. If he's sad, his eyes can't hide it. And if he's needy, desperate with the yearning to be full of despair because he's masochistic and loves to hurt, his actions declare his desires. He gives himself away when his eyes dip down to the hollow of my throat where the second tattoo I got today peeks out the top of my shirt. He doesn't fucking like it. He loathes that I got it, jealous because, on the day I marked myself for him, I marked myself for her, too.

Leigh. The girl from the plane who saved my mind

while I lost hold of it. The 'cool hair' and head of the cobra stares at Soren from my chest, and he's a possessive fool who doesn't want another person's mark on me. His pronounced cheek muscles feather when he clenches his jaw, and his deep blue eyes flicker with distaste, goading me into cutting him so he feels like he belongs to me more than she does. His hypocrisy is sexy because he's so obviously hateful about it.

I don't love that girl. I appreciate her. I don't understand why she came into my hallucination, but I'm grateful that she did because she tethered me to myself. But I don't hold affection for her beyond that. But Soren...

I don't know the definition of love or what it's supposed to feel like. I can't comprehend its depth when I've always been shallow. I can't even wrap my head around the concept of willingly tying myself to one person, cutting off everyone else, limiting my desires and establishing a set of boundaries that prevent me from acting on my instincts. Can't fuck anyone else? Wow. Can't flirt with anyone else? How will I charm? Can't look and wonder and act on sexual attraction without crossing some line I've never had drawn before.

But it drew itself, didn't it? Because I'm firmly planted on this side of it, unwilling to step across because if he ever did... fuck, I'd bury myself under so many layers of masks there'd be no chance left for me to ever find my identity. Soren makes me want to be bare. Raw. Real. I've never wanted to be real with anyone else. Maybe that's love, maybe it isn't. Maybe love is selfless, and I'm simply mimicking what I think selflessness to be.

I could mimic forever for him... Because it's effortless.

I know how I feel despite being incapable of labelling it.

He'd be stupid not to feel the same, but just in case he doesn't...

I grab his jaw, tilt it upward, and press him back until he's steady against the bedroom wall. I take my time carving three words along the chiselled line of his jaw, not wanting to rush them because they took a long time to mean something. I want them clear, precise, and able to be read so that everyone who sees them can ask what they mean. And whenever someone does, Soren will blush, trying to explain 'just in case' without giving anything away until he tells them to fuck off and mind their business.

He doesn't move or hiss or breathe any harder. The pain is the stinging kind because the blade is so sharp, but Soren takes it with pride. Because these words are prideful to him. I don't have to tell him what words I etched into his skin forever because he knows. *He knows.*

We know. The words and what they mean. A meaning without a proper definition.

When I'm done, I slide my thumb through the blood to get a better look at my art. I'm a clear, neat writer, and adrenaline fills me when I see the words, clear as day. They'll scar perfectly. Sucking my bloody thumb into my mouth, I let the tang of him rest against my tastebuds, looking him straight in the eyes.

Just in case, sweetheart. Here's my declaration, written on your skin because we're now forever.

Soren's eyes are full and anticipatory. His dark blond hair is pushed off his forehead, giving me an unimpeded view of his expression. It's another finite one, something that portrays exactly how I feel without either of us having to speak a word. This moment connects us, ties us, sets our lives on a path neither of us ever saw coming. But fate is weird like that.

Maybe he's always been mine. Maybe he's simply mine from this moment on. Either way, he's mine, and I'm his, and if he wants this as much as I do, he'll take the blade I offer him. I hold it up in front of me, watching his eyes dip down to it. Soren doesn't hesitate. He takes it, leans in to press his lips to mine for one quick and savage kiss, and then pushes me back.

"Take your shirt off. Now."

His voice, so authoritative and dominant, turns me on, but the energy coming off him sets me on fire. Because he's the Ghost of Moros, but right now, he can't settle himself down enough to be silent. He doesn't want to be silent. His vibrations are dramatic, his energy is loud, and as I take my shirt off, he gets a full look at the King Cobra. His jaw clenches again, a bit of blood leaking from his new wounds, but he doesn't dwell. He turns me around and runs his fingers down my healing back.

I've looked. My Vile House tattoo is mangled. The skull is visible, and most of Vile House at the top is clear, but my name is almost completely gone, and that's the part that hurts the most. Instead of carving me over my fresh burns, Soren bends, and his lips hit the healing skin instead.

I fucking tremble. It's such a declaration, but so soft that I can barely hold myself back from exploding. He's kissing me better, and no one has ever done that for me. Not too long ago, I wouldn't have even trusted him at my back. Now I want him there because he respects my trust, and I don't know exactly when or why that happened, but he's the only person I can put my back to. Especially my warped back and the burns that ruined me.

Soren's lips caress every burn. He starts at my lower back and moves upward, causing emotional pain because I appreciate it so much, but soothing pain because he cares so much. When his lips hit my nape and his hands touch my ribs, he pauses to breathe me in. His nose tickles my hair, his breath soothes my skin, and his hands trace my sides. I close my eyes to feel the whole moment.

I have the sudden urge to play piano. To express... *this.*

After sinking into this calm yet charged lapse in time, Soren kisses the back of my neck before pushing my hair aside. He starts carving, and I'm almost grateful it's on the back of my neck so I don't have to see it. His writing is fucking atrocious. The razor stings, the slices smarting as the air hits my welling blood, but it's that cleansing kind of pain that feels relieving. When he's done, he blows warm air against the exposed slices. The same three words. *Just in case.*

I turn to face him, extending this rare moment as long as possible before I turn it dark and unhinged.

"You ever gonna tell me how you feel?" I ask him, pushing his hair back. So silky between my fingers.

"No," he says honestly. "Don't know how." He fights a smile, but it happens anyway, so he hides it by pressing his lips to mine. "You could ask me."

I hold him against me, smiling, too. "You hate me?"

"Absolutely."

"You mine?" I speak against his lips.

"Mhm."

Our foreheads roll together and our smiles connect, eyes closed. "You superior to me?"

"Always."

I lick my lips, wetting his as my nerves grow. "You love me, sweetheart?"

Soren's fingers dig into my back, making pain scream out. It's washed away when he whispers, "Yes."

My exhale isn't meant to be shaky, but it is. Beyond shaky. Entirely stuttered because... he loves me. I'm loved. By Soren Sauder. The declaration is a single word to a loaded question, but it's tremendous all the same. I'm brimming with something new. There is so much pressure inside me that I don't know how to contain it all. My chest is full, my head is pounding, there's way too much air in my lungs, and my throat is backed up with emotion. There is water in my eyes!

"Do you?" he asks so quietly I barely hear him. "Love me?"

I exhale everything. The new feeling, all the pressure, the water in my eyes, and the word. "Yes." I fucking love him.

And I don't know how to handle it.

GHOST

38

DECLARATION MURDER

HE'S GOING TO EXPLODE.

I'm going to explode.

Emotions were expressed *with words spoken* this time, and holy fuck, it's heavy. The heaviest thing I've ever felt. But it's weightless, too, like the weight of it can't be determined. It's blanketing me comfortably, but also suffocating because of what it means.

The word 'yes.' Just in case...

Mine, mine, mine, my soul screams.

Run, run, run, my vulnerability demands.

Stay, stay, stay, my heart requires.

We both step back at the same time, the scared look in his eyes also reflecting from mine. I don't know why it's terrifying. It's new, something rare, something that has never happened before, and the casual way we declared it doesn't fit the volatile way we feel it. We're twisted up, caught somewhere between sentimental and detrimental, unsure which reaction is right.

I wanna love him.

I wanna fight the love, deny it, take it back because it's horrifying.

I want to throw love at him in droves because I feel it so strongly.

I don't know how to be soft right now. My puzzle no longer sits on the table. The pieces are scattered all over the floor, my foundation is crumbled, and I'm not the illusionist who projects the mirage of me. I'm just some boy, standing in front of another boy, feeling things with my heart for the first time.

Put me back together!

"I—" I swallow down words, wanting to say them but not wanting to *need* to say them. "I need the ninety... I need—"

"Death," Killian says for me. "You need Death."

Yes. Take me to her.

Because I unmasked Killian Hallows, and unmasking him is the epitome of breaking him. I've always wanted to break him; it's been my goal for so long. I don't crave it anymore. I don't want him to be broken, but I don't have it in me to express how beautiful he is without anything hiding who he is. Not right now. I'm way too vulnerable to start talking about beauty, and I need a brush with Death to stabilize me.

Me. Me. *Me.* Always me first. Because nothing proves my self-worth more to me than defying Death. I need to prove that I'm stronger than her.

I need it right fucking now!

Killian delivers. Because he's feeling the same intense pressure and out-of-control vulnerability as I am. I see it in his turbulent eyes, the clouds brewing, readying to unleash their storm. On me.

He balls his fists and tries to tamp down his breathing, but when he snaps, it's in my direction. He comes at me fast, charging like he has no control over his feet. When his body impacts mine, the air knocks from my lungs, but I don't have time to think about that. His force carries me, my feet tangle in a random rope, and the bedroom's single-paned window shatters against my back.

I break through it.

Fear strangles me, but not hard enough that I can't still laugh. Gravity disappears and my stomach rises to my throat as I explode through the second-story window. Glass shards surround me, and Killian lets go. A joyous, terrified scream rips through my vocal cords, Death watching me closely. Her hellions and demons all come forth, creeping out of shadows and crevices to bear witness to my fall from rancid grace.

The cool night air is fresh and shocking, the sky lit up with stars and a moon that's only a sliver. As my legs scrape the sill, I fall backwards. My body tilts, the treetops and neighbouring houses come into view, and when I roll my eyes as far back as they can go, the ground and certain injury stare back at me. I smile at it because I'm sicker than Krypt. I laugh at it because I'm going to mar it as much as it's going to mar me.

I jar to a stop, my teeth clacking so hard my mouth fills with blood and my stomach keeps falling while the rest of my body stops. The world goes still as I hang from the window, my calves still hooked over the ledge. I can't see him, but Killian's hands hold my shins, preventing me from falling but having the power to drop me whenever he sees fit. He once called himself my god...

My life is in his hands. I've never felt safer and in more danger than I do right now.

I throw my arms back, letting them hang as blood fills my head and puts pressure on my eyes. Upside down, Moros looks even more twisted. The trees sprout from the sky and the empty windows all blink at me, Death's minions in each pane of glass. My heart is pounding hard, but Killian's grip is a tether I didn't think I'd want but feel assured to have.

I love him...

Just in case...

Fuck. I really don't want to die now.

When my body jostles, I look up to see him tying my ankles to something. "I'm not close enough."

"I know," he says, continuing to wrap something around my feet while he pins my shins down with the other arm. *He knows...*

"What're you doing?"

"I'm showing you off to that bitch Death. Stay there, sweetheart. I'll be right back."

When he lets go, I drop another few inches as the rope's slack tightens, but the window above me is empty, no grey eyes looking down at me. So, I hang. Because I like the perspective.

But I like it more that Death is watching me. I've lured her here, and I'm in no rush to lose all her attention. Wickedly, I smile.

WHEN KILLIAN RETURNS, it's with an angry mob.

I hear the shouting first, angry voices coming down the street so loudly that they startle me from my deathly slumber. I can't feel my legs anymore, and I should have pulled myself up long ago because the muscles in my abs won't function now that they're deadened with immobility. My fingers are numb, but my arms are tingly, asleep, limp, and out of my control. But my eyes still work.

I open them, looking at the street upside down. Killian leads the charge while a trail of angry people follow behind, yelling words I can't yet make out. Killian is dragging someone, not slowing his pace at all, entirely blocking out whatever the mob is shouting at him. The parade and party on Death Row still sounds in the distance, but it's washed out as Killian's personal procession gets closer.

I swing a bit, trying to get a better view. My body groans, and the blood that has rushed to my head makes me exhausted and dizzy. Death is still here, waiting for my brain to give up on me, my heart to stop ticking, and my body to die because it's stopped getting blood where it needs. At some point, my legs slipped over the windowsill and the only thing keeping me dangling is the rope he tied.

"Sweetheart!" Killian shouts, and when I look, I pull my body in as close as I can get it, crumpling in on myself because knives are flying my way. He throws three of them, the first two thudding into the windowsill and the third making the rope around my feet fray. "Tuck and roll, Soren!" He throws the fourth, and the sound of the rope shredding only gives me a two-second head start to get my body into position to make a two-story drop.

It snaps, and I fall. My heart thunders and my useless limbs don't tuck like they're supposed to. That roller coaster sensation disorients me, but when I slam into some hedges, the pain disorients me more. Branches scratch at me everywhere, and I'm grateful for the numbness because I don't feel it all right away. I tuck, trying to roll out of the bush, but I don't tuck enough. I land on the hard-packed grass, my shoulder popping right out of joint from the impact.

"Fuck," I groan, holding it with my numb hand and rolling onto my side. "Fucking fuck, Killian!" I curl into the fetal position, cradling my shoulder so it doesn't break entirely.

"Sorry, sweetheart." His voice is impatient but amused when he takes my good arm and pulls me to my feet. I sway, off my axis and riddled with pain. His gaze finds the new words on my jawline before he holds eye contact with me. "Answer still yes?" he asks.

"You're—" I cry out in agony when he grabs my scapula and my arm, snapping my shoulder joint back into place. "Fuuuck!" My eyes water and my stomach heaves, nauseous as the onslaught of torture peaks. "What the fuck, Kill?"

Killian lifts my chin, forcing me to block out the other people here. "You're mine, Sauder. You said it."

Okay? Where's he going with this? The crazed look he's throwing me isn't putting me at ease.

"The fucking curse can't have you. I don't share."

That's when I look beyond him, seeing that the mob he's led here is a group of fifteen Sauders. My back straightens and the pain fades, the numbness in my limbs only a mild irritation now. There they all are, the inferior family members I don't want to be like. My cousins, at least ten of them, and three uncles. Two widowed aunts. They're here, angry, glaring at me like I'm at fault for whatever Killian did.

"The fuck are you talking about?" I look at Killian.

"Pick one."

"What?"

"Fucking pick one, Soren. I'm killing one of them right now to end this curse."

The group erupts, pulling weapons, shouting their anger, and pleading for their chance to outlive the curse. I'm... goddammit, am I swooning?

Is he really so possessive that now that I've confessed I love the bastard, he won't even let me half-ass belong to a curse? Fuck, why is that so hot? How is my cock hard through all this pain and numbness?

"Pick one," he snaps at me.

But I can't form a name right now because I'm staring at his lips, feeling his brand on my jaw, noticing my bitemark tattooed on his. My dislocated shoulder is nothing compared to how much it hurts to love him. On instinct and nothing more, I step forward, grip his rolling throat, and kiss the fucker like I'm falling for him even more for doing this.

Is it even true love if he doesn't kill your cousin to keep you from a curse?

I wrap my fingers around his neck, digging them into his nape because I can't get enough of him. He hisses when I press on the words I carved there, but he grunts against my lips and kisses me back.

"Stop fucking stalling and pick one or I will."

I wanna fuck so bad right now. I've been turned on

before, especially by him, but this is something else. This is a need so strong I don't think I'll survive without it. It's a pull from deep in my core, emanating an energy so fiery the world will burn if I don't get what I want. I've never flirted with Killian, but my tingling hand reaches down, rubbing his cock and feeling it so much more than I did that night in my grave.

He groans, biting my lip while a riot breaks out behind him, reaffirming his Vile given name. I'm fervent, unable to stop, needing to fucking feel him against my skin. I reach up, trying to shove my hand down his pants, but he grabs my wrist to stop me.

"Fucking hell, sweetheart. I will fuck you in front of them and then kill all your cousins if you don't stop."

The messed-up part is, I'm happy. Not because he wants to end my family curse, but because he wants to own me so completely that even it can't hold a part of me. He's snatched up all my pieces and hoarded them for himself, and with them in his hands, I'm falling apart yet so put together. I don't care about the curse. I care that he's possessive of me.

Because I'm fucking worth it and someone is finally appreciating me how I should be appreciated.

"The one in green. He's a dipshit who blamed Remi for our dad's—"

He moves fast and with authority. A dagger flies into my cousin Tim's shoulder, and another knife is held out in front of Killian to warn everyone away when he grabs the one in green. My extended family shouts, but no one tries to stop my man. I grin at that, and then I grin wider when Killian drags him over to me, a knife pressed to his throat.

My cock throbs with need, adrenaline pounds in my chest, and his eyes roil with more storm clouds than I've ever seen him possess. I don't even watch the knife drag across Tim's throat. I watch Killian Hallows kill my cousin as an act of possessive love. I bite my lip into my mouth as blood soaks into Tim's shirt and the rest of the family goes silent. Tim is choking and gurgling the last seconds of his life away, and I pant ragged, desperate breaths as he slices from one ear to the other, Tim's throat smiling as he dies.

I can't smile. I'm too busy trying not to come in my fucking pants.

Blood coats his hand, dripping down his scarred and tattooed forearm all the way to his elbow, and still, he doesn't look away from me. Fuck, he's mine. *He. Is. Mine.* Has a man ever looked hotter than he looks right now? Hair dishevelled, body muscled and coiled, eyes riotous, and demeanour calm. He might murder with ease, but one move from me and his casual grace will snap in half as animalistic savagery barrels through.

And that's my very own power to hold on to. The power to wield this man however I choose.

Death is still here. She's watching, admiring me for defying her for so long and thanking me for bringing her to this show. She has a soul to take with her, and as Tim hits the grass, the weight of the Sauder curse rises from my pores, leaving me as nothing but the Ghost of Moros and Killian's *just in case.*

The night stills, my family stops breathing. Killian grips the knife he used, but he steps over Tim's corpse and flings it to the ground, the point sticking into the lawn. My thighs clench harder than my stomach, and my throat dries, so thirsty for him I can't even swallow.

"The curse is lifted!" someone shouts. "I feel it! Oh my god, I can feel it lifting!"

"Thanks to him!"

"Killian Hallows!"

But I fling my own dagger at my uncle, glaring at him as Killian steps closer to me. "Don't say his fucking name," I snarl, pointing at him. "He's mine."

"Leave," Killian seethes, eyes on mine.

I don't know where they go or if they stay, but when Killian gets to me, my last speck of restraint shreds, and I give in to my base needs.

Death. Desire. Despair. They all come from Killian now.

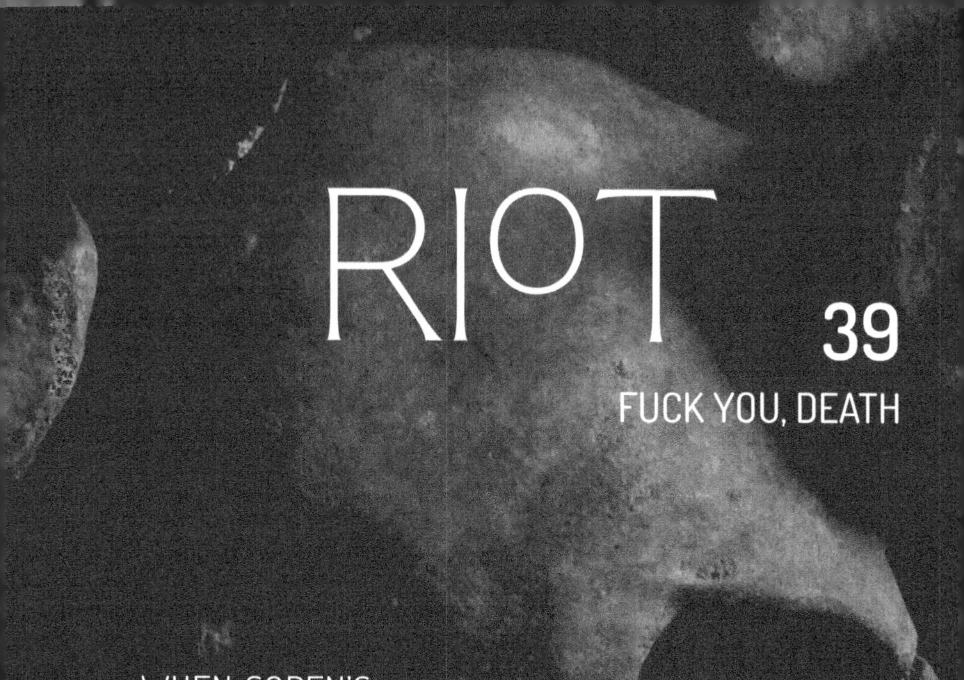

RIOT

39

FUCK YOU, DEATH

WHEN SOREN'S hand goes down my pants and his teeth bite my neck, I look at the sky and revel in my earned status. *That's right, sweetheart. Deny it all you want, but I am your god, and the way you worship me proves it.* He's all over me, needy and uncoordinated, and I've never seen him so desperate before. It feeds my ego and amplifies my murder high, turning me into a chasm of ominous power I know he can withstand.

But the neighbouring lights are on, and there have already been too many murders on this property. My mom. My dad. Brady. Tim Sauder.

Four deaths with impeccable purpose. Four deaths to advance *my* plot.

I push him out of sight, forcing him into the shadows at the side of the house. His back slams against the siding, and the groan that comes out of his throat is purely guttural, unhinged because he lets it slip out instead of tamping it down. His glassy eyes flash in the reflection of a streetlamp, and his lips shine with spit, chest heaving and heart hammering. We're making music again, and this time, it's a fucking ode to me.

"Show me," he demands breathlessly. "You killed my cousin. Fucking show me what all this death chasing got me, Killian! Show me you!"

I spin him around and grip the back of his head, holding his face pressed to the siding. He snarls at me, but there's a laugh in it that makes my cock firm up even more. I love him when he's insane, and there's no sanity left in him tonight.

It turns cruel, an evil cackle. "You're pathetic! You just ended my curse because you're fucking possessive, and now you can't even take what you fucking claimed."

Fury burns. No one questions my authority but me. I *am* his god. His devil. His deity.

I pin him in place, lips by his ear as I undo his belt with one hand. "And you're the desperate attention whore finally begging for what you want." I rip his belt free and force his wrists behind his back, strapping them together with a technique Menace taught me.

"Pathetic," he laughs again. "Know you can't handle me so you have to—"

I kick the back of his knees and force him to kneel. Lording my strength over him, my chest vibrates and my stomach clenches, ready to make this man I love my slave for the night. He wants me to show him what all this death chasing got him? This is it.

Because his curse doesn't own him anymore, I do.

Soren hisses when I rip his pants down below his ass, and he curses when I slam his face off the side of the house to bend him over more. I rip his shirt to shreds and toss it aside, needing to see all of him. Unable to restrain myself, I smack his perfect ass, ready to ruin it by turning it red and raw. I smack it again, watching colour bloom on his pale ass cheek. My aversion to red skin is demolished by how well he wears it.

He groans, trying to hide a whimper, but it turns to a necessitous moan when I bend over and spit, letting it fall down his crack. Biting my lip into my mouth to watch my spit slide down, I bend, running my fingers through it to press it to his tight hole. So pink. So firm. So thoroughly mine.

Using the hand that isn't coated in his cousin's blood, I push my saliva inside him with one finger, feeling the way he clenches around me. He's so warm compared to the cool night air, but when he whimpers for real, I burn hotter than he does. I add a second finger, spitting again to fuck it into his ass. Soren's forehead thumps against the siding and his ass presses back against my hand, stoking my fire.

"You my sweetheart now?"

"Fuck me," he rasps. "Hurry up."

I can't hurry up. Because I confessed my feelings, killed his cousin, ended the Sauder curse, and made him mine for real. All this time, I chased him, nipping at his heels like a hellhound, and he's finally exactly where I manipulated him to be. There's conflict in the power of knowing that. I want to hold it over him and remind him how much control I have, but I want to appreciate him because he helped get us here. I don't share credit, but fuck, here we are.

"Who are we right now? Riot and Ghost or Killian and Soren?" I kneel, grabbing his bound wrists and pausing my fingers in his ass.

"So pathetic," he groans. "You need me to say it?"

I do, but I can't admit that, so I tug on the belt until his recently dislocated shoulder makes him cry out.

"Fuck!" he seethes. "Killian and Soren. Fucking Killian and Soren!"

My new teeth chatter.

Bending, I let go of his wrists and spread his cheeks apart, burying my face between them to tongue fuck his hole. He writhes in my hold, pushing back and pulling away together, humping the air as his cheek rests against the house. I push my tongue inside him before flicking it over his rim until he's panting. I'm panting harder, my cock pressing hard against the material of my pants.

"Holy fuck," he mumbles. "I'm gonna come from this."

I pull back, spreading him apart to admire his open hole. The streetlamps aren't enough, and I wish I could see every little detail about him. The flush to his ass, the dimples in his lower back, the crescent divots in his palms from his nails digging in so hard. The bloody handprint on his ass from my hand. Shiny and wet, I plunge my fingers inside him again, running my tongue around his rim until I'm the one who's close to coming.

Soren moans, body going slack, barely able to hold himself up. "Killian, my god."

Yes. His god. I tongue and finger fuck him at the same time, rutting against the air to appease my untameable cock. When he breathes harder, on that precipice of coming, I pull back and spit again, fascinated by the sight of it leaking down his crack.

"Please," he whines. "Don't make me fucking beg, Killian."

It's music to my ears. Better than music. Something I've

wanted from him since the beginning. I free my heavy cock, leaking and thick with the need to be buried inside the man I own.

"One more time, sweetheart." I press against his hole, slicking spit all around him.

"Ugh," he groans, trying to fuck my cock without any balance. "Don't make me."

"Soren."

He pants, head dipping forward. His back rises as he talks himself into giving me what I want at the cost of his pride. Our egos are well-matched, which makes us a hellish match as a couple. "Please."

I barely hear it. "Soren."

"Shit." He pushes his shoulder off the wall to lift himself up. Turning his head to glare at me with big eyes and beautifully pink cheeks, he snarls, "Please. Please fucking fuck me."

Simultaneously, I thrust inside him and wrap my hands around his throat from behind. He cries out, and I pull him back, eyelids fluttering from the pleasure of being buried inside him. All my recent wounds ache, and the stab wound in my hand stings as I grip his neck.

"Death," I tell him, bringing his back to my chest. His bound hands press against my abs, but he tilts his head back to rest against my temple. "That one or two second precipice. You ready for it, sweetheart?"

He moans so lowly. "Yes."

I squeeze his throat. Restricted blood flow *and* airflow. My sweetheart is about to see the afterlife, and when he's there, experiencing a thrill he's longed for since he became obsessed with taunting Death, I'll let him live in it for two seconds before I drag him back to my realm. The one I reign over with him by my side.

I fuck him hard and grip him harder. His dick slaps off his abs with every hard thrust, and his moans turn more choked the harder I squeeze. I bask in all of it, tainted bliss invading my veins and harmony filling my mind. Because again, this is us. Volatile and vulnerable, caught somewhere in between, thriving in the way we both hurt and harness one another.

His fingers dig into my abs and his head goes slack against the side of mine. He wheezes, and I look over his shoulder to see his dick red and hard, a bead of precum leaking from the tip.

He's almost there.

I clench my abs and pull all the way out, feeling every inch of my cock pushing into him languidly as he dies in my grip. It's hard to fuck and kill someone at the same time, but I need him to have this experience.

"You looking at her?"

Weakly, he nods in my hold.

"You there? Between life and death?"

He tries to swallow against my braided fingers. A strangled sound comes from his throat. His eyelashes flutter as they close, and I know he's seconds away from passing out.

Lips against his ear, I remind him of what's more important. "Laugh, sweetheart. Laugh in her fucking face and slam the goddamn door."

I look at his face. His eyes spring open, bloodshot and wild, and his popped-open lips try their damndest to pull into a smile. Sounds work their way up his constricted throat, and even though they don't come out sounding like a laugh, I know he's laughing. I close my eyes to hear it with Death, watching my psychotic man laugh in her snide face as he stands on her doorstep, gripping the door.

His body goes slack, fingers losing their grip on my abs, cock flagging just a little.

"Slam it, Soren. Defy death."

In his head, he does. I feel the moment he laughs the loudest, slamming the door and closing that chapter of his life as he finally wins the prize he's been after. To outsmart Death herself. To be better than her. To prove to himself that he's stronger than the only sure thing in life.

I give him a split second to revel in his accomplishment as his body slackens further. My cock is buried in his ass, and even those muscles loosen their grip now that he's not resisting. Time to bring him back.

I clamp my teeth to his shoulder and bite down hard at the same time I release his neck. "Not today, sweetheart."

Soren gasps, rasping in a lungful of air. Panic grips him for a second, and when I spread my hands over his bare chest to hold him up and remind him where he is, he laughs.

Sickly. The sound is so twisted and warped that I know he's experiencing true joy mixed with pure pleasure. So I laugh with him.

"Fuck you, Death!" he screams, voice abrasive and raw. "Fuck you!" He hacks out coughs and words together.

I pull out and thrust back in, cutting off his words as he moans.

"You fucking won, sweetheart."

"I fucking won," he repeats, laughing even harder. "Holy fuck, I won!"

I drag my hand down his chest, grip his cock, and fuck

him. Three more thrusts, the thrill of his death chase and the peak of his pleasure rattling my teeth. Pressure builds inside me, coiling low in my stomach and burning through my nerves.

"Fuck. Fuck, Kill. Ahhh." His ass squeezes my cock, making me erupt before he even does. My mouth opens on a silent groan, and my eyes roll back as my hips stutter. I jerk his cock as he comes, painting the house with his pleasure. His head tilts back to rest on my shoulder as his body trembles against mine. The moan makes him cough, his throat sore and raw, and each cough constricts the fuck out of my cock, pumping cum from me so hard I buckle forward as he falls backwards.

We lean against each other, the power of the moment staying strong as the intensity simmers to something comfortable. He slumps down, ass hitting my thighs, unable to hold himself up any longer. My cock pops out, cum leaking down on my legs, warm and silky.

"Holy fuck, you just killed me."

I huff out a laugh, forehead resting on his shoulder as I catch my breath and get my heart to slow down. "Was it worth it?"

"Thank you," he says softly. "Just... fuck." He wiggles his hands. "Untie me."

With shaky hands, I undo the belt and pull it off. Soren wobbles to his feet, pulling his pants up as he turns to face me. I'm too spent to stand, so he kneels in front of me, lifting my face by cupping my cheeks. My one hand is coated in blood from killing his cousin, so half his neck is tinged red when I look up at him. I don't like another man's blood on him, so I scowl at it.

"No masks?" he asks me.

"No cracks?" I ask him.

He smirks shyly. His eyes meet mine before he looks down at my mouth. "Answer still yes?"

Moths take flight in my heart. "To what question?"

He groans. "Don't make me fucking say—"

"Yes." I nudge his cheek with mine, angling him so I can press my lips to his. "Just in case, sweetheart."

He melts. Dies. Comes to life. I don't know, but it's the single best moment of my life.

Until Remi ruins it. "You killed Tim!" he screams, running at us as Krypt casually strolls behind.

"Killed Soren, too," I say, eyes on Soren's blue gaze. "Guess I broke the curse and our bargain."

"Worth it," Soren whispers, kissing me with a smile. "Sauder curse is over, Rem."

Thanks. To. Me.

GHOST

40

IT'S FUCKING GETTING IT

WITH A BAG of chips and a packet of peanuts, I lean against the stone wall of Mom's cell and look at the unopened snacks. Killian brought them to me. Because he found the calling card that told him I like salty snacks.

Now I've brought him a smoothie and he's brought me snacks, and it's all so fucking soft that... that I like it when I didn't think I would. I'm getting too comfortable with him, relying on him for things I'm telling myself I'm just owed. Which brings me back to love and how people know they feel it.

"You ever love dad?"

Mom's hair is stringy because she refuses to use her shower. I mean, her room is a cell with a gate for a door, but it's updated enough to have some amenities. Why is she here? Because Remi and Selena thought it'd be a good way to keep her out of the path of the Reaper Corp war, especially after Axel tried getting her mind back with no luck. But me? I want her locked in here as a prisoner now that I know what she did to Dad. Something still ain't right in her head. I don't know if that's Axel's fault or if she just snapped at some point, but she went from being an alright mom—or so I thought—to a useless sack of skin with a somewhat functioning mind. I haven't liked her since she cut Remi's wrist.

"Yes," she says, leaning against the opposite wall but sitting on her bed. "I love all of you."

"Why'd you kill him then?"

"He killed himself."

"You helped him along." I stretch my legs out straight, cross my ankles, and open the damn chips. "Tell me why?"

"I never intended..." She cries, burying her face in her hands, and I tilt my head, wondering how much of it is a show and how much is real. "I never meant to do it! He told me to!"

The gate creaks open and Krypt comes in, sitting down next to me and stealing my peanuts. He doesn't say shit, but he crosses his ankles, leans back against the wall, and watches my mom. We snack while Mom cries, neither of us uncomfortable with other people's sadness.

"Axel told me some shit while he had me," he says, chewing nuts. "That your mom and Malone were high school sweethearts or something. That your dad was taking too long to succumb to the curse, so she helped him get there faster."

"I know that part." I crush the bag of chips, but Krypt keeps talking.

"He also said that she was born into a cult, married a cursed man, left a cult, relied on another cult, and all that time, Malone whispered shit in her ear. Her mind isn't fucked because of Axel. It's fucked because she's been manipulated all her life. She's just snapping now because no one is forcing her thoughts and she can't think on her own. Can't hide it anymore."

Then how could she hide it all our lives? I've heard parents have superpowers, but if she's been fucked up all this time, she can mask better than Killian can. Perhaps her puppeteer was the one telling her how to be a parent. What's made her slip up now? Maybe because we're all grown and she doesn't have to hide it anymore in order to be our mom. Or maybe she doesn't have anyone to hide behind now. No more master.

Mom's still crying, and I don't know why Krypt is telling me this. Chatting has never really been our strongest point.

"You defending her?" I ask.

"No."

"She made my dad kill himself."

"So kill her. The fuck do you want me to say? I don't give a shit." He tosses peanuts into his mouth. He sucks at remorse more than I do, so I brush it off and shake my head, eating a few more chips.

"Is love just another form of manipulation?" I ask him, since... he must know, right?

He shrugs. "Fuck if I know. At least it's the kind that feels good."

But does it? Because Killian sacrificed his damn life for me back in Reaper City, and if that was love, I can't handle how terrifying it is. I can't live through that again. It hurts, and as much as I enjoy a brush with danger, I've never willingly hurt myself like this before. Whatever this feeling is, it's horrifying because it's so strong and out of my control. I wish I could shut it off, tell myself that I don't give a fuck about him, and let it all go. But he's stuck in me, and no matter how many times I remind myself it's a weakness, the feeling doesn't budge.

"Remi okay after, uh, Tim?"

"He likes to play the hero. He's fine. Relieved, I think." Krypt's knee bumps mine when he shifts his leg. "Bargain's over now, Ghost. Where does that leave us?"

The back of my head thunks off the wall and my jaw itches with healing words. "Fucking each other's brothers, I guess."

"I guess," he repeats.

The moment slows, Mom keeps crying to herself, and we chew our salty snacks. Am I settled? Did the curse really lift? Am I, god-fucking-forbid, happy? My toes twitch out a soundless beat in my boots, wiggling in front of me because there's more I want to say, but I don't know how to say it. Or if I even need to.

I clear my throat.

So does he.

"It's more," he blurts.

"Not just fucking," I blurt at the same time.

"Yep." He stands, uncomfortable as fuck.

"Yeah." I stand with him.

His eyes meet mine. I look away first. I nod. Krypt nods. He leaves. God, that was awkward, but at least it's out there.

"You love the other Hallows boy?" Mom asks.

"You love Gregory Malone?" I snap back. "The man who haunted three of your sons and helped push two of them into early graves?"

"No," she cries. "No! I don't. Please, let me out of here!"

"Then why do you keep asking for him?"

Her face crinkles in confusion, like she doesn't think

she's been asking for him and doesn't know what I'm talking about. Wow, she's messed up.

She's not sane. Neither am I, but at least I can function. Maybe she's telling the truth, and maybe Krypt is right, but I'm not the one who is going to make this judgement call. If Remi and Selena want her to stay here, she will. If they want to check her into the legitimate part of the asylum, they can. If they want to send her back home to potentially die in this upcoming war, great. I'm washing my hands of it. I don't give enough of a fuck anyway. I just want the bitch to suffer for what she did to our dad.

I grab the empty chip bag and swear at it as I leave. "Fuck, he's soft." I head back to Vile House for the meeting Director called.

FACTS IS extra jittery since the parade on Death Row last night. I didn't get the chance to introduce him to Novak, but he eavesdropped without butting in, so at least he has some sort of idea about the guy. I grin at him, and he blinks at me, mouthing 'hello' to himself, before looking away like I don't exist. Normally, that would piss me off. I snort instead, amused at how awkward he is about sexual interests.

"With the keycodes you two got," Director says, nodding at me and Riot. Killian? The fuck do I call him here? "We've been able to read the Reaper Corp chips in every one of their brains. The three prisoners we got from Misfit Hall were part of a breach task force."

“What?” Menace cuts in. “They were literally bred and trained just to breach places?”

“Seems so,” Director answers. “Axel is still going through their encrypted files, and Glitch has been helping.”

Glitch nods. “Yeah. The keycode gives us access to their patient and training information, most of their breeding program traits, and their rank level. The only thing it doesn’t have is real names; they’re mostly code names. Reaper Corp works in specific DNA traits and then trains their people through levels until they reach a useful status. It’s like everyone born from the Reaper Corp program is bred for a specific purpose, but the civilians who lived in the city they took over just got put through mass brainwashing to believe Reaper Corp rule. It’s impressive, even though it pisses me off.”

It's bullshit if you ask me. I mean, if I was the puppeteer, sure, I’d be into it. But I couldn’t imagine being a puppet to serve a purpose in someone else’s show. I live by my agenda, and performing for Vile House furthers it. I do shit for me and only me. Mostly...

I look to my right, where Riot’s knee bounces next to mine under the table. He calls me sweetheart and I’ve slipped a baby out here and there, and maybe I do things for him, but they’re also for me. Can I be in a relationship when I’m this selfish, or will he understand because he’s self-obsessed, too? It’ll probably lead to massive fights because I’ll want him to live by my agenda, and he’ll want me to live by his, and when neither of us give in, the battle will be brutal. Like it always has been. Kinda looking forward to that part. When his knee bounces right into mine, he stops, pressing us together. Glancing up at him, he grins without looking at me, and then his stupid hand moves up my thigh and my fucking asshole clenches.

Jesus.

"And that woman who blew up Death Row was listed as," Director pauses, looking at Glitch for confirmation.

"Infiltration and scarification." Glitch shakes his head. "Bitch was literally bred to be a suicide bomber."

Ransom leans forward, elbows on the table. "What about Benton Wentworth? Anyone scan his brain?"

"You think he's Reaper Corp?" Facts asks.

Ransom shrugs. "We thought Axel was working with Reaper Corp at the start, and Wentworth was funding his research. He's a billionaire, seems to evade everyone, met with Yates that night in Janie's Woods, and now he's interested in Remi's house? Why?"

"Because he's a nosey prick who doesn't know what team to bat for, so he's putting spoons everywhere," Seven says. "I say you just kill him when you meet with him, Director. Off the bastard, take his money, and be done with him. We already held him as a prisoner, so it's not like he's going to work with us."

"There is information I need from him first." Director inhales through his nose while Killian's hand slides up my thigh, cupping my cock and rubbing. "He will work with us if he wants property in Moros. We need his money, and we need to know what pokers he has in whose fires. We want him close so we can keep an eye on him. Just like we're keeping an eye on Lock's three potential insiders. We leaked the info, and now we wait."

My lips part and my breath comes out wobbly when my cock firms up and my body sweats. Killian keeps rubbing gently, subtly, and I can't even help that my thighs have spread.

"I don't need to tell you all again how proud I am of you for unifying the town. Everyone is working together, on the same page, and allied in this fight. Alas, I'll say it again. I'm proud of you."

Kyd's smile is full of pride. "Awww, thank you, poppa bear!"

"Don't call me that."

"Love you." Kyd stands. "Love all of you!"

"But," Director butts in. "Another body ended up in the morgue late last night. Being prepped for a funeral and burial." Director looks right at me and Killian. "Anything to say?"

All I do is breathe when my hips subtly thrust against Killian's hand. I can feel my face getting red, so I lean forward to brace my elbows on the table to hide my lap. "I'll be at the funeral," is all I say.

Killian laughs when Director looks at him. "What? I was keeping my end of the bargain. Sauder curse is over. You're fucking welcome."

Everyone groans at his ego, but Director shakes his head again. "Alotta dead bodies turning up from you lately, Riot."

Killian gives my cock a smack, making me choke. "It's called romance."

"Romance?!" Menace cackles. "The fuck do you know about romance?"

I know he's rubbing my cock so perfectly that I can't think straight, and if he doesn't stop, I'm going to come in my pants.

"Who are you romancing?" Director asks.

"This one," Killian says, tilting his head at me. "Not my fault his love language is murder and death."

"You might wanna hang back after this meeting," Director tells us both. "So we can talk about what love means to you both."

Ransom leans back in his chair, refusing to leave. Menace grabs a bag of candy from his pocket. Kyd plants his chin in his palms to stare at us. Krypt rolls his eyes, and Facts looks like he's interested in the answer for scientific purposes. Glitch grins at us, and Seven kicks his feet up.

"Fuck all of you," I snap at them, trying to bat Killian's hand away. He grabs my thigh instead.

Everyone laughs, but they still don't move, so I look at Monster. Instead of being interested in mocking us, he looks interested in hearing what love is. For some reason, my heart cracks in half at that. He doesn't know. None of us really know, but he's so warped he tries to pick up any bit of information he can about things he was twisted into believing mean something different from what they really mean.

"I fucking know what love is," Killian says.

"What is it?" Director asks. "Are you sure you want to do this with an audience?"

"Ashamed?" I look at him.

"Fuck you, sweetheart. I ain't ashamed of shit." He squeezes my thigh. "It's picking someone to be yours because they're too fucked up to survive on their own, so you take them under your—"

I kick his shins. "You're the one who's too fucked up. You drowned me, paralyzed me in my own fucking grave, and hung me in the music shop."

"Oh my god," Director's voice barely breaches my attention.

"And you loved every second of it." Killian grins, and shit, I did love every second of it. Even the seconds I hated.

Menace laughs hard, and Kyd pulls out a journal—I don't want to know where from—to jot this down. Everyone else either smirks or snickers, and my cheeks flame.

"Love is owning someone," I declare.

"Like I own Remiel?" Krypt baits me.

I growl at him. "You don't fucking own him. He owns you."

"Not denying it." He shrugs.

"Okay, I think you both need an appointment with Psych. Maybe get some insight into how you feel love. Yeah?" Director looks at us hopefully.

Well, screw this shit. I really don't feel ashamed, even though it's embarrassing. I stand up, dick still hard in my pants. Not ashamed of that either. "It's fucking getting it. That's love."

The room goes quiet, my eyes on Killian's cocky face. His smirk morphs into something kinder, more understanding, and his eyes meet mine. "It's fucking getting it," he repeats.

Yeah. It is. That's what love is to me.

Quietly, with a raspy voice, Monster asks, "Getting what?"

"Each other," Director tells him, eyes widening. "Understanding each other."

"All the parts. Dark and depraved. Volatile and vulnerable," Killian tells Monster. "Don't hide the sinister shit, Monster. Someone gets it."

Ransom watches Monster so intently, but Monster never looks his way. He nods and then stands, looking at the door to ask if the meeting is over.

Director nods. "Yeah, you can all go. Everyone has to be there tomorrow night, though. Final town meeting, and Lock is bringing Yates for his final judgement."

Everyone gets up, and I start to leave. But fucking hell, I linger. Which makes everyone else linger. And I hate that I'm lingering because it makes me pathetic! I linger so hard that I can't make myself leave, so I glance back at Killian to find him still in his chair, leaning back with a cocky as hell grin on his face.

"Waiting for something, sweetheart?"

Holy fuck, I hate him. I hate him even more when everyone laughs at my expense again. I'm burning from embarrassment when he gets up, casually walks over to me, and breaks the one rule I told him to abide by: not to kiss me in front of the Vile Boys.

He grips my chin gently, whispers, "Just in case," and kisses me the way I lingered for.

When the guys all break out in sounds I decide not to decipher, I no longer care if it's mocking or prideful. This asshole conditioned me to expect the 'just in case' kiss, and now I do. Because love is 'fucking getting it' and that's what this kiss is to me. He better not be better at gaslighting than I am.

"Need something else from me?" he asks against my lips, everyone watching.

"I need you to finish what you started when you rubbed my cock." I kiss him, just in case. Because I want to. "Baby," I finish.

He smirks, gripping my wrist to drag me from the con room.

Letting go, he plants his palm against my chest, pushing until my back hits the hallway wall. His energy isn't volatile right now, and when his hand comes back to cup my cock through my pants, I blow out a breath right in his face. As everyone disperses, Killian's eyes dip down to my once again bruised neck, his handprints almost permanently etched into my skin under my new cuts.

"You know what turns me the fuck on?" he asks as he caresses my cock.

I lean against the wall, dry humping his palm. "Your ego."

He grins. "Yours. It's so hypocritical."

Groaning when he rubs a little harder, getting right in my face, I pant through the pleasure and try to pay attention to his words. "How?"

"Remember how fucking hard you pretended to hate your pet name."

"I do hate it."

"Now you beg for it. Like your ego finally clued in and said it's allowed. Call me baby again, sweetheart. I dare ya."

My hips wriggle and my head tilts back. "Fuck you."

"True or false, Soren? You love being called sweetheart." His hand pauses when I refuse to answer.

"Ugh." My chest heaves when I look into his grey eyes. "It grew on me, okay?"

He smiles so charmingly and continues groping me. "You my sweetheart?"

I thrust against his hand.

"Answer me."

"Yes. Fuck."

His lips brush mine when he asks, "And who am I?"

I taste him on my tongue, breathe him in through my nose, and feel his hand so thoroughly that my balls tighten and my abs tense. "My baby." I moan through it, my boxers dampening with cum. My head falls forward, pressing against his. I look down, watching his hand slow, rubbing me through my orgasm gently, so fucking perfectly that I shiver from head to toe. "Mine, baby."

Killian presses his lips to mine as his hand stops moving. He doesn't say *just in case*, but I know he's thinking it, so I feel it. He's answering yes, and I'm answering yes right back. I slump, going limp against him and the wall.

"I got your salty snacks," I mumble, unsure why. I'm not thanking him, but...

"I'll give you another salty snack later," he says, laughing. Ruining the moment. I hate that I'm laughing, too.

RIOT

41

UNCONTROLLABLE NEW MASK

PULLING on the energy from the parade, the Moros Cemetery is thrumming with adrenaline and unity. The Death for Life Cult mingles with The Misfits, and the business owners celebrate with low-level gangs. Everyone is out for a good time—a deadly good time. Because this is Moros' version of court, and Yates is the one on trial. The locals play judge and jury, and Lock will play executioner. The Moros PD sit back, admire the show, and feel no guilt about not stepping in.

To blend in with the locals, we're all here as ourselves. All except Ransom, who is clad in black and wearing his haunting red Vile House mask, standing next to Lock to show allyship. And since we're being all 'just in case' and answering yes to tough questions, I've got my arms around Soren's neck to stake my claim on him publicly. I revel in the whispers about us being together when our brothers are together because I'm sick-minded and can get on board with the family ties taboo aspect of it.

"Get off," Soren snips at me, trying to remove my arms.

"It's like you're pissing all over me when we both know I'm the alpha."

"Do we both know that?" I ask, pulling his back to my chest. "Because from where I'm sitting, you're the bitch in heat and I'm the top dog in this dynamic."

He snaps his teeth together, half-ass attempting to shrug me off again. "You're just jealous I can top from the bottom. If the roles were reversed, you'd be submissive as fuck."

Maybe. Not sure we'll ever find out. Submission is hard for me, but he's never asked and I'm too selfish to offer. "You want that, sweetheart?"

Soren grabs my arm and switches our positions. Behind me, his lips press to the phrase he carved into my nape, and his voice vibrates against my skin. "Do you?" He reaches down, cupping my cock. I groan, rocking into it. "Because, top or bottom, I'm the one fucking you, baby."

I smile, looking at the cemetery but feeling only Soren. "You know, Willow Olenna told me something else the night we hunted Yates."

"What's that?" His lips dip to the side of my neck, and his cock firms up behind my ass, grinding forward.

"That you and Menace tag-teamed Richelle Ulrich at a Misfits party a few years ago."

He keeps humping me, rubbing my cock, and nipping at my neck. "So?"

"A party I was at."

He stiffens, pulling his mouth away from my neck. "So? What of it?"

Oh, but he knows. His rapid heartbeat—that I can feel in my chest again—tells me he knows exactly what I'm going to call him out on. Because that party was around the same time our competitive games started, and I was on Soren's mind one hundred percent of the time. "You fucked her while her and Menace spouted off fantasies, didn't you?"

He shoves me, but I spin, grabbing him by the hair. His eyes flare bright blue, and his cheek muscles tense.

"Fantasies about me. While you watched me at the party and got off on it from the balcony above. You came because of me."

He shakes his head, denying it. "She's wrong."

"She's never wrong." I smile wide. "Should I ask Menace?" I look over his shoulder. "Mason!" I shout since he's unmasked.

Soren grabs my jaw. "Don't."

"Embarrassed, sweetheart? It's okay if you had a best friend's brother thing going on."

He squeezes my jaw, making my newly healed teeth ache. "Killian."

"Shit, you two are explosive," Menace says as he walks up, draping his arms around both of our shoulders. "Can I get in on this?"

"No," we both snarl.

"But you can tell me about that night you two fucked Richelle—"

"Menace, shut your fucking mouth," Soren warns him before I can get the full demand out.

I laugh, but Menace laughs harder. Soren pushes us both away, cheeks flaming. "Goddamn, that night was hot. You were the inspo," Menace says to me with a sexy wink. "I got off to you, bud. Scouts honour."

"Menace, fuck off." Soren glares at him, seething quietly

enough that no one overhears. "You might have, but I didn't."

"Like fuck, Sauder. You were so into it you couldn't look away from him." Menace snorts. "Guess you got what you dreamed about, yeah?"

I lick my lips and watch my man contend the urge to either fight Menace, fight me, or disappear into the crowd like the ghost he is. He squares off with me, making the right choice.

"So fucking what? It was a fantasy about ruining you. Guess dreams really do come true."

If he thinks I'm ruined, he's more delusional than I thought. But that's okay because Soren is a narcissist, and narcissists love lying to themselves. "Guess so," I agree with a chuckle. "You're welcome."

Soren scoffs and Menace laughs right as the crowd starts shouting their votes for Yates' punishment.

Kill him!

Toss him in the asylum!

Make him your bitch, Lockan!

Ransom and Lock listen to the locals, letting them make this call. They wait for everyone to finish shouting, so we turn to pay attention. If Yates is gonna die right here and now, I'd like to watch. And jerk Soren off while he dies.

Yates is a mess. Half-eaten by crows, only partially alive, and barely recognizable. He's tethered to the lamp post near one of the biggest mausoleums, but he doesn't look scared. That pisses me off.

"What's wrong with him?" Soren asks.

"Too dead to feel fear anymore," Menace says.

"Or... up to something." I study him. His eyes are open,

and I recognize chaos when I see it. He's about to do something, cause a riot, set the town on edge, but I don't know how. I grab Soren's wrist... just in case. Yates isn't an intelligent man, but something smart is rolling inside his head right now.

As everyone shouts, his face breaks into a clandestine grin, and my skin prickles with unease. I pull Soren closer, latching onto his wrist to steady myself. Yates keeps laughing, louder and louder as the townsfolk quiet, startled by his sinister hysterics. He laughs so loudly that the cemetery grows hushed while the crows and ravens stop their flapping. The fog settles into something thick and ominous, filtering Yates' laugh and warping it into an omen of something to come.

Lock smacks him across the face, blood flying to the stone platform. "Something to say, old man? Get on with it." He pulls two short daggers from his belt.

"Moros!" Yates shouts.

Everyone boos, throwing shit at him and calling him a traitor. Menace closes in on my other side, and Monster and Kyd weave through the crowd to join us. Kyd's unmasked, not typically allowed out in public without his mask, but he's blending in enough as Monster's friend. His smile is gone tonight, no joy emanating from him at all.

"You think I don't know you, Moros!" Yates shouts, shushing the crowd. "Kill me if you want, but I know."

"Know what?" Agatha of Death For Life shouts. "The fuck do you know about anything, you bastard?"

Yates' smile splits his bloody lips. "I know every traitor. Every Reaper Corp plant. Every person in this town who is your enemy. Every spy! You can't trust anyone!"

Whispers and chatter break out through the crowd as family members look at one another skeptically and friends take steps back. Soren bristles, but he masks it, slipping into a silent form of energy that can disappear into the shadows to tame this beast of a crowd if he needs to. Tonight, I don't want to let him go.

"You're the traitor!" Lock shouts at him. "You're the enemy."

"I am," Yates agrees. "But so are they." He nods into the crowd, and every person believes he's nodding at someone different. A different family, group, cult, or gang. They see what they want to see, buying into Yates' bullshit. I sense it in my bones: mass hysteria is about to break out.

"Soren," I warn him, my voice quiet but deadly. "We're unmasked."

His fingers link with mine. "I know."

"Ransom isn't. He can call us in for backup." Menace looks at the crowd, gauging what's about to happen.

"You can't just disappear or people will notice," Kyd says. "I can, but you can't."

Because him and Monster aren't that well known around town, but the rest of us are. I scan the crowd, seeing Krypt, Remi, Seven, and Facts closer to the platform where Yates is. Glitch is by himself, off to one side with his parents, moving himself in front of them in a way they won't notice. We're all on edge, unsure which way this thing is going to crack.

"He's a liar!" Seven shouts, trying to calm the crowd. "He brought Reaper Corp into Moros."

"So he really does know who they all are!" someone else

shouts. "Let him talk before you kill him. Pull names from his traitor lips!"

"Think about it," Yates says, quieting everyone again. "Think of the people who have played roles and no longer keep them."

"Fuck," Menace seethes, bouncing on the balls of his feet. "He's getting to them."

"There are traitors in this crowd!" Yates shouts right before Lock punches him in the face and knocks him out.

"Don't let him poison your minds!" Lock yells.

But the people are already spooked. An incoming war, one attack and a bombing, the threat of retaliation from what I did to Reaper City, and the downfall of an established gang all have everyone on edge.

"Like Soren Sauder!" a guy in the crowd shouts, making my fingers grip Soren's harder. "He was in The Misfits, and as soon as Yates got overthrown, he disappeared! He's not even in the gang anymore!"

"He's a traitor!"

"He's working for Reaper Corp."

"You're covering for Sauder!" someone else shouts at Lock. "That's why you knocked Yates out." The crowd chants agreement, and Lock can't muzzle them this time.

My vision spots, black invading the edges of everything I see. Every mask I've ever worn flits over my personality, passing by because I don't fucking need them. I create a new mask, one I'm building right here, right now. It's a protective, lethal mask that paints me as a ruthless killer with no mercy. There's no charm, no manipulation, no understanding, and definitely no empathy. It isn't subtle or vague in tone, and as I don it, I feel it take hold of my body—my soul. I become the man who defends and protects Soren. At any and all costs. There isn't a price I won't pay.

As all eyes turn towards us, I hear fucking Fabrizio roar in the distance. Kyd's lion startles the town, but my roar of absolute rage startles them more. Their eyes snap back to me, the threat they've now triggered and the consequence of their actions. My fists tighten, Soren's fingers bending in mine.

"He's not even in The Misfits anymore!" a guy I went to high school with snarls, coming towards us. "Sauder is a spy!"

"Fucking say that again," I snarl at him, nothing human left in me.

"Killian," Soren says, voice trembling with a mix of rage and fear. His shame breaks me most.

"Sauder sold us out!"

My new facade settles into place, wrapping me in a fury born of protectiveness. When that asshole opens his mouth to spew more accusations, I slam my fist through it and make him choke on his teeth. My knuckles swell, bleeding down my fingers, but my fist is already flying at the next guy coming for Soren. His eye socket shatters alongside my knuckles, but the pain only fuels me to dip deeper into my spiral.

"Killian!" Soren shouts from behind.

I can't place the tone of his voice, and when I turn back to check on him, I get hit in the side of the head with a tree branch. My world tilts, and all I see is Soren reaching for me. He knocks someone out, catching me before I tumble all the way to the grass.

"Fuck, we gotta get outta here." He hauls me upright, holding me steady.

I shake the disorientation away, flexing my fingers to keep them from stiffening. "Fuck that. We need to kill every one of these cunts for turning on you." I spin, shoving a chick away from approaching. Her ass hits the grass, and I step over her, joining Menace, Kyd, and Monster in a fight.

I keep Soren at my back, sinking deeper and deeper into my new persona the more shit I hear about him. How fucking dare they turn on him? He saved this goddamn town from Reaper Corp the night they attacked Misfit Hall, and he saved them again when we went to their city down south.

"Why isn't he in the gang anymore then?" Sadie, Cain's girlfriend screams, a blade clutched in her hand.

"Watch your mouth, woman," Menace snarls at her. "Or I'll rip your jaw open and—"

Monster touches Menace's shoulder, shutting him up.

"Get him!"

A surge of hysterical idiots head our way. They're our people, but they're turning on us like we're nothing. Like Yates holds all the power.

"Stay the fuck away from him or you won't see sunrise," I warn, and there must be something in my voice because everyone stops advancing. "Want him? Get through me."

"Stop." Krypt rushes up, getting in my face. "Fucking stop."

"They're turning on him."

"They're scared, and Yates is winning. Fucking stop."

I look past my brother, who is never the level-headed one. Yates is still hanging from the lamp post, Ransom standing guard next to him with Remi nearby, not obvious enough to be considered together. Lock is in the crowd, fighting alongside Glitch and Seven. Fuck! Fuck this whole situation. After everything we did to bring this town together, Yates blew it up with a few words, and now I don't know what to do.

I always know what to do! I am the master manipulator, for fuck's sake.

All I need to do is fight. Stop anyone and everyone from getting to *my sweetheart*. He's all I give a shit about, and the angry mob glaring at him from behind the wall of unmasked Vile Boys is setting my teeth to chattering in a rage so strong it's about to burst out of me.

"Soren," Krypt says, and then Soren's hands grip me around the middle. "Get him out of here before he kills our own people."

Soren starts to pull me away, and I get a second's reprieve because I let him. But then a rock flies, hitting Soren in the side of the head, and it's all over from there.

I black out. Give in. Lose myself to my new mask. I've created riots before, but this is one for the record books because I'm attacking the very people I set out to protect. I am the fucking Riot of Moros. My fists fly, my shoulders barrel through, and my forehead clacks off noses. My knuckles are close to breaking, and my heart is seconds from beating out of my chest. There's blood all over me—I don't know whose it is. I don't care, as long as it isn't Soren's.

"Moros!" Ransom's authoritative, modulated voice distracts the crowd. "We will find the traitors, I promise you that. But I know for a fact it isn't Soren Sauder. This is not the time to turn on one another!"

I'm yanked backwards, my fist rising. Soren grabs it to

stop my hit, dropping it just as fast to press his hands to the sides of my head, forcing me to look at him and only him.

"Killian." He swallows, blue eyes on mine, blond hair all sweaty and blood-soaked. "I need the ninety seconds."

That shocks me, and I stumble back a step.

"With you. I need ninety seconds *with you.*"

Oh. I look straight into his eyes, trying to understand. The ninety seconds have always been a safe reprieve... from each other. A way for us to settle so we don't kill each other. But now... am I his safe reprieve?

My chest thumps and my lungs heave, but I grab Soren's hand and let him lead me out of the cemetery. Ransom has the crowd somewhat listening when we make it to the edge, but my nerves won't settle and this new mask won't fall away. I can't shake it. I've wrapped myself in a hundred charming personas, worn even more murderous masks, and perfected the art of acting and morphing to twist my surroundings to meet my needs. But this one is different. I don't have any control over it, and it's the strongest one I've ever worn.

"Look at me." Soren stops us on the edge of the woods, hand on my chest to settle my heartbeat. "I'm fine."

I breathe.

"I'm right here."

I exhale.

"They're our people."

I vibrate.

"They're wrong, but they have a point. Yates got in their already messed up heads and made everyone doubt each other. I took the brunt of it, but they're still our people."

I try to blink. I can't.

"Killian, look at me. Look at me standing right fucking here. You're the one who's hurt." He touches my bloody knuckles. My eyes shift to the blood dripping down from his temple. He touches it, and I bristle, jittering worse than Facts does. Soren smirks at me, and I don't understand why. Pressing his blood to my lips with his fingers, he says, "Oh, please. You've brought me way closer to death than any of them ever have, baby."

Baby.

A crack in my character. Enough of one that I can rip the persona away and see something more than encroaching blackness. I suck in a quick breath, my throat spasming around it.

"Ninety seconds, Kill. I need it with you." He leans in, wrapping his arms around my neck and holding me there until I settle enough to hold him back. I pull on his lower back, pressing us flush together so I can feel his heart in my chest, physical proof that he's here, alive, okay.

Still mine.

I lean my temple against his bloody one and breathe.

RIOT

42

HIS STRINGS, MY KEYS

SOREN'S FINGERS ARE GENTLE, but the antiseptic stings. He's quiet as he cleans my knuckles, and I'm quiet because no one has ever taken care of me before. I figured I never needed it. I can take care of myself, and no one is good enough to fix me, but this is nice. He's doting on me... because he brought me to the patient ward of the asylum, so we don't have to go back to Vile House yet.

"You worried a few split knuckles are gonna do me in? I'm tougher than that, sweetheart."

Soren pours acidic liquid onto my open wounds and I hiss through the pain. "Don't be a dick right now. I need... I just need you not to be a dick."

I smile as he cleans up the last knuckle but doesn't let my hand go. "Tell me. Uh, what do you need?" I ask. When he looks at me weird for asking, I add, "Never been good at that part. I know what I need. Not anyone else."

Though that might be a lie because I've always understood when he needs a brush with danger and death.

He drops the gauze and leans back against the stone

wall of the empty family visiting room we're hiding out in, hand in mine, resting on my thigh. The room is mostly dim, the only light coming from a few lamps in the corners. I've spent a lot of time in the asylum, but never in here. It's quiet and empty, big enough for hiding in and open enough to contain our energies.

He rubs the scabs still healing on his jaw, the three words grounding him. "I'm trying to keep a level head and believe what Krypt said about everyone just being scared."

"But?"

"But it fucking guts me when I'm doubted. I had to tolerate that gang for years and now that I'm out I'm still fucking paying for it. They doubt me. Again," he snaps, eyes closing and breaths deepening to calm himself. "So, just don't doubt me."

"I don't."

"You once mocked me for being the guy who craves the spotlight but succeeds in the dark."

"I did."

Slowly, Soren leans over until his cheek rests on my shoulder. It's so jarringly perfect that I stop breathing, loving this moment more than I ever thought I would. "Right now, I just want to hide in the dark with you."

I'm conflicted. On one hand, I want to ask him why he picked me. On the other hand, I *know* he picked me because I'm strong enough to handle him. He sees himself as superior to his family, and I see myself as superior to him. Soren is a mindfuck because he lies to himself, believes in himself to an ungodly level, and sees literally every other person as beneath him. But somewhere along the way, he unknowingly put me on a pedestal. I'm eager to stand on it, but I wonder if he knows how many different masks I wear while looking down at him from my platform.

He wanted Death? I got it for him.

He wanted someone to not stop when he said no? I did that.

He needed the Sauder curse to end? I fucking ended it.

He wanted to stop trying so hard to hold himself together? I fucking gave him that.

He wanted to hold my hand? You're goddamn right I manipulated him into wanting it by holding that little girl's hand.

He wanted to be superior? I did that for him when I sacrificed myself in Reaper City, putting him first just to be the stitch in his side for the rest of his life. *I'm* his saviour!

The room is silent and still despite how tumultuous my thoughts are. I'm making this about me again, but fuck, I can't help it.

Because I've led him to where we are *on purpose.* I turned him into my loyal little lapdog. For as long as I've been rivalling him, I've wanted this power so I can hold it over his head. So, why the fuck am I not doing that? Why am I not forcing him to bow down to me? Why does he get away with things I'd never let anyone else get away with?

Why does his flushed skin excite me rather than repulse me? Blushing is a weakness. I've mastered the art of morphing my face into the exact expression I want it to wear, and anyone who blushes doesn't have that skill. It means he's mundane, not in control, and beneath me. I am superior to all these pathetic fools who can't master their facial expressions, so why do I give him a pass? Maybe because it feeds my ego to know I'm the one who makes him blush...

Inwardly, I worry that he's simply the coerced man I turned him into. I tricked him into loving me, so it can't be real, can it? But maybe he tricked me, too. I've never been a protective person—at least, not towards another person. Sure, I helped save my brother, but I did that for selfish reasons. I wanted to be able to say I did it. But I protected Soren tonight without a selfish thought in my mind. Or did I? Maybe I publicly made him mine, and it embarrassed me to be tied to a man the town doubted.

Fuck. What is real?!

How can I be sure?

He asked for ninety seconds with me, and the pressure of that is too much. These are his ninety seconds, yet I'm the one freaking out because everything I know about myself doesn't align with this version of me who loves a man. Something changed, and I don't know whether to blame him for it or take credit for it.

Because whatever piece of me got left behind in Krypt's bedroom that night we played piano... Well, it got added back to me when Soren said he loved me in the same room. I'm unfamiliar with this old part of me, resenting it as much as I'm cherishing it.

"What're you freaking out about?" he asks.

"Nothing." I shrug my shoulder to get him off it. Standing, I pace the room, giving him my back because I don't want him to see my face. I can feel his eyes on me, though, and it sets me on edge enough that I leave the room. Walking into the adjoining room, my boots scuff the stone floors and my throat tightens up, questions and answers and insecurities getting clogged there because I refuse to let them out.

The town is turning on him. He loves me. I love him. I don't understand any of it. He says love is 'fucking getting it' and now I'm doubting my ability to love because I sure as hell don't get it. It just happened. Was Psych right? Do I use love as a strategic tool to further my own agenda?

But other than giving me attentive praise, good sex, and a god complex, what the hell does Soren do for my agenda? He's nothing but a pain in the ass who entices my mind. But… I sought him out years ago *because* he's a pain in my ass who entices my mind. My life was stagnant, and then he started fighting back, and things have been exciting since. I'd be bored without him constantly challenging me, but I never saw the feelings coming. I just wanted to prove to him that I'm a more worthy opponent than Death, and now look at where we are.

In an abnormal relationship that has no boundaries and no real goals. No definition. No idea what love means for us, yet claiming to feel it regardless. We're liars and hypocrites for declaring an emotion we can't grasp, yet we're both too stubborn to admit we don't know what it is.

I've wandered so far that my feet stop in front of the grand piano in the music room. I fucking hate it. I love it. I want to play it but I don't want to touch it. What will my music say? Will I know what it's implying?

I sit, confused by the feel of the bench beneath my ass. It's nostalgic, yet unfamiliar. Holding my hands above the keys without touching them, I look down to take in the whole picture. My swollen knuckles, split and still bleeding, above ivory keys so aged but pristine. How do the two go together? My hands cause harm when balled into fists, but if I spread my fingers and place them on the keys, they create such beauty.

I know Soren is listening. I'm trying not to care.

When I place my fingertips on the keys, my ribs crack open and my heart pours out. Horribly, at first. The notes are all wrong, misplaced and stuttered. The music isn't flowing. My fingers are too swollen to reach where they need to. But as they loosen and my heart bleeds, I begin to create music. It's real, honest, from the depths of me that I haven't touched in so many years. I bring life to feelings that don't make sense.

Love conflicts with my personality. Shame hurts my ego, but compassion feels foreign and right. Self-appreciation is my main setting, but appreciating Soren becomes natural.

I'm all twisted up, doubting myself when I haven't doubted myself since before I killed our parents. That night I played piano with my brother and lost a part of me to that music. It's returning to me now, savage and abrupt. It hurts because I want it, but heals because I need it.

My music turns into a song, and when I close my eyes to feel the notes, I realize what they're saying. They're telling me it's okay to be vulnerable with him, that it's not a weakness to love a man who doesn't know how to love because neither do I—our version of it can be different. The song tells me that together, we'll live forever, even if we die. It'll be a twisted trip from here to there, the afterlife he seeks and the control I crave. And the hardest part about all of it is the realization that I don't have to manipulate him into any of it. He's here willingly, and I think that might hurt the most.

I'm worth it. He sees me as worth it.

The piano music bounces off the echoey walls of the asylum, and the hush that falls over the halls is respect. Because the patients are listening, and whatever they're hearing from my music is the same way I feel in bed, listening to Soren play the violin from his room. The ability to feel and heal in private.

My bloody, busted knuckles aren't hurting anyone but me at the moment, and as I shift the sadness into something dark and beautiful, my eyes water while they stay closed. Especially when Soren's back presses to mine, his ass behind me on the wide bench seat. He sits there, listening, breathing, letting me feel his heart beating in my chest while I remember what it feels like to play piano.

I sense it. His music is desperately hoping to join mine. I'm so afraid of it that I play louder, hoping to drown out the sounds of his violin if he attempts to play with me.

But then I hear it. The strings of his violin mix with the keys of my piano. I choke on some sense of self, a feeling of home like I've never had before as our music melds, meshing together seamlessly despite how deeply it hurts.

Then he plays *with* me, and our music becomes a real song.

And the notes of his violin are declarations, so I press the keys and step on the pedals, admitting to everything that's hard to say. And it feels good, so good it hurts more, that healing kind of pain that rejuvenates your soul but drains your energy.

Because the town turned on Soren.

Because I love Soren.

Because I don't know how to cope with either.

But mostly because loving him has given me this gift

back, and I credit myself for that. For being strong enough to open up to him, and for letting him see me without any of my masks.

I don't know who leads, his strings or my keys, or maybe we're just building off each other, but the music we make starts off slow and emotional. The music room becomes our stage, the asylum becomes our amphitheatre, and Moros becomes the one and only stop on our tour. The stone walls absorb our melancholy, not letting it leach out to ears beyond, but when the dark tones and slow sounds become something more, I press my back to his and create music with the man I love.

We play together for so long that the moon disappears from one window and reappears in another. A raven pecks at the glass pane, and seconds later, rain taps on the window to join our beat.

And then we stop. Together. Breathing.

Because there's nothing left to say.

Back-to-back, I lean on Soren and he leans on me, letting the sound of the light rain wash away the overwhelmingness of the night. Looking down to my hands still resting on the keys, I notice that I've bled all over them. My split knuckles are shiny and wet, the keys are turning sticky, and my regrowing fingernails are bleeding again.

Somewhere in the ward we're in, a patient cackles and doors slam, but the sounds don't jar me as much as Soren's soft question. "Did you get it back?" he asks.

I remove my fingers from the keys and stare at the stains. The white and black keys and the light wood no longer seem so daunting. Did I get music back tonight?

"Yeah."

He doesn't take the credit like he normally would, and he doesn't ask anything else. Instead, he leans against my back, rests the back of his head to mine, and sighs contentedly. And because he's so calm, so silent and supportive, I let go of everything that just happened at the town meeting and put my trust in him. In us. In music and the ability to interpret it again while the sounds around us simmer along with us.

Later, after my heart has settled and my breathing has regulated, my knuckles ache when Soren says, "It was a confession."

I try to think back on the music I played. "Confession of what?"

"Guilt."

"No." I shake my head.

"Shame."

I shake my head again.

"Acceptance, then."

I start to shake my head, but I stop. Yeah, maybe it was an ode to acceptance. Maybe I am okay with where my life has gone. Maybe all the tricks and the lies and the manipulations have benefitted me in a way I never thought they would. Because I'm here without a mask, and I have my brother, Vile House, a town to protect, and Soren.

I'm seen by him. As me, Killian and Riot all meshed into the sole version of who I really am. And I'm not a nobody like I feared I might be.

But because I don't know how to say all that, I reach back, grab Soren's arm, and pull him around until he's straddling my lap. The piano keys all snarl when his back leans against them, but I bring his mouth to mine to block it out.

Maskless, I lose myself in the man who defies death.

GHOST

EPILOGUE

THIS IS the most embarrassing shit of my life. It's pissing me off to sit here, watching him pick the scabs on his knuckles and grinning like he doesn't give a single shit about any of it, while I feel my cheeks flush so harshly that my neck even feels hot.

My medical file is thick, but his is thicker, and it's yet another region of our dynamic that makes it seem like he's winning. Like, *oh, look at poor Riot who has to overcome so many more mental blockades just to be with you.*

Pathetic.

"Why the fuck are we here?" I bark, my patience dwindling to nothing. "We don't need this. I don't need this."

Director lifts a brow at my outburst, leaning against the treatment room wall with his hands in the pockets of his lab coat. "No?"

"Fuck no. I know what I'm doing."

Killian snorts at that, and I'm so on edge I can't hold back my punch. My fist flies at his gut, but he grabs my wrist and pulls me close, lips against my ear. "You never know when to shut your mouth."

I shove him back and try to leave the room, but Director stops me with a look. The only thing keeping me in this pleasant as fuck therapy room is the fact that he told me I need to be open about it if I want to stay in Vile House.

"Two of my masked members are together. Do you see how this is a risk for all of Vile House?" Director asks, nodding at the relaxing little couch I'm supposed to be sitting on. "Have a seat, Ghost." Looking at Killian, he adds, "You, too."

Reluctantly, we squeeze onto the tiny couch with all its plush cushions and fuzzy blankets. This feels like couple's therapy, and to be honest, the best couple's therapy I can think of is a bloody fight that ends with his cock in my ass and a few new battle scars.

Director stays standing, but Psych, the doctor who manages all our mental issues, sits in the bucket chair across from us. She's around Director's age, might even be his cousin or something, if I recall that introduction, and is too pretty for my current mood. Not yet haggard and worn down by our twisted town. Probably because she spends most of her time in the asylum, letting her crazy out in the comfort of these stone walls.

"This isn't a study," she starts, since we both refused to take part in some learning experience about why our personality traits decided to attempt a relationship together. Apparently, we're so alike that it's basically unheard of for people like us to choose to be a couple. "But we want to understand what a relationship means to the two of you.

Mostly so we can support you, but also to ensure the safety and continuation of Vile House."

My turn to snort. "Really? We've been trying to kill each other for years, and now that we actually half-ass like each other, you wanna talk about safety?" I stand up, done with this.

Killian pulls me back down. "The fuck you mean by half-ass, sweetheart?" His arm wraps around my lower back, squeezing my hip. "You're full-ass in love with me."

I glare at Psych. "Get on with it then. There's a fucking town-wide manhunt for me, and we're sitting here doing this bullshit?"

"Yes," Director says, all blunt. "You're both prone to defying orders because of your self-absorbed tendencies, and now that you're in it together, I want to know where your society ranks on your priority list. Can I still trust you both as leading members of Vile House?"

Oh, the rage. We both bristle at that. Because fuck anyone who questions our authority.

"Fuck you, Director!" Killian snarls. "You like to focus on our fuck ups and blame it on whatever iffy diagnosis we have, but you never give us credit where it's fucking due. We got through the Reaper City job together, didn't we? And what about the night Death Row was bombed? You think I wasn't losing my shit that he was at Misfit Hall? I didn't abandon the other guys and go running to him, did I? I fucking stayed where I was supposed to stay and let him almost die. So fuck off with all your accusations."

I'm about to cut in and remind him that I didn't almost die and had a lot of fun killing that Draco guy, but Director's grin stops me.

"You did. And Ghost, I'm proud of you for getting Riot out of there before he killed someone last night. You two work together really well when you drop the attitude and stop competing."

"No, we don't. We only work together well *because* we're competing." I lean back, crushing Killian's arm.

"Oh? Like the night you blatantly defied your job orders and killed a guy because you thought he was part of your sex games?"

Fuck. I won that night, so I'm not even mad.

Director comes over to sit beside Psych. She leans back, letting him lead this 'appointment' or whatever the hell it is.

"You have sociopathic tendencies, so how can you love him?" he asks Killian.

"He feeds my ego and gets me exactly what I want."

I hate him, but Director moves on. "And you? You have narcissistic tendencies, so what makes you love him above yourself?"

"Never said shit about 'above myself,'" I scoff.

"Say it," Director tells us. "You claim to love one another, so say it."

"We don't do that."

"Why not?"

Because my pride can't form the words and Killian's confusion about it won't let him either. But maybe that's not it. Maybe it's terrifying to say those words because no one else gets what they mean. What if they mean something different to me than they do to him, and what if that means Director is going to kick us out of Vile House?

Killian leans forward, knuckles bleeding again. "You

want us to be like everyone else. That's your problem. Not ours."

Director nods like he agrees. "For years, I've watched you two war with one another. I'll admit, this isn't how I saw it concluding, but I'm happy for you if this is what you want. But we have to come to some sort of an agreement. I need to be able to trust you together, mostly on jobs and while we're gearing up for this war. Can I?"

"Yes," we both snap.

"Then tell me what it means to love each other."

"Why?"

"He wants to know you aren't going to kill each other with your love. He's worried about you," Psych says. "Especially if you consider how your relationship started. You chased death, didn't you? You're... harsh together."

I glance at Killian to find him already looking at me. Because yeah, we did chase death. More accurately, I did, and he helped me get there. But as much as it pains me to admit, he gave me a gift I'll never forget. Killian granted me that one-or-two-second precipice between life and death, and when I was there, staring Death straight in her evil eyes, he didn't pull me back. He let me do that on my own, and that's all I've ever craved.

Looking at Killian, I say, "I'm not chasing death anymore."

"Because he ended the Sauder curse by murdering your cousin?" Director asks.

My fists clench, not liking that he gets all the credit for that. Killian grins, but he keeps watching me. "Because I'm chasing him instead."

The moment is charged with a million ways Killian can turn this on me, but he doesn't. He leans forward, embarrassing me more by pressing his lips to mine with an audience, and asks, "Still a yes, sweetheart?"

I think it'll always be a yes. Because I live by the 'just in case' mentality now. He trained me to, but I'll never admit it. I kiss him because I own him. My kiss is my version of yes.

Director is smiling when I look at him, my cheeks red because this is so awkward. "There. Was that so hard?"

We both look at him, confused.

"That's your love. Volatile. Vulnerable. And trust me, I don't want you to be like everyone else. This is your thing, your way of acting on it and feeling it, so don't let anyone tell you it's wrong." He leans forward. "As long as you're both still Vile Boys."

Well, if I've learned anything about possession, it's that I feel it strongly. Killian might be mine, but Vile House has been mine longer. I grin at Director, all warped and sick, and he smirks back. "Fucking try and take my mask from me, I dare you."

Director's grin widens, enjoying my twisted mind. He looks at Killian next. "Riot?"

"Only mask I need, Director. You ain't getting it back."

Turning his smirk into a proud smile, he stands. "That's all I needed to know. And boys?" He looks at us as he starts to leave. "I'm proud of you."

VOLATILE AND VULNERABLE. I feel both inside me. The turbulence of feeling so offended by the town turning on me is soothed only by how good it feels to be vulnerable for Killian.

"Don't hide from me," Killian says, busted knuckles under my jaw to lift my eyes to his. "Don't fucking hide from me. I can't take it right now."

Because something big is coming, putting all our lives at risk, and for the first time, the risk is hitting me differently than it normally does. I don't want to lose this, whatever it is. I don't want to be taken from him or have him taken from me. I don't want this budding relationship to be stomped on by Reaper Corp and whatever they have planned as retaliation.

For right now, I want to hide away with Killian in my room at Vile House. I want to forget that the town lost their trust in me, that my mom is in a patient room at the asylum, and that Moros is in danger.

I look into his grey eyes and see the storms I build within them. Admiring the way I turn him into something he never thought he could be—maskless. I did that. I brought him this comfort level. I stripped him bare and made him expose himself to me.

His other hand slides down my spine, tilting my body as I rock on his cock. I'm mixed up somewhere between slow-building pleasure and a fear I won't admit to. Because his eyes are as vulnerable as I feel, and I'm picturing them swollen shut, his mouth missing teeth, and his body burned and bloody in that torture chamber in Reaper City.

I'm afraid. Of something ripping him away from me.

And maybe he is, too. Maybe that's why he doesn't want me to hide from him.

Staring straight into his eyes, grey on blue, I lift onto my knees and feel my lips part at the drag of his cock. I moan when I slide back down, Killian's fingers digging into my hips. It's all so slow and intimate, and I've never had sex like this before. It's as hot as that night we fucked over Brady's body, and it's hotter than the night we fucked with masks on. He's fucking my ass, but I'm on top, and whatever skewed logic our brains work on lets this be a level playing field. He's not dominating me and I'm not dominating him. No one is inferior because we're both superior when we work together.

I press my forehead to his, riding him as his hands hold onto me tighter than anyone or anything ever has. Tilting my hips is the only way he attempts to control me, and a part of me craves more. I want him to take control so I don't have to think so hard or put forth any effort.

"I got you, sweetheart." He smirks against my lips, kissing me swiftly before he flips me onto my back and settles between my legs.

I sink into the bed and wrap my calves around his hips, digging my heels into his ass. I run my hands down the marred flesh of his back burns, panting through each thrust and swivel of his hips.

"You know," he starts, voice authoritative yet more playful than usual, "there's something I've been wanting to try."

"Finally gonna let me fuck your ass?" I tease.

He grins, eyes glinting. "You haven't earned that yet." He pulls out and kisses me at the same time. My fingers end up in his hair and then move down with his head as he kisses my jaw where the carved words heal, my neck where he's choked me so many times, and my chest where my heart beats out of tune for him.

"What have I earned?" I look down at him, so sexy and dark as he looks up at me. Fucking hell, he's sinister and hot, and I like not knowing what he's going to do at any given moment. Killian doesn't need masks because he only needs to wear the Riot mask with me. "Wasn't there a time when you jerked off with my blood on your cock? Hmm? Didn't you say you were gonna coat yourself in my blood?"

He nips my hip then licks the tip of my cock, making me shiver. "I did say that." He sucks the head into his mouth and I shiver harder. When he pops off, licking down the side of my shaft, I breathe so hard my cheeks flush down to my jaw. "I also said I hated when you blush. Rather fond of it now."

"Rather?" I laugh, fingers raking through his dark waves.

"Rather," he repeats. "Because you do it for me. You're so collected and poised for everyone else, and I'm the only one who gets to see you fall apart."

"Blushing isn't falling apart. It's just my skin tone."

So fast I don't see it coming, he slaps my thigh. I jolt upright, but I'm stopped when he sucks my cock into his mouth again, rubbing where he slapped. "This skin tone?" he asks, tongue still lapping. "This perfect handprint on your sexy thigh? That I caused."

I groan when he slaps me over the same place, the red bloom perfectly showing two different layers of his fingerprints. I settle back, propped up on pillows so I can watch him be fun and playful, but obviously still cocky.

He swallows my cock, and I hold my breath, watching him hold himself there. Fuck him because his face doesn't even get red. But when he pulls off, he lets his teeth graze me slowly as his eyes meet mine and he starts to grin. The scrape of it feels fucking amazing, a slight bite of pain, but more so the anticipation of him tightening his jaw.

"Should we add teeth marks to your dick, sweetheart?"

"Absolutely not."

"Come on. I tattooed your bite on my jaw. The least you could do is tattoo mine on your cock." He licks.

Tempting, only because he says it as a dare, but no part of me wants to get a cock tattoo. I'm not as insane as Kyd. "Sure. And Menace can strap you to the chair while you have to watch him basically give me a handjob to do it."

Killian growls, nipping the tip of my dick.

I laugh. "What's this thing you've been wanting to try?"

"Who are we right now?" he asks, gripping the base of my cock.

So insecure while trying to be cocky. "I think you know the answer to that."

"Well," he says, kissing his way back up my body. "It's this super rare kink. Basically, you lay there and take it while looking into my eyes, and we don't fucking talk. It's all kissing and bodies grinding and panting. No dares or challenges or death chasing or anything. Not even breath play or a blood buzz."

What a dick. I pull him flush against me, spreading my legs to encourage him to thrust inside me. When he does, it's slow and purposeful, deep and settling. "Never heard of it," I whisper, my lips against his. "Does it have a name?"

Killian's fingers wrap around the side of my neck and his

thumb pushes up on my chin. He kisses me and our bodies rock together, a slow build of pure bliss turning us sweaty and needy.

"I think it's called sex," he says against my lips. "And if we're getting really specific with it, I think it's called missionary sex."

"You're sick, you kinky bastard."

"You love it."

Fuck, I do. "You sure that's what it's called?"

"No," he whispers, but neither of us will call it what it really is.

There's no *making love* in Vile House, so I sure as fuck won't be the one to say it. Regardless, our bodies grind together, and we start to sweat, just like he said we would. When our mouths latch together in messy kisses full of panting breaths and hitched groans, I know that's what we're doing. Making some sort of love.

I'm disgusted with myself, but not enough to stop. Because the euphoria of it comes from the process, not the finish line. It's complete trust and a connection that comes from an emotional level, amplified by a physical level. It's him and me, us together, chasing something so much healthier than death.

When I'm rasping against his lips and he's groaning against mine, our bodies hit their musical crescendo, and everything pauses to give respect to the moment. I don't even have to touch my cock. I come from him in my ass and his body all over mine, and when he thickens, releasing his pleasure deep inside me, I open my eyes to look at my reality.

This isn't Hell.

It's not Death's doorstep.

It's volatile and vulnerable love with the devil I picked and won to stand by my side.

I. Fucking. Won.

"You love me?" I ask.

"Yes," he breathes against my neck. "And now I'm gonna fuck you bloody."

RANK

+++ DIRECTOR

MY TEMPLES HAVE BEEN THROBBING for months, a low-grade headache pounding with all the stress I'm under. Reaper Corp coming to take over Moros is second in the stress line to having Ghost and Riot finally combust. I'm still not convinced they won't kill one another in some lover's quarrel or a sex game neither of them will be willing to lose, but the boys are on it. The rest of them know to keep an eye out.

"Trust them," Ransom says to me outside the con room. Everyone else is already inside, waiting for me to start the meeting. "They're sick and twisted, but they're smart, too. You brought them into Vile House for a reason."

He has a point...

"Plus, you should have been more worried about Krypt accidentally killing Remi instead."

"Remi is rational."

Ransom snorts. "Is he?"

I hate it when he has two points in a row. "Get in there

so we can start this meeting." But before he does, I touch his elbow to stop him. "How's Monster?"

Ransom and Monster are my two child experiences. They both came to me young, too young to know what Vile House was or what it meant to grow up in this house. Ransom has lived here since he was an infant, and Monster came when he was eight, which meant they were the only two young people around and spent a lot of time together growing up, despite their age difference. I thought they'd have a brotherly bond, and they do, but I'm also more in the know about their odd relationship than any of the other Vile Boys.

"Just going through it right now," Ransom answers.

"Anything set him off?"

Ransom glances into the room, watching Monster sit with Kyd at the table. Monster listens while Kyd rambles, barely reacting, but I know the two of them have a good relationship, too. Kyd has done a lot to teach Monster how to enjoy things, be a person, and understand the world he doesn't otherwise understand.

"Nightmares."

"You let me know if there's anything we can do."

"I've got him."

"I know you do, but I'm here for you. I know he won't accept help, but if *you* need it, let me know."

Ransom purses his lips, but he nods and heads into the room.

I've got nothing but bad news for the boys today, so I wait, listening to them laugh and bicker and banter. Most of them are goading Ghost and Riot into spilling who the top and bottom are, or if they flip fuck, whatever that is, but it's lighthearted and fun. There won't be much fun around here for a while, and I want to grant them this moment. This breath of time to enjoy the new relationship and their bond as a family. Most of them don't understand the concept of family, but whatever Vile House and the other members have become to them, it's what they consider familial bonds to be, and I'd like to think I had a part in encouraging that.

"Director." I turn, seeing Media coming my way. "Bad news got worse." She shows me the tablet and as soon as I see who the video message is from, my blood runs cold.

"Thanks. Keep it quiet for a few more minutes. I want to assess how they're all doing before I show them this."

She hands me the tablet and gives a weak smile. "I'll let you do it. Good luck."

Sighing, I pinch the bridge of my nose and feel defeated, but I still morph into the Director role as soon as I step through the door. "Rank! Line up!"

It's still strange for me to see Ransom so close to the end of the line, but I try to ignore it as they line up. Ghost and Riot shove each other, fighting over the second to last position, and Kyd is still rambling uselessly about something Monster doesn't give a shit about as they get into rank.

In my opinion, rank is so stupid. It means nothing, but when this group of ten formed and became a unit, I couldn't figure out how to get them to cooperate unless they were challenging one another.

Seven might be the most responsible with the initiates, but he absolutely does not deserve to be at the head of the line. He's more of a shit disturber than half of them, but he's not the bragging type, so he gets away with a lot more. Still, I step up in front of him, a brow raised and the sternest expression I can muster on my face.

"How'd the meeting end last night?"

He looks down the line at the rest of the Vile Boys, shaking his head. "Town's all fucked up. Manhunt for Ghost. Well, Soren. Ransom calmed them down a bit, but..."

"Everything we did to bring all the besties together has gone to shit, Director!" Kyd shouts. "Locky has to defend Ghost, The Misfits are getting all the extra hate, and soon, I'll have to drop out of the asylum theatre program." He huffs. "Everything was so fun and now it's not so fun." His hands go to his hips, he shakes his pink hair, and he huffs again.

I need to tell them it's going to get even worse. Instead, I look at Ghost and Riot. "But at least these two are finally on the same team." I smile at them.

"End of the line butt buddies," Menace goads. "How's it feel to be at the bottom... Riot?"

Riot simply grins, shrugging. "Wouldn't you know?"

"Not yet," Menace answers honestly. "Top dog around here, baby." He winks. I make a mental note to keep tabs on Cain Carson because I don't think the boy knows he's caught the attention of a killer.

Krypt scoffs at Menace, or maybe at his brother and best friend. It's hard to tell with Krypt since he usually dislikes everything and everyone. Me, a lot of the time. "Are we here to talk about—"

"Oh, fuck off, Krypt," Soren snaps, bending forward to look down the line at his best friend. "We all had to hear about you and my brother. Had to take a fucking vote on it, for shit's sake."

"Oh!" Kyd shoots out of line. "If we're voting again, I vote that Ghost moves into Riot's room and we do a tradesy! I want Ghost's room."

"You have the most rooms out of all of us," Glitch weighs in. "One at Vile House, one in the long-term patient ward, and one in our ward of the asylum."

"And the floor in Axel's lab," Seven adds with a laugh. "Like a little puppy following his owner around."

"No denials because this puppy bites," Kyd says, waving them off. "But Ghost's room has the best floorspace for my theatre practice, and Facts has been teaching me how to ballroom dance. Please, Ghosty!"

While they bicker about rooms, I watch them fondly. I enjoy seeing my boys like this, brotherly and giving each other a hard time for fun reasons rather than dire ones. They're all so harsh and intense that it always brings a smile to my face when they remember to have fun. Kyd might have the darkest, most deranged side out of all of them, but half the reason I brought him into the ten was because he's lighthearted and reminds the others to work together and enjoy the little things.

I don't know how the debate ends, but somehow, Kyd is smiling and Monster even smirks a little.

"Sit down, boys. We've got a shitstorm coming." The fatigue and stress creep into my voice, and they all stop laughing as they sit down.

"Because of me?" Ghost asks. "Because I'm the town traitor who brought Reaper Corp into Moros?" He slumps back, and Riot must touch him under the table because, with a heated scowl, he looks at his new... boyfriend?

"More than that," I tell him, sitting at the head. "I've got bad news and worse news. Which do you want first?"

No one says anything, but their attention is focused.

"They still haven't figured out what we stole from Reaper City, which means they're putting new codes and protection on everything. All their data is being encrypted, and Axel is having a harder time trying to crack the prisoners we have." I look at Glitch, letting him take over.

"I'm trying to hack as fast as they're switching everything out, but... I wouldn't be surprised if they block me out entirely. Really soon. I'm only one guy, and they have whole teams on it."

"Which means we're switching tactics," I say. "Back to Axel's original plan."

"Capture. Brainwash. Release back to Reaper City," Kyd says.

"Hello." Facts raises his hand. "We also verified two rats in The Misfits. Lockan Tate is aware, and he's awaiting a meeting with us to sort out the best method of dealing with them."

"Like, use them or kill them?" Ransom asks.

"Exactly," Facts answers.

"We also just received this." I cast my tablet to the screen. "It's not an idle threat." I press play.

As the video threat from Reaper Corp plays, I pay attention to their reactions. Anger, vengeance, god complexes, rage and protectiveness, and under it all, fear.

"You may have poisoned our city," the modulated voice behind the shadow person on the video says, "but we've been poisoning your town for years. We're coming for you,

Moros, and we've been slowly taking you out right under your noses."

Fists clench and snarls resound, but before the video even ends, the con room door bangs open.

"The town has gone mad," Axel says, breathless like he ran here from the asylum, his eyelid fluttering like crazy. "Come look."

"Masks on!" I remind them all as we rush out of the room to look through the front windows of Vile House.

Town citizens are on the lawn, down the street, and banging on the front door, shouting aggressively. Business owners and cult members, even some of The Misfits, an angry mob of everyone we've been trying to protect. Glitch's parents are out there, faces skeptical. And right there, in the middle of all of them, with wide sad eyes and an innocence about him that's going to get him killed, is the boy whose dead dad is still cooling in my morgue.

"The fuck are they doing?" Ransom asks. "Are they after Ghost?"

I look to see where Ghost is, but he's gone. Vanished into thin air.

"Vile House! Unmask and show us who you are!" someone shouts.

"How do we know they aren't Reaper Corp members?" someone else yells.

"Reaper Corp killed the Vile Boys and now they're parading around in their masks!"

"Fuck," Facts gasps. "Why didn't I see this coming? I should have fucking predicted this!" Before he can beat himself up too hard, he gasps again, and when he whispers, "No," it's a word full of dread. I follow his gaze to one of the Moros firefighters, not understanding his reaction.

The knot of dread in my stomach worsens, tightening and twisting as rocks and bottles and eggs hit the house. Never in Moros history has Vile House been doubted. I look at my boys in their masks, watching the hysteria unfold and reacting to it in different ways.

They've thrived as hunters. Now we see if they'll thrive as prey.

"We're unmasking you, Vile House!" someone declares outside.

And the town cheers.

THE END.

END RANK:

1. Seven
2. Menace
3. Facts
4. Glitch
5. Monster
6. Krypt
7. Ransom
8. Kyd
9. Ghost
10. Riot

VILE BOY COLOURS

RANSOM	->	RED
SEVEN	->	ORANGE
GLITCH	->	GREEN
GHOST	->	TEAL
KRYPT	->	PURPLE
MENACE	->	BLUE
RIOT	->	WHITE
KYD	->	PINK
MONSTER	->	YELLOW
FACTS	->	COPPER

VILE BOY NAMES

RANSOM	–>	
SEVEN	–>	
GLITCH	–>	MAKOA KAMAKA
GHOST	–>	SOREN SAUDER
KRYPT	–>	KEEGAN HALLOWS
MENACE	–>	MASON ....
RIOT	–>	KILLIAN HALLOWS
KYD	–>	(KYD)..... KOPITAR
MONSTER	–>	
FACTS	–>	

MORE REVEALED AS THE SERIES GOES

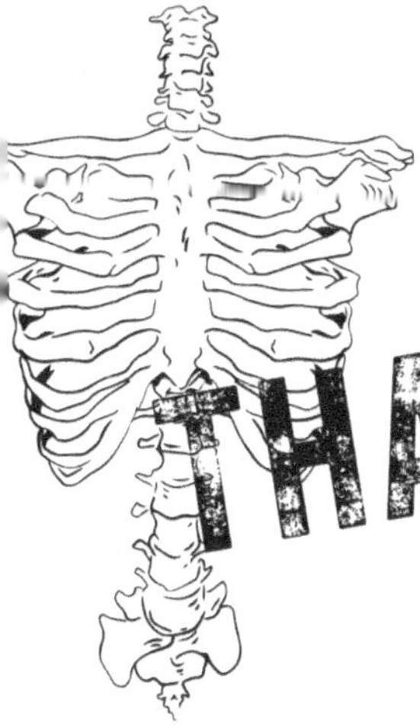

THANK YOU!

Thank you for reading FRAGILE FACADE!!

It took me a few attempts to get these two right. When I first started writing this book in April 2024, I figured Ghost and Riot would be extremely ruthless and volatile. Which they are, but I had not been expecting their vulnerable, softer side to come out like it did. I even tried to make them less gentle and more dark, but it wasn't flowing right. They just want to have some softness thrown in there, and who am I to change their minds?! They're pretty stubborn, and Ghost wasn't gonna let that girl be the only one to hold Riot's hand, thank you.

While they did end up learning to think about the needs of each other, they still motivated themselves with selfish reasons, and that felt important. So-fucking-what if Soren brought Killian a smoothie, right? He just needed to prove he was important! It had nothing to do with wanting to take care of his man... right?! *eyeroll* It was tough to pair these two together, and their personality traits made it harder, but it was fun trying to merge two like-minded people and force them to consider the feelings of the other.

As the series continues, we'll get to know so many more characters, unpeel all their layers, and learn their motivations. Good and evil are pretty blurred lines in Moros, and so many of our boys like to tread that line, which has become a favourite part of mine to write. Actions and the motivations behind them differ from person to person, and I love that difference!

My baby FACTS is up next! And oh boy, he's a complicated one, but he's so resilient. With the town out to unmask the Vile Boys, he takes that threat personally. Because he's the one who usually sees the bigger picture, and he didn't see this coming because lust distracted him. He loathes himself for that, and getting rid of the lust is his first priority.

His story is a tough one because of the way his mind works, the upbringing he's had, and the warped way he sees the world around him. We'll finally learn why he says 'hello' so often.

Because it's a series, things mentioned in this book might not come back until later books. We still have an extra Initiation Night to address, that kid with the dead detective dad, and the rebuilding of The Misfits under Lockan Tate's new leadership. Is Menace ever gonna get Cain's girlfriend out of his way? What is Reaper Corp going to do to retaliate, and who the hell are the spies in town? Anyone we know? It's all coming and more, don't worry!

I hope you're enjoying the series so far. Riot would expect it, so let's all bow down to him for ending the Sauder Curse like the God he is.

As Remi says, "You killed Tim!"

And Riot just says, "You're welcome."

As always, thanks for being here!

Nordika

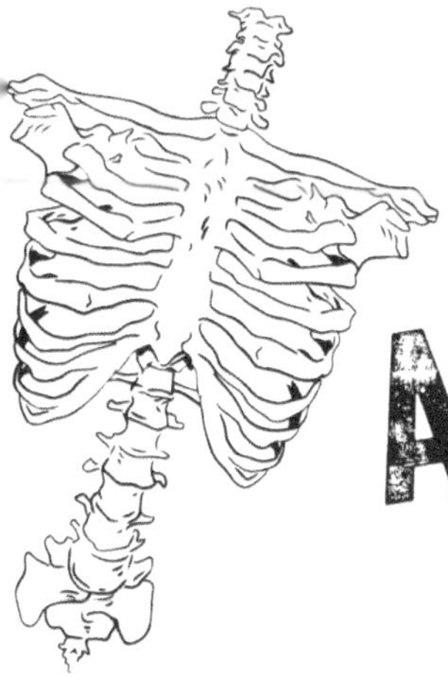

ALSO BY

DARKER READS:

Alter Arlo —> click here

- So, you're craving something dark and twisty, eh? Well, come to this dark dystopian world and meet the boys! This one is psychological, has 2 couples, and comes with a twist that you might see coming. Might not. Go find out! The clues are all there if you look for them.

LIGHTER BUT STILL GRITTY READS:

THE WEEKDAY WEIRDOS SERIES:

- **RED FLAGS & TUESDAYS —> click here**

Reid and Atticus are battling a slew of Tuesdays and a whole bunch of red flags! Atticus is hard to get, but Reid isn't gonna stop trying. Together, the learn what romance means... to them. It isn't conventional ;)

- **SOBER DOPE & SUNDAYS —> click here**

Gage is out of rehab for the 8th (!!) time, and he's bound

and determined to keep his shit together. Luckily for him, his new neighbour is a neurotic rambler that becomes his perfect sober companion. They try to fight it, but fate has other things in mind :)

Garron Park & Lot 62 —> click here

- Meet Maddox and Devon, two rivals. Both in life and motocross. Their trailer park lives aren't easy, but together, they find a way to make things a bit more exciting.
- Not only do they start as rivals, but they stay rivals. This enemies to still enemies but also lovers story is full of tension and aggressive love languages.

Little Demon in the Details —> click here

- Craving a snarky brat that loves button pushing? Come meet Mercer! He's a little demon by nature, but he meets his match in Blake, the lethal man with the patience of a saint. Don't you dare call him daddy, though. Seriously. Don't. Blake doesn't like it.
- Their story is all about empowerment and a rise to the top despite all that is against them. There's spice, brattitude, and a burnt grilled cheese sandwich.

NORDIKA NIGHT

++

++

Nordika Night doesn't know wtf she's doing most of the time, but that's life.

Writer of gritty MM romance in all tropes and hopefully lots of genres, she's still finding her lane.

Canadian.
Coffee lover.
Writing buddy: Waylon, her mastiff!
www.nordikanight.com

I'm looking forward to what's next, grateful to the past, and trying to enjoy the present without letting it overwhelm me!

Nordika Night xo

Printed in France by Amazon
Brétigny-sur-Orge, FR

31686070R00284